Scots on the Rocks

ALSO BY MARY DAHEIM

Scots on the Rocks

A Bed-and-Breakfast Mystery

Mary Daheim

HARPER LUXE

An Imprint of HarperCollins*Publishers*

SCOTS ON THE ROCKS. Copyright © 2007 by Mary Daheim. All rights reserved. Printed in the United States of America. No part of this book may be used or reproduced in any manner whatsoever without written permission except in the case of brief quotations embodied in critical articles and reviews. For information address HarperCollins Publishers, 10 East 53rd Street, New York, NY 10022.

HarperCollins books may be purchased for educational, business, or sales promotional use. For information please write: Special Markets Department, HarperCollins Publishers, 10 East 53rd Street, New York, NY 10022.

FIRST HARPERLUXE EDITION

HarperLuxe™ is a trademark of HarperCollins Publishers.

Library of Congress Cataloging-in-Publication Data is available upon request.

ISBN: 978-0-06-126039-1
ISBN-10: 0-06-126039-8

07 08 09 10 11 ID/RRD 10 9 8 7 6 5 4 3 2

Acknowledgments

Special thanks to Jim Bilsand of the Grampian Police for his generous assistance. If there are any deviations from fact, I alone stand convicted.

1

Judith McMonigle Flynn put a fifty-dollar bill on the table, glared at her husband, Joe, and said, "I'll take that bet."

"Sucker," said Joe, the gold flecks dancing in his green eyes. "Since when has your mother ever called me by name? It'll be 'Knucklehead' or 'Lunkhead' or 'Dumbbell' before she ever refers to me as Joe. We've been married almost fourteen years. If you can remember when she ever used my real name, I'll give you fifty bucks right now."

"I can't. But," Judith went on, crossing her arms and looking mulish, "Mother's mellowing. Last night she said your barbecued spareribs were delicious."

Joe chuckled. "They came from Nicky Napoli's rib joint."

"Mother didn't realize that," Judith countered.

Joe pocketed his fifty-dollar bill. "Why bet against each other with our own money? Change the stakes. Who gets to choose our next vacation?"

Judith was still glaring at Joe. "Vacation? What's a vacation?"

Joe pulled out a kitchen chair. "Sit. Look," he said earnestly as Judith reluctantly eased herself into the chair, "I realize you've been under a lot of pressure lately. Except for St. Valentine's Day, February's always a slow month at the B&B. March won't be much better, with Easter not until mid-April. Why not take some time off to go somewhere wonderful?"

Judith grimaced. "My state B&B board review is next week."

Joe had sat down at the kitchen table opposite his wife. "It's Tuesday, right? We'll have the rest of the month for a getaway."

Judith looked glum. "If I feel like it. For all I know, they'll yank my innkeeper's license."

"Don't think negative," Joe admonished. "It's not your fault you've found a few dead bodies in your career. It's happened to me, too."

"You were a cop," Judith pointed out.

"True." Joe looked down at the green-and-white-striped tablecloth. He seemed to be having trouble finding the right words.

"I've never gone out of my way searching for victims," Judith asserted. "They usually come to me. Furthermore," she continued, gathering steam, "not that many people have been killed on the premises in the sixteen years since I turned the family home into Hillside Manor. I'd guess that any inn, motel, or hotel would have a similar fatality ratio."

"You've had your share of bad luck." Joe didn't sound convinced.

"I could use some good luck." Judith reached across the table. "I'll take that bet. I want to go somewhere with sun and a beach and rooms fit for royalty. What about you?"

Joe's high forehead creased in concentration. "Somewhere I can fish. Fresh- or saltwater. I'll research possibilities."

Judith nodded. "Done."

The Flynns shook hands.

"Done" was probably not a good choice of words for Judith.

I figured," Cousin Renie said late Tuesday morning, "you needed cheering up before you get the verdict from the B&B board later this afternoon. I've made lunch reservations at Queen Bess's Tea Shop."

"That sounds nice," Judith said in a small voice.

"I'm paying."

"That's nice, too."

Renie, formally known as Serena Jones, glanced at Judith. "How's the bet coming?"

"It's not," Judith replied as they crossed the bridge that spanned the city's ship canal. "Mother hasn't called Joe anything since we made the bet. She's so quiet lately. It worries me."

Renie turned right off the bridge. "Face it," she said, "our mothers are *old*. They can't live forever." She frowned as she braked for a five-way stop. "Or can they?"

"They may outlast us," Judith responded with a wan smile. "When my artificial hip bothers me, I get so worn out going back and forth to the toolshed with Mother's meals and medications and whatever else, not to mention my job at the B&B and keeping track of Mike and his family and going up and down, down and up all those stairs in a four-story house—"

"Tell me about it," Renie broke in. "At least your mother is on the premises. Mine's almost a mile away and you know how she phones me six times during my waking hours and expects me to jump whenever she needs a spool of thread or has a twinge in her neck. I average one trip a day to her apartment—and still work as a graphic designer."

"You sound as if you need a vacation, too," Judith noted.

Heading east, Renie steered the Joneses' Toyota Camry—affectionately known to its owners as "Cammy"—above the city's main freeway. "I probably do. January and February are always hectic with annual reports. But once my concepts are ready to be filled with useless, boring copy, things slow down. Did you choose your spot yet?"

Judith nodded. "Dana Point. Why don't you two come with us?"

Renie made a face as she headed past the tree-lined streets north of the University. "I may not be a sun-and-sand person, but Bill, as a native Midwesterner, gets glum when the days are still gloomy. I'll think on it."

"It'd be fun," Judith asserted as Renie started down a narrow street on a steep hill. "Dana Point has a whale watch during March. The beaches are wonderful and we could go over to Catalina."

"It's still California," Renie said, and yawned. "I prefer a swanky mountain resort at Bugler in British Columbia."

"At Dana Point, Joe and Bill could charter a boat," Judith argued as Renie made a quick turn to park on the verge of the cemetery that was located by the tea shop. "The deep-sea fishing there is excellent."

Renie parked across from the tea shop on the edge of the Catholic cemetery where both of the cousins' fathers and several other Grover family members were buried. "We'll toast them with an Earl Grey," Renie said. "Let's eat."

The tea shop was busy, but Judith and Renie were seated almost immediately. The cozy comfort lifted Judith's spirits only a trifle. Her dark eyes scanned the surroundings—flowered draperies, framed photos of English royalty, past and present, sketches of famous castles, stuffed animals, and live doves in a cage by the front window. Dana Point seemed a world away.

"Tea," Renie said. "A brisk cup of tea will do you wonders. Stop acting like you're on a permanent trip to the cemetery."

Judith smiled weakly. "Sorry. I'm kind of tired."

Renie glanced up at the white-aproned waitress. "A pot of Earl Grey with steak and kidney pie," she said, closing the menu.

"Uh . . . the same," Judith said, not having studied the selections.

"Okay," Renie said, after their server left. "Pay attention, heed my advice. Cheat."

Judith was aghast. "Coz! Our parents taught us never to cheat!"

The waitress returned with a bone china teapot that had a pattern of purple flowers. "Get your mother in on it," Renie said, pouring tea through an antique strainer. "Cut a deal."

"How?"

Renie stirred cream and sugar into her Royal Worcester cup. "It's March, baseball spring training. Bet Joe he can't hit a ball over the Rankerses' hedge."

Judith was puzzled. "So?"

"Have your mother watch. When he hits the ball—doesn't matter where—have her cued to say, 'Good one, Joe.' For DiMaggio, get it? Aunt Gert can remember that. It's from her good old days."

Judith shook her head. "It sounds complicated. Before I can set it up, she's bound to call him some awful name. If she does, I lose."

"Then act fast. Right after we finish lunch." Renie paused to sip her tea. "Have you chosen a place to stay at Dana Point?"

"One of my weekend guests from San Diego suggested the St. Regis Monarch Beach Resort," Judith replied. "It's pricey, but worth it."

Renie gave a nod. "Maybe we could come along. Bill loves to walk the ocean beaches. Now eat, sip, and relax. Victory's in the bag."

Judith, however, had her doubts.

————————

An hour and a half later, Renie pulled into the Flynns' driveway. She insisted on staying until Judith heard from Ingrid Heffelman. "Bring the cordless phone," Renie said. "Joe's MG is gone, so he's not home. Let's tell your mother about our plan so you can win the bet."

Somewhat reluctantly, Judith picked up the receiver and headed out the back door. "I tell you, Mother's not herself lately. Last Friday night, she wouldn't even play bridge with those retired schoolteachers."

"Yes," Renie said. "My mom had to get a sub for her—Nora Plebuck, who can't drive and lives out north. I got stuck picking up my mom, collecting Nora, and taking them home. I felt like a damned taxi."

Judith nodded in sympathy. "I figured you'd end up being the patsy. But I couldn't talk Mother into going." She tapped once on the door to the converted toolshed, then turned the knob.

Gertrude was in her chair behind the cluttered card table. The TV was turned off. It struck Judith that the old lady had been sitting and staring. Or perhaps catching one of her many catnaps.

"Hi," Judith said cheerily. "Renie's here."

Gertrude's faded old eyes focused briefly on her niece. "So?"

"So," Renie said, kissing her aunt's cheek, "you should be agog."

Gertrude snorted. "I should be a dog? Louder, Serena. I'm deaf."

"Never mind," Renie said. "How do you feel?"

"With my fingers," Gertrude said. "When I can bend 'em."

"Is that why you didn't play cards the other night?" Renie inquired.

Gertrude's expression was glum. "Maybe."

Renie and Judith exchanged anxious glances. Gertrude's lethargy was upsetting. "Want to come for dinner tomorrow night at our house?"

"Why? You can't cook."

"I actually can," Renie said. "Lamb steaks and greenie noodles?"

Gertrude shook her head.

"Pot roast?"

Gertrude again shook her head.

"Fried chicken?"

Gertrude didn't bother to respond.

"We could play cribbage after dinner," Renie suggested.

Gertrude's head jerked up. "Never!"

"Oh, come on, Aunt Gert," Renie said, putting a hand on the old lady's shoulder. "You know you'll beat me. I haven't played crib for so long that I'll have to relearn the game."

Gertrude pulled away from her niece's touch. She was so upset that her head began to shake and she clamped her lips shut.

"Mother," Judith said with concern, "what's wrong? Are you sick?"

There was a long pause before Gertrude spoke. "Sick at heart."

Judith leaned down closer to her mother. "About what?"

"I won't tell you."

"Okay," Renie said, moving away from her aunt. "Don't. But we've got something to tell you."

Gertrude's face brightened. "You're both getting a divorce?"

"No, Mother." Judith sighed. "It has to do with . . . " She frowned and glanced at Renie. "Maybe we shouldn't."

"Shouldn't what?" Gertrude demanded, looking more like her usual prickly self.

Renie gave her cousin a warning look. "Make a bet. Judith against Joe."

"I like that part," Gertrude said.

"Good," Renie said. "Here's the deal and what we want you to do."

The old lady listened attentively, but didn't comment until Renie had finished relating her plan to have Gertrude refer to Joe DiMaggio's hitting prowess. When she did speak, she sounded confused. "I don't get it. I always liked Lou Gehrig better. You know his nickname?"

Renie nodded. "The Iron Horse, because he never missed a game."

"Oh, that's so," Gertrude agreed. "But he had another nickname—Biscuit Pants. I forget why, but I like it."

"Interesting," Renie remarked. "I didn't know that. Remember—all you do is say, 'Way to go, Joe,' when he hits the ball."

"Sounds screwy to me," Gertrude muttered. "Do I win a prize?"

Renie nodded. "You don't have to eat dinner at our house."

"Sounds good to me," Gertrude said.

The cordless phone rang, making Judith jump. Swiftly, she picked the receiver up from the card table and answered.

"You got a reprieve," Ingrid Heffelman announced. "Not that I agree with it."

"What do you mean?" Judith asked, moving away from her mother and Renie to hear more clearly.

"The board deadlocked, with one abstention," Ingrid said in disgust. "They'll have to vote again next month. Consider yourself on probation. Meanwhile, if you find another damned corpse, your innkeeping goose is cooked."

"I won't," Judith asserted. "I promise."

What a relief!" Judith exclaimed after the cousins left the toolshed. "I was sure that Ingrid would convince the board that I'm a blight on the profession."

"Now you can focus on your vacation," Renie pointed out.

"I will," Judith promised. She looked through the window over the kitchen sink. "Darn. It's starting to rain. I won't be able to coax Joe out to the backyard to hit baseballs until tomorrow."

"That's okay," Renie said, picking up her big black handbag from the counter. "It'll give you time to remind your mother what to say."

"True." Judith followed Renie as she headed for the back door. "I thought you'd mention why we were making the bet—like asking Mother why she hasn't called Joe by any of her more insulting names lately."

Renie shrugged. "I assume that's part of her recent lack of pep. But she perked up after she heard our plan."

"You didn't specify what the bet was for," Judith pointed out.

"Of course not." Renie slung the handbag over her shoulder and opened the back door. "Then I would've had to explain about the usual names she calls Joe and she might've turned ornery."

"Oh." Judith nodded. "And just as well you didn't mention the vacation part. Mother might have balked. She hates it when I go away."

"So does my mom," Renie said. "Like to my own house instead of her apartment. See you."

When Joe arrived at five-thirty, Judith was preparing appetizers for the guests' social hour. "Where've you been all afternoon?" she asked.

"Research," he told her, hanging his jacket on a peg in the hallway between the kitchen and the back door.

"I thought you turned down your last two cases."

"I did," Joe said, kissing Judith's cheek. "Defend me against the infidel. As in 'infidelity.' I'm sick of following husbands and wives who stray. Why don't suspicious spouses just ask?"

Judith mixed hard-boiled egg yolks with mayonnaise and tiny shrimp. "So what kind of research were you doing?"

"For our vacation," Joe replied. "Sporting goods stores, the travel agent on top of Heraldsgate Hill, checking with Bill and his resources."

"Have you made a choice?"

Joe took a bottle of Harp lager out of the fridge. "I've narrowed it down to three places. Bill says he'll go along with any of them."

"The Joneses will definitely come with us?" Judith asked.

"So it seems." Joe removed the lid from the lager and eyed the deviled eggs Judith was sprinkling with paprika. "May I?"

"Just one." From overhead, Judith could hear some of the guests stirring. Four of the six rooms were occupied—not a bad number for a Tuesday in early March. "What about dates?"

Washing down a bite of egg with the beer, Joe strolled over to the calendar on the bulletin board. "That's tricky, since we don't know our destination. The third week of March would work. But," he added, "the bet's still on, so nothing can be firmed up."

Judith shrugged. "We can't force Mother to say what each of us wants to hear. Maybe," Judith said, avoiding Joe's gaze, "we should have made a different kind of bet."

Joe chuckled. "You're waffling. You know I'm going to win."

"Well . . . given Mother's history, the odds are in your favor."

"You bet they are," said Joe.

But, Judith thought smugly, Joe didn't know the deck was stacked against him.

The rain stopped during the night. Wednesday, the third of March, dawned with mostly blue skies and only a thirty percent chance of rain. Of course the local forecast changed approximately every half hour. As a native, Judith trusted her instincts, not the meteorologists.

When her cleaning woman, Phyliss Rackley, arrived, Judith informed her that the plan for the day would be slightly altered.

"I've asked Joe to help clean out some stuff from the garage," Judith explained, "so I won't have time to fold the laundry when you get done. Leave it in the pantry and I'll get to it later."

"Later?" Phyliss's beady eyes scrutinized Judith. "It's later than you think. Saint Peter's going tick-a-lock with those pearly gates for me even as we speak. I'm poorly. Very poorly."

Judith feigned sympathy. "Really? That's a shame. Maybe you should take the day off to see a doctor."

Phyliss's eyes practically bugged out. "Are you serious? You think I'm . . . terminal?"

Judith shrugged. "You know your own body. You've had so many close calls that I'm hardly surprised if The End Is Near."

"Well." Phyliss swallowed so hard Judith could see her Adam's apple move on her scrawny neck. "I might be able to last the day if I take my tonic."

"Good idea." Having dismissed her cleaning woman's latest bout of hypochondria, Judith headed outside to find Joe in the backyard, swinging a golf club.

"Where'd you find that?" Judith asked.

"In the cupboard on the side of the garage," Joe replied. He took another swing. "There's almost a complete set. They aren't mine."

"They belonged to my father," Judith said. "He golfed. The clubs must be seventy years old."

"They're not exactly the latest graphite type," Joe noted, looking up at the gray clouds that were gathering overhead. "It's going to rain. We should put off this job until afternoon. Or tomorrow."

"No." Judith's tone was unusually sharp. "I mean, it could rain until the end of June. We'll be in the garage most of the time anyway."

Joe looked resigned. "So what should I do with these clubs?"

"Get rid of them, I guess. Bill used to golf once in a while but he hasn't done that in years." She paused. "Let me show them to Mother. Did you find Mike's Louisville Slugger yet?"

"I saw it in there," Joe replied. "Does he want it back?"

"He might—for the boys," Judith said. "Our grandsons are getting old enough to play ball."

"Okay." Joe handed Judith what looked to her like a club that might be some kind of iron. He went back to the garage; she hurried to the toolshed.

"Mother," she said, "it's time to strut your stuff."

"What stuff?" Gertrude retorted, looking glum. "My stuff lost its stuffing a long time ago. What's with the golf club? Are you going to beat me with it if I don't do whatever I'm supposed to do?"

"It's part of the set that belonged to my father," Judith said, showing the club to her mother. "Remember?"

With a tentative hand, the old lady reached out to touch the club's shaft. "Oh yes. I remember," she said softly. "He was no Bobby Jones, but he tried. And he never cheated like some golfers do."

"Ah . . . that's true. My father was the soul of integrity."

Gertrude nodded. "More than you can say for some." She shot her daughter a sharp glance. "Well? What do I say when Lunk—"

"You say," Judith interrupted quickly before Gertrude could finish the derogatory nickname, " 'Way to go, Joe.' "

"Huh. Okay, help me to the door. I can do it from there, can't I?"

"Sure."

After getting Gertrude positioned in the doorway, Judith went back outside and retrieved the baseball she'd found in the garage and hidden under a fuchsia bush by the toolshed. Joe was coming from the garage with the baseball bat, an infielder's mitt, and a pair of badminton rackets that needed to be restrung.

"I assume," Joe called to his wife, "you've given up smacking the birdie around."

"Yes," Judith replied. "Toss those rackets. My hip has benched me. See if you can hit this." She cocked her arm to throw the baseball.

"Whoa!" Joe cried. "Let me put this other stuff down." He noticed Gertrude watching from the toolshed door. She had been joined by Sweetums, whose big orange and white body was curled up at the old lady's feet. "Hi there, pussycats," he said.

Gertrude didn't say anything. Sweetums yawned.

Judith lobbed the ball to Joe. He swung and missed. "Oh, come on," she said with a smile, "you can do better. How do you expect to coach Joe-Joe and Mac when they start Little League?"

"That was too low," Joe complained, picking up the ball and tossing it to his wife. "It was so far out of the strike zone that it practically grazed my ankles."

Judith tried to put more oomph on the second throw. Joe connected. The ball sailed off to the left, narrowly missing the statue of Saint Francis of Assisi.

Gertrude leaned forward, watching the ball land under a rhododendron bush. "Way to go!" she cried as Judith held her breath. "Way to go," she repeated. "Good swing . . . Biscuit Pants!"

Joe stared at Gertrude. "What did you just call me?"

"Biscuit Pants," Gertrude repeated. "Lou Gehrig's nickname." She looked at Judith. "What are you staring at? Lunkhead's foul ball?" The old lady tottered precariously as she turned to go back to the toolshed.

"Mother!" Judith shouted. "Wait!"

Joe raised his hands, making a Churchillian victory sign. "I win!"

Judith barely glanced at him as she hurried to steady Gertrude. "What's wrong with you?" she hissed. "You ruined everything!"

Gertrude took a couple of deep breaths and glared at her daughter. "I ruined you, that's for sure!"

"That's what I . . . how do you mean?"

With Judith's help, Gertrude hobbled to her armchair. "By not raising you right," Gertrude said in disgust. "For setting a bad example."

Puzzled, Judith eased her mother into the chair. "I don't understand."

Gertrude let out a big sigh. "Didn't I teach you never to cheat?"

"Ah . . . yes." Judith grimaced.

Sadly, Gertrude shook her head. "But you cheated today. You pulled a shenanigan. No matter what I've done, I won't have it."

Still not sure what her mother was talking about, Judith sat down on the arm of the small sofa. "You didn't do anything. I mean, you called Joe by the wrong name and then referred to him as—"

Gertrude waved a hand. "Hush! I . . . " She started to cry.

"Mother!" Judith got up and put an arm around the old lady's shoulders. "You what? You haven't been yourself lately. What is it?"

Tears slipped down Gertrude's wrinkled cheeks. She took a handkerchief from her housecoat's sleeve. "You better hear the worst."

Judith hugged her mother gently. "Tell me."

Clearing her throat, Gertrude made a swipe with the handkerchief. "Two weeks ago at SOTS bridge club."

Judith recalled helping Gertrude get into Angie Mazzoni's car for the card game with Our Lady, Star of the Sea—or SOTS, as the parishioners were more familiarly known. Afterwards, Gertrude had seemed glum even though she'd won the quarters.

"Go on," Judith urged when her mother fell silent.

"You know what a blowhard Mary Clare O'Malley can be," Gertrude finally said. "Bossy, too. On the last hand, she bid a small slam. I was pretty sure I could set her—if I knew if she was finessing on the second trick. She was bragging, and I hate showing off. Anyway . . . " Gertrude made a wretched face. "I peeked at her hand. She *was* finessing, so I played my high card and she went set, doubled and redoubled."

"That's it?" Judith said in obvious relief.

Gertrude scowled. "Isn't that enough? I've never cheated in my life! Granted, she was waving her cards around along with her big mouth, but even so, I had to lean a little to see them all. I don't know why I did it. I've been sick inside ever since. I'm probably going to hell."

"Oh, Mother," Judith said with a laugh and another hug, "don't be so hard on yourself. Mary Clare is a pill."

"That's no excuse for what I did," Gertrude insisted. "I feel like I should give back the quarters. They came to three dollars."

Judith patted her mother and stood up. "You probably sensed she was finessing. I'll bet you'd have played that high card regardless."

"Don't mention 'bet' to me," Gertrude snapped. "And then you do the same thing—cheat. I couldn't believe it, even if it meant you'd lose to Knucklehead. I couldn't go along. What was that all about anyway?"

Judith sighed. "It was a silly wager about the names you call Joe."

Gertrude stuffed the handkerchief back into her sleeve. "So? He should be used to it."

"He is," Judith said. "It's not a big deal. The winner gets to pick where we go on vacation."

Gertrude looked worried. "You're going away? Where?"

"I don't know yet," Judith said. "Not too far. Joe wants to fish."

"How long will you be gone?"

"We haven't decided," Judith replied. "A week or so."

Gertrude grew thoughtful. "The Rankerses are coming back from California in a couple of days, right?"

Judith nodded. "I'm sure Carl and Arlene will take wonderful care of you. They always do."

"You bet," said Gertrude, and bit her lip. "Forget I said that. No more bets. Arlene and Carl are fun. They treat me right."

"I know," Judith said, grateful as ever for her next-door neighbors. "Are you feeling any better?" she asked as Sweetums seemed to appear from nowhere and jumped up onto the back of Gertrude's chair.

"Well . . . maybe." She smiled faintly at Judith. "I guess it's true. Confession's good for the soul."

Judith had no intention of admitting to Joe that she'd attempted to sway the wagering odds in her favor. But her husband had seldom been fooled by liars and cheats during his career as a police detective.

"Nice try," he remarked as Judith entered the garage.

"It was . . . sort of a . . . joke," Judith said lamely. "Besides, Mother's been down in the dumps lately. I thought it might cheer her up."

Joe chuckled. "You're a wonderful liar, but I'm not buying it. I'm going to call Bill after I finish this corner of the garage. We need to firm up our plans ASAP."

"So where are we going?" Judith asked, wondering why they'd kept a rusty old lawn mower that must have belonged to Grandpa Grover.

"It's a secret," Joe replied. "We want to surprise you and Renie."

"Can I have a hint?"

Joe wiped his grease-stained hands on a rag. "No."

"Oh, come on!" Judith begged. "Renie and I have to know something about our destination or we can't pack the right clothes."

Joe thought for a moment. "You get three questions."

"Is there a beach?"

Joe nodded.

"Good. Ocean view?"

He nodded again.

"Quaint shops and restaurants close by?"

A third nod confirmed Judith's hopes. "Great!" she exclaimed, and kissed her husband's cheek. "How soon do we leave?"

Joe frowned slightly. "I'm not sure. A week, maybe two." He shook a finger at her. "No more questions."

"That's fine," Judith agreed. "I'm going inside to make sure all the guests have left and to check on Phyliss. I'll be right back."

But the first thing Judith did was to call Renie. It was well after ten o'clock, and her antimorning cousin should be up and fairly alert.

"It's not a sinus infection," Renie shouted into the phone. "It's my damned pollen allergies. Stop fussing, Mom. I'm naked."

"I hope you're inside the house," Judith said calmly.

"Of course . . . Coz? Oh," Renie said with relief, "I thought you were Mom calling me for the third time already this morning to make sure I don't have a terminal sinus infection. She woke me up the first time at nine. I wanted to sleep in longer than usual because I went to the opera with Madge Navarre last night. It was Verdi's *Don Carlo*—the uncut version. It was great, but I was really tired by the final curtain call."

"Sorry I bothered you. Do you want to get dressed?"

"I didn't want to get undressed," Renie responded. "I was cozy in bed in my nightgown, but when Mom called—and you know Bill, he never takes calls—I had to answer it because I'm always sure that one of our three children who live in far-flung places is hanging by his or her thumbs from a steep cliff over shark-infested waters."

"I'll make this quick," Judith said, hearing someone on the main stairs. "I lost the bet, but I'm almost certain I know where we're going."

"Going? Oh—the supposed trip. Where?"

"Dana Point! Just what I wanted! You will come, won't you?"

"Well—if Bill wants to. I assume he does if he and Joe have been hatching plans. But I'm not sure we can afford any big expenditures. If only Bill wouldn't have such hard luck with his inventions. If he could ever sell one, we wouldn't be semi-broke."

A month earlier Renie revealed that Bill had been spending part of his retirement not just counseling a few of his longtime mental patients, but also dreaming up inventions. He was embarrassed about the activity, especially since every time he tried to find a backer for ideas such as his circulating hospital mattress and lightweight collapsible Rollo-Bag for shoppers, he discovered they were already patented.

"Excuse me. I just heard the postman." Renie hung up.

Judith smiled as she set the receiver on the dining room table. She hoped Renie would remember to put on some clothes before she went out to the mailbox.

After bidding farewell to her departing guests, Judith found Phyliss in the living room about to turn on the vacuum. "Moses and I are ready to roar," the cleaning woman said with an eager expression.

"Wonderful," Judith remarked, smiling slightly. Phyliss referred to the vacuum as Moses, and pretended she was parting the Red Sea or leading the Israelites out of captivity. "If you need me, I'm in the garage."

"All I need right now is Moses," Phyliss declared, turning on the vacuum. "On to Mount Horeb! We want to see that burning bush!"

Judith went back outside. As she helped Joe finish cleaning the garage and then attended to her other routine chores, she dreamed of California's warm sun, sandy beaches, and fine cuisine.

The dream kept her going all through the busy day and into the evening. During the night she woke up once, thinking she could hear the soft surf caressing the pristine sands. The sound was only the rain pattering on the windows. She smiled, rolled over closer to Joe, and went back to sleep.

2

The rest of the week passed quickly, but that following Monday as the wind picked up and the rain slanted down, Judith's mood turned sour. Joe had told her they'd be leaving in a couple of weeks, but he hadn't mentioned a date or anything else about his plans. Judith had alerted Ingrid Heffelman about the need for a B&B sitter. Ingrid had been cantankerous, though she'd agreed to find someone reliable. Monday afternoon, Ingrid had called to confirm the dates. Judith was unable to tell her anything concrete. Ingrid had hung up in a huff. Judith didn't blame her, but Joe wasn't forthcoming. He merely went around the house humming and looking pleased with himself.

"At least," Judith said to Renie the next day as the cousins met for coffee at Moonbeam's on top of

Heraldsgate Hill, "the Rankers are back from California, so Mother is taken care of. Thank heavens she's in a better mood since she unburdened herself about the bridge game."

Renie sipped her mocha and nodded. "I've rounded up the usual suspects to watch over Mom. She's convinced we're going to some ghastly place where we'll need shots and mosquito netting and get kidnapped by white slavers."

Judith blew on her espresso. "Bill hasn't let anything slip?"

Renie shook her head. "You know how tight-lipped he can be. Bill's the only person I know who could withstand any kind of torture before revealing a secret. Even threatening to make homemade soup for dinner won't get him to open up. He's very strong."

Judith recalled many years earlier when Renie had made soup—for the last time. One of their children had thrown a dirty gym sock in it, hoping to improve the flavor. Renie had taken the hint.

"But," Renie went on, "I've got the tax stuff in to our CPA, I'm winding up loose ends with my graphic design business, and I'm virtually packed. So is Bill, but I can't tell what he's taking because he locked his suitcase and probably swallowed the key."

Judith smiled at two mothers who were pushing high-tech strollers between the tables. "Mike and Kristin and the boys are coming for St. Patrick's Day dinner tomorrow, so I know we aren't leaving before that."

"You're lucky," Renie said for what Judith figured was the hundredth time. "Your son and his wife and the grandchildren live only an hour away at the ranger station. Our three and their unfruitful spouses are whole continents and oceans away."

As usual, Judith commiserated. "Think of the bright side," Judith said. "In probably just a few days we'll be relaxing under the sun with margaritas at our side."

"I'm not so fond of sun," Renie muttered. "I'm the essential Pacific Northwest native. Gloom is good."

"I'm a native, too," Judith countered, "but I wouldn't mind some warmth and clear skies. It seems like a long winter."

Renie, who had a foam mustache on her upper lip, shrugged. "Fair enough. Getting away will be nice. So will being waited on. A spa session sounds good, too."

Judith replied. "I printed out the St. Regis Monarch Beach Resort in Dana Point web site and taped it to the bathroom mirror. It isn't cheap, but we don't go anywhere that often."

"Nor do we." Renie raised her cup. "To relaxation and pampering."

Judith smiled. "My, yes. And to us."

Mike and his family left Hillside Manor Thursday night full of corned beef, cabbage, carrots, potatoes, and soda bread. Judith was loading the dishwasher when Joe came up behind her and leaned over her shoulder. "Set the alarm for six o'clock."

"I always do," Judith replied, "so I can get the guests' breakfast."

"You're not getting breakfast tomorrow," Joe said, tightening his arms around Judith's waist. "The airport shuttle's coming at seven."

Judith whirled around and angrily regarded her husband. "Joe! I can't just walk out the door! I have to arrange for—"

He put a finger to her lips. "It's covered. Your B&B sitters arrive at six-thirty. I talked to Ingrid Heffelman Tuesday. She's a good sport."

"Since when?" Judith snapped. But the mischief in Joe's eyes softened her temper. "You took care of everything? Ingrid was . . . nice?"

"Sure. You're kind of hard on her. She has a cute giggle."

Judith shook her head in disbelief. "I've never seen Ingrid smile, let alone giggle." But she could understand the usually dour überführer of innkeepers melting under Joe's Irish charm. "Where are we going?"

He grinned at her slyly. "It's still a surprise. You'll find out when we get there."

Having waited this long, Judith stopped asking questions. She still had a lot to do, but first she had to call Renie.

"Don't," Joe said. "She won't know anything until Bill wakes her up at five-thirty."

"But . . ." Judith goggled at Joe. "At that time of day Renie won't be fit to deal with anything that doesn't include a pillow and a dark room."

Joe stepped away from Judith and shrugged. "That's his problem. After forty years of marriage, Bill can handle it."

Judith considered. "So we're flying. If Renie doesn't realize that, she won't be a nervous wreck and therefore won't have time to drink herself into a stupor like she did before we flew to San Francisco."

"Very true," Joe said. "And don't worry about your mother. I talked to Carl and Arlene. I also told Mike where we're going."

Excitement began to build. "Oh, Joe, this is going to be wonderful!" She hugged him and planted a big kiss on his lips. Suddenly she tensed. "Does Mother know?"

"She knows we're going," Joe said.

"Does she know where and for how long?"

Joe looked vague. "Not exactly. A few days at the beach was the way I put it. She may have the impression we're . . . ah . . . visiting Auntie Vince and Uncle Vance up on the island."

"Just as well." She smiled. "Oh, this is going to be amazing!"

Judith had no idea how right she was.

Renie was clearly smashed when the Flynns boarded the shuttle. But at least she was smiling, which wouldn't happen in the early morning unless there'd been several shots of Wild Turkey involved.

Bill acted as if he'd never seen his wife before in his life. The trip to the airport was uneventful, however. Judith had been impressed by the older couple who had shown up to take over the B&B. They'd owned their own establishment for years in Idaho, but had sold it and moved farther west to be closer to their two sons and their families. Full retirement hadn't suited either of them, so they'd become substitutes for absent innkeepers.

As usual, the airport was under construction. Judith couldn't remember a time when it wasn't being expanded or altered. When the Flynns and the Joneses got off the shuttle, she paid no attention to the overhead signs designating the various airlines. Judith was too busy watching Renie stagger slightly as she exited the vehicle.

"Thank you, doorman," she said to the driver. "Put my purchases on the porch, okay?"

Bill was already at the curbside check-in desk. "Yes," he said wearily in response to the woman who was checking their tickets. "She's my wife. There's nothing I can do about it. We're Catholics."

Joe was behind Bill. The process went smoothly except for Renie, who managed to get herself entangled in the ropes designating the passenger line. Judith managed to free her, and Renie managed a loopy smile and murmured, ". . . Crazy place for a jump rope."

The husbands led the way to the escalators. Both men were walking faster than Judith could manage, but she thought it best to stay close to Renie, who was wandering this way and that.

"Hang on to me," Judith said softly to her cousin.

"'Sa matter?" Renie asked. "Your hip hur'?"

"Yes."

"Poor you."

Judith kept the husbands within sight, but was puzzled when they headed for the tram that went to the far-flung airline waiting areas.

"Odd," she murmured. "The California flights are in the main terminal."

"You sure?" Renie asked.

"Yes." Judith thought for a moment. "But I think some of the Hawaii flights are on the tram route." She beamed at Renie. "Do you suppose we're going to the islands?"

"What islands?"

"The . . . " But Judith had to hurry, hauling Renie along with her. The tram had arrived and the husbands were boarding. The cousins entered just before the doors slid shut. Recorded announcements were made while Judith scanned the stops listed above the doors.

"I was right," she told Renie. "The first stop is for the Hawaiian-bound airlines. The second one, too. Oh, I'm so excited!"

"Unh," said Renie.

But when the tram doors opened, Joe and Bill remained in place. Nor did they budge at the second stop.

"Golly," Judith said, "we're going to the international terminal."

Renie gave a start. "Are you kidding?" she asked in what sounded almost like her normal voice. "You're right. It's the last one. Are we going to Polynesia or the Caribbean?"

"Australia or New Zealand, maybe," Judith said. "It's late summer or early fall down there, and we've had guests who've raved about the fishing—and the beaches."

As the tram glided to its final stop, Joe nodded at Judith. The Flynns and the Joneses got off along with a half-dozen Asian businessmen, a couple of bearded Sikhs in turbans, an elderly cleric, and three exquisite young Japanese women whose beauty wasn't the least bit marred by their giggles.

Only the cleric and one of the Sikhs headed in the same direction as Joe and Bill. Judith's eyes grew huge as she realized they were going to the British Airways desk. She and Renie nudged their way in front of Joe and Bill as they waited to go through security. "London!" Judith gasped, and pointed to the departure listings. "Oh, I'm thrilled!"

"I thought you wanted sun," Renie said. "The weather in London is the same as it here. Which, of course, is fine with me."

Joe turned around. "London's not our final destination."

Judith stared at him. "What is?"

"You wanted beaches and an ocean view, right?"

"Yes, of course." Judith jabbed Renie. "The Riviera—or Spain."

"Really long flight," Renie said under her breath. "Damn."

Judith and Renie passed through security without any glitches. Joe and Bill, however, were stopped.

"Men," Renie muttered. "Too many keys and other suspicious metal objects. It always happens."

Joe was cleared after only a couple of minutes. Bill, however, was still being detained. But finally he was allowed to move on.

"What was that all about?" Renie demanded of her husband.

Bill frowned. "Do I know you? Are you a patient, or were you in one of my university classes?" He turned on his heel and walked away.

"Why have I not killed him in forty years?" Renie mumbled. "And why isn't the bar open in this part of the terminal?"

For the next hour, Judith did her best to avoid Renie, who spent most of the time pacing around the waiting area. Joe and Bill had gone off to buy magazines. At last, the boarding call was announced.

"I wish I'd changed my will," Renie murmured as she got into line. "I'd have left Clarence to Madge Navarre."

"You know Madge hates animals," Judith retorted. "She'd hardly want a bunny running around her condo. And don't be so pessimistic."

"Our husbands aren't sitting with us," Renie said as they moved up a few places in line.

Judith looked at her boarding pass. "You're right. You and I are in a completely different part of the plane."

"I can't blame Bill," Renie said. "The last time we flew I brought some small liquor bottles in my purse. The flight attendant said it was illegal and threatened to throw me off the plane. Bill offered to help."

The cousins displayed their boarding passes and walked down the corridor to the plane. Inside the cabin, Judith saw Joe wave at her from his seat several rows away. Judith waved back but didn't smile. Having Renie as a seatmate during a twelve-hour flight to London might be trying.

But as soon as she buckled her seat belt, Renie dug around in her purse, took out a pill caddy, extracted four small yellow tablets, and chewed them up. They had just begun to taxi for takeoff when Renie put her head on her cousin's shoulder and said, "G'night."

Judith also dozed off. The initial excitement had worn off and the long walk in the terminal had tired her. When she woke up, it was dark.

Renie also opened her eyes. "Where are we?" she mumbled.

"Thirty-five thousand feet above Planet Earth," Judith replied.

Renie shuddered and went back to sleep.

Joe came by to check on his wife. "I saw you limp a bit when you went to the restroom," he said, leaning across the aisle seat, which had remained blessedly empty. "Are you okay?"

Judith nodded. "Sitting so long bothers me sometimes. What time will it be in London when we arrive?"

"Around noon." Joe checked his watch. "I'm already on UK time."

"How much time between flights?"

"A couple of hours," Joe said.

"How long is the second flight?"

"Not long." He smiled mischievously. "See you at Heathrow."

Judith couldn't get back to sleep. She'd finished the novel she'd been reading and had flipped through the British Airways magazine. She was making a trek to the restroom when the pilot announced that they were beginning their descent.

By the time she reached her seat, Renie was awake. "I thought you left," Renie said. "I heard the announcement. I like the descent part. If we crash, we don't have so far to fall. Besides, we can jump up and down like people do on plunging elevators. If you're up in the air when it lands, you won't get hurt."

Judith didn't comment. Instead, she got out her compact and reapplied her makeup.

"You want to be a pretty corpse?" Renie asked. "I forgot—you can't jump with that phony hip."

"Shut up, coz," Judith said. "We have only a two-hour layover. That means we can't go into London. I'm kind of disappointed."

"Maybe we can do that on the way back," Renie said.

A half hour passed before the plane landed on the tarmac. Tired and stiff, Judith exited into the blur that was Heathrow. She didn't feel as if she'd traveled ten thousand miles from Hillside Manor. She simply felt as if she'd had a very bad night.

"Sun," she murmured to Renie as they waited in the customs and immigration line. "I can't wait."

This time there were no delays. The foursome was cleared in short order. Judith tried to hear Joe's response when he was asked about their next stop, but he elbowed her out of the way and lowered his voice.

"Now what?" Renie demanded. "Hey!" She tugged at the sleeve of Bill's jacket. "Remember me? We once took sacred vows in a church."

But neither of the men would reveal anything. Judith didn't pester Joe, conserving her energy to walk to their connecting flight.

Twenty minutes later, the cousins discovered the next stop.

"Aberdeen, Scotland?" Judith gasped.

"Why?" Renie asked in a bewildered voice.

"Sun-drenched beaches?" Judith muttered. "Not this time of year." She turned to Joe, who was studying what looked like an itinerary. "Is Aberdeen our final stop?"

Joe didn't look up from the printout. "No."

Exasperated, Judith walked back to Renie. "We keep going."

"How? By spaceship?"

Judith shrugged. "I'm beginning to lose my enthusiasm."

The flight, however, was relatively short. By three o'clock, they were in misty Aberdeen. Renie complained that she couldn't see the city from the airport.

"Don't worry," Bill said. "That's not where we're staying."

Joe had rented a car. Fifteen minutes later, they were driving away from the city. Traffic was heavy. The Friday commute, Judith thought, and finally reset her watch.

"Are we there yet?" Renie asked sullenly from the backseat.

There was no answer from Joe behind the wheel nor from Bill, sitting beside his wife. After almost an hour, they left the highway where the mist began drifting onto the narrow, winding road.

"Are we there yet?" Renie asked again.

No answer.

"Where is there?" Judith inquired.

"You'll see," Joe said.

"I won't see anything in this weather," Judith retorted. "As much as I hate to use the words 'husbands' and 'idiots' in the same sentence, this is some terrible practical joke, or else . . . " She left the rest unspoken.

It had grown dark. Joe rolled down the window. "Smell the sea?"

"I smell a rat," Judith muttered, she sniffing at the air.

Joe began to slow down, obeying the road signs giving the legal speed not in miles, but kilometers. "We're getting close."

"I'm starved," Renie declared.

Moments later, lights glowed through the mist. "The village," Joe said. "St. Fergna."

"Who?" Judith asked.

"Fergna the White," Joe replied. "A seventh-century abbot."

"Who was Fergna the Black?" Judith asked dryly. "Or maybe Fergna the Black-and-Blue?"

"Fergna better have started a restaurant," Renie grumbled.

From what Judith could see of the village, it was small and probably had a certain charm if it hadn't been shrouded in mist. She spotted a half-dozen people on the winding cobbled streets. But Joe didn't stop. He kept going seaward until they were on a steep dirt road.

"We aren't there yet?" Renie demanded.

Joe stopped the car on the flat sands. A thick fog hid everything but their immediate surroundings. She knew they were near the North Sea. Not only could she smell it, but she could also hear the surf.

"Didn't I promise you beach with a water view?" Joe asked.

Judith stared at him. "We're camping?" Her tone wasn't pleasant.

"No," he replied. "Just wait." He sat behind the wheel, hands folded on his slight paunch. After a few minutes, a light glowed in the fog. Joe flashed the head-lamps. "Here's the ferryman."

"The ferryman?" Judith asked, aghast. "We're going to an island?"

"Not quite," Joe said. "Only when the tide's in."

Judith saw an elderly man approach carrying a lantern. He wore a peacoat, dark pants, and heavy boots. A fisherman's cap covered most of his longish white hair.

"Gibbs here," he said with a Highland accent. "Ye be Flynn?"

"Yes," Joe replied. "Flynn and Jones."

Gibbs peered inside the car, gazing with sea blue eyes at Judith and Renie. "These be your ladies?"

"Yes," Joe repeated. "Mrs. Flynn and Mrs. Jones."

"Come along," Gibbs said.

Judith stepped out onto the wet sand and sank about half an inch. "I'm stuck," she informed Joe. "Help me." She refrained from adding, "Before I kill you."

Renie disdained any assistance, her shoes squelching in the sand as she tromped toward a small skiff about ten yards away from the car. She swore several of her father's favorites oaths along the way.

"Ah," Gibbs said softly. "She be a rough 'un. Sounds like a sailor."

"It's hereditary," Bill said.

Joe took Judith's arm. She refused to look at him. When she was settled into the small craft, the wind changed and the fog began to roll out to sea. While Gibbs plied the oars, Judith could make out a rock formation with craggy, sheer cliffs. Her heart sank. She was sure they were going to stay in a lighthouse. With any luck, maybe the boat would sink, too.

Gibbs, who seemed very strong for his age, rowed the little group to the bottom of the rocks in less than five minutes. "Up ye go," he said.

Joe helped Judith get out of the skiff and onto flat granite stones set in the sandy ground. "How," she asked pointedly, "do we get up?"

"We follow these stones," Joe said in a reasonable tone. "Look. There's the lift."

The elevator was an iron-grilled cage on cables that seemed to disappear into the clouds. Judith stared—and shuddered. "Is it safe?"

"Gibbs came down in it," Joe said. "So now we go up in it."

Renie was balking. "No way. I'll sleep on the beach."

"Move it," ordered Bill, giving his wife a push. "Let's go, let's hit it, let's boppin', let's—"

"Let's shut the hell up," Renie snarled. But she moved.

The foursome went inside the cage. Joe found a lever and pulled it. The conveyance rumbled and shook—and moved slowly up the face of the cliff. After about a minute, it stopped. They got out and took in the sight before them.

"My God!" Judith cried. "It's a castle!"

Joe chuckled and put his arm around her shoulders. "Didn't you want something fit for a queen?"

3

G ood Lord!" Judith gasped. "It's real? It's not a mirage?"

"It's real." Joe offered Judith his arm. "Shall we enter, milady?"

"What's it called?" Renie asked, looking suspicious.

"Ah . . . " Joe hesitated. "Grimloch, Gaelic for 'green' or 'grass.'"

"No," Renie countered. "It comes from Old English for 'fierce.'"

"Are we waiting for a dictionary?" Bill asked impatiently.

Judith and Joe moved toward the arch. She noticed a raised portcullis and saw that the castle's building stones were a weathered dark gray, covered in patches of lichen and moss. Indeed, water seemed to seep out of the masonry cracks. The outer wall was only one story, though the inner U-shaped section had at least two levels aboveground. Since the castle sat high on an outcropping of rock, there was a drawbridge and a moat. Judith noticed twin towers, the castle keep, the battlements, and a few narrow windows on the ground floor. The inner courtyard was planted with grass and shrubs.

"There's only a couple of lights inside," Judith said, then peered at her watch. "It's a little after seven. Where is everybody?"

"I told you, we're the only guests," Joe replied. "Isn't that great?"

The social animal in Judith reacted. "I don't know if I like that."

Joe ignored the comment. He had led the others to a heavy oak door on their right. The iron knocker was a boar's head, which he banged three times.

Judith felt chilled as the wind picked up and the damp air crept into her bones. Like Renie, she was hungry, but she was also very tired.

Finally a rotund white-haired woman with pink cheeks opened the door. "Welcome," she said with a tight little smile. "I'm Mrs. Gibbs, the housekeeper."

The housekeeper didn't offer her hand. She merely stepped aside with what might have been a little bow and allowed the visitors to enter. A shield showing three muzzled boars' heads on a blue background hung on the opposite wall. Above it was draped a predominantly green and blue tartan plaid. Judith could feel a draft coming from somewhere in the narrow stone-walled passageway.

"You're the ferryman's wife?" Judith said, unable to restrain her friendly—and curious—nature.

"Aye."

"When's dinner served?" Renie asked.

"Bide a bit," Mrs. Gibbs replied.

"Bite a bit?" Renie retorted. "I'll bite more than that if you—"

Bill tugged at Renie's arm. "Mrs. Jones's feeding time is past due."

"We should probably change," Joe put in. "Perhaps you could show us to our rooms."

"Aye."

Mrs. Gibbs led them down the narrow passageway to a winding stone staircase. Judith regarded the steps with trepidation.

"How many flights?" she asked.

The housekeeper turned slightly. "Flights? Oh. One."

The stairs were narrow but spaced close together. Judith realized that when the castle had been built hundreds of years ago, people had been shorter and smaller. That, she thought, was a blessing for her hip. She also noticed that the torches in the wall sconces had been replaced by electric lights shaped like flames. Maybe the accommodations weren't as grim as the castle's name implied.

Mrs. Gibbs stopped at the first door on their left. "Flynn," she said, taking a set of keys on a metal ring from the leather belt she wore over her gray dress. Unlocking the door, she handed the key to Joe. Then she moved across the hall. Judith heard her say, "Jones."

The Flynns' room was large, with a huge fireplace ready for a match to light the logs. The windows were tall and recessed, with facing stone benches. A canopied bed stood opposite the fireplace. There was a desk, a table, two armchairs, and a settee.

Mrs. Gibbs returned. "The garderobe," she said, pointing to another oak door.

"That would be the . . . bathroom?" Judith said.

"Aye."

Mrs. Gibbs left.

"Quite a view," Joe said, looking out the double window with its ancient glass. "That is, when we can see it. We overlook the water."

"How could we not?" Judith murmured. "This is a virtual island."

"Shall I light the fire?"

"No. Wait until after dinner. I'm only semifreezing now." Judith opened the garderobe door. "At least it's a real bathroom. Toilet, sink, and tub. Even a shower, thank goodness. I won't have to worry about getting in and out."

"I know," Joe said, admiring the tapestry of a hunting scene. "I made sure of that. And," he added, "there is an elevator. I think it's at the far end of this passageway."

"Ah." Judith was relieved. "What does a place like this cost?"

Joe grinned. "Nothing."

Judith stared. "How come?"

Joe sat in one of the armchairs. "Remember when Bill and I fished in Scotland while you and Renie stayed with your English friends?"

"They weren't exactly our friends," Judith said. "The connection was my longtime pen pal from high school days."

"Right." He shrugged. "Anyway, while we were fishing, we met a Scotland Yard detective, Hugh MacGowan. He still works, but plans to retire in June. Great guy, an old-fashioned cop who doesn't trust modern technology and relies on solid detective work and his instincts. He still uses a typewriter and won't touch a computer. He knew about Grimloch, and said the owners took in summer guests. I wrote to Hugh even before our bet to ask if we could come earlier in the year. Being a canny Scot, he coaxed them into a free stay for us."

"Mr. and Mrs. Gibbs own this place?"

"No. It belongs to a whiskey distillery owner," Joe replied. "He spends his winters in Spain, but comes here for part of the year."

"Good," Judith said. "You didn't have to plunder our savings." A knock at the door sounded as she studied a handsome armoire.

Gibbs arrived with their luggage. Joe proffered a tip but was refused. "Butler rings gong at eight," Gibbs said, tipping his fisherman's cap. "A wee dram awaits in the drawing room near where ye came in."

Judith hurriedly unpacked, hanging their clothes in a capacious wardrobe. Joe showered first. When Judith's turn came, she was elated to discover that although the bathroom fixtures looked old, the plumbing was modern. She had no problem pulling the toilet's chain as long as it flushed; she didn't mind the outdated faucets if they poured hot and cold water. Maybe, she thought, just maybe, she might succumb to the castle's charm. After all, the sun might come out in the morning.

"Good grief!" she cried, coming out of the garder-obe wrapped in a large white towel. "I just realized I don't have clothes for this kind of weather! I packed for California. Or someplace like it."

Joe looked puzzled. "If you didn't know where we were going, why didn't you bring clothes you could wear anyplace?"

Judith heaved a big sigh. "Women don't pack like that. I'll bet Renie's having a fit."

"Renie was almost over the limit on her luggage," Joe pointed out. "I'll bet she's brought along some . . . ah . . . warmer stuff."

Judith was shoving garments this way and that in the wardrobe. "This purple and white orchid dress with the ruffled sweater," she muttered. "That'll have to do for tonight. I'll call Renie and Bill to find out how soon they'll be ready." Judith looked around the big room. "I don't see a phone."

"Um . . . they don't have one in the guest rooms. No TV, either, but," Joe went on cheerfully, "that's be-cause there's so much else to do."

Judith started to dress. "Such as?"

"Well . . . the village, shops, history. Oh—dolphins. They call them bottlenoses—or something like that."

"You left out fishing," Judith said sharply.

Joe looked surprised. "You want to fish?"

"Never mind." Judith applied lipstick and blush. "Let's eat."

By chance, Renie and Bill were leaving their room. Renie was wearing a wool emerald green sweater with a long black wool skirt.

"For sunny California?" Judith asked with sarcasm.

Renie shrugged. "Once the sun goes down, it gets chilly in Southern California."

"Nice room," Bill remarked as they headed for the staircase. "Too bad it's not on the ocean. We see the village."

"All those bright lights," Judith retorted. "All four of them?"

"I built a fire," Bill said.

"That must be pleasant," Judith responded. "Joe's going to try that after dinner. If he can find the flint."

They started down the circular stairs. "I'm taking the elevator back up," Judith declared.

"What elevator?" Renie asked.

"There's one somewhere," Bill said vaguely.

They reached the ground floor. "The gong," Judith said. "Have we heard the gong signaling dinner?"

"It's two minutes after eight," Judith said, looking at her watch. "How could we hear it through these thick stone walls?"

"Good point," Joe said. He gestured straight ahead. "That's where we came in. The drawing room is—" He stopped. At the far end of the passageway, a small, furtive figure skittered into view, paused, turned around, and disappeared.

"Who was that?" Judith asked.

"What was that?" Renie said. "A kid? The butler? Our waiter?"

The door to the drawing room opened just before the foursome moved on. A man in proper butler's attire beamed at them. He looked familiar to Judith.

"Gibbs?" she said.

"Aye," he replied, still smiling. "The finest Scottish whiskey awaits ye. Did ye hear the gong?"

"Aye," Judith said. "I mean—nae. No."

Gibbs nodded. "I thought not. Nobody ever does."

The drawing room made Judith catch her breath. Some of the furnishings looked very old, perhaps from the seventeenth or even sixteenth century, but they had been lovingly restored. Brocades, silks, and velvet covered the chairs and settees. Many of the pieces were heavy and solid. The walls were paneled in oak; the ceiling was coffered. Judith immediately moved to the fireplace hearth where logs were ablaze. The chimney, she noticed, was decorated with a stag's head, proper.

"The family crest?" she inquired as Gibbs stood by a satinwood table where decanters, glassware, and an ice bucket had been set out.

The ferryman cum butler smiled. "Aye, the Forbes clan. The master is a Fordyce, a sept o' the Forbes. There's a Castle Fordyce to the southeast, but distant kin, ye ken. Now and again, folks get confused, come to the wrong one."

"That's understandable," Judith said. "Did this Fordyce inherit Grimloch Castle?"

"Nae." Gibbs's face turned stony. "The master . . . bought it some twenty-odd years ago." He cleared his throat. "Will ye be drinking his special malt?"

Judith, Joe, and Bill said yes. Renie looked apologetic. "Do you have any Canadian whiskey—or Pepsi?"

Gibbs nodded and reached into a glass-fronted cabinet next to the table. "Set aside for our colonial cousins."

Judith accepted a flared crystal highball glass. "May I please have some ice?"

"Ah." Gibbs's blue eyes twinkled. "Yanks. Ye must have yer ice."

After the drinks were poured, Gibbs announced that he'd retire to assume his other duties. "Cook serves at half past the hour," he said.

Judith sipped her drink and explored their surroundings. "Some of these paintings must be very
valuable," she said to Renie. "Is that Venice scene a real
Canaletto?"

"Could be," Renie replied. "There's a Turner Grand
Canal on the other wall. The portraits are excellent,
too."

"Mostly ancestors, I suppose."

"Maybe, but not all of them," Renie said. "I spotted
Mary, Queen of Scots, and her son James VI—James I,
if you only count him as an English king."

"Fascinating." Judith looked at Renie's wool sweater
and skirt. "You were smart to pack at least one warm
outfit."

"Ah . . . well, you know . . . " Renie looked away,
ostensibly studying an inlaid chess table on a pedestal.
"The weather's always unpredictable."

Judith eyed her cousin suspiciously. "But wool?"

Still avoiding Judith's gaze, Renie shrugged.
"Wool . . . breathes."

"Only when the sheep's wearing it," Judith snapped.
"What else did you pack that you couldn't possibly
wear in eighty-degree heat?"

Renie grimaced. "A couple of other sweaters. Wool
slacks. Hooded jacket. Furs."

"Furs?"

"Faux fur," Renie said. "Except for my raincoat's real fox lining."

Judith moved closer to Renie, forcing her to back up against a mahogany settee. "You knew?"

Renie shot a quick glance at Joe and Bill, who were standing on the hearth at the other end of the room. "Bill had to tell me. Otherwise he wouldn't have been able to get me on the plane. But he figured that if we were headed for Scotland, I'd be willing to fly. You know I love Scottish history. And," Renie added lamely, "Scottish weather. It's just like home, only more so."

"You lied to me!" Judith exclaimed softly. "How could you?"

"I didn't really lie," Renie insisted. "Bill didn't tell me until the night before we left. Please don't let Joe find out. Until now, I had to act clueless. Bill felt terrible about breaking his promise to Joe, but he realized I might stay home even if I had to fake my own death."

Judith shook her head. "I'm speechless—and flabbergasted."

"Hey." Renie wagged a finger at her cousin. "This whole thing started because of your dumb bet, and the—"

"It wasn't dumb," Judith interrupted. "At first, it was fifty—"

"Never mind that part. I mean," Renie clarified, "the vacation stakes. Why on earth would you, a Pacific Northwest native, want to seek sun? It's unthinkable."

Judith considered her cousin's words. "Honestly, I don't know why I said Dana Point. I'd been there a couple of times with Dan, and it was very pleasant. For a few hours. Maybe when Joe asked me where I'd like to vacation, I didn't think it through. Maybe I forgot how much I hate heat and constant sunshine."

"That's okay," Renie said in consolation. "Everybody has an occasional lapse."

The cousins' attention was diverted as a tall, handsome young man in classic tweeds entered the drawing room. Joe and Bill nodded as the newcomer went directly to the cabinet where the liquor was stored. He poured out a generous measure of whiskey and rather insolently gazed from the husbands to the wives.

"Do I know you?" he asked in a slightly drawling voice that sounded more English than Scots.

Joe offered his hand. "We're guests. Joe Flynn and Bill Jones. Our wives are over there." He nodded in Judith and Renie's direction.

The young man's handshake lacked enthusiasm. "Oh. I heard you were coming. Or did I?" He frowned. "I'm Harry Gibbs."

Judith and Renie had approached the young man. "I'm Mrs. Flynn, and this is Mrs. Jones."

Harry Gibbs's hazel eyes darted from cousin to cousin. "Oh." He drank his whiskey neat.

Judith was taken aback by Harry's ungracious manner. "Are you related to the Gibbses?" she asked to cover the awkward moment.

"Grandson," he said, and finished his drink in one big gulp. Harry returned to the liquor cabinet and poured a refill. Without another glance at the visitors, he sauntered out of the drawing room.

"Not exactly the warm and fuzzy type," Judith remarked. "I wanted to ask him who we saw at the end of the passageway. Whoever it was almost looked like a child. I should've asked Gibbs."

"Maybe," Renie suggested, "it's another—younger—grandson. Harry's parents may dump their offspring on Grandpa and Grandma."

"Harry's no kid," Joe pointed out. "I'd figure him for over twenty. And he was wearing a wedding ring."

"He's old enough to drink," Renie said. "A lot, it seems."

"Unbalanced," Bill declared in his most authoritative psychologist's manner. "Something's off."

Renie grinned at Judith. "Lucky us. Your husband notices details like wedding bands and mine diagnoses a nut job at fifty paces."

"Hmm," Judith murmured. "Maybe there are enough people around here to keep us intrigued."

Joe put an arm around Judith. "People—my wife's favorite hobby."

Renie gazed at the drawing room door. "Dinner—my favorite hobby. Shall we dine?"

"I think," Joe said, "we'll be summoned. It's not quite eight-thirty. Anybody want to freshen this most excellent beverage?"

Judith and Bill requested just a jot more. Renie shook her head. "I've hardly touched my Canadian. Liquor is off-putting after my bout with Wild Turkey. I can barely stand the smell, let alone the taste."

"Serves you right," Bill said.

At precisely eight-thirty, Gibbs reappeared. "Dinner is served," he announced. "Cook will present."

The dining room was long and rather stark with its stone walls, two recessed windows, and an open fireplace where logs burned fitfully. The single table for sixteen was covered with a white linen cloth. The settings were handsome, however, with gleaming silver, elegant plates, and sparkling crystal glasses. The chairs were quite plain, though upholstered with faded brown damask. A candelabrum burned at the end of the table where the place settings had been laid.

A swinging door opened. Cook appeared, delicately balancing two soup plates on each arm.

"Mrs. Gibbs?" Judith said in surprise.

"Aye." Mrs. Gibbs, who was attired in a flowered frock protected by a big white apron, adroitly set Judith's soup in front of her. "Feather fowlie. Granary rolls in covered bread basket." She delivered the rest of the soup and presumably returned to the kitchen.

Judith tasted her soup. "It's delicious," she said, accepting the roll basket from Bill. "The fowlie must be chicken. I wonder if Mr. and Mrs. Gibbs take care of this entire castle themselves."

Joe shrugged. "Could be. It's the off-season."

Renie looked across the table at Bill. "Cute," she murmured. "But not now. I'm eating."

Bill looked up from the roll he was buttering. "What's cute?"

"You," Renie said. "With the kneesies."

"Kneesies?" Bill looked puzzled. "I'm sitting five feet away from you. How could my knees stretch so far? You know I'm a thirty-inch long in the leg and a thirty-four waist."

"I know the thirty-inch part," Renie said dryly. "The waist measurement is . . . Hey!" She turned to Joe and then to Judith. "Who's bumping me? Cut it out! I almost slopped my soup."

"So what?" Bill inquired. "You're a messy eater."

"My knees aren't near you," Joe asserted. "I'm a thirty-two long and a . . . ah . . . um . . . "

"Forget it," Judith snapped, almost saying that her husband couldn't count that high. "It's not me. You must be hitting something."

"No," Renie declared. "I haven't moved my . . . Yikes!"

The table rocked and the fine white linen cloth flew up at the corner between Renie and Joe. A head of short, curly dark hair poked out and turned to gaze at the startled diners.

"Hello. I'm Chuckie."

Judith gasped—and stared. The boy looked like a gnome, with small dark eyes, a long chin, and a big, cheerful grin.

Joe was the first to recover. "Hello, Chuckie. Do you live under this table?"

Chuckie shook his head before crawling out and sitting on his haunches. Judith guessed him to be in his early teens, but small for his age. She assumed he was the person who had skittered across the passageway earlier.

"I live lots of places," Chuckie said. "I'm rich."

"That's good," Joe said. "How about living somewhere other than where we're having dinner?"

Chuckie scowled. "Where?"

"Do you have more than one castle?" Joe asked, his mellow voice even softer, as if he were interrogating a juvenile offender.

Chuckie shook his head. "Sometimes I sleep in a barrel." He got to his feet and surveyed the table. "A roll, please."

Bill passed him the basket. Chuckie studied the remaining rolls closely before making his choice. He began picking the roll to pieces, dropping the bits on the floor as he moved away.

"So I won't get lost," he said, and left the dining room.

"The short one's crazier than the tall one," Bill said.

"He's certainly creepier," Renie asserted. "How old?"

"Twelve, thirteen," Joe guessed.

Bill disagreed. "He's older, but very small for his age, barely five feet. I'd estimate him as closer to twenty."

"Is he developmentally disabled?" Judith asked.

Bill, who rarely answered serious questions without a great deal of careful thought, considered the query. "That depends on what you mean. I'd have to study him much longer to decide."

"Is he dangerous?" Renie asked.

Again, Bill took at least a full minute to respond. "I don't know."

"That's not very reassuring," Renie said.

Mrs. Gibbs entered the dining room, bearing prawn cocktails. "Ye done with yer soup?" she asked.

Judith nodded. "It was delicious. Thank you."

"We had a visitor," Joe said as Mrs. Gibbs removed the soup plates. "A young fellow named Chuckie."

"Oh?" Mrs. Gibbs wasn't surprised. "Was the wee laddie hungry?"

"He wanted a roll," Joe said.

Mrs. Gibbs espied the crumbs on the stone floor. "Ah."

Judith couldn't resist. "Who is he?"

"The master's son and heir," Mrs. Gibbs replied. "Chuckie Fordyce." She placed the prawn cocktails on the table. "The laddie will one day run Glengrim distillery." She smoothed her white apron. "Unless . . . " She shrugged. "Main course is next." She made her exit.

"Don't buy stock in Glengrim," Renie cautioned. "The company's future looks. . .grim."

"We have locks on our doors," Bill said. "I think we'd better use them. The residents seem to show up without warning. Both of them."

"There could be more," Judith pointed out. "I must ask Mrs. Gibbs about the tall young man who told us he was the grandson. If Harry is married, maybe there's a granddaughter-in-law living here, too."

"According to the layout of the castle that I got from Hugh MacGowan," Joe said, "the rooms in our wing are all for guests. There must be another section where the family quarters are located."

"I'd like to see that layout," Judith said. "Do you have it?"

Joe nodded. "It's in the pocket of my big suitcase."

The rest of dinner was uneventful. Since Mrs. Gibbs was looking harried from her exertions, Judith refrained from asking any more questions. After the Flynns and the Joneses had finished their excellent Angus beefsteak, partaken of Bonchester and Cadoc cheeses, and finished with a crème brûlée, they were stuffed—and sleepy.

Mrs. Gibbs had a final word for her guests. "Breakfast at five," she announced.

"Five what?" asked an astonished Renie.

"For the gentlemen," Mrs. Gibbs replied.

Joe looked sheepish. "Bill and I are meeting Hugh at seven to go over our fishing plans. Maybe we'll try out a stream nearby."

Renie looked relieved. "For a moment I thought . . . Never mind."

"The ladies may come down anytime after eight," Mrs. Gibbs informed the cousins. "Breakfast is served from the sideboard in the other part of the dining room."

When they returned to their room, Judith was too tired to chide Joe about his early departure in the morning. "Just don't wake me up," she said, and kissed him good night.

She fell asleep before her husband could start the fire or even begin to undress. Judith had worried that her fatigue might bring on strange dreams, even nightmares, but she slept soundly. When she woke up the only dream she could remember was sitting in a beach tent looking at a gigantic thermometer that registered eighty-five degrees. That was as close to a nightmare as she got.

But of course they'd only been at Grimloch Castle for a few hours.

4

It wasn't surprising that Renie wasn't on hand when Judith went down to breakfast at nine o'clock. The food, including kippers, toast, rashers of bacon, scrambled eggs, fruit, and flat, soft rolls was tasty. When Judith finished eating, she couldn't resist seeking out the kitchen.

It wasn't difficult. She opened the door Mrs. Gibbs had used, and faced a second baize door. Judith knocked. Mrs. Gibbs responded.

"Aye?" the cook said. "What would ye want?"

"I shouldn't intrude," Judith apologized, "but I run an inn. I was curious to see how you manage your kitchen. I serve only breakfast."

"Come along," Mrs. Gibbs said with a resigned air.

The kitchen was huge, with an open fireplace and a spit that looked as if it was used regularly. The cast-iron stove had eight round cooking spaces of varying sizes, not unlike the smaller version Grandma and Grandpa Grover had used for years in the family home.

"Wood-burning?" Judith inquired.

"Wood and coal," Mrs. Gibbs replied.

The counters were made of old, well-worn wood, fragrant from decades of cutting fruit and vegetables. There were two sinks, both enamel with old-fashioned faucets like the ones in the guest bathroom. The big black refrigerator, however, looked new. The only hint of nonfunctional decor was a framed tartan on the far wall next to a glass-covered cupboard.

"You do all this yourself?" Judith said with admiration.

"Aye. That is," Mrs. Gibbs explained, "except for summer when the regular guests come. I have a daily or two to help."

"I should think so. What about cleaning? This place is vast."

Mrs. Gibbs agreed. "Daily help for that, too, in summer."

"Does your grandson live here all the time?" Judith asked, admiring the heavy cookware that hung from a circular rack.

Mrs. Gibbs frowned as she used a wooden spoon to stir what looked like cake batter. "He's paying us a visit."

"Oh." Judith smiled. "That's nice. Where does he live?"

The frown deepened. "Close by."

"Do he and his wife have children?"

Mrs. Gibbs dropped the spoon and bent down to retrieve it. "He told you about his wife?"

"No," Judith admitted. "But he's married, isn't he?"

"Aye." Mrs. Gibbs wiped her forehead with the back of her hand. "They had a wee bairn, Jamie, last November."

"That's wonderful. You must be thrilled."

Mrs. Gibbs didn't respond. Judith changed the subject. "What are those flat soft rolls? I ate two. They're delicious."

"They're baps," Mrs. Gibbs replied, "from an auld recipe. Tomorrow I'll make bannocks. You call them . . . what?"

"Pancakes or flapjacks," Judith said. "I remember bannocks from when my cousin and I were in Scotland many years ago."

Mrs. Gibbs nodded once and stirred the mixture in the bowl. "No lunch. High tea at four, if you like."

"My cousin and I will probably go into the village to explore," Judith said. "We'll eat there. What do you recommend?"

"A tearoom, a Chinese restaurant, a curry house, two pubs, pizza. Take your pick." Mrs. Gibbs kept her eyes on the dough.

Judith pointed at the tartan on the wall and moved for a closer look. "That's different from the Forbes and Fordyce green and blue plaid in the hallway. I like all the red. Is that the clan's hunting colors?"

"Nae." Mrs. Gibbs still didn't look up. "That's my family, the MacIver tartan."

"Oh." Judith peered at what she assumed was the clan motto. "*Nunquam obliviscar.* What does that mean?"

The other woman finally glanced up, her eyes narrowed and her tone bitter. "It means 'I will never forget.'" She turned back to the dough and gave it a hard thump with her fist. "I must finish this."

Judith sensed that she was being dismissed. "Thank you." Without another word, she returned to the dining room. Renie was at the sideboard, heaping food onto her plate.

"I thought you'd run off with Chuckie," she said.

"I was trying in vain to befriend Mrs. Gibbs," Judith explained.

Renie was surprised. "If you flunked, she can't be human."

"The only thing I found out is that Harry is just visiting, and his wife had a baby boy last November," Judith said, pouring herself a third cup of coffee. "He lives nearby, which, I assume, given the smaller distances between places in Scotland, could be the village."

Renie topped her scrambled eggs with a couple of kippers. "So?"

Judith shrugged. "Nothing, I guess."

"I'm more concerned that our husbands will be arrested for poaching," Renie said, sitting down and sprinkling salt and pepper on her food. "Land along the UK's rivers and such are usually owned privately."

Judith had also sat at the long trestle table. "Joe mentioned that MacGowan had permission to fish in certain spots around here. He's going to serve as their ghillie, which is what the locals call a guide. Apparently you don't have to buy a fishing license, only some kind of permit that gives you the property owner's approval."

"Good. So what do we do for amusement?" Renie asked.

"Explore the village? We may need Gibbs to row us ashore."

"You could make it up that hill?"

"I think so," Judith said. "It isn't very far, though I couldn't see much in the fog. I found Joe's castle layout and a local map. We're close to several interesting places and not all that far from Inverness."

When the cousins were ready to leave, they found Gibbs by accident. He was in the courtyard, armed with a trowel and a rake, doffing his cap when he spotted the cousins. "Bulbs coming up," he said. "Got to make way for crocus and daffodils."

"Ours are in bud at home," Judith said. "They should be blooming by the time we get back. Do you do all the gardening?"

"Aye." Mr. Gibbs straightened up, a hand pressing his back. "Stiff I get, o' times." He smiled at the low gray clouds. "Spring's coming."

"Also true where we live," Judith said. "We're going to St. Fergna. It looks as if the tide's out."

"It is," Gibbs agreed. "Harry can drive ye. Here he comes now."

Harry Gibbs was coming out through a door on the other side of the courtyard. He was dressed casually, if stylishly, in a black jacket that displayed a Burberry plaid lining, and well-cut corduroy slacks.

"Do ye mind passengers?" Gibbs called to his grandson. "These ladies want to plunder the shops in the village."

Harry paused to survey the cousins. "Well . . . why not?"

"We passed muster," Renie murmured.

"I need to buy warmer clothes," Judith said, indicating her navy blue linen jacket and white cotton slacks.

Harry snickered. "You thought it'd be warm in the Highlands?"

"She thought it would be seasonably warm in California," Renie responded. "The plane forgot to make a right-hand turn."

"Awkward," Harry remarked. "Follow me to the lift."

In the daylight, Judith could see the sheer cliff below the castle and beyond the sandy beach to the village. She could hear the surf and smell the salt-scented air. There were no dolphins, but gulls swooped above them, coming to rest on the castle's watchtowers and battlements.

Time seemed to recede, two thousand years a mere tick on the planet's clock. The Romans moving north to build the barrier of Hadrian's Wall; Saint Columba setting foot on a nearby shore, bringing Christianity to the Celtic tribes; the Vikings come to raid and plunder; Robert the Bruce and William Wallace fighting for Scotland's sovereignty; union with England under King James; the religious wars, the clan wars, the foreign wars—so many battles, leaving the land soaked in blood to make way for oil rigs and distilleries and pizza parlors. Judith sensed the irony.

"This is quite a view," she said as they stepped inside the lift.

"I find it bleak," Harry said. "I prefer the city."

"Inverness?" Judith said as they began the slow, noisy descent.

Harry laughed derisively. "London. I grew up there."

"Oh. Is that where your parents live?" Judith asked.

"Yes. When they're not traveling the globe." He yawned, as if the subject—or the cousins—bored him.

Judith wondered how Harry's mother and father seemed to be living a life of leisure while his grandparents toiled away as virtual servants at Grimloch Castle. But she thought it best not to bring up the subject. In any event, the lift had clattered to a stop.

"That's my Range Rover," Harry said, pointing to a metallic silver SUV parked on a stretch of concrete in front of a small wooden shed by the narrow road to the village. "Where shall I let you off?"

"What should we see?" Judith asked. "We drove through St. Fergna after dark last night."

Harry opened the back door of the expensive vehicle. "There's not much of interest, in my opinion."

"Where are you going?" Renie inquired. "We could get out where you park."

"I'm not stopping," Harry replied as the cousins settled themselves into the comfortable leather seats. "I'm going beyond St. Fergna." He closed the door with a click that was more like a whisper.

Judith and Renie exchanged bemused glances, but kept quiet as Harry got behind the wheel. "There's a very old church," he said, "if you're into that sort of thing. Presbyters and all that."

"We may explore it," Judith said. She looked around the beach where a couple of wading birds foraged for food. "Are those sandpipers?"

"They're called turnstones here," Harry replied. He suddenly took a sharp turn to the right. "That's odd," he muttered.

"What's odd?" Judith saw nothing except for a couple of people much farther down the beach.

Harry slowed down. "That bird on the rock beyond the castle cliffs is a great northern diver. They're rare around here. They go north to the Orkney and Shetland Islands in the summer. I hate them." He honked the horn, but the big bird didn't move. Harry swore under his breath and turned the car back toward the track from the beach.

"It looks like a loon to me," Renie remarked.

Harry didn't respond. He seemed to tense at the wheel as he approached the steep bank.

Judith caught a glimpse of fishing boats at anchor about a hundred yards down the strand and decided to change the subject. "Do they fish commercially around here?"

"Some do," Harry said, cresting the hill in less than a minute.

The cobbled street was narrow and fairly steep. Harry drove past several small old shops that featured fish, meat, and woolens. Judith also espied a cobbler, a confectioner, and a draper.

"You can let us off at the woolen store," Judith said as they reached an unmarked intersection. "We haven't changed our money yet. Do they take credit cards?"

"Yes. I never carry cash. Too much bother." Harry put on the brake. "There you go," he said, stopping in the middle of the street. The SUV wasn't blocking traffic. There wasn't any, except for a small car coming slowly from the opposite direction.

The cousins thanked Harry and got out. Only a handful of pedestrians strolled past the shops.

"Nice," Judith remarked. "Nobody rushing, no heavy traffic, no vying for parking places."

Renie smiled. "They have cell phones, though." She nodded in the direction of a young woman pushing a pram with one hand and holding a phone to her ear with the other. "We aren't living in medieval Scotland even if we are staying in a castle."

Judith paused to look in the fishmonger's window. Mussels, salmon, crab, oysters, and plaice were displayed on beds of ice. "I wonder if our husbands have caught anything," she said.

The woolen shop was small but well stocked. Judith perused the tartan skirts, wool slacks, and various types of sweaters. "Not cheap," she murmured. "Don't you talk me into buying more than I need."

"I won't," Renie said. "I feel guilty for not warning you."

After half an hour, Judith had purchased a lamb's wool baby blue twin set, two pairs of slacks, a heavy ecru turtleneck, an eggshell ruffled silk blouse, a forest green cashmere sweater, a black mid-calf skirt, and a dark plaid hooded cape.

"I've always wanted a cape," Judith said as the sales clerk rang up the bill on an old-fashioned cash register. But she was aghast at the total, which came to almost eight hundred American dollars. "Maybe I don't need the cape," she said to Renie.

"Coz." Renie looked severe. "You have to wear something warm around here. The cape's lined. Its dark colors won't show dirt. At home, it'd cost twice this much."

The young sales clerk, who had dark brown streaks in her fair hair, giggled. "That's so," she agreed. "We don't have many visitors, so our prices aren't so dear."

Judith reached into her black handbag and handed over her Visa card. "Oh well. It's Joe's fault for not warning me I might need warmer clothes. At least our lodging's free."

"Darn," Renie said, tossing a couple of cashmere sweaters she'd been fondling on the counter. "I can't *not* buy something."

"You've friends in St. Fergna?" the clerk asked in a chipper voice.

"Our husbands know someone from around here," Judith explained, "but we're not staying with him. He's put us up at the castle."

The clerk's blue eyes grew wide. "The castle!" She pursed her magenta lips. "It's said to be haunted."

"Really?" Judith responded. "Who's the ghost?"

The clerk looked disappointed. "You Americans are skeptical."

"Not all Americans are," Renie pointed out. "We have some of our own ghosts. Does this one have a name?"

The clerk nodded. "Some say it's Mary, Queen of Scots. Others describe a child. He's prankish."

"What sort of pranks?" Judith asked.

The clerk handed over the receipt. "I'm not sure . . . " She stopped, china blue eyes on the door. "It's Mrs. Gunn. She's fussy but spends her money. I'd best see to her."

A small, stout woman with graying dark hair entered the shop. The clerk hurriedly rang up Renie's sweaters and greeted Mrs. Gunn. "A fine day, ma'am! I put aside those items you took a fancy to last week."

"I've changed my mind," Mrs. Gunn said, eyeing the cousins with suspicion. "No pleats. Herringbone, not tweed."

Judith and Renie took their parcels and left the shop.

"Definitely not pleats," Renie said when they got outside. "Mrs. Gunn would look like a small ship sailing into port."

"This stuff's heavy," Judith complained. "I don't want to lug it all over the village. What were we thinking of? We should've left it at the shop and picked it up on the way back."

"Here," Renie said. "Give it to me. I'll ask the clerk if that's okay. You sit and wait." She pointed to a stone bench in front of a crafts store.

Gratefully, Judith sat. The air was misty, but the sun peeked from behind gray clouds. Two cars and an ancient bus went by. There were still no more than a half dozen pedestrians. She considered what it would be like if they'd gone to Southern California: hordes of suntanned people, beach volleyball, endless sunshine, blaring rap and hip-hop music, cars everywhere, strip malls, outlet malls, supermalls . . .

Church bells rang the hour. Judith looked beyond the cluster of uneven roofs and spotted a steeple some fifty yards away. Maybe they could explore the church, as Harry had suggested. By the time they finished, it would be time for lunch. Across the street, Judith saw a green sign that read rose's tea shop in flaking gold letters hanging above a canopied doorway. The windows on either side of the doorway had lace curtains. Judith watched two middle-aged women in sensible shoes enter. Yes, she thought, it was a perfect spot to eat.

Renie stomped out of the woolen shop. "Next time, I'll bring a weapon!" she cried. "Mrs. Gunn is a real horror!"

"What happened?" Judith asked, surprised.

Renie rearranged her black trench coat and smoothed her short, disheveled hair. "She threw her purse at me. All because I interrupted her monologue about a present her ex-daughter-in-law had given her."

"What happened to our new clothes?"

Renie checked her makeup in a compact mirror. "The clerk put them in the back while I held Mrs. Gunn down on a display case."

"Good grief! You really went at it?"

Renie shrugged. "I didn't have any choice. I couldn't stand around listening to the old bag bad-mouth her ex in-law. If I'd had that woman for a mother-in-law, I'd have ditched Sonny Boy, too."

"We'd better get out of here before Mrs. Gunn leaves the shop," Judith said. "Or calls the cops. How about the church?"

"Seeking sanctuary sounds right," Renie replied. "Where is it?"

Judith pointed to the steeple. "It must be off the village green."

The cousins moved along, though Judith checked a couple of times to make sure that Mrs. Gunn—or the local constabulary—wasn't in pursuit. They paused by the parklike green with its granite cross and memorial to various locals who'd fallen in battle from the days of Robert the Bruce through World War II. The list was mercifully short, considering that it spanned over eight hundred years.

The church, which bore the name of St. Fergna, looked almost as old as the castle. It was small and its stones were weathered, but, as Renie pointed out, it hadn't suffered the cruel destruction that had befallen so many Scottish churches during the various wars of religion.

"It's Protestant," Judith remarked, noting the wooden sign that proclaimed united church of scotland. "We'll have to find a Catholic church in Inverness for Sunday Mass."

"Maybe they have a five o'clock today," Renie said as they walked along a stone pathway that was partially covered by moss. "Then we could sleep in tomorrow."

Judith paused halfway to the church entrance. "This cemetery is really ancient. You can hardly read some of the markers." Several Celtic crosses were broken; many inscriptions had blurred with time.

Renie stopped by what looked to Judith like a worn gray slab. "This thing is really old," Renie said. "It's engraved with a late Pictish version of the Celtic cross. Eighth, even ninth century, about the time the Picts merged with the Scots. Look, you can hardly see the outline."

"I wouldn't know it was supposed to show a cross," Judith admitted, but, as always, deferred to her cousin's artistic eye.

"Crosses are fascinating. They're one of the first symbols I studied in graphic design." Renie took Judith's arm and turned her to face the sea. "Did you notice the two flags at Grimloch when we came outside?"

Judith shook her head. As usual, she'd been more interested in people than things. "I can see the red and yellow national flag of Scotland," she said. "What's the black or blue one with white?"

"The yellow flag with the red lion is the national flag of the Scottish government and the Scottish monarchy," Renie explained. "The national flag is blue with what looks like a white X but is a Saint Andrew's cross."

"Interesting," Judith said, though her focus had been diverted by matters at hand. "On your right—someone's putting flowers on a grave."

Renie turned to see the tall, leggy redhead in a short fur-trimmed coat arranging red and white roses by a marker that looked quite new. Curiosity drew Judith like a moth to the flame. The young woman straightened up just as Judith got a few feet behind her.

"Are you lost?" the redhead asked in a lilting voice.

"You can tell we're tourists?" Judith said with a smile.

"Oh yes," she replied, pointing to Judith's lightweight jacket. Her deep-set amber eyes seemed to miss nothing. "You must be freezing."

"I am a bit chilly," Judith admitted. "I bought warmer clothes at the woolen shop on the High Street. That's what it's called, isn't it?"

"It usually is," the young woman said with a charming smile. She was an inch taller than Judith's five nine, and leaned gracefully when she spoke. Her manner might have been taken as condescending, but Judith assumed she was used to talking to people who were shorter. "At least in most Scots towns and villages. You're American . . . or Canadian?"

"American," Judith said. "I'm Mrs. Flynn and this is Mrs. Jones."

The young woman put out a long white hand. "I'm Moira Gibbs."

Judith shook Moira's hand. "We're staying at Grimloch Castle. We met your . . . relatives there."

"My husband's grandparents," Moira said without enthusiasm. "However did you manage to go there? It's off-season."

"It's a long story," Judith said, "involving our husbands knowing a local fellow fisherman."

"Who?" Moira asked a trifle sharply.

Judith was surprised at the blunt question. On previous visits to the United Kingdom she'd found most strangers to be reticent when it came to talking about themselves and consider it virtually taboo to exhibit anything that might be mistaken for nosiness.

"Hugh MacGowan," Judith answered.

"Ah." Moira nodded. "Our law enforcement chief. The MacGowan has a way with him." She gave a last look at the roses by the grave. "I must go. My brother has come looking for me." Moira made a face. "He thinks I'm scatterbrained and got lost in the graveyard." She raised a hand and called out to the tall, bearded man who had entered through the lich gate. "I'm coming, Jimmy. Don't get your knickers in a bunch!"

As Moira hurried off, Renie read the inscription aloud: " 'David Pietro Piazza. And Christ receive thy soul.' He died last October first, at twenty-nine. An Italian in a remote village?"

"Americans aren't the only ones who move around," Judith said, gazing at some of the other graves. "There's another new—and rather ostentatious—monument under that yew tree. It must be a local bigwig."

The cousins trudged closer to the old stone arch. "It's the Gunn family plot," Renie said. "Same name as the pushy old bag in the shop."

"You're right." Judith studied the monument, noticing that some of the letters were chipped, and ivy crept up its twin columns. Still, it was obvious from the neatly clipped grass that the plot was well tended. "Here's Eanruig Gunn, who died four years ago at fifty-five. Maybe your Mrs. Gunn is his widow. There's a ship on the marker." She looked to her left where a statue of an angel overlooked another grave. "This one's from three years ago, maybe a son, Francis Gunn, twenty-two. No wonder Mrs. Gunn is crabby. She's had her share of tragedies."

"I've had my share of graves," Renie said. "Let's eat."

The cousins strolled out of the cemetery through the lich gate. Judith smiled. "Weird, huh? Our first tourist stop is a cemetery." She paused, waiting for a couple of bicyclists to pass. "Nice," she went on, breathing in the sea-tinged air. "No heat, no hurry, no murders."

"That's a dumb thing to say," Renie chided.

Judith grimaced. "Yes. I wonder why . . . " She gave herself a shake. "That's what I get for standing on top of a bunch of bodies. Oh well."

Renie refrained from saying the obvious.

5

As Judith and Renie finished a lunch of smoked salmon tarts with cream cheese and capers, one of their cell phones rang.

"Yours," Renie said. "Mine's not on."

Judith scrambled for the phone in her large travel purse. "Hello?" she said breathlessly.

The voice at the other end was faint and almost unrecognizable. "Joe?" Judith said so loudly that three elderly ladies at an adjoining table stared—discreetly. "I can't hear you," she said, lowering her voice. "Should I go outside to . . . What? You've been spayed?"

Renie was looking alarmed. "Where's Bill?"

"Oh." Judith slumped in relief. "You're at Speyside. When will . . . Why not? . . . Joe, I can't hear you very well . . . Okay, fine, goodbye." She clicked off. "The husbands are fishing in the morning," she informed Renie. "They're on the River Spey and won't be back tonight."

Renie received the news with unusual calm. "Sure. The river's probably hot. They can't possibly leave. That's why they're there."

Judith sighed in resignation. "Your father was an avid fisherman. Mine wasn't. You understand the species better than I do."

"My father considered fishing a religion," Renie recalled. "He told me it was no accident that so many of Jesus's disciples were fishermen, especially Saint Peter. Really, the whole fishing thing is a spiritual experience. It must be magic on these local rivers and streams."

"You're being too nice," Judith pointed out, trying to calculate the tip for their lunch. "That's not like you. We have no car, so how do we get to church for our own religious experience?"

"Don't we get a dispensation when we're traveling?" Renie asked with a quizzical expression. "We're strangers in a strange land."

Judith calculated an adequate tip and stood up. "Let's collect our new clothes and go back to the castle. Frankly, I'm still tired."

Renie checked her watch. "It's going on three. The tide's probably halfway in. Let's call Gibbs to see if he can pick us up. Didn't Joe say there was a chauffeur?"

"Who is also probably Gibbs," Judith pointed out. "Strange—I didn't see any other car parked on the beach except Harry's."

Renie frowned. "You're right. But maybe we didn't look far enough. For all we know, there's a freight elevator somewhere on the cliff and they park their vehicles in the castle garage. Or stable."

"I doubt that," Judith said as they exited the tea shop. "Maybe the clerk at the woolen store knows how it's done."

The clerk was looking slightly frazzled. "Oh, hello," she said in a voice that was no longer chipper. "I suppose you want your purchases." She went to a door at the far end of the counter and disappeared.

"We'll have to exchange our money Monday when the bank is open," Judith said. "I can't put everything on my credit card."

"I saw a Royal Bank of Scotland on the corner by the village green," Renie said. "I haven't spotted an American Express office, but maybe there's one off the High Street."

"I don't think there's much more to the commercial section than what we've seen. The rest of the village looks like cottages and other private homes.

I doubt that more than a few hundred people live here."

"Probably not," Renie agreed. "It's off the beaten track."

For a couple of minutes, the cousins waited in silence. Renie looked through a rack of tailored jackets; Judith resisted the old urge to bite her fingernails.

"What's taking so long?" Judith finally said. "This place isn't big enough to lose our packages."

Before Renie could answer, the clerk reappeared. "Sorry," she apologized, "but I had to lock your purchases in the safe. I use it so seldom that I never get the combination right the first few times."

Judith was curious. "Do you have a problem with theft?"

"Oh no," the clerk asserted. "Only in the summer when the visitors come to the beach. Especially the young ones. But . . . " She blushed and avoided looking at Renie. "Mrs. Gunn was a mite upset."

"Who wasn't?" Renie retorted. "What did she do after I left? Threaten to cut up our clothes with a cleaver?"

"Ah . . . " The clerk winced. "Rather like that, yes."

Judith nudged Renie. "We must apologize. I hate coming across as typical rude American tourists."

"Yeah," Renie mumbled. "But Mrs. Gunn pushed me first."

"Please," the clerk said. "My name's Alison, by the way. Mrs. Gunn is sometimes difficult."

Judith felt compelled to play peacemaker. "We visited the church graveyard. Mrs. Gunn has suffered recent losses."

"That's so," Alison agreed. "Her husband was killed in a hunting accident. Then her eldest son died very young. It was some sort of fever he'd picked up on a trip to Africa. He was never strong. His wife—still just a bride, really—had done her best to nurse him back to health, but . . . " Alison stopped and shook her head. "It was all so sad. I admired Moira's devotion."

"Moira?" Judith echoed.

"Moira Gibbs," Alison responded, "now that she's remarried." The clerk's expression had turned sour.

"We met her at the cemetery," Judith said. "She was putting flowers on the grave of a man with an Italian name."

Alison nodded. "Davey. He worked for her."

"Oh?" Judith couldn't rein in her natural curiosity. "Moira looks so young. What does she do?"

"She inherited Blackwell Petroleum," Alison explained. "Her parents are both dead. Her father died young, and her mother ran the company for many years until she passed away about the same time that Frankie—Moira's first husband—died. Moira's half brother helps run the company. Davey was her personal assistant."

"And now," Judith said, "Moira's married to Harry Gibbs. Does he work for Blackwell Petroleum?"

Alison frowned. "Well—Harry's not one for working."

After nineteen years with Dan McMonigle, Judith understood. She was about to ask how Harry's parents could afford to travel so much, but two young women entered the shop. Renie hurriedly asked Alison if she knew how to get back to the castle when the tide was in.

"You can use this phone," Alison said, bestowing a friendly smile on the newcomers. "Here, I'll do it for you." After a pause, Alison informed whoever had answered that the American guests needed transport. "Gibbs will be along shortly," she told the cousins.

Judith thanked Alison and exited the shop with Renie, who was already standing by the door.

"Well?" Renie said. "Is your curiosity satisfied?"

"You can hardly blame me for wanting to get to know some of the locals," Judith said in a defensive tone.

Renie shook her head. "Coz, by the time we leave you'll be on a first-name basis with everybody in this village."

"So?"

"Never mind." Renie paused as a midsize sedan came up the hill. "Maybe this is Gibbs." But the car kept going. "Maybe it isn't," Renie murmured. "I wonder what he's driving?"

"He can't miss us," Judith reasoned. "There are only about ten other people on the High Street."

An older man on a bicycle went by and doffed his cap. A van that bore the lettering macbean meat purveyors came up the street and stopped in front of the butcher shop. The sun had come out again. Judith gazed down the hill toward the castle where the flags hung limp on their standards. "It's fairly warm," she remarked.

Renie nodded. "Probably fifty degrees. Still in my comfort zone."

The quiet of the street was broken by the oncoming roar of a motorcycle heading in their direction.

"Bikers," Renie said in disgust. "I understand they have problems with them over here, too."

Before Judith could respond, the cycle slowed and stopped. She stared at the helmeted man leaning on the handlebars. "Gibbs?"

"Aye." He pointed to a sidecar. "Who goes first?"

"Who," Renie retorted, "doesn't have to go at all?"

Judith considered her artificial hip. "Is the ride . . . bumpy?"

"Nae," Gibbs replied. "I'll drive slow."

Renie nudged Judith. "You go. I'll find an inn and stay here."

Judith ignored the sarcasm. Gibbs dismounted to help her get in the sidecar. After securing her parcels with a rope, he started the cycle, and with a mighty roar they made a U-turn and headed down the hill.

Gibbs wasn't going fast, though the cobbled street made for a rough ride anyway. But as soon as they left the High Street and started down the road to the beach, the track turned smooth. Gibbs assisted Judith in getting out of the sidecar, and then unloaded her packages.

"Be back anon," he said, and hopped onto the motorcycle.

Judith gazed out to sea where a freighter sailed across the horizon. Far down the beach she saw children playing among the rocks. And before her, the castle loomed in its solid age-old mass.

Looking to her right, she noticed Harry Gibbs's Rover. Apparently he hadn't spent very long wherever he'd been going after dropping off the cousins. Perhaps he'd met his wife Moira for lunch. Judith frowned. Harry had said he didn't intend to stop in St. Fergna. She couldn't help but wonder about the younger Gibbses' marriage. They were virtual newlyweds, judging from the date of Moira's first husband's death. They also had a new baby. Her curiosity couldn't be squelched.

At that moment, the Rover's door opened and Harry got out. To Judith's astonishment, he was stark naked. He didn't look her way but walked straight into the sea and began swimming.

Or, Judith thought suddenly, was he trying to drown himself?

But Harry seemed to be staying close to shore, bobbing up and down on the occasional wave, backstroking toward the beach, diving briefly underwater. Maybe he was a member of what they called the Polar Bear Club at home: hardy souls who went swimming no matter how low the temperature dropped.

Harry was still splashing about when Gibbs returned with Renie.

"Wow," Renie said softly, "that was kind of fun. Thanks, Gibbs."

Judith waited for Gibbs to help Renie get out of the sidecar. "Does your grandson often go swimming this time of year?" she finally asked.

"Och," Gibbs said with a nod, "the madness of youth. Better than taking those devilish drugs. Into the boat with ye, ladies. I'll come back for Beams later."

"Beams?" Renie said.

"Aye. 'Tis an older BMW bike."

"You don't have a car at the castle?" Judith asked, still watching Harry swim hither and yon.

"Aye, we do, but 'tis in the shop. Brakes need fixing." Just as he was about to help Judith get into the skiff, he looked up. "Och! The Master has arrived!"

Judith turned toward the road where a handsome wine-colored sedan was creeping onto the beach. "Do you mean Mr. Fordyce?"

Gibbs suddenly seemed agitated. "Aye, I do. Lord help us!" He glanced out to sea where Harry was still frolicking. "We must bide."

"Sure," Renie said. "I've always wanted to meet a master."

Gibbs was hurrying to greet the newcomer. The middle-aged man in the dark-colored windbreaker looked ordinary to Judith—close to six feet, graying black hair, a mustache, and a long, lean face.

The woman who got out on the passenger side was far from ordinary. She was young and slim, with long black hair floating over her shoulders. Her features weren't perfect, but the slanting brown eyes were lively and she exuded self-confidence.

"Phil!" she cried in an amused voice as she pointed toward the water. "Is that Harry?"

Philip Fordyce peered in the direction his companion had indicated. "Damn fool!" he exploded. "Reckless and stupid!"

Harry swam toward shore. Gibbs muttered to himself. Philip swore under his breath. His companion laughed so hard she had to lean on Philip. Judith and Renie felt like excess baggage.

Harry floated a few more feet before standing up.

"Oh, he's starkers!" the young woman cried. "How terribly funny!"

Harry walked nonchalantly toward his car but stopped halfway, turned around, and mooned the little gathering.

"What a prat!" the girl cried, and laughed some more.

"Despicable," Philip declared, refusing to look at Harry. "To the castle, Gibbs." He scrutinized the cousins. "Are these . . . ladies with you?"

"Er . . . aye, they're the MacGowan's friends, Mrs. Flynn and Mrs. Jones from the States."

"I see," Philip said, his keen hazel eyes surveying the cousins.

"We didn't ken ye'd be back from the islands so soon," Gibbs said.

"Cyclone warnings," Philip replied. "Come, Beth, get into the skiff."

Judith overcame her awkward feelings. "Mr. Gibbs, are we a problem?" she whispered as Philip and Beth climbed into the little boat.

"Nae, nae," Gibbs said softly. "The Master can be a wee bit tetchy."

As Gibbs gave Judith a hand, she looked for Harry but he wasn't in sight. Maybe, she thought, he was getting dressed in the car. Certainly he wouldn't have gone into the village in the altogether. Or, she wondered, would he? Harry Gibbs seemed unpredictable.

The girl called Beth was sitting next to Philip, clinging to him like paste. "I'm glad we came back early," she said. "I was bored at Palma."

"I noticed," Philip said dryly. But he smiled and patted her hand.

"Hospitality," Renie murmured, and sighed. "Scotland is famous for it. We thank you for yours, Mr. Fordyce. Or do I call you 'Master'?"

Judith tensed. Renie didn't like being ignored. Trouble was already brewing.

"Mr. Fordyce will do," Philip replied. "The title is honorary."

"And deferential," Renie noted. She smiled, the phony, toothsome smile that usually spelled impending disaster. "How quaint."

The little boat plied the waters in silence for the rest of the short trip. Judith was relieved that Philip Fordyce hadn't risen to the bait. After all, Renie couldn't swim.

The cousins immediately retreated to Judith and Joe's room.

"Trophy wife," Renie said. "Big-shot CEO dumps wife number one and lands beautiful raven-tressed bimbo."

Judith stretched out on the bed. "I'm not sure she's a bimbo. The only thing I was sure of was that you were trying to provoke Philip Fordyce. Wasn't decking Mrs. Gunn enough brutality for you today?"

Renie shrugged. "Did Mrs. Gibbs say they had high tea?"

"She did, in fact," Judith said. "At four. It's a few minutes after."

"Better late than never," Renie said. "Let's go."

"Oh, coz, I'm tired! You go. I think I'll take a nap."

"You sure?"

"Yes. Head for the trough. Let me know when you're finished."

It didn't take long for Judith to fall asleep. Maybe she was still suffering from jet lag. Maybe she'd walked too much in the past couple of days. Maybe the excitement of the trip had tired her. But, she'd told herself when she stretched out under the down comforter, the reason she'd gone on vacation was that she was already worn out. It was time to relax and recreate. Sleep was necessary; sleep was healing.

Upon awakening, Judith looked at her watch. To her astonishment, it was going on six. She'd slept for almost two hours. Even Renie couldn't take that long to gobble up high tea.

Judith cautiously got out of the canopied bed and stepped onto the furry area rug instead of the cold stone floor. After slipping on her shoes, she went across the passageway to see if Renie was in the Joneses' room. There was no response to Judith's knock, so she opened the unlocked door and called her cousin's name. No one answered. Perhaps Renie was still enjoying a hearty tea meal. Or she'd gotten into a row with Philip Fordyce. Maybe there was a note. Judith glanced at the parcel containing Renie's new sweaters. There was nothing on the bureau except for Bill's assortment of small change, travel information, and a new pair of shoelaces. The empty suitcases were stored in the wardrobe. The mantel revealed nothing. Judith gave up.

Halfway to the door, she was startled by a voice. Judith stopped to listen. "Open the gate," said the high-pitched voice. "Open the gate."

There was no one in the room and the tall windows were shut, so Judith assumed the voice was coming from the passageway. She went to the door. The corridor was empty. The other guest rooms were supposedly vacant. Judith stood on the threshold and listened. But there was no further sound. Puzzled, she crossed the passageway just as Renie came up the stairs.

"Wow," Renie said in an awed voice. "That was some tea! Scones and shortbread and sandwiches and . . . What's wrong? You look weird."

Judith shook herself. "Nothing. I was looking for you in your room and I heard somebody talking. But nobody was there."

Renie laughed. "Are you nuts?"

"No. No, of course not."

"Come on," Renie said. "Let's go into my room so I can put away my sweaters."

"I haven't put my own things away," Judith said, indicating the summer clothes she was still wearing.

"Okay," Renie said, "I'll come with you. Opening bags and boxes of new wearables is one of my favorite things, right next to buying them."

As Judith removed her items from their wrappings, she asked Renie if Philip and Beth had shown up for tea.

"No," Renie said, sitting on the bed and dangling her feet over the side. "They're staying on the other side of the castle. For some reason, Philip wanted to see Chuckie, but he couldn't be found. The Fordyces are definitely married. And that's a Daimler Super Eight that he drives. They're really expensive. The whiskey business must be good."

"I suspect it is," Judith agreed, hanging up one of the pairs of slacks she'd bought. "I think I'll wear the other slacks and the twin set for dinner tonight. It'll seem strange eating without Joe and Bill here. Do you think the Fordyces will join us?"

"I doubt it," Renie replied. "Mrs. Gibbs mentioned that they might drive into Inverness tonight. The lovely Beth wants to go to a jazz club. I'm kind of full. Will I be hungry by eight-thirty?"

"Probably," Judith said. "It just drives me nuts that your metabolism lets you eat like Petunia Pig and you never gain an ounce while I constantly wage the weight battle."

Renie shrugged. "It's not my fault. My hair won't turn gray, either." She twirled a short strand of her chestnut curls. "Freak of nature, that's me."

Judith ignored the remark. "Did you find out how we're going to get to Mass tomorrow?"

"Oh—yes," Renie said. "I almost forgot. The castle's original chapel is still in use because Philip is a Catholic. They row a priest from somewhere, usually around eleven."

"Good." Judith shook out the mid-calf skirt. "This is really handsome. The workmanship is excellent.

Aren't we lucky to end up in such a cool, interesting, and quiet place? I think I can hear the sea."

Renie cocked her head to listen. But it wasn't the sea she heard. A sudden loud noise shattered the peaceful evening.

"What was that?" she asked, jumping off the bed. "It sounded like an explosion."

Judith and Renie went to the tall windows in the alcove.

"I only see water," Judith said. "Was it inside the castle?"

"I don't know. Maybe it was fireworks."

Judith suggested that they investigate from Renie's room. "It overlooks the village."

The cousins trooped across the hallway. Even from across the room, they could see an ominous glow outside. "A fire in the village?" Judith said as they approached the window embrasure.

Her guess was only partly accurate. The fire was on the beach where the high tide was beginning to ebb. Judith and Renie stared at the orange and red ball of flame.

"Isn't that . . . " Judith began in a hushed voice, "where . . . ?"

"I . . . think . . . so," Renie said. "But," she added quickly, "we shouldn't jump to conclusions. It could be just a bonfire. Maybe somebody threw a battery or an aerosol can into it. You know how they explode."

"You're right," Judith said. She laughed, though the sound was jagged. "I'm so used to foul play that I assume . . . you know."

"Right." Renie's smile was forced. "Who'd want to blow up Harry Gibbs's car?"

6

The fire was burning brighter. Judith and Renie were transfixed. After a couple of minutes had passed, they could see figures running on the beach, coming from the direction of the castle and the village. Moments later, they saw the flashing lights of an emergency vehicle.

"It's not just a bonfire," Judith declared. "Something bad has happened. We should go downstairs and find out what's going on."

The cousins hurried out into the passageway. Judith stopped. "Maybe I should get my jacket, in case we go outside."

"Where would we go?" Renie asked. "The tide's still partially in."

"I'm getting my jacket anyway. This place is drafty, especially in the hallways." With Renie trailing, Judith went into her room and opened the wardrobe where she'd hung her lightweight jacket. She was reaching for it when a curly head popped out between Joe's sports coat and flannel slacks.

"Hallo!" cried Chuckie. "What went bang?"

Startled, Judith put a hand to her breast. "You scared me! What are you doing here?"

"I took a nap," Chuckie replied, crawling out of the wardrobe. "So did you."

Judith was flabbergasted. "You were here all the time?"

Chuckie brushed some lint from his corduroy pants. "Time? I don't believe in time. What does it mean? It's always passing."

Renie looked as if she was about to pounce on Chuckie. "Why don't you pass out of here? If your family owns this castle, your rooms must be somewhere else. Try to find them."

Chuckie looked unperturbed. "Someday I'll own all this. And more, when I marry my true love." He grinned at Judith, skittered past Renie, and went out into the passageway.

"Really, really weird," Renie murmured. "I hope he's harmless."

"Maybe he's the voice I heard," Judith said, putting on her jacket. "No—I heard it from your room, not ours. Let's go."

As they descended the winding staircase, they could hear voices. It took Judith a few seconds to realize that Mr. and Mrs. Gibbs were in the passageway near the foot of the steps.

"We must know!" Mrs. Gibbs cried, leaning against the stone wall for support. "I feel faint. It canna be!"

"Becalm yerself," Gibbs exhorted. "We'll hear soon enough."

"But if . . . " Mrs. Gibbs began, and broke off.

"It should be Moira," Gibbs said.

His wife didn't respond but dabbed at her eyes with her apron. She finally looked up and saw the cousins.

Judith hesitated before approaching the distraught couple. "I'm very sorry," she said, "but what's happened?"

Gibbs set his face in stone. "We dinna ken. We must bide."

"Bide for what?" Judith asked. "Can't you call someone from St. Fergna? Like the police?"

"Nae!" Gibbs cried. "Not wi' The Master here!"

"But . . . " Judith's patience snapped. "We saw an emergency vehicle arriving. The police may be there already. What's wrong with you people? Where is the . . . Mr. Fordyce?"

"Gone," Gibbs replied without expression.

"Then," Judith said emphatically, "he's not here."

"I'm getting my cell phone," Renie muttered.

"No!" Mrs. Gibbs wrung her hands. "Ye'll cause only harm!"

"Shove it," Renie snarled, and rushed back up the stairway.

Judith didn't blame her cousin, but Mr. and Mrs. Gibbs were in obvious distress. "We only want to help," Judith said quietly. "It's frustrating not to know what's happened."

Mrs. Gibbs was sobbing, her pink cheeks pale and her fingers pressing her forehead. Ignoring Judith, Gibbs moved closer to his wife.

"Come, come, lass, let's have a wee dram." Gently, he guided Mrs. Gibbs down the passageway.

Judith heard their footsteps echo on the stone floor even after they were out of sight. She guessed they had retreated to the kitchen. The walls seemed to be closing in. Her thin cotton jacket didn't ward off the drafts. She tried to imagine nobles and servants, soldiers and clerics, all engaged in their routines in the castle precincts. Grimloch had been built for protection, but its old stones felt menacing to Judith.

A sudden sound startled her. She let out a little yip before she saw Renie coming from the stairwell.

"This phone doesn't work well inside these walls," Renie declared. "Here," she said, tossing Judith's new cape at her. "We're going outside."

Judith saw that Renie was wearing her fur-lined raincoat. "And?"

"We call the cops," Renie replied, leading the way to the main entrance. "We look over the ramparts to see what's happening on the beach. We find out what blew up. We get chilled and catch bad colds and ruin our vacation."

Mist was settling over the courtyard. There was no moon, but Judith could still see the fire's glow lighting up the night sky. She could hear voices but couldn't make out the words.

"I should've brought a flashlight," Renie muttered. "Oh well. Let's take the lift down to the beach."

"I thought we were going to watch from the ramparts," Judith said.

"We can't," Renie responded, "because of the mist. Oops!" Renie stumbled on an uneven stone but caught herself. "Aren't you curious?"

"Well . . ." Judith paused. "I had this crazy idea that I was going to relax and enjoy myself. No worries. Just R&R instead of B&B."

"You'd be bored," Renie pointed out as the lift doors opened.

"It may be nothing serious," Judith said as the cage rattled and clattered. "It may not have been Harry Gibbs's car that was on fire. For all we know, this is a public beach."

"It doesn't work that way over here," Renie asserted. "It's staked out with the cement parking areas for the castle's visitors' cars. Didn't you notice the 'Trespassers Will Be Prosecuted' sign at the top of the beach road when Gibbs brought us back from the village?"

"No," Judith answered as the lift lurched to a stop. "I was too busy trying to hang on in the sidecar."

Stepping onto the beach, the cousins saw that the tide had receded several yards since their return from St. Fergna. It was, however, still impossible to reach the mainland without getting soaked to the knees.

"The fire's burning out," Judith said, peering through the mist. "Is that an ambulance or a fire truck parked off of the road?"

"I can't tell," Renie admitted.

She had barely finished speaking when more flashing lights could be seen coming down the track to the beach.

"Damn!" Judith swore softly. "This is frustrating. If that was Harry's car that caught fire and—or—blew up, where's Harry?"

"Harry—and his car—may have left a long time ago," Renie pointed out. "It's almost seven o'clock. For all we know, it's a prank."

Judith looked at Renie. "You know it's not."

Grim-faced, Renie nodded once.

Judith rearranged her cape, which she'd donned in a hurry. "This is very warm. The tags are still on it."

"I didn't have time to cut them . . . " Renie stopped. "Can you row?" She pointed to the skiff that was tied up near the lift. "Why don't we go ashore? Frankly, we could almost wade through the water."

"Not in my new cape we don't," Judith replied. "And we can't row with your virtual shoulder replacement and my artificial hip."

"We don't have to," Renie said. "The shore's coming to us."

Two men were moving toward the cousins through the outgoing tide that splashed no higher than the ankles of their mid-calf boots.

"Hallo!" one of them called. "Stay as you are, please."

As the pair came closer, Judith saw that they were both in police uniform. Constables, she guessed, as the mist cleared enough so that she could see firefighters extinguishing the blaze on the far shore.

"What's happened?" she asked when the men were closer.

"Names, please?" the shorter policeman queried in a soft burr.

The cousins spoke simultaneously:

"Judith Flynn."

"Serena Jones."

"We're guests at Grimloch Castle," Judith explained, noticing that their name tags read adamson and glen.

"From the States?" Glen inquired.

Judith nodded. "We got here yesterday."

"You'd best go back to the castle," Adamson said.

Judith noticed that they were both young, probably not yet thirty. "Can you tell us what happened? We heard an explosion."

"No need for concern," Glen said stoically.

Judith persisted. "Was it a . . . bomb?"

"Please return to Grimloch." Adamson's voice turned sharp.

"But," Judith countered, "we must tell Hugh Mac-Gowan."

The policemen exchanged glances. They seemed surprised that Judith knew the name. "Detective Inspector MacGowan?" said Adamson.

Judith assumed that was MacGowan's title. "He's our host. Right now he's fishing with our husbands. Have you spoken with him?"

Renie brandished her cell phone. "I'll call Bill so he can tell Hugh."

"No!" Glen turned red. "That is, we'll do it. It's police business. Ma'am," he added, and tugged at his cap, "there's been an accident."

"We realize that," Judith said calmly. "Did it involve injuries?"

"Yes." Adamson grimaced. "A fatality."

"Who?" Judith asked.

"I'm sorry," Adamson said. "We can't say until next of kin are notified. We're waiting for assistance."

Judith looked over to the bank where the fire had practically burned out. Flashlights played around the area, probably wielded by emergency personnel. "Was it Harry Gibbs?"

Neither constable replied.

"If so," Judith said, "you must inform his grandparents."

"Regulations," Adamson said. "Next of kin first."

"Of course." Judith nodded. "Moira, his wife."

Again, the men said nothing.

"How very sad," Judith said softly. "With a new baby and all. He had everything to live for."

The constables both touched their caps in salute. "If you'll excuse us . . . " Glen said politely.

"Sure," Renie said. "I guess it's over for Rover."

Adamson looked puzzled. "Eh?"

Renie waved at the sputtering flames. "The Rover. Harry's car."

The policemen walked away. Up by the track that led to the beach, several people had gathered to gawk. Apparently they weren't being allowed to come closer. Of course, Judith realized, the sands weren't only an accident scene, but private property.

She flipped the cape's hood over her head as a breeze picked up off the water. The salt air was strong; the receding surf was muffled. "The victim must be Harry. He's so young. Moira's a widow twice over."

"Are you thinking 'accident'?" Renie asked.

Judith frowned. "Just once, I'd like to avoid a murder."

Renie laughed harshly. "With your track record, don't count on it."

Judith's expression was bleak. "I won't. What should we do? We can't go back and face the Gibbses," Judith said. "They suspect the explosion involved Harry, and we have no official word."

"Are you up to walking into the village?" Renie asked. "It's either that or spending the night on the beach."

Judith considered their options. "I suppose we could have dinner in St. Fergna. But we still have to get back to the castle." She stared as another vehicle drove onto the sands. "Somebody else just arrived. Let's see who it is. The tide's out enough that we won't get our feet wet."

Judith and Renie proceeded with caution in the wet sand, watching for rocks or any debris that might cause them to stumble. As they grew closer to the accident site, they saw the constables' footprints. Adamson and Glen were approaching the car that had just come to a stop. A man wearing a raincoat and hat got out from the driver's side.

Judith assumed he must be the local detective chief inspector—if that was indeed the correct title. But as the cousins moved closer, it was apparent that the new-comer was arguing with the constables.

"Don't patronize me," he warned in a stern voice. "If it's Harry, I'll tell Moira."

Judith recognized Jimmy, Moira's brother, from seeing him at the cemetery. The constables were trying to reason with him, but he brushed them aside. "Where's the body?" he demanded.

Adamson glanced at the other emergency personnel who were finishing their part in the disaster operation. At that moment, Jimmy spotted the cousins. "And who are you?" he asked in an imperious tone.

"Does it matter?" Renie shot back.

"Of course it does!" Jimmy exploded, striding closer to Judith and Renie. "Are you witnesses?" he asked in a calmer tone.

"Are you a cop?" Renie asked.

"No." He jammed his hands in the raincoat's pockets. He was over six feet tall, with a dark goatee and hooded dark eyes. "I'm an attorney."

Renie smirked. "We call them ambulance chasers in the States."

"You're not in the States," Jimmy said dryly. "I understand the pejorative term. I represent Blackwell Oil, as well as my sister, Moira Gibbs. Did you witness the accident?"

Judith tried to nudge Renie out of the way. "We heard it. We're staying at Grimloch Castle."

Jimmy looked displeased. "You're friends of Philip Fordyce?"

"Not exactly," Judith said. She hesitated mentioning Hugh MacGowan. "It's complicated."

"But you saw nothing? Were you here or at the castle?"

"The castle," Judith replied, as Renie wandered toward the track leading to the village. "You're here because Moira's husband is—"

Before Judith could finish, Jimmy turned swiftly and raced to meet a man wearing a leather jacket and Levi's. "Patrick!" Jimmy shouted. "Where . . . ?" The rest of the question was lost in the mist.

The two men engaged in deep conversation. After a minute or two, they walked over to the place where the Range Rover had burned into a smoking hulk. Judith noticed that the crowd at the top of the bank had grown. Half the village's population had come to learn what caused the big bang.

"Do you expect Bill and Joe to come back tonight?" Judith asked.

"Only if MacGowan is called in because of this mess," Renie said. "I don't know the Highlands very well. Everything's much smaller than at home in terms of distances. I don't do kilometers."

"Neither do I," Judith admitted. Her attention was diverted by the man in the leather jacket who was storming away from Jimmy and heading in the opposite direction from the track to the beach. "Jimmy must have said the wrong thing to that guy, too. He seems angry."

"He disappeared," Renie noted. "There must be another way up from the beach."

Judith gazed at the steep track. "I don't want to try climbing up that tonight. We'd have to go through the spectator section and then get back to Grimloch. I won't pester Mr. and Mrs. Gibbs when their grandson has probably been killed. Let's walk back to the castle and try to avoid the Gibbses until they get official notification."

"What about dinner?" Renie asked. "You must be starving."

Judith gave Renie a wry look. "I tend to lose my appetite when tragedies occur. You, on the other hand, could've eaten your way through a torture session with the Inquisition."

"I like Spanish food," Renie said.

"What do you suppose happened? Did Harry stay in his car the rest of the afternoon after his swim? Or did he go somewhere and come back later? Did you see him at the castle while I was napping?"

"No," Renie said. "His name wasn't mentioned."

Judith slowed her step as the mist grew thicker. "I can't see the castle but we must be almost there."

"We'd better be." Renie finished speaking when the cousins were able to make out the dark stone walls rising above the rocky cliff. "Let's hope we can summon the lift. It strikes me as problematical."

Judith grimaced at the sheer cliff with its rugged face covered in moss and lichen. Despite the darkness, a movement about ten feet above the ground caught her eye. She looked up.

"It's that bird Harry hated," she said, "perched above us on a rock."

"Where? I can't see it," Renie complained.

At that moment the great northern diver let out an eerie, haunting cry and flew off into the night. Judith shivered. "Never mind. It's gone."

The lift arrived a few seconds later, heralded by the contraption's creaks and groans. Moments later, Judith and Renie were moving across the courtyard. To their relief, the door was unlocked.

"They must not need much security here," Judith murmured.

An eerie silence echoed through the empty passageway. Despite her cape, Judith could feel a draft. "Let's go to your room," she suggested as they wound their way up the stone staircase. "Maybe we can watch what's happening on the beach."

After the cousins reached the Joneses' room, Judith checked her watch. It was almost eight o'clock. She wondered if she should call Joe to tell him what had happened, but decided against it. If he and the other two men didn't know, the news might ruin their fishing expedition. They'd find out soon enough, when they got back Sunday afternoon.

"Where are Philip and Beth?" Judith asked as the cousins sat in the window embrasure. "Where's Chuckie?"

"Have you looked in the bathtub?"

Judith sighed. "Beth can't be his mother. She's too young. And what did Mr. and Mrs. Gibbs mean when they said something about 'it should be Moira'?"

"Oh, coz," Renie said resignedly, "you're already turning this into a murder case. You don't know if foul play was involved."

"Range Rovers don't blow up on their own." Judith resumed her speculations. "It should be Moira who blew up Harry? It should be Moira who was blown up? It should be Moira and Harry?"

"Any or none of the above." Renie leaned closer to the window. "Somebody's coming. A car's driving onto the beach parking area."

Judith peered through the old, irregular glass. "An unmarked car, dark color. But it's not the Fordyce Daimler."

Two men got out and walked toward the lift. "Cops?" Renie said.

"Could be."

The men disappeared, hidden by the cliff's outcropping. "Should we go downstairs after they deliver the bad news?" Judith asked.

"Wouldn't that be intrusive?"

"Mr. and Mrs. Gibbs aren't young. No one else seems to be around except for Chuckie," Judith reasoned. "We may be virtual strangers, but we could offer some kind of support."

Renie considered. "And forage for food. Okay. Ten minutes?"

"That sounds about right. Besides," Judith went on, "we have to find out what happened." She looked at her watch again. It was 8:06. Renie got up and began pacing around the room. Judith stayed by the window.

The mist thinned and thickened, blown to and fro by the wind. The activity on the beach appeared to have diminished, and the onlookers on the bluff had dwindled to only a dozen or so curious souls.

At fifteen minutes past eight, a knock on the door startled the cousins. Renie hurried to answer it.

"Alpin MacRae," the older of the two men announced. "Detective chief inspector, Moray division headquartered in Elgin. This is my sergeant, Malcolm Ogilvie. You must be the guests, Mrs. Flynn and Mrs. Jones."

"Right," Renie said as Judith joined her. "I'm Jones, she's Flynn."

"No matter," MacRae said easily. "We won't tarry. The constables told us you were on the beach after the explosion."

"Yes," Judith said. "Would you like to sit?"

"No, thank you," MacRae said politely. "This won't take long. Do sit." His keen blue eyes studied Judith. "You look quite tired."

"Well . . . I am, I guess," Judith said, and sank into an armchair near the hearth. "I have an artificial hip. Walking too much wears me down. Not to mention the long flight." She stopped speaking. MacRae was a big man whose solid presence invited confidences. His sergeant was no more than thirty, with fair hair and a skimpy mustache. He seemed somewhat intimidated, either by his surroundings or by his superior.

MacRae had moved to the hearth, hands clasped behind his back. "You know Hugh MacGowan, I understand."

"Our husbands do," Judith replied. "They're on a fishing trip with him now. My husband is a retired police detective."

MacRae nodded and looked at Renie, who was sitting on a large oak chest at the foot of the bed. "Mr. Jones is a psychologist, I believe."

"I believe that, too," Renie said hastily. "I mean—yes, he is."

MacRae smiled slightly. Judith figured he was accustomed to rattling even the most hardened of criminals. Obviously he'd done his homework on the Flynns and the Joneses.

"I'm afraid," MacRae said in an appropriately somber voice, "that Harry Gibbs was killed this evening."

"We guessed as much," Judith said quietly. "It's very sad."

"Indeed." MacRae paused. "We understand you heard the explosion. What time was that?"

"A little after six," Judith answered. "I'd taken a nap and woke up just a few minutes before the hour."

She looked at Renie. "You came in a few minutes later."

MacRae nodded and glanced at his subordinate. "That agrees with the other reports, eh, Mal?"

"Yes, sir."

The DCI gazed at the cousins. "You met Harry Gibbs?"

"Yes," Judith said. "Not long after we arrived yesterday. He came into the drawing room while we were having our predinner cocktails. He didn't talk much—he had a couple of quick drinks and left."

"He was friendly?" MacRae's question invited candor.

"Friendly?" Renie echoed. "Not really. I thought he looked at us as if we were some kind of virus."

MacRae chuckled; Ogilvie's smile was tense.

"That was the only time you saw him?" MacRae asked in a tone that indicated he already knew the answer.

"Mr. Gibbs—his grandfather—had Harry give us a ride into the village," Judith explained. "He dropped us off and told us he was going on beyond St. Fergna. Later, when we came back to the castle, he was on the beach, swimming in the nude."

Again MacRae nodded. "That was a habit of his. No harm in it, really, but rather foolish this time of year. Did you see him after that?"

"No," Judith said, "not after he came out of the water and went back to his car. At least I assume that's what he did, probably to dress."

"You didn't see him drive from the beach?"

"No." Judith shook her head. "We returned to Grimloch with Philip and Beth Fordyce, who'd just arrived."

"Harry mooned us," Renie said. "Is that a motive for murder around here?"

MacRae regarded her curiously. "You think Harry Gibbs was murdered?"

Renie grimaced and shot Judith a quick glance. "Well . . . it usually is when my—" She broke into a coughing fit.

But Judith knew that Renie had already said too much.

7

Alpin MacRae didn't miss a beat. "It's early days to render an opinion," he said smoothly, covering Renie's gaffe. "When an explosion is involved, it's natural to conclude there was foul play. We prefer to err on the side of caution."

"Very wise," Judith said. "How are Mr. and Mrs. Gibbs doing?"

"They're shocked," MacRae replied, "and grieving. Mrs. Gibbs asked us to tell you that she won't be serving dinner tonight, but breakfast will be ready by nine tomorrow morning."

"Please tell her that's not necessary," Judith asserted. "We can manage our own. We won't burden them at such an awful time."

"The Gibbses appear to be practical folk," MacRae said. "Harry's parents will be informed, though that may take time. They're surviving."

"Surviving what?" Renie asked.

MacRae was impassive. "Apparently they enjoy going to exotic locales and living off the land. Mr. Gibbs thought they might be somewhere on the Amazon River."

Renie shuddered. "How horrible. My husband refuses to go anywhere that doesn't have digital cable. Except for fishing, that is."

"It seems Harry's parents are adventurers," MacRae said.

Judith couldn't help but raise a hand, as if she were a student and MacRae the teacher. "Have the Fordyces been notified?"

"Yes," the DCI answered. "They were contacted on their cell phone. They'd gone into Inverness for the evening. We expect them back soon."

"What about Chuckie?" Renie inquired.

MacRae looked puzzled. "Chuckie? Who is that?"

"We understand," Judith said cautiously, "that he's Mr. Fordyce's son. He lives here—at least part of the time—at the castle."

"You've met the laddie?" MacRae asked.

"Y-y-yes," Judith said. "He's a bit . . . odd."

The detective seemed faintly amused. "And how might that be?"

Judith frowned. "He seems small for his age. That is, his face looks older than his size would indicate. I doubt that he's much over five feet tall. His behavior is . . . unusual."

MacRae gazed at Renie. "Has your husband met him?"

"Briefly," Renie replied. "Chuckie tends to pop up unexpectedly."

MacRae nodded. "Has Dr. Jones made any sort of evaluation?"

"Yes," Renie said. "Bill says he's nuts."

Ogilvie had to put a hand over his mouth to keep from laughing, but MacRae merely nodded again. "Not a clinical diagnosis," he remarked, "but evocative. Unstable, in other words."

Renie shrugged. "Probably."

"We'll have to speak with this Chuckie," MacRae said, more to Ogilvie than to the cousins. "That will be all for now, ladies. Thank you for your cooperation." The DCI led the way out but paused to turn back to Judith and Renie. "We understand you'll be staying here for at least a fortnight. If you see or hear anything of interest, please keep us informed." His expression was somber. "And do be careful."

Well," Judith said after the detective and his sergeant had left, "MacRae certainly knows more about us than we do about him. I wonder if MacGowan filled him in before we ever got here."

"You mean MacGowan expected somebody to get killed just because you arrived at Grimloch?"

Judith was annoyed. "Of course not! I mean, conversation. You know—MacGowan is taking two Americans fishing, and their wives will be staying at the castle—and so on."

"Possibly," Renie said. "What do we do about dinner?"

"You have a one-track mind," Judith chided. "I'll admit I'm getting hungry. The Gibbses may expect us to forage for ourselves. Shall we?"

"You bet," Renie said, sliding off of the chest. "Let's go."

Mr. and Mrs. Gibbs were nowhere to be seen in the passageway that led to the ground-floor guest area. "I know how to get into the kitchen through the dining room," Judith said. "Follow me."

"Can't you walk any faster? I'm practically stepping on your heels. Good thing I'm not wearing shoes."

"You know I can't walk much faster," Judith replied, hearing her cousin's feet slap against the stone floor like scattered applause. "It's been a long day. And why aren't you wearing shoes?"

"My feet got wet. I think my shoes are ruined. I left them to dry out on what looks like a heater in our room."

The dining room was dark. "We'll have to feel our way," Judith said. "I've no idea where the light switch is located." She began groping her way toward the table and chairs. Renie kept a hand on her cousin's back. "I found a chair," Judith said. "When we get to the end of the table, we keep going almost straight ahead. There are two doors." She reached the end of the long table, proceeding more slowly since there was nothing to grasp. "It's not far," she reassured her cousin, and touched the wall. "I think the door is a little to the—"

"Open the window."

Judith gave a start. "What?"

"I didn't say anything." Renie moved closer to Judith. "Who's there?" she called.

"Open the window."

Judith tried to figure out where the voice was coming from. "Except for the window instead of the gate part, that's what I heard in your room," she whispered to Renie. "Who is it?"

"Chuckie?" Renie guessed.

"That's not how he sounds. Too high-pitched, even for Chuckie."

The cousins didn't budge, standing in silence. But they heard nothing more.

"Where did that voice come from?" Judith murmured.

Renie hazarded another guess. "The far end of the room?"

"The fireplace is there," Judith said, no longer whispering. "There's a door, too, as I recall." She edged along the wall. "Ah! The kitchen."

Both the door into the dining room and the baize door into the kitchen were unlocked. The lights were already on in part of the big kitchen. Renie headed straight for the refrigerator. Judith took time to stroll around the area, discovering a pantry, a scullery, and a large cooler stocked with fresh fruit and vegetables. She took out a head of lettuce, a tomato, scallions, and a rosy apple.

"I'll make a salad," she volunteered.

Renie was slicing a big ham. "Hot or cold?" she asked.

"A sandwich is fine with me," Judith said. "I'll find bread."

She was looking for the bread box when Beth Fordyce entered the kitchen from a door off of the old scullery.

"Oh!" Beth exclaimed. "You're the guests. I wager you're sorry you ever came to Grimloch."

"We're so sorry about Harry," Judith said. "Was he a close friend?"

"No," Beth replied. "I know Moira. She married my brother."

"You mean," Judith said, "her first husband?"

Beth removed a bottle of bicarbonate of soda from a cupboard. "Yes, Frankie. He died." She gave the bottle several hard shakes, careful to keep it away from what looked like a very expensive pleated cream jersey top and putty-colored cropped pants. "I don't know why Phil doesn't bring his own medicine when he knows he's got a bad stomach."

"So your maiden name is Gunn?" Judith inquired, recalling the headstone marking Francis Gunn's grave in the local cemetery.

Beth nodded. "Poor Moira. She's had horrid luck with husbands."

Judith found the bread. "What caused the explosion that killed Harry?"

Beth looked at Judith curiously. Her features had the kind of animation that indicated she wasn't as empty-headed as Renie had guessed. "It wasn't the explosion that killed him. Who told you that?"

"Well . . . we inferred it, I suppose," Judith said. "We heard the big bang. The police were here and they didn't say otherwise."

"The police are still here," Beth said, making a face. "Why do you think Phil's stomach is upset?" She shook her head and departed the same way she'd come into the kitchen.

Renie was gazing at Judith. "So how did Harry die?"

"That's what I'd like to know," Judith said, finding a tub of butter in the cupboard by the bread box. "Maybe he drowned."

"So why was his car blown up?"

"I don't know." Judith buttered the bread and started searching for mustard. "He may not have been in the car when the bomb went off. That would make sense. If he'd been . . . well, literally blown up . . . nobody at the scene would be sure how he died unless it was the result of the explosion. They might not even know if the remains were Harry's."

Renie had found a bowl for the salad. "I wonder how Moira's faring on this latest voyage into widowhood. She must feel hexed."

"I wonder where she lives," Judith said. "Not always with Harry, since he seemed to spend time here at the castle."

"The rich are different," Renie pointed out, "as we have discovered. They don't live conventional lives like the rest of us poor persons."

"Maybe Joe can learn more when he and Bill get back tomorrow," Judith said, cutting up the tomato. "I gather MacGowan hasn't been called in on the case."

Renie had returned to the refrigerator. "I see five kinds of salad dressing. What's your choice?"

"Blue cheese?"

"Okay. Me, too." Renie brought out a small crock. "This is homemade. See the handwritten label with the fancy letter G?"

"Very nice. Mrs. Gibbs, I suppose."

"Who else?" Renie spooned the thick dressing into the salad bowl. "Do we eat here or in the dining room?"

"Let's not do either," Judith responded. "We don't know where the dining room lights are and there's really no place to sit in here. We should check out the drawing room and maybe have an after-dinner drink from the liquor cabinet."

Judith and Renie put their meals on a pewter tray and carried them out through the door Beth had used. They found themselves in a small hallway by the indoor elevator. Around the corner was the passageway that led to the drawing room. The lights were on. Someone had recently used the room. Cigar smoke hung in the air.

"Philip Fordyce?" Judith said as they settled onto a Regency sofa covered in dark green velvet. "I can't imagine Gibbs sitting around smoking cigars."

"Maybe it's Chuckie," Renie said. "He'd do just about anything."

"I wonder if the police have tracked him down for questioning," Judith mused. "Want half of this apple?"

"No, thanks." Renie took a large bite of sandwich. "AhwunnerufChuggienosowtomakabum."

"Chuckie may be the type who'd not only know how to make a bomb, but would enjoy setting it off to hear it go bang," Judith said, accustomed to hearing Renie talk with her mouth full. "Although he did ask what the noise was, indicating it surprised him."

The drawing room door opened. A tired-looking Philip Fordyce entered, appearing surprised to see the cousins. "Pardon," he said, going to the liquor cabinet. "Did I leave my drink in here?"

Judith scanned the large room. "I don't see it. Do you remember where you were sitting?"

"I wasn't," Philip answered tersely. "Never mind. I'll pour a fresh one." He went to the cabinet and got out a bottle of Scotch.

"I understand," Judith said, "you own the Glengrim distillery. I had some of your whiskey last night. It's excellent."

Philip didn't look up from the glass he was filling halfway. "Yes."

Judith glanced at Renie, who was chomping away at her sandwich. She hoped her cousin would keep her mouth shut about her dislike of Scotch. Philip remained by the liquor cabinet, savoring his drink.

"How long will you be?" he inquired after a long pause.

Judith turned to look directly at him. "In here?"

"Yes."

"As long as it takes," Renie said, fortunately not with her mouth full. "Why? Isn't this the guest part of the castle?"

"I'm expecting someone momentarily," Philip explained.

"We're almost—"

Judith was interrupted by Renie. "Anybody we know?"

"Doubtful," Philip replied with a severe look for Renie. "You arrived only yesterday, did you not?"

"Right, but my coz and I get around. You'd be surprised." For emphasis, Renie wiggled her eyebrows.

"If you don't mind . . . " Philip began, but at that moment the door opened and a haggard Gibbs showed Mrs. Gunn into the drawing room.

"A fine mess this is, Philip," she declared, though her manner seemed almost jubilant. The sparkle in her eyes dimmed when she saw Judith and Renie. "My word! What are they doing here?"

"Told you so." Renie chortled and flexed her bare toes.

"You're acquainted?" Philip asked Mrs. Gunn, who was eyeing Renie's unshod feet with disgust.

"We've met," Mrs. Gunn said through taut lips. "I'd no idea you were offering them hospitality."

"It's rather involved," Philip said. He raised his voice and addressed the cousins. "Would you mind? Mrs. Gunn and I have private matters to discuss."

Judith gathered up the remains of her dinner. "Of course," she said, wishing for once that she could be as rude as Renie. There was nothing she'd like more than to hear what type of "private matters" Philip Fordyce and Mrs. Gunn wanted to talk about. "Is it possible that we could take a small bottle and glasses to our rooms?"

"Please." Philip took a backward step, as if he was afraid the cousins might contaminate him.

"No Scotch for me," Renie said. "I'd rather drink motor oil."

Judith went to the cabinet and got two glasses, a pint of Glengrim Scotch, and an airline-sized bottle of Drambuie. Renie was already out of the room. With her hands full, Judith had trouble closing the door before she joined her cousin in the passageway.

"You were awful," Judith declared. "Though I don't actually blame you. Despite your loathing of Scotch, I got you some Drambuie, which, as you damned well know, has Scotch in it."

"The other ingredients disguise the taste," Renie replied blithely. "Here, let me take your food. I finished mine and left the dirty plate in the drawing room."

Judith handed over everything but the Scotch. She and Renie were almost to the stairs when Judith stopped. "I'm going back to take your plate to the kitchen. I'm also going to apologize for your big mouth."

Renie sighed. "You're going to listen at the keyhole. If there is a keyhole. Go ahead. I'll see you upstairs in your room."

Judith didn't care if a keyhole existed. She hadn't been able to shut the door tightly because of her burdens. Her only concern was if Philip or Mrs. Gunn had closed it after the cousins' departure.

But, no doubt because of what Judith perceived as their sense of urgency, the door remained slightly ajar.

"Journalists!" Mrs. Gunn was saying in her husky voice. "If that's all you're worried about . . . " The rest of the sentence was lost to Judith.

"Harry must have died on our property," Philip said. "I don't like scandal attached to Glengrim. It's rotten publicity. Why couldn't he have stayed at Hollywood?"

"Because of his flu," Mrs. Gunn replied impatiently. "Moira didn't want Harry near the baby. She's very protective, a natural nurse. Moira was a pillar of strength for my poor Frankie when he became ill."

"Come, come, Kate," Philip said so loudly that Judith figured he must be near the door. "Harry seemed quite recovered when Beth and I arrived this afternoon. He took one of his bare-bum swims."

Mrs. Gunn chuckled. "I didn't say he was clever. Harry has always behaved foolishly. What would you expect with his parents half a world away most of the time he was growing up? A poor choice on Moira's part, I must say. Still, the lad had charm and looks."

"That's all he had," Philip said as Judith heard the sound of glassware and pouring liquid. "Some might be relieved that he's dead."

A brief silence followed. "True," Mrs. Gunn finally said. "I don't trust Moira's judgment. She may act imprudently again."

"Patrick?"

"Yes."

"He has a wife. Jeannie's a lovely girl. Wealthy in her own right."

"Not as wealthy as Moira."

"Not many are," Mrs. Gunn pointed out. "Where does Harry's death leave us? If he was an obstacle . . . " Her words became inaudible.

Judith could only catch phrases of Philip's response. "The plan is . . . Jimmy's influence is . . . if Beth can . . . out of the way . . . "

Judith had stood still for so long that her joints were stiff. Lurching slightly, she fell against the door, causing it to open.

"Excuse me," she said as a startled Philip and Mrs. Gunn looked up from their chairs near the unlit fireplace. "I came to collect my cousin's things. I don't want to make more work for Mrs. Gibbs."

"By all means," Philip said.

Judith didn't dare look at him—or at Mrs. Gunn. She sensed they were both suspicious. She also had the feeling that suspicion of others was only one of the traits they shared.

"I must apologize," Judith said as she gathered up Renie's plate, silverware, the pewter tray, and the salt and pepper containers. "Mrs. Jones was ungracious. She's very distraught, of course. My cousin and I," Judith added, lying through her teeth, "aren't used to violence."

"Oh?" Mrs. Gunn said with irony. "I thought you were Americans."

Judith glanced at Kate Gunn. "Contrary to media reports, we don't live in constant dread of finding corpses on our doorsteps." *Oh,* Judith thought, *I really am telling a whopper, but I have to defend my country.*

The other woman said nothing. Judith left the drawing room and headed for the kitchen via the door near the elevator. She had just entered by the old scullery when she heard voices from somewhere in another part of the kitchen.

"Forget about it, Chuckie," a woman said firmly. "You always think you're falling in love. I don't care how old Phil is. I married your father because I wanted to. Please leave me alone."

"You're unkind," Chuckie said. "Now I won't tell you my secret."

"You always have secrets, Chuckie," Beth said in a weary voice. "You shouldn't listen at doors or hide in closets."

"I don't always have to do those things to have secrets," Chuckie declared. "But I won't share my secrets with you anymore because maybe I never loved you. Maybe I love Moira. Maybe I always did."

"Then I'm pleased for you. I wish you well." Beth Fordyce was coming straight toward Judith, who was forced to duck inside the scullery. Beth sailed by and went out of the kitchen. A moment later, the dining room door closed. Beth and Chuckie were gone. Judith put the dinner things on the counter and went back the way she'd come. The elevator seemed like a good idea. She was extremely tired.

But Judith's brain wasn't ready for rest. "Philip and Mrs. Gunn are conspiring," she announced upon arriving in her room.

"About what?" Renie, who was setting off a fire in the grate, stood up. "Are you saying that's relevant to Harry's death?"

"Maybe," Judith said, setting the bottles and glasses on the dresser. "I don't know what they're up to."

"What would Harry Gibbs have to do with Glengrim distillery or Mrs. Gunn?" Renie asked.

"It sounds like it's all connected to business," Judith explained, pouring the drinks.

"You know," Renie said, taking the Drambuie snifter from Judith, "this isn't any of *our* business. For once, can't you back off?"

Judith thought for a moment. "No. For me, that would be morally reprehensible."

"Be practical," Renie urged. "You're a visitor in a foreign country. You're the guest of a local cop. The police in the UK are very competent. You don't know any of the people involved. Let Scotland's criminal justice system do the job. Otherwise you're just in the way and probably in danger. You know how Joe's going to react to that. It'd spoil the whole vacation. This is our long-planned getaway."

"That's the problem," Judith said bleakly. "I can't let anybody get away with murder."

8

The rest of the evening proved uneventful. Renie retreated to her room around eleven. Judith set her travel clock for eight-thirty. But it was well after midnight before she finally settled down. Upon awakening, she couldn't remember what she'd dreamed, but knew she'd passed a restless night. The comforter was half off the bed and one of the pillows had fallen on the floor. Maybe, she thought, she'd been haunted by poor Harry and the life that had been cut so short.

After showering, putting on her makeup, and dressing in her new slacks and twin set, she went across the hall to Renie's room. There was no response to her knock. The door was locked. Judith didn't blame Renie; she'd locked her own door, too. Her cousin must be sleeping in, as was her habit. It was after nine, and if they were to eat breakfast before Mass in the chapel at eleven, Renie had better get going. Judith knocked harder and called out. "It's me! Wake up!"

A full minute passed before Renie staggered to the door. "Is the sun up yet?" she asked in a groggy voice.

"It's cloudy, but it's not exactly dawn. You missed that," Judith said, closing the door behind her. "Come on, we have to eat."

"Oh. Eat." Renie was wandering around the room in her flannel nightgown. "Breakfast. I remember. Good concept." She wove her way to the garderobe.

When the cousins arrived in the dining room half an hour later, the sideboard held another generous repast.

"Porridge," Renie said. "Real Scottish porridge. I read somewhere that they have an annual porridge-off around here. Inverness, maybe. They go for the Golden Sprutle."

"The what?" Judith asked.

"Sprutle," Renie repeated. "It's the stick used to stir porridge."

"Only you would know that," Judith said, shaking her head.

"True," Renie agreed. "I'm a font of useless knowledge."

"I'm going to try the tangerine marmalade," Judith said. "It's in another crock like the salad dressing with the fancy *G* on it. Mrs. Gibbs must be a wizard in the kitchen."

"Putting up preserves is a lost art," Renie noted. "Remember how our mothers did it every year? I tried it when I was first married, but it was too much trouble. Canning was always in August, the hottest time of the year, standing at the stove and getting even hotter."

"You're babbling," Judith declared. "I like it better when you don't talk before ten o'clock."

Just as the cousins were finishing, Mrs. Gibbs entered the dining room. Her cheeks were pale and there were dark circles under her eyes.

"Father Keith will arrive before eleven," she said in a toneless voice. "Do ye know where to find the chapel? It's in the southwest tower. Look for the cross over the door."

Judith's expression was compassionate. "We're so sorry about your grandson. If there's anything we can do—"

Mrs. Gibbs cut her off with a sharp gesture. "What's to be done? The laddie's gone to God. Pray for his poor soul, that's what to do."

"Of course," Judith said. "Have you reached his parents?"

"An impossible task," Mrs. Gibbs said. "They never should o' had the bairn. Free spirits, they call themselves. Worthless, I call them." She turned and went back to the kitchen.

"Not fond of Sonny," Renie remarked, stirring sugar into her tea. "Why can't parents take responsibility for ending up with rotten kids?"

Judith shook her head. "Sometimes kids are just bad apples."

"Maybe." Renie checked her watch. "Ten-twenty. I wonder how many people attend Mass in this Scottish Reformed Church country? Which reminds me, speaking of parents. It was Saint Margaret of Scotland who had six kids, and three turned out fine but the other trio was awful. She once remarked that even Ted Williams never batted five hundred."

Judith smiled. "I doubt she used those words, since she must've died about nine hundred years before Ted Williams was born."

"Oh?" Renie feigned innocence. "Maybe Saint Margaret meant shooting from the field. Or pass completions. You get the point, though I'm not sure I agree with it."

The dining room door from the passageway opened. Beth Fordyce entered, wearing a very short yellow nightgown. "Coffee!" she exclaimed, her slanting brown eyes widening. "Where?"

"Try the silver urn," Renie said. "We're drinking tea this morning."

"What a ghastly night," Beth said, taking a cup and saucer from the sideboard. "I hardly slept. I've never been interrogated by the police. What do I know about Harry's death? It'd be like him to blow up his own car, from what I've heard. He craved attention." She poured her coffee and sat down a couple of places from Judith. "Phil is wild."

Judith was puzzled. "You told us the explosion didn't kill Harry."

Beth nodded. "That's what I was told. The autopsy's tomorrow. The Sabbath is sacred around here." With delicate fingers, she picked up her cup and saucer. "I must dress for Mass."

After Beth left, Judith looked at Renie. "So she's RC. Who else?"

Renie shrugged. "We seem to have fallen into a nest of papists."

"Ordinarily, that'd be fine with me," Judith said, "but at the moment, I have my doubts about whether these people practice what they preach. Especially," she added grimly, " 'Thou shalt not kill.' "

Father Keith was elderly, white-haired, and rail-thin, but he zipped through the liturgy at top speed. The only reference to Harry Gibbs was during the intercessions when the priest asked the small congregation to pray for the dead man's soul.

Despite the brevity of the service, Judith had time to take in the age-old beauty of the chapel. The statues of Jesus, Mary, St. Joseph, and St. Fergna probably weren't the originals, but they definitely dated from the eighteenth or even seventeenth century. The Stations of the Cross in bas-relief also looked as if they'd been added later. Behind the altar the stained-glass windows depicted various saints Judith couldn't identify. The workmanship looked very old, though a few sections looked as if they'd been replaced after attacks by enemies or Mother Nature. The tabernacle was crafted from ancient gold and studded with jewels.

Philip and Beth Fordyce, Mr. and Mrs. Gibbs, and—to Judith's surprise—Mrs. Gunn were in attendance. So were a dozen strangers, though she couldn't help but notice a pretty young woman in the back pew wearing a gorgeous sable coat. As Father Keith concluded the Mass after the final blessing, he all but darted out of the chapel. Judith surmised that he was a kind of circuit-riding priest who still had at least one more Mass to celebrate in another nearby village or town.

As the worshippers left the chapel, Judith noticed that Beth had paused to light a votive candle.

"Hold it," Judith whispered to Renie.

"Why?" Renie shot back. "Father Speedo skipped the sign of peace. I wanted to take the opportunity to deck Mrs. Gunn again."

"She might have decked you," Judith said. "Here comes Beth."

"Is there a priest shortage in Scotland, too?" Judith asked.

"Oh yes," Beth replied, "especially in the Highlands. The few younger priests who are ordained all seem to want to teach. Pardon, I must speak with Will and Marie."

The cousins trailed behind Beth as she called to the couple Judith had noticed in the last pew. The woman, who apparently was Marie, exuded a lush air with her fair skin, masses of auburn hair, and all that expensive fur. The man at her side was of average height, with a receding hairline, a long, lean face, and a slightly hooked nose.

Judith's observations were cut short by a commotion on the cobbled walkway to her left. Philip and Chuckie were arguing. Or rather, Chuckie was screaming at his father and jumping up and down.

"I'm not going to hell!" Chuckie shouted. "I get bored in church! That's why I threw oranges at the priest during Christmas Mass!"

Philip grabbed his son by the collar, dragging him away from the others. Judith couldn't hear what Philip was saying, but Chuckie wore a truculent expression and kept shaking his head as he leaned against the half-timbered wall. Judith noticed that Beth had abruptly stopped talking to Will and Marie. Except for Mrs. Gunn, the rest had left.

"Phil!" Beth shouted. "Let me speak with Chuckie!"

Chuckie took a couple of swings at his much taller father but missed. With a weary expression, Philip walked off. He'd gone only a few feet before Chuckie raced up from behind and tackled the older man. Philip fell flat on his face. Chuckie sat on him and hooted in derision.

Beth headed toward her husband and her stepson. "Chuckie, Chuckie, what are you doing?" she asked in a resigned voice. "Get up. I'll make you some cocoa."

"Really?" Chuckie grinned at her as Philip tried to dislodge his errant son. "With biscuits?"

"Of course. Come along now. Be my good boy."

Chuckie sprang off of his father and hurried to take Beth's outstretched hand. "What kind of biscuits?" he inquired.

"Your favorites," Beth said, leading Chuckie away.

The man called Will was helping Philip get up. The woman named Marie strolled over to Judith and Renie. She spoke in an undertone. "Chuckie's quite mad, you know."

"No kidding," Renie retorted.

"He should be institutionalized," the woman said, brushing her chin against the sable collar of her splendid coat. "These days they treat crazy people with pills. I don't think it works very well."

Philip was brushing himself off while Will looked the other way, perhaps to save them both from the embarrassment of the moment.

"Are you friends of the Fordyces?" Judith inquired.

Marie smiled slightly. She was several years younger than her husband who appeared to be close to forty. "Beth and Moira and I all went to school together. My husband, Will Fleming, is the Blackwell Petroleum comptroller. That's how we met." Her smile widened, showing dimples. "Will's very clever. Believe it or not, he can be quite funny."

Judith glanced at Will, who was looking anything but amused at the moment. He'd finally walked away from Philip.

"We should go, Marie," he said. "The tide will be changing shortly."

Marie nodded. "Of course, darling." She turned to the cousins. "Beth says you're guests here. You've had rather a rude welcome."

"We're used to it," Renie said.

"Really?" Marie giggled, then suddenly sobered. "I shouldn't laugh. It's quite dreadful about Harry. Still, it's the sort of thing one would expect of him." She scooted away to join her husband, who was already at the arched entrance to the castle.

"Harry's not getting a lot of sympathy," Renie noted. "I'm beginning to think I was right the first time—he was a jerk."

"I pity him," Judith said, but shut up as Philip approached.

"I apologize," he said stiffly, "for my son. He's unwell. You mustn't think ill of him. He has a genetic defect, causing physical and emotional growth problems. I've sent him to the best doctors and clinics. When he takes his medication, he's well behaved and quite bright."

"It must be very hard on you," Judith said before Renie could open her big mouth and spoil what must be a difficult admission for a man like Philip Fordyce. "I sympathize."

"Very kind of you," Philip murmured. "Excuse me, I feel a need to walk the beach."

Judith watched him move away, hampered by a slight limp. "Maybe we should go someplace, too," she said.

Renie frowned. "Where?"

"The village? I think I can walk that far."

"Everything's probably closed on the Sabbath," Renie pointed out.

"True." Judith gazed around the courtyard. The sun had come out from behind the clouds. Judith noticed an old sundial in the flowerbed near the door where Beth had left with Chuckie. She strolled toward it with Renie following her.

"No hands," Judith noted. "It's symbolic, don't you think? This place is really timeless."

Renie disagreed. "It's marking time, a millennium's worth of centuries. So many people have come and gone, yet the castle remains."

Renie stopped as a strange, eerily familiar sound captured the cousins' attention. Judith looked up. Near the top of the castle's second story, the great northern diver was perched on a corbel, emitting his haunting cry. The bird preened a bit before flapping its wings and sailing off over the courtyard and out of sight.

"That weird call," Judith said softly. "It sounds like the bird is mourning."

"Maybe," Renie allowed. "Or uttering a cry for help."

Despite the sun, Judith shivered. "I'm not a fanciful person, but there is something spooky about this place. Maybe it's all the history."

"History is nothing but old gossip," Renie declared. "Who did what to whom and why and how it all turned into a war or a revolution."

Judith frowned. "Maybe. I wonder if there really is a ghost here. Certainly there's a voice, telling us to open the gate or the window. Where does it come from?"

"TV," Renie said. "For not being fanciful, you're sounding a little loopy. Remember on our first trip to Europe we reached Deauville the night before taking ship for home, we got to the cheap B&B and were terrified before we rang the bell?"

Judith's mind traveled back to that chilly October night in Normandy. "Yes. The house was dark, it looked run-down, and when we finally rang the bell nobody answered. We almost grabbed our suitcases and ran off."

"Oh yes. It was raining and blowing like mad. We were sure the owners were inside plotting our imminent demise." Renie grinned. "Instead they had the lights out and wouldn't come to the door because they wanted to finish watching a rerun of *I Love Lucy*. In French."

Judith smiled. "So I'm imagining the atmosphere at Grimloch?"

Renie was studying the daffodil and hyacinth greenery that was poking its way out of the peaty ground. "I can't dismiss the murder that's occurred since we arrived, but we should be used to it."

"If people knew about my track record when it comes to dead bodies," Judith said, "they'd avoid me like the plague."

"But they don't," Renie pointed out. "As I told you years ago when the first homicide happened at Hillside Manor, it was good advertising."

Judith grimaced. "I've never been convinced of that. Most people don't pay attention to anything that goes on outside of their own little world." She looked around the courtyard again. All seemed quiet except for the flags that fluttered gently at half-staff in the occasional wind from the sea. "There's a third flag today," Judith noted. "It's got the stag's head on it. They must hoist it when The Master's in residence."

"Makes sense," Renie said. "So what are we going to do with ourselves until Bill and Joe get back later today?"

Judith considered. "Do you suppose there's a taxi?"

"Land or water?"

"We can walk to the beach now," Judith pointed out. "Let me use my cell. I'll call local directory information. I wonder if I just dial zero. . ."

Renie was sorting through her wallet. "I've got a number on my bill from the woolen shop. Try that." She handed the invoice to Judith.

"They won't be open," Judith said, but tried the number anyway. There was neither a live response nor a recorded message. "Drat."

"Hold on," Renie said. "Bill gave me a list of helpful contacts before we left home. You know how thorough he is. I forgot I had it in my . . . Ah!" Renie read from her husband's hand-printed list. "Directory assistance for Scotland is 192."

Judith dialed the three digits. An operator answered, asking for what city or town. Judith said St. Fergna. The ring changed to a different sound but was picked up on the third beep. The voice at the other end sounded strangely familiar.

"I'm calling from Grimloch Castle," Judith said. "Is there a taxi service in the village?"

"Mrs. Jones? Or is it Mrs. Flynn?" asked the female voice on the other end. "This is Alison, from the woolen shop."

Judith laughed. "I thought you sounded like someone I knew," she said. "It's Mrs. Flynn. We feel stranded. Are you the local directory service person in addition to working in the store?"

"I have two jobs," Alison said. "I'm saving to get married. There's not much to do here in winter. There's no taxi as such, but my fiancé, Barry, can give you a lift. He's bored. Where do you want to go?"

"We're not sure," Judith admitted, "but we'll make up our minds by the time he gets here. How soon, do you think?"

"Let me ask him." Alison turned away from the phone. Judith could still hear her voice, followed by a brief male response. "Five minutes, if you like, Mrs. Flynn."

"That sounds fine," Judith said. "We'll pay, of course."

"Well. . .you don't have to. Barry's not a very good driver. But we can use the money."

"Of course," Judith said. "We'll head for the beach. Thank you so much." She hung up and grinned at Renie. "A local lad who apparently has no connection to the castle and its crew. He may prove very helpful."

Renie sighed. "Here we go again."

When Judith and Renie got out of the lift, they noticed that there were several people on the beach in both directions. Families, couples, young, old, and in-between—but no one was within a hundred yards of the strand in front of the castle. Although there was no visible barrier, apparently there was an understanding between the villagers and Philip Fordyce. It might be the twenty-first century, but when his flag flew over Grimloch, The Master still reigned in his fiefdom.

The cousins had almost reached the parking area when a small old car came rattling down the track. Judith couldn't distinguish the make or model, but parts of it were painted blue, other parts red, and the rest of the exterior was rusted out.

"Hallo!" called the driver, leaning out through the window. Except, Judith realized as she approached the beat-up vehicle, there was no window. A clear plastic flap was held in place by a big piece of masking tape. "I'm Barry MacPherson. You must be the American ladies."

"We are," Judith said. "Thanks for coming to get us."

"Gives me something to do," Barry replied cheerfully. "Which of you is which?"

The cousins introduced themselves. Barry nodded. He was in his early twenties, with a crown of dark red hair shaved into a mullet. He had freckles, and although he was sitting, he struck Judith as the lanky type, with long fingers and big knuckles.

"So," Barry said, "you being the tall one, Mrs. Flynn, sit up front, please. Mrs. Jones, you'll have to make do in the backseat. Just move the trash. I didn't take time to tidy up as I wanted to collect you before the tide came in much higher."

Judith glanced at the backseat. Or in the area of the backseat, since it wasn't visible, but was covered with discarded fast-food boxes, CDs, items of clothing, and a small cage containing a dwarf hamster.

"That's The Bruce," Barry said. "He bites. Mind your fingers."

"I bite, too," Renie said, showing off her large front teeth. "And I'm much bigger." Reluctantly, she crawled into the backseat and started making room for herself. "The hamster's cute," she said. "He smells like fish and chips." Seeing the grease-stained newspaper wrappings, she went on: "Everything smells like fish and chips. Or worse. We have a dwarf lop bunny named Clarence. We keep him very fresh. He doesn't bite, but he's got a mean left hook."

Barry chuckled good-naturedly. "The Bruce goes everywhere with me, even to work."

"Where do you work?" Judith inquired, settled into the passenger seat despite the feel of broken springs poking her bottom.

"At Tonio's Pizza," Barry replied, gunning the car into gear before attempting the climb up to the village. "I deliver."

Renie had settled into the backseat. "I smell pizza, too."

Judith gritted her teeth at the grinding of gears. "I didn't see a pizza parlor in the High Street yesterday."

"One street off the High," Barry replied, leaning into the steering wheel as if to coax the car up the steep track. "Where are we going?"

Fortunately, they were going up at the moment, slowly and noisily, but the hill was finally crested.

"We'd like to know what's in and around the village," Judith said. "We arrived Friday night, so we couldn't see our immediate surroundings."

"Arrived just in time for the murder," Barry remarked. "Very exciting for these parts. Just like the telly. I don't think we've ever had a murder before, at least not in my time. Maybe the Mafia's moved to St. Fergna." The young man sounded thrilled at the prospect. "You're not . . . what's the term? 'Mobbed up'?"

"No," Judith replied. "We're very respectable." They were moving up the High Street's incline. "Did you know Harry Gibbs?" she asked.

"Me?" Barry laughed. "Harry and Barry, a couple of mates. Not bloody likely. Excuse my language. Harry was a cut above. No chum for the likes of me."

"Where did he live when he wasn't at the castle?" Judith asked.

Barry glanced at Judith. "You don't know?"

Judith shook her head. "We're not friends of the family. Our stay was arranged by a fishing companion of our husbands."

"Awkward," Barry remarked, braking at the fork in the road by the village green. "That is, you must feel peculiar being caught up in this murder thing. What have we here?"

Barry was looking at the green where at least fifty people had assembled. A stout middle-aged man in tweeds appeared to be giving a speech from the bandstand.

"It's ruddy Morton," Barry murmured. "I'll be frigged. He's back."

"From where?" Judith asked. "Who is he?"

"Jocko Morton," Barry replied, letting the engine sputter and idle. "He's Blackwell Petrol's CEO, but he did a bunk a while back, called it taking a leave, and went to Greece. What's he carrying on about?"

Judith tried to roll down her window but it was stuck. A florid-faced Morton was waving his pudgy hands. "Can you hear him?" she asked Barry, who was leaning his head out on the driver's open side.

"Some. He's telling the crowd how wonderful he is and what he can do for Blackwell Petroleum and for St. Fergna and for God and country. Full of wind, that's Jocko Morton. He likes to be the pukka sahib, thinks he knows how to run everybody's life better than they do."

The gathering gave a great shout. Several people were pumping their fists in the air and others were jumping up and down. Barry's expression turned curious. "Riled up, I'd say. Why, I wonder?"

"Flyers are being passed around by a man who looks like Jocko," Judith noted. "Can you get us one?"

"That's Jocko's brother Archie," Barry said, starting to get out of the car. "He runs the local garage. Be right back."

Barry jogged off to fetch a flyer. The car started to inch forward, heading toward the green. "Why are we moving?" Renie asked.

"I don't think Barry set the emergency brake," Judith said, leaning across the front seat. "I found it."

The car kept going, despite Judith's hard tug on the brake. "Damn! I don't think it works."

The car kept crawling along, edging ever nearer to the oblivious gathering that spilled out almost into the street. Judith pulled again on the brake lever. It still didn't stop the old rattletrap from moving. "Look out!" she cried in warning. But the crowd couldn't hear her. Just as she was certain they were going to mow down a half dozen villagers, Barry sprinted back to the car and jumped in.

"Sorry," he said, fumbling under the dashboard and pulling on a rope. "I should get this fixed, but then I don't have many emergencies." The car stopped six inches short of any would-be victims.

Judith was aghast. "You use a rope to pull on the brake?"

Barry shrugged. "It works, doesn't it?" He handed Judith a flyer, his face grim. "Kind of ugly. They're calling Mrs. Gibbs a murderer. Or would she be a murderess?"

"Let's hope she's not either one," Judith replied.

Renie leaned over the seat to look at the white sheet of paper with the bold black lettering. "Jezebel? Whore? Scorpion? As in the critters that kill their mates?"

"Jocko Morton doesn't seem to be in his company owner's corner," Judith said. "This is inflammatory." She looked up from the flyer. Jocko used a bullhorn to call for quiet. The crowd finally stopped spewing what sounded like venom, but not before Archie Morton emerged from the fringe and appeared to make some threats.

"Save your strength for the inquest," Jocko shouted. "Let the rich know that they can't get away with murder!"

The crowd burst into another round of cheers and chants. Even from a distance, Judith could tell that Jocko looked smug. "I don't get it," she remarked. "He's Blackwell's CEO and he wants Moira arrested?"

"That's not so mysterious," Renie said. "There must be a fight over top-level decision-making, and Jocko thinks Moira's an obstacle to his position and livelihood. I've seen it before with some of my graphic design clients. Dog-eat-dog, and it's not always the money, but ego."

Judith turned to Barry. "Where's Hollywood?" she asked as the name suddenly popped into her head.

"To the left," Barry said, and turned in that direction. "That's where Harry lived when he wasn't at the castle. It's Moira's house. Very nice, though I've only delivered there twice."

The elderly car made several strange noises as they passed whitewashed cottages and a row of stone houses. Moments later they were going through the rather flat countryside. Judith didn't recognize all of the trees that flanked the road, though she saw several tall rowans in bud and a few wild rhododendron bushes.

She judged they'd gone about two miles when Barry slowed down. "The gate to Hollywood's on your right. We can't go in, but you can get a glimpse of . . . Oh, bloody hell! I'm out of petrol!"

The car began to go even slower as Barry fought the wheel to reach the narrow verge. "Sorry. I'd have checked the gauge, but it broke."

Judith turned to look at Renie, who had been unusually quiet during the ride. Her cousin was petting the hamster in her lap.

"He reminds me of Clarence," she said. "He's so soft, and he only tried to bite me once."

"Great," Judith murmured. Her thoughts weren't with Clarence or the hamster or even Renie. She'd been given a golden opportunity and intended to seize it. "Would Moira Gibbs have any petrol to spare?"

Barry chuckled. "Aye, she does at that. But we mustn't bother her at such a time. I can walk back to the village." He snapped his fingers. "I forgot. The petrol pump's closed for the Sabbath."

"How far are we from the gate to Hollywood?" Judith inquired.

"Just up there," Barry said, pointing to a stone marker less than twenty-five yards away.

"We have no choice," Judith declared. "We'll have to walk to Moira's house. We met her yesterday at the graveyard." She turned back to Renie. "Put the hamster in his cage, coz. Let's go."

Barry, however, proved reluctant. "We shouldn't, truly," he insisted. "Mrs. Gibbs must be all weepy and sad."

"Then we'll console her," Judith said, getting out of the car.

The door fell off.

"Oh no!" she cried. "I'm so sorry!"

"Never mind. It does it all the time," Barry assured her. "I can tie you in with the emergency brake rope on the way back. I don't know what I'd do without that rope. Really handy, it is."

Judith and Barry walked up the road. Renie trailed, having taken the time to restore The Bruce to his little wire home. Turning in at the stone marker, which bore the engraved name hollywood house, Judith noticed that the iron gates were shut. She could see a Georgian house with a circular drive where a red BMW sports car was parked.

She could also hear laughter.

It didn't sound to Judith as if Moira Gibbs was mourning her late husband.

9

Moira Gibbs and the man named Patrick were holding hands as they started up the steps to the elegant three-story house. Judith recognized Patrick from his sturdy build and the leather jacket he'd worn when he met Jimmy on the beach after the explosion.

The couple apparently hadn't seen the trio at the gate. Judith called to them while Renie looked for a buzzer or an intercom. Barry, however, simply gaped in disbelief at Patrick and Moira.

"That's no way to act," Barry muttered. "If somebody blew up Alison, I'd feel quite glum."

Judith's shouts were ignored by the couple, who headed inside the house without turning around. Renie, however, had found a keypad. She poked a button labeled visitor. Judith could hear a stilted masculine voice respond.

"You got gas?" Renie asked.

"Pardon?" the masculine voice said, sounding affronted.

"Gas, petrol, whatever you call it here. We're stuck," Renie said. "Tell Moira that Hugh MacGowan wouldn't like us having problems. The name's Jones, by the way. The other one is Flynn. Moira knows us."

Judith was leaning over Renie's shoulder. She heard a woman respond but couldn't make out the words. After a brief pause the stilted voice resumed speaking. "You may enter. The mistress will see you."

"Nice work," Judith said to Renie as the gates opened smoothly.

"Amazing!" Barry exclaimed under his breath. "I wouldn't have dared in a million years!"

"Pushy Americans," Renie said. "That's why everybody hates us. We have no manners."

The cousins started up the drive until Judith realized that Barry was still standing outside the gate. "Aren't you coming?" she asked.

He shook his head. "I'll stay by the car. I wouldn't want anyone to steal it. Ha-ha."

" 'Ha-ha' is right," Renie murmured. "Nobody would steal that crate even for spare parts."

"He's obviously intimidated by his so-called betters," Judith said.

"That's the problem," Renie said. "We think we're better, too."

"I think it's called equality," Judith pointed out.

Renie shrugged. "It's the same thing."

Moira Gibbs stood in the open front door, which was painted a bright blue. She was wearing a white wool dress with a glittering ruby brooch. "Come in," she said, with a touch of warmth in her voice. "Pay no attention to Fergus. He's beyond stodgy, but it's difficult to find butlers these days. He's been with the family since before I was born."

She led the way past the colonnade and into the main hall with its soaring ceiling, marble statuary, and elegant plasterwork. "We'll go into the library," Moira said. "I arrived only a few ticks ahead of you."

The library was large, complete with a balcony, wood paneling, and ladders to access books on the top shelves. Since no one was in the handsome room, Judith figured that Patrick was being discreet and making himself scarce.

Moira invited the cousins to sit in the leather chairs that formed a semicircle in the middle of the room. "A drink, perhaps?"

"We're fine," Judith said. "We want to offer our condolences. This must be a terrible shock for you."

"Oh, it is," Moira said, sitting down. "I'm muddling through on sheer nerve—and handfuls of tranquilizers."

Judith wanted to believe that Moira was grieving. Surely a young woman with a baby who had been widowed twice would be devastated.

"I've been widowed, too," Judith said with compassion. "I was left with a teenage son. That's a difficult stage under any circumstances."

"I would imagine," Moira said. "Poor you. Now," she went on, leaning forward and folding her hands on her knees, "you must tell me about your gas problem. Is it some sort of leak?"

Renie made a face. "I should've said petrol. We ran out. I keep forgetting that we're two countries separated by a common language."

Moira laughed. "Three," she pointed out. "We have many Scots words the English don't understand. I'll have Fergus provide you with a five-liter can. Will that be enough?"

"Ample," Renie replied. "Thanks. We'll reimburse you."

Moira waved a slender hand. "No, no. That would be inhospitable of me. We keep an extra supply on hand. Did you hire a car?"

"Not exactly," Renie said. "It's like a car . . . but . . . "
She made a helpless gesture.

Moira frowned. "I heard the castle's Morris saloon is being repaired."

"It is," Judith said, then changed the subject before Renie could lead their hostess further astray. "How old is your son?"

Moira smiled tenderly. "Almost five months old. He's utterly adorable and quite good-natured." A soft rap sounded on the library door. "Yes, Fergus?"

After the butler informed his mistress that her brother was on the telephone, he made a stately exit. Moira got up and went to a desk that looked as if it had been inspired by Chippendale.

"Pardon," she apologized to the cousins. "Yes, Jimmy," Moira said into the phone. "What is it now?"

Judith tried to pretend she wasn't eavesdropping. "This is a wonderful room," she said to Renie. "Look at all the leather-bound books encased behind glass."

Renie gazed at her surroundings. "Valuable, maybe. Some are probably collectors' items."

Judith rose and walked over to the nearest bookcase, which was just opposite Moira.

"Oh, Jimmy, just take care of it!" Moira said testily. "You're so good at handling this sort of thing. It's hardly the first time. Don't pester me with details. I'm sick of the whole thing." She rang off. "I'm so sorry for the interruption," she said, sitting back down. "My brother is extremely competent and very clever. I've no idea why he has to bother me with problems he can easily solve for himself. Where were we?"

Judith also sat down again. "Talking about your son?"

Moira smiled. "Oh—little Jamie. I named him for my father. He's trying to crawl. I'd let you see him, but he's down for a nap."

"Never wake a kid from a nap," Renie warned. "Mothers deserve some peace and quiet." She grimaced. "Sorry. That's an unfortunate thing to say, given what's happened."

"You mean to Harry?" Moira shook her head. "It was bound to. He brought it on himself."

Judith tried to hide her astonishment. "He had enemies?"

Moira's smile was ironic. "I suppose we all do, when we're in business. But I can't imagine . . ." She grew serious. "Like his parents, Harry was a risk-taker. Hang gliding, jumping out of airplanes, mountain climbing, rock climbing, hunting wild animals with a bow and arrow—he tried everything. He was fortunate not to have gotten himself killed long ago." She noticed the curious expression on Judith's face. "Please, make no mistake. It's a terrible tragedy, but one has to face facts. Harry lived on the edge. He didn't use good judgment."

Judith began to understand. "You think it was an accident?"

Moira shrugged. "What else? We should have an official verdict after the autopsy. Jimmy set the funeral for Wednesday. I doubt that his parents will be—"

Another soft rap at the door interrupted her. "Yes?" she said.

Fergus stood stiffly in the doorway. "Mr. Cameron is here, ma'am." His lips barely moved. Judith wondered if he could do ventriloquism.

"Tell him to wait in the west drawing room," Moira said. "Would you please fetch five liters of petrol for these ladies?"

Fergus nodded and left.

Moira stood up. "This is awkward. I'd forgotten Mr. Cameron was coming by. He's Blackwell's head of engineering and also in charge of security. No matter what else happens, business must be done, with the oil world so vital and volatile. Fergus will get the petrol and see you out."

"She's smooth," Renie remarked after Moira had left. "She must have inherited the petroleum company from her family."

"I doubt that Moira's more than twenty-five," Judith said. "Jimmy looks quite a bit older. If their parents are dead, why didn't he inherit the business along with his sister?"

"That is odd," Renie agreed. "Jimmy mentioned he was an attorney for the company as well as for Moira. I wonder where the head offices are. I thought most of the North Sea oil business was around Aberdeen."

"Let's find out," Judith said, going to the desk. "There must be a letterhead in here somewhere." She opened the middle drawer but found only pens, paper clips, postage stamps, scissors, and other utilitarian items. The top drawer on the right yielded the company stationery. "The main offices are in Inverness, but there are branches in Aberdeen, London, and Copenhagen."

"I suppose the family wanted the headquarters closer to where they live," Renie conjectured. "Judging from the architecture, this house was probably built in the late eighteenth or early nineteenth century."

Just as Judith moved away from the desk, Fergus appeared holding the five-liter gas can far away from his body as if he expected it to explode like Harry's car. "Your petrol," he said solemnly.

"Thanks, Fergus," Renie responded, taking the can from him. "You're a good egg. I'll remember you in my will."

Fergus coughed slightly. "Pardon, ma'am?"

"Never mind," Renie said blithely. "We can let ourselves out."

The butler seemed dubious. "I'll escort you to the door."

"Why not?" Renie retorted. "As my husband would say when he wants us to move along, 'Let's boppin'!'"

Looking pained, Fergus stepped aside as the cousins walked out of the library. He accompanied them through the entry hall and on to the front door. With a barely perceptible nod, he wished them good day.

"Right back atcha, Fergus," Renie called over her shoulder.

"Coz . . ." Judith murmured. "Can it."

"Can it yourself," Renie snapped as they descended the steps. "This thing's heavy and hard to carry with my bum shoulder."

"Keep your mouth shut and your eyes open," Judith declared.

"Why?"

"Because," Judith said, "if you'd been paying attention instead of showing off, you'd have been able to peek into the parlor. The door wasn't completely closed. I saw Mr. Cameron."

"So?"

"Mr. Cameron is Patrick," Judith said. "The announcement of his arrival was a sham. Moira didn't realize we'd already seen her with him from the road. She doesn't want us—or anyone else—to know how chummy they are. Philip Fordyce and Mrs. Gunn talked about rumors concerning Moira and Patrick. Tranquilizers or not, Moira doesn't seem overcome by losing husband number two."

"How do we get out?" Renie asked as they walked down the driveway. But before Judith could respond, the gate swung open. "Ah—remote control from Fergus," Renie murmured.

Barry was dozing in the car. Through the glassless window, Renie jabbed him in the shoulder. "Fill 'er up!" she called.

"Oh!" The young man awoke with a start and threw his hands up in the air, banging his fingers against the car's roof. "Don't shoot me! I haven't got any money! I'm stony broke!"

"It's us," Renie said. "The American battle-axes. Go ahead, put the gas in the tank. I'm setting the can down here by the door."

"Wow!" Barry exclaimed. "How'd you manage to get that?"

"Sheer charm," Renie said, getting into the backseat. "Hi, Bruce. How are you doing?"

The hamster jumped onto his wheel and began to run like mad. Barry got out of the car. Judith stood watching him as he coped with the gas tank—no easy task, since it looked as if the original cap had been replaced with a cork.

"How," she inquired, "did Moira inherit Blackwell Petroleum?"

"Her mum and dad died," Barry replied as bits of cork broke off while he attempted to unplug the tank. "Mr. Blackwell's been gone since before I was born. Her mum passed on two, three years ago."

"But why didn't Jimmy get the company?" Judith asked. "He must be at least ten years older than Moira."

The cork finally came out. "Jimmy's a bastard," Barry said.

"You mean he was disinherited because he was . . . what?"

"A bastard," Barry repeated, pouring gasoline into the tank. "His dad—Moira's dad, too—played around."

"Oh," Judith said, enlightened. "Jimmy's illegitimate."

"Right. No way was Moira's mum going to let Jimmy have part ownership. He could work for Blackwell, but no owning it for the likes of him, a mere by-blow. The missus was that put out."

"That must rankle," Judith said.

"Aye, especially after Harry got a plush job with the company."

A Jaguar sedan had slowed to see what was going on by the side of the road. Judith thought the driver was Jocko Morton, the man who'd been giving the speech on the village green. He looked, he saw—and sped on. Curious, she followed the car with her eyes, wondering if it would turn in at Hollywood. But Morton kept going. "What did Harry do at Blackwell?" she asked, turning back to Barry.

He shrugged. "I don't know." Finishing with the tank, he put the cork back in and screwed the cap onto the petrol can. "Anyway, Harry and Jimmy got into it at the Yew and Eye pub last week. A regular brawl, it was. What should we do with this can?"

"We'll drop it off at the gate," Judith said. "You mean a fistfight?"

"Aye, with chairs thrown and bottles broken and pints spilled."

"Were you there?" Judith asked as Barry escorted her to the passenger side.

"Aye, me and my mates. Quite a show they put on until Will Fleming broke it up. Here," he said as Judith got into the seat, "move a mite to the right and I'll fetch the rope to keep you in."

While Barry went to get the rope from the boot, Judith turned to Renie. "Did you hear that about Jimmy and Harry at the pub?"

Renie nodded. "I wouldn't have known who to root for."

"I don't understand much about any of this," Judith admitted. "I always think of the oil business as a Middle Eastern thing—or Texas."

"I don't think about it at all," Renie said. "Bill takes care of Cammy. For all I know, gas could cost a hundred bucks a gallon."

Judith shot her cousin a dirty look. "It's a global concern. You shouldn't be so cavalier."

"Is there something I can do about it?" Renie demanded.

"No," Judith allowed as Barry struggled with securing the rope, "but this Blackwell business may be the reason why Harry was killed."

"Moira thinks it was an accident," Renie reminded Judith.

"I don't believe it," Judith countered.

Barry finally fastened the rope and came around to the driver's side. "What's your fancy, ladies? We could drive to John O' Groats with this much petrol. 'Course we couldn't drive back."

"Bill made a list," Renie said, taking a small notepad out of her purse. "Culloden, where Bonnie Prince Charlie was defeated. Cawdor and Brodie Castles. Moray Firth for dolphin sightings. Nairn, where the sun shines more than anywhere else along the northern coast. Culbin Sands, to watch a bunch of birds. We might also consider food. It's been a long time since breakfast."

"Um . . . " Judith stared out through the windscreen, which had several squiggly cracks. "Barry, why don't you just drive us around this area? I'm a people person, not a nature or history lover. Where does Jimmy live? Or the Flemings? And tell us more about Jocko Morton." She ignored Renie's groan.

"Jimmy and his wife live on the other side of St. Fergna," Barry replied. "Nice house, modern-like. The Flemings have a place down the road here. You can't see either of them from the car. Morton has a condo in Inverness and a shooting lodge somewhere—I forget."

"Oh." Judith was disappointed. "What about Mrs. Gunn?"

"Ah, she's got a grand house on Spey Bay. I hear she took it from her husband's ladylove."

"My, my," Judith said. "Do all businessmen here have mistresses?"

Barry looked genuinely puzzled. "I don't know. We could ask." He turned a serious face to Judith. "Might be cheeky, though."

"I mean," Judith clarified, "Mr. Blackwell and Mr. Gunn both played around, right?" She saw Barry nod. "Who is Jimmy's mother?"

"Lucy Morton," Barry answered. "I forget her maiden name. Later on, she married Jocko's cousin, Rob. They live in Inverness."

"Please tell me that Rob doesn't work for Blackwell Petroleum."

"Nae—he's a dentist."

"And Mr. Gunn's girlfriend?"

"She's not a dentist."

Judith sighed. "I don't mean that. Who was she?"

"A ladyship," Barry replied. "Let me get this right . . . the Honorable Diana Porter-Breze. Bonniest woman I ever saw, though not young, not at all. Older than Mr. Gunn, much older than Mrs. Gunn. Nice, too."

"Does she still live around here?"

Barry shook his head. "She moved to Inverness. Or Paris."

"Gee," Renie said plaintively, "The Bruce and I are fading away back here. Any chance of finding a restaurant?"

"There should be pizza in one of those boxes," Barry said.

"The Bruce may like cold pizza," Renie said, "but The Cousin doesn't. Try again."

Judith checked her watch. "It's almost three. When's high tea?"

"How about the village tearoom?" Barry asked.

"We went there yesterday," Renie said. "What else is nearby?"

Barry considered. "There's a fine place down the road. Cummings House, it's called. Alison and I ate there once. It's pricey, though."

"Money's no object," Renie declared. "I'm starved."

Barry struggled to start the car, but eventually the engine caught and the vehicle lurched forward. They passed the gate to Hollywood and continued on the road for at least a mile. Judith admired the rowan and birch trees, though after another mile or two, the road climbed slightly. Now they were winding among alder and pine. Then the road dipped precipitously. The car sped down the hill into a glen.

Judith saw a two-story timber-fronted building up ahead. As they raced along the road, she saw the sign proclaiming Cummings House. "Is that the place?" she asked.

"Aye," Barry said, and gulped.

"I thought we were stopping there," Judith said.

"I thought we were, too," Barry agreed, pumping the brakes, "but I guess not. The car won't stop. Oh well."

The road had flattened out. "You don't have seat belts in this thing!" Renie shouted. "You're going to get us killed!"

"Nae," Barry responded, turning around to look at Renie. "Mind The Bruce. Don't let his cage slip off the seat."

"Watch the damned road!" But Renie put a steadying hand on the cage as the car began to slow down.

On the next bend, Barry aimed for a hedgerow. The car thudded into the barrier and groaned to a stop. Judith hazily guessed they were going only about ten miles an hour. She caught herself on the dashboard; Renie was holding The Bruce's cage and cussing her head off.

Barry was slumped over the wheel. "Whew!" he exclaimed, and whistled softly. "Sorry. How's The Bruce?"

"He's filing a lawsuit for whiplash," Renie snapped. "How are we getting to the restaurant? Afoot?"

Before Barry could answer, Judith's cell phone rang.

"How's it going?" Joe inquired in a cheerful voice.

Judith gritted her teeth as she peered through the windscreen and saw a goat peering back from the other side of the hedgerow.

"Uh . . . we're not going at the moment," she replied, mouthing her husband's name for Renie's benefit. An acrid stench filled Judith's nostrils— no doubt, she figured, the odor of burning brakes. Or the goat. "Where are you?" she asked Joe. "At the castle?"

Joe's chuckle sounded forced. "No. No, actually we're at Invergarry by Loch Oich. We had some luck on the Spey, but Hugh thought we should try some of the other nearby streams and lochs. He's on leave, you know, so he doesn't have to get back to work for a week or so. We'll go from here to the River Beauly and Beauly Firth, maybe on Tuesday. Hugh says the salmon fishing there is amazing."

"You mean," Judith said, looking at Renie, "you and Bill aren't returning to Grimloch anytime soon?"

"Well . . . this is a once-in-a-lifetime chance to fish these waters," Joe explained. "Not just anybody can access them. Since Hugh's offered us the opportunity, we could hardly turn him down."

"Hardly," Judith said dryly. "Are you camping out?"

"What? Oh—no, you know Bill. He's not one for camping."

"Neither are you," Judith pointed out. "Your idea of camping is a rustic five-star lodge with a jazz combo for your evening entertainment. Where are you staying tonight?"

"We just checked into the Glengarry Castle Hotel. Hold on," Joe said. "Bill, you got the remote? Thanks." There was a pause. "Great digital TV reception here. Tell Renie that Bill's eating a banana ice cream sundae. I think I'll talk him into giving me a taste."

"I won't mention that," Judith said as the goat wandered away.

"Lots of other stuff around here, too," Joe said. "There's a ruined castle right by the hotel and we're not far from Ben Nevis and—"

"Stop," Judith interrupted. "You're breaking up at this end." It was a lie, but Barry had gotten out of the car and was trying to push it away from the hedgerow.

"Oh—sorry," Joe said. "Everything okay with you and Renie?"

"It's swell," Judith replied. "We've gone for a country drive."

"Great," Joe enthused. "I knew you and Renie would find plenty to do around St. Fergna. Bill sends his love. Talk to you later."

Judith shoved the cell phone back in her purse. "I don't know whether to be relieved or peeved. Joe and Bill and even Hugh MacGowan don't seem to know anything about Harry's death. Hugh's taking a short leave to cart our husbands around the Highlands—in style, I might add."

"The Bruce doesn't like that goat," Renie asserted. "It sounds like the husbands have gotten our goat. Why are they having all the fun?"

Judith ignored the question. "Let's get out of the car. Barry can't budge it with us sitting here."

"I'm not helping," Renie warned Judith. "I have a bad shoulder. I'm also weak from hunger. I wonder how that goat would taste?"

"I have an artificial hip," Judith said, undoing the rope. "Barry's on his own."

"That restaurant's within walking distance," Renie said, gesturing at the site, which looked about a quarter of a mile up the road. "I really don't enjoy riding in a car with no brakes."

"No window, no door, no—" Judith stopped as a car coming around the bend slowed down. But after taking a good look at the battered beater and the trio on the verge, he stepped on the gas pedal and sped away.

"Jerk," Renie snarled. "Couldn't he see we're a couple of middle-aged ladies in dire distress?"

"I think that's why he left," Judith said. "Didn't you recognize the Jag and the driver? It was Jocko Morton. I don't think he's a very nice man. I wonder why he left the country?"

Renie shrugged. "When in doubt, think Enron."

Judith's expression was ironic. "Or murder."

10

Barry borrowed Judith's cell and called his father to rescue him. After assuring the cousins that the brakes would be fixed in no time so that he could pick them up after they ate at the restaurant, Judith succumbed to Renie's pleas and agreed to walk to Cummings House.

The road's incline was gentle; the distance was short. They went slowly, though Renie had to stop several times to allow Judith to catch up. The cousins arrived at the restaurant just after three-thirty, and were seated immediately by a cheerful older woman wearing a ruffled apron and a broad smile.

"Tourists, eh? Lovely!" she exclaimed. "Do sit by the fireplace."

The dining room was small and cozy. The decor was minimal, and on this Sunday afternoon, only a handful of the dozen or so tables were occupied. There was a bar, however, which was marked by a sign with an arrow pointing off to the right.

Cummings House didn't offer a high tea, but Judith and Renie both found items that pleased them.

"Haddock and chips for me," Judith said.

"I'll have the homemade lamb and kidney pie," Renie declared.

The cheerful waitress went off toward the kitchen. Sitting in the comfortable high-backed chair, Judith stretched her legs toward the hearth. "Nice," she remarked. "Just the sort of place you'd expect to find in the Highlands."

"As nice as where the husbands are?" Renie asked suspiciously.

"Well . . . I'm not sure. They have TV and good food."

"What's the place called?"

Judith jogged her memory. "Hotel Glengarry?"

"Don't con me," Renie snapped. "I've gone through Bill's guidebook. It's Glengarry Castle Hotel and it's supposed to be one of the elite places to stay in the Highlands. Those creeps! They're off having a wonderful time and we're stuck in the middle of nowhere while you play Sherlock Holmes! Some vacation!" She leaned forward. "Tomorrow will be different. We're going to hire a car from wherever we can get one and see the sights on our own. I refuse to sit around the castle and watch you try to solve a murder case involving people you never heard of until forty-eight hours ago. This is my vacation, too."

Judith studied Renie's obstinate expression. "You're the one who always says that fishermen should be able to do as they please."

"As long as they're fishing," Renie retorted. "Watching high-definition TV or whatever in a plush hotel and eating their way through a gourmet menu doesn't count. That's for us, not the husbands."

"This is nice," Judith argued. "The prices are reasonable and—" She paused as a hearty laugh burst out from nearby, followed by a masculine voice:

"What's our advantage without Gibbs?" The man's voice was deep and halting.

Leaning on the side of her chair, Judith tried to see who was coming out from the bar area. "Morton," she whispered, "with a fair-haired man I don't recognize."

"Oh, damn!" Renie swore. "There's no escape!"

Jocko Morton and the taller, younger blond man walked by the cousins and sat down in an inglenook across the room by the window.

"Morton must have parked in back," Judith whispered. "I didn't see his Jag when we came in the main entrance."

"I don't care if he parked on the roof like Santa Claus," Renie snapped. "Could we eat a meal without a side dish of sleuthing?"

Judith sighed. "After all these years," she said in a low, earnest voice, "you know that when somebody gets killed virtually before my eyes, I'll try to figure out who did it. I can't help it. It's like you, studying everything you see with your artist's eye. Just now, when you saw the menu, you frowned. I knew it wasn't the food, it was the menu's design."

"Wrong type font for this kind of place," Renie said. "Too modern. They should have gone with a Monotype Corsiva, not an Arial Black. There's no warmth, no history."

"You see what I mean?"

Renie looked faintly repentant. "Okay. You have a point. I just wish your talent wasn't for finding killers. It'd be nice to go somewhere and not stumble over a dead body."

"You mean and not care if I stumble over a dead body," Judith amended. "Everybody encounters dead bodies every day." She saw Renie start to protest. "Hold it, coz—let me finish. At home, the morning paper often has a homicide victim in the news. The obituaries may contain someone whose death is unnatural. We're untouched by them. But when someone is killed within my purview, I have to act. Get it?"

Renie nodded wearily. "I've always gotten it. I just . . . get fed up with it. Or maybe I get scared. It's a dangerous avocation."

"Life's a risk," Judith said. "Now will you shut up? Here's the food, and I'd like to try hearing what Morton's saying across the way."

Renie was content to keep quiet as she delved into her lamb and kidney pie. But Morton and his companion were speaking quietly. Seriously, too, Judith noticed, except for Morton's occasional hearty—if harsh—laughter. His companion was more solemn, rarely managing even a smile. Finally, they were eating what looked like puddings. Morton put aside the napkin on which he'd been scribbling some notes.

The waitress came over to Judith and Renie, asking if they were enjoying their meal.

"Very much," Judith said. "The haddock and chips are excellent. My cousin would say the same about her meat pie if she'd stop eating long enough to talk. By the way," she continued, dropping her voice, "the fair-haired man in the inglenook is familiar. Should I know him?"

The waitress glanced discreetly at Morton and his fellow diner. "You mean you know him from the States?" she asked.

"I'm not sure," Judith fibbed. "Maybe he reminds me of someone. Is his name . . . Rankers, by any chance?"

The waitress shook her head. "Nae. He's Seumas Bell, an attorney for Blackwell Petrol. Comes here often when he has business with poor Mrs. Gibbs. But you wouldn't know her, not being from these parts."

"We do know her," Judith said. "It's a shame about her husband."

The waitress's eyes grew round as she leaned closer, exuding a lavender scent. "Oh, isn't it though? That laddie met a cruel fate! And now Mrs. Gibbs has taken to her bed, a nervous wreck, I hear. She's never had good health or good luck with men." The waitress grimaced. "I mustn't tell tales out of school, but you're acquainted so you know."

"Yes," Judith said with compassion, ignoring Renie, who had spilled gravy on her new cashmere sweater. "Two husbands dead, her parents dying fairly young, and a big oil company with no one to lean on except her half brother, who strikes me as resentful of her inheritance."

"I suppose you can't blame Jimmy in a way," the waitress said. "He's very capable. Some would tell you he'd be a much better . . . what do you call them? . . . chief executive than his sister. She's so much younger and hasn't had his experience. But there it is." The waitress looked up as a young couple entered the restaurant. "Pardon, I must see to these people. Will you be wanting a sweet?"

The cousins declined, and the waitress hurried off. Renie was dabbing at her sweater with a wet napkin. "Well?"

Judith frowned. "Who said that Moira took to her bed?"

"If she has," Renie said, "Patrick's in it with her."

Judith shot a surreptitious glance in Morton's direction. "Maybe he told the waitress. Or the other man, Seumas Bell."

"It could be anyone," Renie said. "Gossip travels fast in small towns. They all know each other and don't have a lot of things to do."

"True." Judith chewed thoughtfully on her last chip.

Morton and Bell were getting up, making ready to leave. They paid no attention to the cousins. Morton's small piglike eyes glittered with something that might be pleasure. Bell, however, looked worried.

"They left the napkin," Judith said after the two men departed.

"So?"

"Morton was writing on it." Judith got up, looked around to see if anyone was watching, and went to the vacant table. With a swift gesture, she grabbed the napkin and returned to her seat.

"Let's see what he wrote." She unfolded the paper napkin and smoothed it out on the tablecloth. "Numbers, mostly. I don't know what to make of them. There's a name, though. Morton's handwriting is wretched. See if you can read it." She passed the napkin to Renie.

"They might be stock prices," Renie said. She studied the jumble of letters. "The closest I can come is 'Venus Goo.' That can't be right."

Judith took the napkin from Renie and put it in her purse. "Just in case," she murmured.

Renie didn't comment.

The waitress presented their bill. "I have a message for you," she said, looking apologetic. "Barry— the pizza lad from Tonio's—rang up to say he can't come get you. His brakes are bad, and must be fixed at the auto repair tomorrow. He said he hoped you could wait."

"For what?" Renie retorted. "A bus?"

"There is a bus," the waitress said. "It's due here"— she paused to look at the watch pinned to her apron— "in six minutes."

"It stops at the restaurant?" Judith inquired.

"If you flag it," the waitress said.

Renie flipped her credit card onto the table. "We're on our way."

The cousins had been standing for only a minute or so when an old green and yellow bus lumbered around the bend.

"We'll assume it has brakes," Renie remarked, waving at the driver. "Windows and a door are a start."

Only a dozen or so riders were on the bus, which was eventually going to Inverness. As she started to pay the fare, Judith suddenly realized she had only U.S. coins.

"We haven't changed our money yet," Judith whispered to Renie. "Do you have any we can use here?"

"No," Renie said bleakly. "That change Bill left on the bureau was American." She gazed inquiringly at the driver. "Do you take AmEx?"

The driver scowled. "No."

"Bribes?" Renie asked.

"How far?"

"St. Fergna," Renie replied.

The driver sighed. "Pay me next time." He started the bus.

The ride was only slightly less jarring than the one in Barry's beater. Ten minutes later, the cousins got off at the village green. Children were flying kites and playing soccer. One family was cleaning up the remains of a picnic. An amorous young couple nuzzled each other on a wooden bench. The air felt soft as a faint breeze blew through the rowan and birch trees that sheltered the green.

"When do you figure the tide will be back out?" Judith asked.

"It's going on five," Renie said, looking at an iron post clock a few doors down the High Street. "Between six and seven, I think."

"So we've got an hour to kill," Judith noted. "I wonder if the pubs around here are open on Sunday."

"They are," Renie said. "For some weird reason I remember that they finally changed the law back in the seventies to keep up with England. The Scots figured it was time to move into the twentieth century, at least as far as drinking was concerned."

"Then we should have a drink," Judith said, starting across the street. "The Yew and Eye is only a couple of doors beyond the tea shop."

"Ah. The site of Jimmy and Harry's brawl. I should've known."

The weathered sign hanging outside showed a faded tree and a chipped eyeball. Inside, the pub was busy. Judith and Renie managed to find a tiny table near the restrooms—or water closets, as the cousins knew they were known in the UK. It wasn't the decor that lured customers to the Yew and Eye, Judith realized, since the interior was singularly lacking in any attempt at charm. A string of Christmas lights with several burned-out bulbs hung across the back of the bar. Kewpie dolls wearing kilts lined a plate rail on one side of the room. Black-and-white photos of mud-spattered rugby players were displayed on the other. The windows facing the street were in need of washing, and somebody had left a crimson lipstick kiss on one of the small panes. Judith decided the attraction had to be the beer.

"I don't recognize anybody," Judith said, disappointed.

"Gee—and you've been here almost two whole days. Tsk, tsk."

"Don't be mean," Judith retorted. "You know I love meeting new people. That's one of the reasons I opened a B&B."

Renie sighed. "I know. You're the kind who's never met a stranger." She swiveled in her chair to look at the list of beers posted in chalk by the bar. "Not being a beer drinker, I'm doing what I do at the racetrack—picking by name. I can't resist a brew called Old Engine Oil."

"They have mead," Judith noted. "I've always wanted to try it."

The barmaid appeared, a far cry from the clichéd buxom, rosy-cheeked vessel of good cheer. She was as old as the cousins, scrawny and scraggly, with a lean build and graying hair that hung in listless strands. Her voice was gruff, her words were terse, her name tag identified her as Betsy.

"Drat," Judith said after Betsy had glumly taken their order. "How can I chat her up about the face-off between Jimmy and Harry?"

"Try some of the regulars," Renie suggested. "Play darts." She gestured at the board on the other side of the crowded room. "I'd do it, but my bad shoulder benched me years ago."

Judith shook her head. "With my luck, I'd hit Betsy." She surveyed the other drinkers. They were of all ages, from very young to very old. At least two tables served what looked like three generations of drinkers, from a fresh-faced girl to a gnarled old man propped up by pillows in his straight-backed chair. Apparently the Yew and Eye was a family gathering spot. "This is a waste of time. Our next move is for you to apologize to Mrs. Gunn."

"Whoa!" Renie held up her hands in protest. "No way."

"Mrs. Gunn must know all the dirt about everybody," Judith pointed out. "If we don't offer a truce, we'll never get to talk to her." She paused while Betsy wordlessly delivered their drinks. "Maybe we could take her a gift as a peace offering. Seek her out where she's most comfortable in the house she took from her late husband's girlfriend."

"For which we'd need a car to get to," Renie pointed out.

"You said you were going to hire one."

"I did?" Renie frowned. "That was when I was going nuts. I'm sane now. I suspect we'd have to rent a car in Inverness." She sipped her Old Engine Oil. "Not bad. It tastes a little like coffee—or chocolate."

"It's very dark, almost black," Judith remarked. "My mead is honey-flavored. It's sweet. I like it."

The cousins sat and sipped in silence. When Judith finally spoke, she looked apologetic. "I hate to mention this, but we should call our mothers. It's nine o'clock at home. They should both be up."

"Can't we wait until we're back at the castle? It's noisy in here."

"Okay." Judith caught Betsy's eye. "I can't resist. I've got to try."

"Oh boy," Renie muttered, "I can't wait to hear the whopper you're going to give her."

"It's good," Judith insisted. "Hello, Betsy. Can I trust you?"

The barmaid looked puzzled. "What?"

"We're from the States," Judith said, and feigned an embarrassed laugh. "You probably gathered that."

Betsy was impassive. "Nae."

"I'm here to look for my lost nephew." Judith looked forlorn. "We heard he'd been seen in St. Fergna."

There was no comment from Betsy.

"His name's Jim. Jimmy, we call him." Judith's lower lip trembled. Renie stared off into the distance, apparently admiring the kilted Kewpie dolls. "He's always had a drinking problem," Judith went on. "He's tall, in his thirties, dark, and often picking a fight."

Betsy's lean face showed only mild curiosity. "He's a Yank?"

"Ah . . . yes."

The barmaid shook her head. The strands of hair swayed listlessly. "No Yanks here since Christmas."

"Oh. You see," Judith said, sounding very confidential, "I heard there was a brawl here in the last few days and that a man named Jimmy was involved. I thought . . . you know, it might be my nephew. We'd like very much to find him and put him back in the Home."

Betsy's plain features finally showed animation. "He's crazy?"

"We don't call it that," Judith replied. "Our family describes him as communally challenged. 'Maniac' and 'outcast' are such cruel words, don't you agree?"

Betsy nodded. "Aye, cruel."

"So you're certain this Jimmy wasn't my nephew?" Judith asked as Renie seemed to slip lower and lower in her chair.

"Aye," Betsy replied. "I know this one—Jimmy Blackwell. Not a brawler by nature, but an attorney." She lowered her voice. "He got into it with the lad who was killed yesterday, Harry Gibbs."

"Really?" Judith evinced surprise. "What did they fight about?"

Betsy said shrugged. "I canna say."

"Blackwell Petroleum?" Judith suggested.

Betsy stared hard at Judith. "Say, aren't ye the ladies staying at the castle?"

"Yes," Judith said, keeping her composure. "That's why we came here. To look for Jim. Jimmy, I mean. My Jimmy."

Betsy stood up straight. "Well, ye willna find him here. And it'll do ye no good to ask about our Jimmy and poor Harry. I dinna tell tales about our own. Do ye want another pint or no?"

"Um . . . no, thank you."

Sharp chin jutting, Betsy stalked away.

"Some sleuth," Renie murmured, sitting up in her chair. "Even I wouldn't believe your nephew story. You know how news of strangers travels in a small town. And even faster in a village like St. Fergna. "

Judith was studying the customers. "Ordinary folk. But close-knit. Clannish, in the true sense of the word. In the face of tragedy, do they all clam up and feel as if the rest of the world's against them?"

"Probably," Renie said. "It's bred in their bones. In centuries past, they'd all hole up in the castle and wait out the siege."

"That makes it hard to learn the truth," Judith said. "Let's go."

"I haven't finished my Old Engine Oil," Renie protested. "Do they take credit cards or do we end up working off the tab as barmaids?"

"I saw logos on the door for Visa and MasterCard," Judith said.

Renie took a final gulp of her beer. "What's the rush? The tide won't be out for another half hour."

"Patrick Cameron just went by," Judith said. "At least it looked like him. It's hard to tell through those dirty windows."

"So we're going to chase him down the High Street?"

Judith was already halfway to the door. "Pay the bill with your AmEx card. I'll see where he's going."

It was almost dark outside, though the old-fashioned wrought-iron streetlights were on. Judith saw Patrick disappear around the corner by the road that paralleled the shore. "What took so long?" she demanded when Renie came out of the pub.

"I couldn't figure out the bill," Renie replied. "Where's Patrick?"

"Out of sight," Judith said. "Let's see if we can spot where he went."

"This is absurd," Renie declared, "like a bad spy movie."

The road ended at a frame building that overlooked the beach. In between and just off the High Street was a whitewashed cottage behind a laurel hedge. The lights were on and smoke drifted from the chimney.

"Patrick must have gone in there," Judith said in a low voice. "That other building is dark. It doesn't look like a house anyway."

"Gosh," Renie mocked, "do you suppose Patrick might live there?"

Judith ignored her. "Can you read that sign over the porch?"

Renie moved closer to the hedge. "This isn't nearly as ferocious as the Rankerses's man-eating shrubbery. I still have all my appendages."

"Never mind the smart remarks. What does the sign say?"

"It says 'The Hermitage.' People here like to name their houses."

"Why would he live here? Somebody said he had a rich wife."

Renie shrugged. "I don't recall hearing that."

"No," Judith said thoughtfully. "I overheard Mrs. Gunn and Philip talking about Patrick. His wife's name is Jeannie, and she comes from money. This is a small house, great view, convenient, but not what I'd consider the kind of place a wealthy young woman would want to live."

"Can we go now?" Renie walked toward the track to the beach. "The wind's come up and the mist's starting to roll in."

"You're not cold," Judith asserted, reluctantly following her cousin. "You never get cold. You're just annoyed."

"Yes, I am. This is silly. We've had a very long day. I'd like to—"

Judith grabbed Renie's arm. "Footsteps," she whispered. "Someone's coming. Pretend we're looking out to sea."

A man turned the corner from the High Street. Judith tried to see who it was without turning around to stare. "Will Fleming," she said softly, and glimpsed him turning in to the cottage.

"Poker night," Renie said. "Maybe Patrick calls it The Hermitage because it's where he goes when he wants time to himself. Or a night out with the boys. So what?"

"They both work for Blackwell," Judith said. "They'll be seeing each other at the office tomorrow in Inverness. Why now?"

"I told you, some perfectly innocent activity," Renie persisted. "If these men are business colleagues, why shouldn't they socialize?"

"I realize that . . ." Judith stopped. "Two more." She strolled away from Renie, ostensibly watching the mist roll in off of the sea. But out of the corner of her eye she spotted the stocky figure of Jocko Morton and the taller form of Seumas Bell.

"They're not parking by the cottage," Judith pointed out after the two men had gone inside. "They don't want their cars to be seen. I'll grant that Patrick and Will and Seumas might hang out together after work, but Jocko Morton? The waitress at Cummings House told us he was Blackwell's CEO. You know how those people keep themselves to themselves in the corner office."

"True," Renie allowed. "They have their own draw-bridge and moat to keep out the riffraff underlings."

"I'm trying to remember how many people we've met or heard about who work for Blackwell," Judith said. "I realize there must be a ton of employees, but the ones at this cottage are top-echelon guys."

"No Jimmy," Renie pointed out. "Or Moira, for that matter."

The cousins strolled back and forth on the cliffside path, keeping an eye on The Hermitage and occasion-ally looking through the vapors to see how far out the tide had gone. After ten minutes had passed, no more visitors had arrived at the cottage.

"I wonder," Judith mused, "if we could hear them from the garden."

"No!" Renie cried. "Don't make me crawl through that hedge!"

"We don't have to crawl," Judith insisted. "The others opened the gate and went down the walk to the front door. The chimney is on this side of the house, toward the sea. The curtains or drapes on each side of the fireplace are closed. That's probably the room where they're meeting. If we got up next to the house, we might be able to hear them."

"Be my guest," Renie said. "I'm staying right here and watching the tide go out. If you get caught, I've never seen you before in my life."

"Fine." Judith headed for The Hermitage. The mist swirled around her and the smell of the sea tingled in her nostrils. The village seemed very quiet, except for an occasional voice or car in the High Street.

The gate was a simple latch. Judith walked along the path that led through a fallow garden that looked as if it hadn't been properly tended for at least a couple of years. The cottage itself was well kept, however, and a bird's nest rested under the front eaves.

Judith moved carefully along the north side of the house, keeping low and trying not to step on anything that might create a noise—or cause a fall. Crouching under the nearest window, she listened intently.

She heard masculine voices but couldn't identify the speakers. Nor could she make sense of what they were saying. Only a few words were distinguishable—"Blackwell," "reserves," "OPEC"—and "Harry." Another ten minutes passed. Judith still could only catch an occasional word or phrase: "global market"; "Shetland and Orkney"; "outsourcing"; and "devastating disappointment."

She was getting nowhere—except stiff in the joints. Cautiously, she started to stand, but felt a hand on her back. It was all she could do to stifle a scream. The hand pressed harder. Judith suddenly felt faint.

"Are you stuck?" Renie asked in a whisper. "Dislocated?"

Judith sighed in relief as the faintness evaporated. "Damn you," she said softly. "You terrified me."

"You have to see something odd." Renie was still whispering as she helped Judith straighten up. "Come on. It's the castle."

The cousins crept out of the garden and back onto the path by the road. "Watch," Renie said, pointing to the castle. "You have to wait until the mist rolls away."

"Watch what?" Judith asked.

"You'll see."

Judith and Renie waited for three, maybe four minutes. "I can barely make out the castle's outline," Judith complained.

"Just wait."

At last the mist floated to the east, revealing Grimloch's bulk on top of the steep cliff.

"Do you see the light on your far right?" Renie inquired.

"Yes. So?"

"It's in our room."

Judith frowned. "Are you sure? Or did you leave it on?"

"This morning in broad daylight? You know I hate bright lights when I wake up. I'm a mole person. Think about the castle layout. That light's coming from the second floor, near the stairway in the guest wing. Bill and I overlook the village and the beach. It's got to be our room."

"Maybe Mrs. Gibbs is cleaning it," Judith suggested.

"At six o'clock on the Sabbath?" Renie shook her head.

Judith stared at the amber glow in the lighted window. Before she could say anything else, the light went out.

11

Mrs. Gibbs looked as if she'd aged ten years in eight hours. She was not only still pale, but her body seemed to have withered. Her hands shook and her lips trembled as she met the cousins at the castle door.

"How are you feeling?" Judith asked with concern.

Mrs. Gibbs didn't answer immediately. She stepped aside, a hand clutching at the fabric of her gray dress. "How should I feel?" she finally responded. "Sad, helpless, angry. Who did this horrid thing?"

"The police will find out," Judith asserted. "I'm sure they're very capable. Have they contacted you today?"

Mrs. Gibbs shook her head. "The inquest is Tuesday. Moira called to tell us. Imagine, being too sick to come to Mass here in the chapel to pray for the poor laddie's soul! She's young, she should carry on, she's not bowed down with age like some of us. Where's her spunk?"

Judith didn't dare look at Renie. Moira had seemed to have plenty of spunk when they'd seen her at Hollywood. "We heard she'd taken to her bed," Judith remarked.

"Aye, Moira's a great one for that when there's trouble." Mrs. Gibbs's voice was uneven. "An excuse, that's all." She wiped her hands on her apron. "God help us, life must go on. Will ye want supper?"

Judith glanced at Renie. "I don't know. We ate a late lunch."

"So we'll eat a late supper," Renie said, adding hastily, "if it's not too much trouble, Mrs. Gibbs."

"In truth, work keeps my mind off my troubles," Mrs. Gibbs replied. "Nine o'clock in the dining room?"

"We'll come get it," Judith volunteered. "We can eat in our rooms."

"Say," Renie put in, "was anyone in my room in the last hour?"

Mrs. Gibbs scowled at Renie. "No. Why do ye ask?"

"We thought we saw a light on in there just before we returned to the castle," Renie explained.

"Oh." Mrs. Gibbs hesitated. "'Twas probably a trick of the eyes. Oftentimes the lights from the village reflect on the castle windows. Excuse me, I must tend to The Master and his wife."

"A quick question," Judith put in. "Can we hire a car?"

Mrs. Gibbs shook her head. "Only if the garage has one to rent out. You might ring them tomorrow."

"Your own car won't be back by then?" Judith inquired.

Their hostess shrugged. "You must ask Gibbs. I canna drive."

The cousins proceeded upstairs where Renie wanted Judith to help her inspect the Joneses' room. "We don't have anything worth stealing," Renie said. "I suspect it might have been Chuckie wandering around. Unless his father grounded him after the debacle in the courtyard."

There was no sign of anything missing or out of order, however. Judith sat on the bed, perusing a list of services and goods in the area.

"I'd forgotten what Barry told us," she remarked. "The local garage is owned by Archibald Morton, Jocko's brother."

Renie sank into an armchair. "No luck eavesdropping at The Hermitage?"

"I'm afraid not," Judith admitted. "Except for hearing Harry's name mentioned, it sounded like business."

"You're working in the dark," Renie said, and yawned. "By the way, if you want to talk to Mrs. Gunn, tell her I'm subject to fits of violence."

"You are," Judith said.

"Only when provoked."

Judith slid off of the bed and went to the door. "I thought I heard someone out in the passageway." She peered out into the empty corridor. "Nothing. I could've sworn I heard a noise."

"I didn't hear it," Renie said with a shrug.

"I'd like to explore the rest of the castle," Judith declared. "Of course I wouldn't want to disturb Philip and Beth."

"Beth seems okay," Renie said. "Maybe she'll give you a tour."

Judith looked at her watch. "It's going on seven. I'm going down to the drawing room for a drink."

"You already had a drink at the pub."

"I never finished it."

"Too bad. I paid for it."

"Are you coming with me?"

"No."

"I'll see you in a bit." Judith went out into the passageway and closed the door behind her.

The drawing room was dark. Judith found the switch and turned on the lights. It wasn't yet seven. The Fordyces still might show up for drinks, though it was possible that, owning a distillery, Philip would keep his favorite Scotch in his suite.

After passing the time by studying the furnishings and other decor, Judith poured herself a small Scotch-rocks. If nothing else, it'd be a conversation starter if and when the Fordyces appeared.

At seven-fifteen, she heard voices in the corridor. Female voices, she realized. A moment later, Beth Fordyce and Marie Fleming entered the drawing room.

"Mrs. Flynn," Beth said with a smile, "did you meet Marie?"

"Yes," Judith said, putting out her hand to Will's voluptuous wife. "We spoke while Chuckie was misbehaving."

Beth shook her head. "I feel so sorry for Chuckie. He's epileptic."

"That's unfortunate," Judith said. "But I assume he receives excellent medical treatment."

"When he wants it," Beth replied, making drinks for herself and Marie. "He's also had a growth problem, a lack of certain hormones. You'd never guess it, but he's almost twenty-three. Naturally, he's bitter, and blames his father for everything."

"What about his mother?" Judith held up a hand. "I'm sorry, I'm prying. But I assume his mother was Philip's first wife."

Beth nodded. "Yes, Bella. She died. So did his second wife. Philip has had bad luck with wives."

"Until now," Marie put in, accepting her glass from Beth. "My Will's first wife passed away, too. The early demise of spouses around here is positively frightening."

"Phil's second wife wasn't really that young," Beth pointed out. "She was older than Phil, and died of cancer. Phil and I hope that the third time's a charm for him. Maybe it'll be the same way for Moira."

"I doubt it," Marie said with bite. "Moira's in love with love. She's shown terrible judgment when it comes to men. If they're good-looking and have a great body, she goes for them. Beth and I are smarter than that. We both married real men, not callow boys."

Judith was reminded of Grandma Grover's advice: "It's better to be an old man's darling than a young man's slave." Marie and Beth might have agreed with her. "Didn't you go to school together?" Judith asked.

"Ah yes," Beth replied. "We three, we merry little band of lassies at a French boarding school. Moira fell for the headmaster, the gardener, and the man from animal control. She was always losing her dog."

"On purpose, I think," Marie said, and both young women laughed.

Judith smiled, thinking about the rich, pretty trio making mischief away from home. It was a world she'd never known, but imagined it as an enchanted life. And knew that it was no preparation for reality.

"I met Moira at the graveyard," Judith said. "She was putting flowers on the grave of a young Italian man."

The young women laughed again. "Davey Piazza was her personal assistant," Beth replied. "She met him when he was playing in a rock band in Edinburgh, but the group broke up soon afterwards, and somehow he ended up in St. Fergna at loose ends. He couldn't decide whether he wanted to play the drums or race sports cars. Moira felt sorry for him—he had wrenching dark eyes—so she offered him a job."

"And bought him a sports car," Marie added. "He drove it over a cliff just beyond the village."

"My goodness!" Judith exclaimed. "What's the average age around here? About twenty-five?"

The remark had a sobering effect on both young women. "Well," Beth began, "several people have died young. My brother Frankie was sickly from birth. My mum worried so about him. She'd waited so long to have children, and even consulted astrologers. She still does, in fact."

"A fertility doctor would have been more to the point," Judith said.

To her dismay, both young women again went into peals of laughter. "You Americans are always so practical," Marie said after overcoming her latest giggle spasm. "Beth's mum enjoys hocus-pocus. But she's a wizard in the kitchen. You should taste her marmalade."

"Maybe," Beth said, "you have. She's always giving it away."

Judith remembered the jars of jams and condiments marked with the letter *G.* "Oh—yes, I thought the initial stood for Mrs. Gibbs."

"No, for Mrs. Gunn," Beth said, and looked at her diamond-studded watch. "It's after seven-thirty. Want another, Marie?"

"Certainly," Marie said.

"Mrs. Flynn?" Beth inquired.

"No, thank you. But your husband's Scotch is wonderful."

"Oh, he runs a fabulous distillery." Beth poured refills from a cut-glass decanter. The Venetian chandelier over the bar created a sparkling effect on the glassware, the diamonds in Beth's watch, the sheen of the satin trim on her tiered georgette halter dress, and even the luster of her fair skin. Judith felt as if she were watching a princess tend bar.

"What time do you expect Will to get here?" Beth asked Marie.

"For dinner," Marie replied. "Poor man, he has to work on Sundays. It's not fair."

"You mean," Judith said, "he has to go into the office? I understand that Blackwell's headquarters is in Inverness."

"It is," Marie said, "but he's working at home. He said he'd leave our house shortly before eight. I got here before the tide was all the way out. Poor Gibbs had to come fetch me in his funny little boat."

Settled in with their second drinks, the young women began to talk of clothes. Judith had finished her own cocktail. She had no excuse to linger. Bidding Beth and Marie good evening, she left the drawing room.

Chuckie was in the corridor, rolling oranges on the stone floor.

"Hullo," he said glumly. "Are you drunk?"

"Not in the least," Judith replied, filled with compassion for the young man. "Where did you get the lovely oranges?"

"My father brought them from Spain," Chuckie replied. "He says they're good for me, but I never eat them."

"Say, Chuckie, could you give me a quick tour of the castle?"

His face brightened. "Really? You want to see my secret places?"

"Sure. Where do we go first?"

"Outside," Chuckie replied.

"Shouldn't we collect your oranges?"

"No. Someone else will pick them up." He paused, his small, bright eyes darting from orange to orange, a total of six scattered along the corridor's cold stones. "My father's very rich. Why doesn't he hire more people here? Only old Gibbs and Gibbs until summer. I'd like a valet and a groom and . . . an orange picker-upper." He smiled broadly.

"I thought you didn't live here all the time," Judith said.

"I don't." He turned slightly sullen. "Didn't, I should say. But the last year or so, I've been kept here. I'm bored." He stared at the oranges. "Oh, come on, let's do the tour." Chuckie scurried down the corridor and waited for Judith by the entrance.

"Hurry up!" Chuckie called. "You're slow. You'd never escape the enemy marauders."

"I'm kind of crippled," Judith responded. "I have an artificial hip."

"You do?" Chuckie frowned. "I thought you were normal."

"Nobody's normal," Judith said. "The worst abnormalities," she went on as she joined him by the door, "are inside."

"But then nobody knows," Chuckie argued.

"Oh yes they do," Judith assured him. "They behave badly and cause trouble."

Chuckie's long face revealed intense concentration as he considered the statement. "You mean, like Harry?"

"Harry? Do you mean what happened to him or what he did?"

"Harry was mean," Chuckie declared, leaning against the heavy door to open it. "He was nasty to me and unkind to Moira. He deserved getting blown up."

"Nobody deserves to be killed," Judith pointed out.

"Yes they do," Chuckie insisted. "I'll show you."

He led the way into the courtyard. Judith felt the damp air on her cheek as soon as she moved outside. The only light came from a half dozen electric lanterns that hung from stanchions along the stone walls.

Chuckie pointed to their left. "See there, by the corner?"

Judith peered into the darkness at a wall fountain where water spewed from the mouth of a stone face resembling Neptune. "Yes?"

"That's where the well was in the old days," Chuckie said. "Sometimes bad people were thrown in to drown. Served them right."

Judith refrained from making a comment.

"The guest rooms are where the barracks used to be," Chuckie went on, strolling ahead and kicking at an occasional pebble. "There was a postern gatehouse in the old days when the castle was still connected to the land. It led to the barracks, where you're staying now. Have you heard the horses stomping in their stalls at night?"

"Not yet," Judith replied. She was tempted to say that she had, in fact, heard a voice saying "Open the gate" and "Open the window." But she decided not to play into what appeared to be Chuckie's fantasy.

"You saw the chapel," Chuckie said. "Did my father make you go?"

"Of course not," Judith replied. "I always attend Sunday Mass."

"You do? Why?"

"I want to receive the sacraments," Judith replied. "They give me the grace to try to lead a good life."

"That's bosh," Chuckie declared. "I wager my father told you that."

"I've been going to Mass since I was a child," Judith said. "I didn't meet your father until yesterday."

Chuckie pointed to the second story of the castle's west wing. "He and bonnie Beth live there, in the apartments for important people."

"Where do you live?" Judith inquired.

"Wherever I want," Chuckie replied. He gestured at the central part of the castle. "That was the great hall.

It still is, in a way. It's used for meetings. The kitchen adjoins it."

"What kind of meetings?"

"Any kind. Sometimes my father holds them there. Sometimes strangers rent them. They go there and plot terrible things. Last month the Rotary Club came to conspire."

"The Rotary Club?" Judith echoed, wondering if she'd misheard.

Chuckie nodded. "They came from Inverness for the weekend. The world is full of evil."

"The Rotary Club does good things," Judith pointed out.

"That's bosh, too." Chuckie nudged Judith's arm. "Look up to the top of the wall," he urged in an excited voice. "See the twin towers?"

"Not very well," Judith said. "They're hidden by the mist."

"Just as well. Along the entire wall on both sides, there were stone spikes where they used to put the heads of their enemies to frighten anybody else who meant them harm. A fine idea, don't you think?"

"I think it's gruesome," Judith said. "And I'm getting cold. I thought you were going to show me the inside of the castle."

Chuckie cocked his head to one side. "Oh. Then . . . if you insist." He started for the area he'd indicated was the original great hall. "Can you see the smaller towers?"

"I've seen them before," Judith said. "I can't see much of anything now except for the courtyard and the walkway."

"The floors were mainly wood," Chuckie said. "They were covered with rushes in the beginning and later overlaid with carpets, but the wood rotted, so it was torn up in the guest section." He stopped by a narrow door with iron hinges and removed a small keychain from the pocket of his khaki slacks. "Do you know why this is locked?"

"Not really," Judith admitted. "I doubt that you have much trouble with burglars."

"To keep the prisoners in, of course." Chuckie laughed merrily. "This smaller tower holds the dungeon. And the torture chamber. That's my favorite place. Come on."

"Ah . . . " Judith didn't budge. "Can we skip that part? I'm not really interested in barbarity."

Chuckie scowled and stamped his foot. "I thought you wanted to see my secret places."

"Not if they're . . . unpleasant. I should go back to meet my cousin. We haven't yet had dinner, and frankly, you're spoiling my appetite."

Chuckie waved his fists. "I thought you liked me!"

Judith was slowly backing away, hoping she wouldn't fall over some unseen obstacle. "I like you," she insisted, though she wasn't sure it was true. "But I don't like tales of cruelty and suffering. I get upset."

"Then you won't know my secrets!" Chuckie asserted, his voice rising in pitch.

Fearing that he might have a seizure, Judith smiled. "Tomorrow my cousin and I will have a picnic with you if the weather's nice. Would you like that?"

"No." Chuckie's voice dropped as he began to sulk. "I don't like that other woman. She has an angry face. Yours is kind, like Beth's and Moira's. Go away. I'll play with the rack in the dungeon."

"Have fun," Judith said, and turned toward the main walkway. "See you tomorrow."

"Maybe."

Judith heard Chuckie slam the tower door behind him. In spite of herself she shivered. Pity mingled with revulsion. Chuckie was a very strange young man in many ways.

She was almost to the guest entrance when she heard footsteps behind her. Had Chuckie changed his mind? Not wanting to turn around, Judith quickened her pace.

Whoever was following her also moved faster. She was almost to the door when she heard a voice:

"Allow me. That door is heavy."

Judith finally turned around. She saw Will Fleming emerging from the mist with a faint smile on his long face.

"You must be one of the guests," he said, removing his gloves. "I saw you at Mass this morning." He opened the door and let Judith enter first. "I don't think we met officially. I'm Will Fleming, the unworthy man who's married to Marie."

Judith put out her hand. "Yes. I was chatting with Marie and Beth a few minutes ago. They're in the drawing room."

Will was taking off his navy raincoat. A package the size of a toddler's shoe box wrapped in brown paper fell to the floor with a clunking sound. "Sorry," he murmured, picking up the parcel. "I was afraid I'd be late to dinner. It's a nuisance to have to bring work home on the weekends—but there it is. A global economy never rests. Will you be joining us?"

"No," Judith replied. "My cousin and I had a late lunch. We'll dine later, probably in our rooms. It's very good of Mrs. Gibbs to do the cooking despite her grief."

"Indeed," Will agreed, cradling the package. "They're a wonderfully old-fashioned pair. Philip is fortunate to have them at Grimloch."

"Apparently their son and his wife are quite different," Judith remarked. "I haven't heard if they've been notified of their son's tragedy."

"Hardly surprising," Will said, taking off his mackintosh. "They prefer not to be found."

"Aging hippies?"

Will's chuckle seemed forced. "Let's say they find it best to keep moving." He nodded to Judith, and headed down the corridor.

When Judith returned to Renie's room, she found her cousin reading a mystery novel.

"Research," Renie said, putting the book aside. "I'm betting that the LAPD detective catches the killer before you do. Where've you been?"

Judith explained how she'd visited with Beth and Marie before running into Chuckie. "He's very disturbed—and disturbing," Judith said. "I wanted him to show me the castle, but he spent most of the time dwelling on the awful things that used to happen here."

" 'Used to'? As opposed to happening since we got here?"

"You know what I mean."

"I do, and speaking of awful, we were going to call our mothers, remember? Your cell phone or mine?"

Judith shrugged. "We can each use our own. But remember, at home it's almost noon. My mother will be about to have lunch."

"Mine, too." Renie got out her cell. "Let's see if these things will work inside the castle. I have doubts after our first failure."

Renie stayed on the bed; Judith took her phone to the window embrasure. This time there was static, but she heard the ring at the other end.

And more ringing. Gertrude refused to pick up the phone until the caller was ready to hang up—or pass out. Finally Judith heard her mother's raspy voice, snarling an unwelcoming "Hello."

"How are you?" Judith asked.

"Who is this?" Gertrude demanded. "Whatever you're peddling, I don't want any."

"It's me, Mother—Judith."

"Speak up, young man. I'm deaf."

"Mother! I'm on a trip, remember?" Judith was practically screaming. She saw Renie motioning for her to lower her voice.

"I can't hear you, Mom," Renie was saying. "Are you sick?"

"A drip in December?" Gertrude said. "The only drip I know of is my daughter's dim-bulb husband. You want to talk to my daughter?"

"Did you call the doctor, Mom?" Renie asked as she rolled over onto her stomach. "What kind of pain?"

Judith tried to open the window to see if the reception would be better. But the panes were sealed shut. She moved toward the garderobe and slipped inside. "Can you hear me now?" she asked just as Renie said in alarm, "What ambulance?"

Judith shut the garderobe door. "I said—"

"Lunch is here," Gertrude interrupted. "Mmm . . . tuna sandwiches with the crusts cut off, deviled eggs, strawberries from California, and oatmeal raisin cookies right out of the oven. You're a doll, Arlene."

Judith could barely hear her neighbor's voice in the background asking who was on the phone.

"Nobody," Gertrude said, and rang off.

Judith swore under her breath. It was pointless to call back. Her mother would be eating lunch, an inviolable occasion. At least the old lady sounded in fine fettle, which apparently was more than could be said for Aunt Deb. Judith exited the garderobe to find Renie tugging at her unmanageable chestnut hair.

"It's probably gas," Renie said in a testy voice. "Mom, you feel puny every time I go more than five miles from Heraldsgate Hill. It's nerves. You're trying to make me feel guilty. It won't work." She put her hand over the speaker part of the phone. "It does work, but I won't let her know it," she whispered to Judith, who'd come to sit on the bed. "No," Renie told her mother, "I'm not taking you to the doctor tomorrow. Ask one of your friends. You've got dozens of them."

Judith wondered what was worse—Gertrude's ornery disposition or Aunt Deb's martyrdom. She waited for Renie to finish listening to her mother's complaints and queries. "Yes, the bed's clean," Renie replied wearily. "No bugs in the food. The white slavers went to Florida. My shoes are sturdy, my nose isn't running, my coat is plenty warm. No contact with germs, I won't eat food off the floor, I wash my hands after . . . I *am* grown-up. I stopped teething sixty-odd years ago . . . Why didn't you say so? Tell Auntie Vance and Uncle Vince hello. I'm hanging up now."

Looking drained, Renie clicked off the cell. "Auntie Vance and Uncle Vince came down from their place on the island and are taking Mom out to lunch. Then they're going to see your mother. My poor ear!"

"I don't even know if my mother knew it was me calling," Judith complained. "She did her deaf bit, and I'm never sure if she really doesn't hear or is just being contrary."

Renie sat up. "Let's eat in ten minutes, maybe have a drink first. That Old Engine Oil didn't see me through the phone call."

"Well . . . okay," Judith said. "I imagine the Fordyces and the Flemings have moved on to the dining room. But . . . "

"What?" Renie said as she slipped into her shoes.

"I thought I'd call Mrs. Gunn about coming to see her tomorrow."

"No apology!" Renie cried. "If you go, it's on your own."

Dialing for directory assistance, Judith shot Renie a look of reproach. "You have no remorse."

Renie started shadowboxing.

Ignoring her cousin's antics, Judith was again connected to Alison. "It's me, Mrs. Flynn," she said. "How long do you have to work?"

"I'm home," Alison replied. "Nobody calls after I leave at five on the Sabbath. The rare request is trunked over to the phone in my bedroom."

Renie continued punching at the air. "Remember the Alamo!" she cried. "Don't Shoot Until You See the Whites of Their Eyes!" "Fifty-four Forty or Fight." She frowned. "Or was it Forty-five Fifty?"

Walking to the window embrasure to get away from Renie's distractions, Judith asked if Alison knew Mrs. Gunn's phone number.

"Yes, she being such a good customer," Alison said, and relayed the number to Judith. "Uh . . . is Mrs. Jones making amends?"

"Mrs. Jones doesn't make amends," Judith said with a stern look for Renie, who had removed a length of green and white twine from her luggage and was fashioning it into a garrote. "She's unrepentant. But I'd like to apologize for her. I didn't want to leave Mrs. Gunn with a bad impression of Americans. Most of us have good manners."

"Oh," Alison said, "I'm sure you do. I'm afraid Mrs. Gunn can be aggravating. And your cousin was in a hurry. Here's the number."

Judith thanked Alison before asking if Barry's car had been towed.

"Aye," Alison replied. "It's gone to the shop. Barry's on his way here now that he's back on his bicycle." She paused. "Well . . . almost here. He just fell off his cycle by the stoop. I must help him get up."

Seeing that Renie was having some of her usual manual dexterity problems with the twine, Judith dialed Mrs. Gunn's number. The voice that answered sounded like Kate Gunn.

"You may remember me from the drawing room at Grimloch last night," Judith said after giving her name. "I'm calling to apologize for the altercation at the woolen shop with my cousin, Mrs. Jones."

Renie had gotten the would-be garrote tangled on the bedstead and was uttering various obscenities.

"Can't she speak for herself?" Mrs. Gunn demanded.

"Ah . . . she's tied up right now." Judith said as Renie stopped cursing and made a rude gesture. "May I drop by tomorrow to bring you a small gift to make up for your . . . inconvenience?"

There was a long pause at the other end of the line. Finally Mrs. Gunn posed an unexpected question: "When were you born?"

"You mean the date?"

"Year, date, time of day," Mrs. Gunn said.

Judith rattled off the day and year, but confessed that she didn't know the actual time. "I think it was in the morning."

"It's better to be exact," Mrs. Gunn stated with a hint of reproach.

"I can't," Judith admitted, warily watching Renie, who had finally disentangled the twine. "Why do you ask?"

"So I can confer with my astrologer," the other woman replied. "This information will have to do. I'll ring you up tomorrow to let you know if and when I'm available." She disconnected, leaving Judith with dead air and a puzzled expression.

Renie, who had been approaching Judith with a menacing look and the garrote in hand, stopped abruptly. "Now what?"

"Put that thing down," Judith ordered, pointing to the twine. "Apparently," she went on, as Renie backed off, "Mrs. Gunn has to confer with her astrologer to figure out if I'm worthy of an audience."

"Why not? Like Bill, you enjoy the occasional nutcase."

"Maybe her astrologer knows who killed Harry."

Renie tossed the garrote in the direction of her luggage. "I leave that up to you. But I'm not apologizing. Now, let's drink and eat."

Judith looked worried. "This is all very strange. We don't even know how Harry was murdered."

Renie seemed about to dismiss the comments, but instead she put a hand on Judith's arm. "Has it ever occurred to you that it might be better if you never found out? Safer, too."

Judith took a deep breath. "I'm all for safety. But I'm against killers. Dead set against them, you might say."

"That," Renie responded, "is what I'm afraid of."

12

To her surprise, Judith slept soundly that night. Despite being wound up in the homicide case, the long and taxing day had worn her out. She and Renie had brought their meal of lamb cutlets, green beans, and fingerling potatoes back to Judith's room. It was after ten when they finished, and they agreed that an early night would serve them well.

Judith came down for breakfast at nine while Renie slept in, muttering that it was barely daylight and pulling the covers over her head. In the dining room, Judith found Philip Fordyce finishing breakfast and reading the *Scotsman*. He glanced up to wish Judith good morning and immediately turned his eyes back to the business section.

The sideboard contained ample offerings, indicating that Mrs. Gibbs was still trying to drown her sorrows in work. Judith selected rashers of bacon, coddled eggs, scones, and fruit compote.

Surreptitiously watching Philip between mouthfuls, Judith wished she'd brought something to read, too. It felt awkward to sit a mere six feet away from another human being and not converse. At home, after preparing the guests' food, she and Joe read the newspaper while they ate and exchanged comments. It was a comfortable way to start the day, usually before the B&B visitors came downstairs.

Philip had finished his coffee—and, apparently, the business section. He folded the paper carefully and was about to rise when Beth appeared wearing a cream lace peignoir.

"Oh, Phil," she began before noticing Judith. "Good morning, Mrs. Flynn. Sorry, but I'm in crisis."

Judith offered the young woman a sympathetic expression. "Do you need privacy?"

"No," Beth replied. "It's nothing like that." She sat down next to her husband. "Marie just called and she's got flu. It's going round. She can't go with me to help Moira."

Philip removed his rimless glasses. "Help Moira with what? The funeral plans for Harry?"

"Not just that," Beth replied. "Moira collapsed. She frequently has some kind of breakdown. Marie felt we should help out. You know how Moira is when it comes to adversity. To be fair, she's had more than her share. But without Marie, I'm not sure I can handle Moira on my own."

Judith cleared her throat. "Would you like me to come with you?"

Beth stared. "Oh, I couldn't possibly let you! You're on holiday."

"I don't mind," Judith insisted. "My cousin and I won't do much sightseeing until our husbands get back from fishing. I'm glad to help."

Beth glanced at Philip. "Well . . . what do you think, darling?"

Philip gazed at Judith for the first time since he'd greeted her upon her arrival in the dining room. "It's a great deal to ask of a visitor."

"Not at all," Judith declared. "I'm an innkeeper by trade. I'm used to taking care of people. In fact, I miss it. The only thing is, I planned to see your mother today, Beth. I wanted to apologize for . . . an incident with my cousin in the village."

Beth smiled. "Oh yes. I gather Mrs. Jones lost her temper with Mummy. A lot of people do. She's used to getting her own way."

"So's my cousin," Judith said.

"I can take you to call on Mummy," Beth offered. "Thank you so much! I'll meet you in half an hour in the courtyard."

Judith went upstairs to deliver the news to Renie, who was still in bed. "Wake up!" Judith shouted. "It's almost ten o'clock. We're going to have adventures."

Renie rolled away as far as she could while Judith jiggled the mattress. "We're going to Hollywood!"

Renie's head popped out from under the covers. Her hair went every which way and her expression was surly. "*You're* going to Hollywood! I don't give a rat's ass!" She stuck her head under a pillow.

Annoyed, Judith left Renie's room and went across the passageway to her own quarters. Maybe Renie wouldn't be able to go back to sleep. Maybe she'd get up, get dressed, and be able to grab some food from the dining room sideboard. Judith's cousin could—apparently without the help of sorcery—make herself presentable in a very short time.

But twenty-five minutes later, there was no sign of Renie. Disappointed, Judith went downstairs and into the courtyard. It was a bright morning, with the sun peeking over the castle battlements. She strolled the path toward the inner gatehouse, keeping an eye out for Beth to come from the Fordyce wing. Five minutes passed, then ten. Gibbs appeared, keeping his head down and walking with a distinct shuffle.

"How are you, Mr. Gibbs?" Judith asked as he approached.

The old man merely shook his head.

Judith knew it would be awkward to pursue the query. "Are you taking us in the skiff?"

Gibbs nodded. Judith took a few steps toward the nearest flower bed. "The hyacinths are coming up. They have a lovely scent."

Gibbs kept silent. Before Judith could say anything else, Beth came hurrying out of the door to the private apartments. "Sorry," she apologized breathlessly, hoisting her black hobo bag over her shoulder. "I'm a bit disorganized this morning."

"Not to worry," Judith assured Beth. "It's pleasant here in the courtyard."

Gibbs was already crossing the drawbridge and heading for the lift. Beth nodded at his stooped figure. "Very sad for him and Mrs. Gibbs."

"It would help if Harry's parents were here," Judith said. "Surely they'd be some comfort, despite their own grief."

Beth kept walking, her eyes straight ahead. "Perhaps."

The descent in the lift and the short ride to the beach were made in silence. The section between the sea and the cliff that had been designated as the crime scene was still marked off. A lone constable stood guard, feet firmly planted in the sand, hands behind his back, and eyes staring straight ahead.

"Oh no!" Beth cried after she and Judith had gotten out of the skiff and were walking to the Fordyce sedan. "The vultures have flown in."

Judith looked up to the cliff's edge. A dozen or more people were congregated, at least two with camcorders and other TV devices.

"I was so hoping the press would keep away," Beth said angrily. "Philip doesn't need negative publicity. We'll simply have to soldier on."

She slipped behind the wheel while Judith sat in the luxurious passenger seat. After making sure that the windows and doors were secure, Beth set her face in an impassive expression and drove up the track. Members of the press immediately pounced, trying to stop the car and shouting questions. Undeterred, Beth kept going.

"Do they know who you are?" Judith asked as the Daimler purred along the High Street while a handful of reporters gave up the chase.

"Probably," Beth replied, annoyed. "The villagers are gossips and some are open to bribery. I apologize for the inconvenience. This must be distressing for someone like you who must lead a very quiet life."

"Uh . . . yes, certainly." Judith stared out through the window to avoid looking at Beth. It wouldn't do to admit that she was an old hand at dealing with the media, up to and including her televised life-and-death confrontation with a merciless killer. "I understand," Judith said as they passed the village green and moved smoothly along the road to Hollywood, "Moira has a history of ill health."

Beth shrugged. "Moira's always been high-strung, even when we were children at boarding school in France. Some of her problems are probably due to stress, but the pains in her side and the fainting spells are no less real because they're caused by emotion."

"She must've gotten ill after I saw her yesterday," Judith said. "Moira seemed in good spirits when Renie and I called on her."

Beth darted a sidelong glance at Judith. "How kind of you."

Judith ignored what she thought was a hint of irony. The sun cast filmy rays through greening foliage as they wound along the road. Judith changed the subject. "Was Chuckie born with his affliction?"

"You mean the epilepsy?" Beth saw Judith nod. "No. He had other problems, but he took a bad fall down a staircase in his early teens. A blow to the head can bring on epilepsy. Chuckie had the best doctors, but they couldn't help him much. The damage was done."

"Will he be able to take over the distillery when the time comes?"

Beth slowed to turn off the road. "Most epileptics lead quite normal and successful lives. But Chuckie . . . " She let the sentence fade as she rolled down the window and punched the intercom buzzer that opened the gates to Hollywood House. Judith could hear Fergus's voice. Beth didn't finish her assessment of Chuckie. "It's a pity," she said as the car glided to a stop, "that Moira and Harry didn't patch things up sooner instead of waiting until Harry got sick."

"I understand they weren't married long," Judith said.

"It was rocky from the start," Beth said with a frown as Fergus opened the front door. "They hadn't known each other very long," she continued, ignoring the butler's stiff stance on the porch. "You're here to help me care for Moira, so you should understand the situation. It was a whirlwind courtship, and after they married, things started to fall apart. Harry wanted a big role with Blackwell Petroleum. Moira didn't mind having him work for the company, but she didn't feel he was ready to be in a decision-making position. Her brother Jimmy agreed with her—one of the few times that they agreed about anything."

"Had Harry any experience in business?" Judith asked.

Beth's expression was wry. "Harry had very little experience with work, let alone the business world.

He grew angry with Moira and Jimmy for being kept in the background, and got it in his head that Moira was carrying on with her secretary, David Piazza."

"Was she?" Judith asked.

"No, I really don't think so. They were close, probably because Harry had gotten so nasty and Davey offered a sympathetic shoulder for Moira to cry on. When he had his fatal car accident, Moira almost miscarried. But the baby was born in November, and before Christmas she and Harry tried to smooth things out. Then he got flu about a month ago. Some of these viruses linger. Moira didn't want him near the baby, so he moved to Grimloch. He was returning to Hollywood sometime this week, but instead he got killed. I'm sure Moira blames herself."

Judith knew the blame game. She'd felt guilty for letting Dan McMonigle eat and drink his way into an early grave. "It's natural."

Fergus still hadn't moved. Beth glanced up at the butler. "I suppose. He's the second husband she's had die, and both very young. I can understand why she feels that way. Come, we'd better go inside before Fergus atrophies."

The butler greeted Beth with a formal bow. Judith swore she could hear his bones creak. "Madam," he said in mournful tones, "is in her boudoir. Elise and Dr. Carmichael are with her."

"Elise," Beth informed Judith as they climbed the curving staircase, "is Moira's French maid. She's rigid, snoopy, and overly protective, but she's definitely loyal."

A short, stout older man was coming down the hall. "Dr. Carmichael," Beth said in greeting. "How is Moira?"

"As usual, nerves," the doctor replied. "I won't over-medicate her." His sharp gray eyes looked at Judith. "A family friend?" he inquired.

"Sorry," Beth apologized, and introduced Judith. "Her husband's gone fishing with the MacGowan."

"I'm at loose ends," Judith said, shaking the doctor's strong hand. "I volunteered to help Beth with Moira."

"Very kind." Dr. Carmichael was completely bald and wore a plaid bow tie. "Don't think me unsympathetic, Mrs. Flynn. My patient has had much grief in her young life. Both parents gone, widowed twice over, her secretary's death—fate's been cruel. But I also don't want to tempt that fate." He turned to Beth. "You understand."

Beth looked pained. "Moira's prone to extremes. She'd have been better off staying in France. She was so happy there. She loved everything French, and spoke the language like a native. She doesn't enjoy living in rural Scotland."

The doctor shook his head. "That couldn't be helped after her mother passed. Nor would Frankie have lived any longer there than here. He was one of those poor souls born with a fatal flaw that wasn't diagnosed properly, and even if it had been, twenty years ago, medical practitioners didn't have the means to correct it. The fever he caught in Africa was the final blow to his weak constitution." He sighed and removed his spectacles, wiping them on his sweater vest. "Born too soon, died too soon." He made a little bow. "I must go."

Beth watched him start down the stairs. "Quite a remarkable man. He had a fine practice in Inverness but gave it up after his wife died six years ago. He moved here where there weren't so many memories. We're fortunate to have him." She led the way to Moira's suite. "Dr. Carmichael still feels guilty for not saving Davey. The accident occurred a short way from the doctor's cottage."

"Had Davey been drinking?" Judith inquired.

"Yes, at the Dolphin, a pub about five kilometers west of St. Fergna," Beth replied, her hand on the doorknob. "Not a lot, but that's a treacherous part of the coast road at night, and of course there was mist. Patrick was lucky to survive."

"Patrick was with Davey?" Judith said in surprise.

Beth grimaced. "That's the oddest thing. I've never understood exactly what happened. Patrick was found near the wreckage, unconscious. He had several injuries, at least one that was quite severe. But he didn't recall being with Davey. Phil and I wondered if Patrick had come upon the scene right after the crash and tried to rescue Davey. Patrick's car wasn't nearby, but his home isn't far from where Davey went off the road. Patrick, you see, has a place in the village, and sometimes he'd walk the two or three kilometers from there to Hunter's Lodge where he lives with his wife Jeannie."

"So late at night and in October?" Judith asked, recalling the time of year Davey had died.

"Oh yes," Beth said with a little laugh. "Patrick is the rugged outdoor type. Very virile, very tough, and yet . . . " She paused to find the proper word. "Very sophisticated. Well educated, too. Come. We can leave our coats and purses here. We must attend to the patient."

Moira's boudoir was part of a sunny suite facing west. The sitting room's predominant colors were yellow, pale blue, and lavender, and furnished with handsome pieces that were both simple and elegant.

The boudoir, however, was in semidarkness with the yellow drapes closed tight. A pale and listless Moira lay with her head propped up by satin-covered pillows. Elise, who seemed to have taken posture lessons from Fergus, stood at attention by the foot of the big bed.

"It's a lovely morning," Beth said to Moira. "You should be sitting in the sunshine."

"Oh, Beth," Moira responded in a pettish voice, "I'm too weak. The pain in my side is almost as bad as being in labor. I couldn't. The bright light would hurt my eyes." She lifted her head slightly from the pillow. The silky cases and sheets were trimmed with delicate lace; the duvet was ecru damask with a rose design. The rest of the bedding was equally lavish, a far cry from the striped Hudson Bay blanket and clearance sale linens Judith had on her bed at home. "Who is that with you?" Moira asked. "Where's Marie?"

"Mrs. Flynn, from Grimloch," Beth replied. "You met her yesterday. Marie has flu."

"Poor Marie," Moira murmured. "Mrs. Flynn? Oh—yes, of course. You were here with your friend."

"My cousin," Judith clarified.

Elise regarded Judith with unconcealed animosity. "Strangers," she murmured, "should keep away from sick rooms. Madam doesn't need more visitors."

"Now, Elise," Beth said in a pleasant voice, "I invited Mrs. Flynn because Mrs. Fleming is ill. Make yourself some coffee. Take your time."

Elise shot Beth a resentful look, but marched out of the boudoir.

"Honestly," Beth said after the maid left, "Elise is too prickly."

"You know I acquired her after my mother died," Moira said. "She's tenaciously faithful to our family."

"I'm not here to quarrel," Beth insisted. "What can we do for you?"

Moira sighed. "Nothing. I'd prefer to close my eyes and die."

"Why?" Beth scowled at Moira. "Harry's death isn't your fault."

Moira turned her head away but said nothing.

Judith tapped Beth's arm. "Should I go into the other room?"

Beth shook her head and mouthed the word "drama."

Judith spoke up. "I lost my husband when he was fairly young."

Moira moved just enough to look at Judith. "Was he murdered?"

"No," Judith said. "It was more like suicide. He purposely lived a destructive lifestyle. I have my share of guilt for what happened to him."

"But nobody blew him up," Moira said.

"He did blow up," Judith asserted. "Medically speaking."

"I don't understand."

"He weighed over four hundred pounds," Judith explained. "He'd developed diabetes, he could barely walk, and his entire system went berserk. I felt it was partly my fault for enabling him. That very morning, I'd brought him a big bottle of grape juice before I went to work."

Moira looked mildly interested. "But you didn't drink it for him."

"No." Judith gazed curiously at the young woman. "You mean . . . ?"

Moira looked at Judith and then turned to Beth. "That's still not murder or suicide." Her tone was bitter. "And," she added, again focused on Judith, "you didn't escape death along with your husband."

Judith was puzzled. "No, of course not."

Beth moved closer to Moira. "What do you mean?"

Moira's fingers plucked fretfully at the lace on the sheet. "Harry asked me to meet him at the beach that afternoon. I thought about going, but changed my mind. I'd been invited to a wedding in Inverness. I couldn't join Harry and get to the reception on time. If I'd gone . . . " She shuddered. "I might have been murdered, too."

13

Moira!" Beth cried. "Why would anyone want to kill you? Or Harry, for that matter?"

"Don't be naïve," Moira retorted. "You know about the power struggle at Blackwell, especially now that Morton's come back." She looked again at Judith. "I'm sorry. You're a stranger, so you have no idea what's been happening. But it's hardly a secret. We've had the media in the UK give us a great deal of negative coverage."

Beth was nodding. "Will complains about how ugly it's gotten. His own position is precarious. The press has hounded him mercilessly about the company's financial status. He won't discuss it, of course. After all, it's a privately held company."

Judith looked apologetic. "I'm ignorant of big business. I was a librarian before I started my B&B."

Moira grimaced. "I wish I'd never inherited Blackwell."

Beth sat down on a tufted satin-covered chair. "You don't mean that. Neither you nor your mum wanted Jimmy in charge."

Moira's color began to rise. "We certainly didn't want Morton. Why didn't he stay in Greece? Why did he come back now?"

"That," Beth said, "is a good question. When did he get here?"

Judith felt like an interloper. She edged toward a divan a few feet from the bed and sat down. It seemed that the two women had forgotten she was in the room.

Beth, however, appeared to have read Judith's mind. "Oh, Mrs. Flynn, this must be so tiresome for you. Let's get Moira up and take her out into the garden. We can have some tea or a cool drink." She shot her friend a sharp look. "What have you eaten today?"

"Nothing," Moira replied. "I couldn't possibly keep anything down. I'm very queasy."

"Nonsense!" Beth snapped. "You can eat toast. Or porridge. I'll have Elise fetch you something. Come, you must get dressed."

But Moira was adamant. "No. I'll try to drink some tea."

Beth looked disgusted. "Frankly, you . . . " She clamped her lips shut. "I'll speak to Elise."

Beth left the boudoir. Judith had been studying Moira. Except for her pale, porcelain-like skin and the dark shadows under her eyes, the newly made widow didn't have the appearance of someone in misery. Certainly she'd been in good health and satisfactory spirits the previous day.

Judith dared to risk a question: "Are you taking medication?"

"A liquid digestive aid," Moira answered. "Aspirin for headache."

"No prescription drugs?"

"No." Moira frowned. "Dr. Carmichael is strict about prescribing them. He's very old-fashioned. He wouldn't renew my tranquilizers." She began plucking at the sheets again. "What's taking Beth so long?"

"Maybe she couldn't find Elise," Judith suggested.

"Elise wouldn't leave her post in the sitting room. I might need her at any moment." Moira gave a start. "I hear voices. Who is it?"

Judith listened but couldn't hear anything.

"They're outside," Moira said. "Look out the window. But don't part the drapes and don't open the casement."

"I don't have X-ray vision," Judith said, getting up and crossing the room to the two tall windows. "You should've hired Superman."

"Ohhh . . . " Moira wadded up the sheet in her fists. "Just see what's happening. I can't endure a disturbance."

Judith peeked between the drapes. The boudoir opened onto a balcony overlooking the front of the house. She slipped through the door between the two windows. Directly below she saw a parked car that hadn't been there earlier. A male and a female voice sounded as if they were arguing. A moment later, Jimmy moved into Judith's line of sight.

"Just tell her I'll be back when I'm able," he said impatiently.

"She needs you," the female voice called. "Don't be so selfish!"

Judith saw Beth step out into the drive. Jimmy kept going, long strides taking him to the car that was parked behind the Daimler. Without looking back, he got in and started the engine. Beth ran up the stairs and disappeared under the overhang.

"Your brother is going away," Judith said, closing the balcony door.

Moira sat up. "What do you mean?"

"Ask Beth." Judith sat down again. "She tried to stop him."

"Why was he here again?" Moira's voice was shrill. "Why didn't he come to see me? Where's Beth?"

"Probably bringing your tea," Judith said.

Moira sank back onto the pillows and covered her eyes with the back of her hand. "Go find her. Get Elise. I'm in pain."

And I'm in a pickle, Judith thought. She wished Renie had come along. Her cousin would have some sharp words for Moira. It wasn't in Judith's nature to be rude, but her patience was wearing thin.

"I have an artificial hip," Judith said calmly. "It's not easy for me to go up and down stairs. Don't you have an intercom or some way you can contact your servants?"

"It doesn't always work properly," Moira said in a sulky voice.

"Where is your pain?"

Moira grimaced and rubbed the right side of her abdomen. "Here. Why would anyone want to kill me?"

"Would it have something to do with your petroleum company?"

"People don't kill people over business issues." Moira bit her lower lip. "Or do they?"

"It's been known to happen."

"Maybe in the States," Moira said. "Certainly not in Scotland." She sat up again. "Where is Beth? Where is Elise?"

"I don't know!" Judith snapped. "What can I do for you that doesn't require searching all over this very large house?"

"Nothing." Moira avoided Judith's gaze. "Why did you come?"

"Beth asked me," Judith replied. "She knew we'd met."

Moira slowly turned to look at Judith again. "You told her you were here yesterday?"

"Of course."

"Did you tell her anything else?"

"Such as how chipper you seemed? No. I tend to be discreet."

Relief swept over Moira's face. "Thank you. Harry's death hadn't sunk in yet. My emotional responses are often delayed."

"That happens. I knew you weren't feeling well enough to attend Mass at the castle," Judith added innocently.

"I couldn't face seeing where Harry died," Moira said. "Or his grandparents. Too, too difficult."

That was possible, Judith thought, but it didn't explain Moira's vivacity with Patrick the previous day. Before Judith could speak, Beth entered the bedroom. She was out of breath and looking annoyed.

"Those press people followed us to Hollywood," she announced. "They're trying to climb over the fence."

"Call the police!" Moira cried. "Those predators must be stopped!"

"The police are on their way," Beth replied. "That detective phoned a few minutes ago to say that he was coming to interview you again."

"No!" Moira pressed a hand to her breast. "Send him away!"

"I can't," Beth asserted. "Don't you want to help the police find who killed Harry? And who may have wanted to kill you, too?"

"Why is Jimmy going away?" Moira demanded.

Beth sat on the edge of the bed. "Jimmy's off to Paris. He didn't have time to see you because he was afraid he'd miss his flight."

"Was Angie with him?" Moira asked.

"No," Beth replied. "You know she's having a difficult pregnancy."

"Jimmy's up to something," Moira said in disgust. "What can it be? Surely nothing to do with—"

A knock interrupted Moira's speculations. Beth got up to admit Elise. The maid carried a tray with an array of tea items. Wordlessly, she set the tray on the bedside table and left. Before she could close the door, Fergus announced Alpin MacRae and Malcolm Ogilvie.

MacRae assured Moira that the press would be dispersed. "I apologize for the intrusion," he said earnestly. "I wouldn't trouble you if this wasn't urgent. You must be desperate to have us find your husband's killer."

"I'm not," Moira replied.

MacRae, who had struck Judith as imperturbable, seemed taken aback by Moira's response. He recovered quickly, however. "That's a peculiar attitude," he said mildly. "I'd like to hear your reasons." He glanced at Judith and Beth. "It will be easier if we speak privately."

"Mrs. Fordyce must stay," Moira insisted. "We're having tea."

MacRae smiled indulgently. "I'm sure Mrs. Fordyce and . . . Mrs. Flynn, isn't it?" he said, looking at Judith and seeing her nod. "The ladies can enjoy their tea in the sitting room and join you later."

"Then my maid must be present." Moira looked beseechingly at Beth. "Please. Send Elise in."

MacRae shook his head. "No, no. This is just a simple chat. Your friends will be outside should you need them. Sergeant Ogilvie and I have no intention of upsetting you."

"We'll have tea later," Beth said, moving to leave. "Relax, Moira."

Judith followed Beth out of the boudoir. The younger woman went to another door and opened it. "I assume you want to eavesdrop, too," she said. "This is Moira's closet. There's a vent in the wall. We can hear some of the conversation coming from the other side in the boudoir."

The offer surprised Judith. "I'm a virtual stranger. I'm not sure I should listen in on such a private matter."

Beth was solemn. "If Marie had come, she'd be in this closet with me. Four ears are better than two. Moira needs any help she can get."

Judith dismissed her qualms. There was no doubt in her mind that she wanted to eavesdrop. The only thing that would be worse, she told herself, was if she were an interloper who was deaf. She studied the capacious closet, which was almost as big as her bedroom at Hillside Manor. Moira's extensive wardrobe hung in zippered bags in two long rows. Three chests contained drawers labeled sweaters, shirts, blouses, and tops. There were ten stacks of shoe boxes, plastic containers marked for accessories, and two more chests for lingerie. The faint smell of mothballs mingled with the scent of jasmine.

Beth noticed Judith's reaction and laughed softly. "These are her transitional winter-to-spring clothes. The rest are in storage, along with most of her furs, and the valuable jewelry is in a bank vault."

"How can she possibly wear all this?" Judith asked.

Beth shrugged. "Clothes are her security blanket. Love hasn't worked out nearly as well for her as Armani and Dolce & Gabbana." She beckoned to Judith. "Come. The vent's above the end of this rack."

The first words she heard were spoken by MacRae. "When did you receive this note?"

"Saturday, around noon," Moira said, though her voice was rather faint. "That is, my husband left it for me then. I wasn't home. I didn't get back until much later."

"Did Mr. Gibbs specify what time he wanted you to meet him at the beach?" MacRae asked.

"Not exactly." Moira paused. "Please, may I see if my baby's awake from his nap? Could you summon his governess?"

MacRae's next words were inaudible. Judith guessed that he had turned away to speak to Ogilvie. "This won't take long, Mrs. Gibbs," he said in a louder voice. "Did your husband mention a time frame?"

"Well . . . that afternoon. Harry loved the beach. He loved to swim. He loved the outdoors. Hunting, fishing, hiking, climbing, all kinds of outdoor activities. Most of them I enjoyed, too. But I was otherwise engaged on Saturday, you see."

"I gather you hadn't been living together at the time of his death," MacRae noted, and paused, apparently waiting for Moira's response.

"A temporary arrangement," she replied after a few seconds had passed. "Due to his recent illness. He had very bad flu, and I felt it unwise to risk him contaminating our baby. A virus can be dangerous to a wee one. Are you sure the governess will bring Jamie to me?"

"All in good time," MacRae assured her. "Are you positive you destroyed the note your husband left for you?"

"Of course. I told you that during our previous interview. Why would I keep it?"

MacRae didn't answer. "Earlier," he went on, "you insisted that your husband had no enemies. Yet we've learned since that he was not on good terms with several of the other executives at Blackwell, including your own brother."

"Half brother," Moira corrected. "His last name is Blackwell only because my father insisted upon it. Jimmy's mother wasn't married to my father. Ever."

Judith heard a door open. "Euphemia," Moira said, "give the baby to me. My governess, Euphemia Beaton."

"Your bairn is handsome," MacRae remarked.

"Yes," Moira agreed. "You must go now. It's time for his midday feeding. I prefer giving the bottle to him myself. I'm sure you understand. Thank you, Euphemia."

Beth pursed her lips. Judith moved to fend off a leg cramp.

"Very well." MacRae's voice sounded strained. "We'll speak again, after the inquest Tuesday."

"Oh—yes, of course." Moira sounded vague.

Beth gestured for Judith to move out of the closet. "My God," Beth said when they reached the sitting room, "what's going on with Moira?"

"You know her," Judith said. "I don't."

Beth threw up her hands. "I shouldn't be talking about all this, but I'm terribly upset. Moira can be the most charming, generous, kindest woman on earth, but she has no common sense. She's doesn't know how to protect herself from predators. I don't give bloody all about Harry. That marriage was a disaster. He married her for money and the power he hoped to get through Blackwell Petroleum."

Judith nodded sympathetically. "Moira has no head for business?"

"She's intelligent, but she's young," Beth said, standing near the door to the boudoir and keeping her voice down. "She likes to party. But she also likes being the nominal head of Blackwell. In time, she could—"

The door opened and the two policemen entered the sitting room.

"Mrs. Gibbs is feeding her baby," MacRae said, and looked questioningly at Beth. "She and the governess need quiet time."

"I'll wait here," Beth said, looking slightly truculent.

"Certainly." MacRae started across the room but turned around. "Mrs. Flynn, may I speak to you for a moment in the hall?"

Surprised, Judith left with MacRae and Ogilvie. "I realize," she said when they were in the hallway, "that I'm a stranger, but—"

MacRae held up a hand. "No need for explanations. Do you have your passport with you?"

Judith felt alarmed. "I left it at Grimloch. I can get it if you—"

"No need. The question was a ruse." MacRae moved a few steps away from Moira's suite but spoke softly. "You know that in this era of terrorism the authorities do background checks on foreign visitors."

"Of course," Judith said, her apprehension mounting.

"Thus," MacRae continued, "we learned who you really are."

Judith's eyes widened. "You did?"

MacRae smiled. "Indeed. Even though you appear to be on vacation, we'd appreciate any help you can give us. This case may have international implications, as I'm sure you realize."

"Oh. Yes. Oil." Judith nodded several times.

"Meanwhile," MacRae said, "just be the keen observer that's made your reputation. Your people skills are, we understand, outstanding."

"Thank you," Judith said, relieved. "I had no idea how thorough these background checks could be."

MacRae chuckled and winked. "Perfect. The American Innocent Abroad." He saluted Judith and turned toward the central staircase.

Judith watched him start down the curving stairs with Ogilvie bringing up the rear. But MacRae stopped after a few steps and reached for his cell phone. He listened for at least a full minute. Judith saw him say something into the phone and signal to her. He rang off, spoke to Ogilvie, and came back up the stairs.

"That was the autopsy report," MacRae said barely above a whisper. "The findings won't be released until the inquest. Harry Gibbs was smothered, probably while unconscious. There was no sign of a struggle, you see, but cocaine was found in his system along with a large quantity of alcohol. He'd probably passed out before his killer arrived. You must act surprised when you hear the official pronouncement," the detective added solemnly. "The inquest is at ten Tuesday in the Women's Institute." He saluted Judith and went down the stairs.

Judith remained in the hallway until the policemen disappeared. Apparently the security agents had checked her out on the Internet and discovered the FATSO site created by admirers of her crime solving. The acronym was actually FASTO, for Female

Amateur Sleuth Tracking Offenders, but had been cor-
rupted into the less flattering nickname, presumably
because it was easier to remember.

Just as Judith was going back into Moira's suite, she
saw Elise come out of a room farther down the hall.
The maid was scowling and wagging a bony finger.

"You must not go in," Elise said with her slight
French accent. "Madame needs rest. Mrs. Fordyce
must also leave. I shall tell her now."

"But I left my purse in the sitting room," Judith
protested.

"I shall retrieve it." Elise's dark eyes hardened. Her
close-cropped black hair looked dyed and her eyebrows were haphazardly penciled in. "You think I am
a thief?"

"Certainly not," Judith said. "I must say goodbye to
Mrs. Gibbs."

"*Non,*" Elise declared, shaking her head. "I shall
tell her for you."

"Fine," Judith snapped. She remained in the hall,
looking over the balcony above the spacious entry area
with its double circular staircases, graceful columns,
and Greek statuary. All seemed calm and quiet. That
was, Judith thought, deceptive. Hollywood was not
a peaceful house. She sensed unhappiness, perhaps
handed down through generations.

The silence was broken by the sound of a slamming door. An angry Beth Fordyce was marching out of Moira's suite. "The nerve!" she exclaimed. "Elise ordered me out! And Moira just lay there with the baby and didn't say a word! Where's her pluck?"

"I got the heave-ho, too," Judith said. "But you're an old friend."

"I thought I was," Beth muttered. "Oh—here's your handbag. Elise practically threw it at me. We might as well go see Mummy."

"Thanks," Judith said, juggling the purse, which seemed unusually heavy. Or maybe she was unusually tired. The vacation had become more stressful than restful.

Judith and Beth got only halfway downstairs when they heard a commotion coming from outside of the house.

"The press?" Judith suggested. "I thought the police were going to make them go away."

Beth stopped with her hand on the gilded balustrade. "It sounds like Morton and . . . Patrick?"

Fergus was moving across the entry hall at a faster pace than usual. He stopped at the door, his ear pressed against the wood.

Beth continued downstairs; Judith followed.

"What's going on out there?" Beth demanded.

Fergus looked down his long nose at Beth. "A dispute, I believe, possibly involving violence."

"Oh, for—!" Pushing Fergus aside, Beth dashed to the door. The startled butler kept his balance by grasping the legs of a marble Artemis.

As Beth opened the door, Judith drew closer. To her astonishment, she saw Patrick Cameron take a swing at Jocko Morton, knocking the heavyset man onto the steps. Seumas Bell jumped on Patrick's back, trying to restrain him. Morton squealed like a pig when Patrick landed a second and third blow.

"Stop!" Beth screamed. "You'll kill each other!"

Her words went unheeded. All three men were rolling around on the gravel drive. Beth shouted at Fergus, "Get a gun! Now!"

"Which gun, madam?"

"One that's loaded, you cretin! Hurry!"

Judith stood in the doorway, watching in horror as Seumas Bell broke free from the writhing pile and yanked a heavy urn off of a pedestal. He was about to bring it down on Patrick's skull when Judith used all her might to throw her purse at him. By a stroke of luck it hit Seumas in the temple, momentarily stunning him. He reeled slightly and looked to see where the missile had come from.

"Who are you?" he asked, blinking several times.

"I'm a peacemaker!" Judith shouted as Patrick jumped up from an apparently unconscious Jocko and decked Seumas, who dropped the urn before falling backwards into the driveway. The urn smashed, strewing chards of concrete and soil onto Jocko's elevator shoes.

Fergus appeared on the porch holding what looked to Judith like a blunderbuss. "Will this do?" he asked Beth.

"Oh, good Lord!" Beth cried. "There must two dozen guns in this house and you bring me a freaking musket? Did you call the police?"

"No coppers!" Patrick looked defiant as he smoothed his dark red hair and rubbed his knuckles. "These two are out of it. I'm going to see Moira." He jumped over Jocko and took the stairs two at a time.

Seumas was coming to, moaning and rolling around in the driveway, getting gravel all over his dark pin-stripe suit. Jocko had opened his eyes, but was staring straight up into the noonday sun.

"Turn out that bloody light," he mumbled. "Pull the curtains. Douse the glim."

For the first time, Judith noticed the red BMW sports car she'd seen on her previous visit. Directly behind it was Jocko Morton's Jaguar sedan. She guessed that Jocko and Seumas had followed Patrick to Hollywood House.

"I think," Beth said calmly, "that you should both leave. I presume at least one of you is able to drive."

"No," Morton said, poking at various body parts. "I'm injured."

"I'll drive," Seumas said, standing up and brushing the gravel from his suit. "But Patrick hasn't heard the last of this."

"I hope I have," Beth said sternly. "Don't you dare get me or Philip mixed up in your squalid affairs."

"Our squalid affairs?" Seumas was indignant. "I'm an attorney, and a highly ethical man."

"How odd," Beth said blithely. "How can you possibly be both?"

"You're on their side," Seumas sneered. "Don't pretend that you and Philip haven't got your own ax to grind. And never try to tell me that the bairn is Harry's! We all know who sired the little bastard!"

Beth kept her lips closed tightly, but her lively eyes shot arrows at Seumas as he helped get Jocko to his feet. Fergus was still holding the musket, cocking the weapon as the two men staggered to the Jaguar.

"Shall I fire now?" he inquired of Beth.

Beth flipped a thick strand of black hair over her shoulder. "Why not? Shoot over their heads, just to hurry them along."

The butler fumbled with the musket. "Wait!" Judith cried. She hurried to retrieve her purse, backtracked inside the house, and put her fingers in her ears. Nothing happened.

"I believe it's jammed," Fergus said dolefully as Morton flopped inside the Jag.

"It probably has no balls," Beth said in a disgusted voice. "There seems to be a serious lack of them around here."

Fergus coughed softly. "Beg pardon, ma'am?"

Beth sighed and turned to Judith. "We may as well go as soon as those two idiots are out of here."

"Why were they fighting?" Judith asked.

Beth grimaced. "Business? Moira?" She shook her head. "I don't know. Phil and I've been out of the country. Moira and Marie and I email each other when we're not here, but it's usually girl talk—mainly about Moira's baby, which, frankly, gets boring since Marie and I don't have children yet. Damn, why doesn't Seamus move that car?"

"Why has Morton been in Greece?" Judith asked.

"His health," replied Beth. "Or so he claimed. He needed better weather. But Will told Marie that Jocko was healthy as a horse, and his leave of absence was to avoid some business problems."

Judith recalled the get-together at the cottage by the sea but wondered how much she should reveal. "I got the impression that these Blackwell executives were fairly tight."

Beth stared at her. "You did? Don't believe it. The one thing they agreed on lately is that the pup, Harry, was a huge pain in the arse."

At last Seumas started the Jag and drove out through the open gates at an accelerated speed.

"Maybe," Beth said, "he'll get both of them killed." She put a hand to her mouth. "I shouldn't say that, not after what happened to Davey."

Driving away from Hollywood House, Judith posed a question. "Was Davey's accident around here?"

Beth nodded. "Up ahead there's a turnoff to the coast road. About a kilometer east is a wicked curve where it happened. Davey liked speed. He had a reckless side, but the official ruling was faulty brakes."

"Wasn't it a new car?"

Beth nodded. "A Lamborghini Diablo. Aptly named, it seems. It crashed onto the rocks below, and was horribly mangled. Of course Davey was . . . " She grimaced. "Moira was too ill to attend the funeral."

The Daimler sped past the turnoff to St. Fergna. "Did I say that when I met Moira she was putting flowers on his grave?" Judith asked.

"Oh?" Beth smiled faintly. "Moira was very fond of Davey. She relied increasingly on him."

"For business decisions," Judith asked, "or . . . emotionally?"

Beth sighed. "Both, I suppose. Moira and Harry were already having problems. After they married, Harry turned into a completely different person. Marie and I felt as if he'd been putting on an act all the time they were going together. He was incredibly rude to Moira even in public. God only knows how badly he behaved in private. It's a wonder she didn't . . . " Beth stopped speaking as her cheeks turned pink.

"Kill him?" Judith finished for her.

Beth slowed down to take a sharp curve. "You know I don't mean that literally."

"Of course not." But Judith knew from previous experience that the spouse was always the prime suspect when it came to murder.

14

The house Kate Gunn had confiscated from her late husband's mistress was a modern, curving structure of glass and stucco set high above the sands. The landscaping looked almost tropical, with tall fronds, exotic grasses, and even a couple of palm trees.

"California style?" Judith said in surprise.

Beth laughed. "You'd be surprised—parts of this area have a very mild climate, due to the land formation and the ocean currents."

Judith nodded. "We have a place like that in our own state on the Northwest Coast. It's called the Sun Belt."

"Exactly," Beth agreed. She paused at the foot of a winding stone stairway. "Let's hear the latest news from Mummy's astrologer."

The double doors were made of beveled glass decorated with intersecting mahogany arcs. Judith and Beth were greeted by a middle-aged woman wearing what Judith thought was a very bad red wig.

"Come in, Miss Beth," she said with a deferential nod. "Mrs. Gunn has a guest in the sunroom, but I'll tell her you're here with . . . ?" She looked questioningly at Judith.

"Hello, Una. This is Mrs. Flynn," Beth said. "Who is Mummy entertaining? It can't be the Wizard of Oz."

"Now, now, Miss Beth," Una said, though her blue eyes twinkled, "you mustn't be unkind about Master Ross Wass. He's a great comfort to your mother. In any case, he won't be here until evening."

Upon entering the sunroom, Judith felt as if she were walking into a jungle. Hibiscus, aphelandra, anthurium, dieffenbachia, philodendron, various ferns, and even orchids were everywhere, some growing from floor to ceiling. The east wall was all glass, and the high humidity as well as the temperature hit Judith like a blast of steam. There was so much foliage, in fact, that Judith couldn't see any sign of Mrs. Gunn.

"Sorry about the heat," Beth murmured after Una had shown them in and departed. "Mummy's somewhere in here, probably between the frangipani and the Venus flytraps."

"Mummy" was sitting in a white wicker armchair. Her guest apparently was seated across from her, but was concealed from Judith's sight by the chair's high back.

"Beth!" Kate Gunn exclaimed. "I didn't know you were coming. How nice. Do sit." She peered at Judith. "Is that Mrs. . . . ?"

"Flynn," said a voice coming from the other chair. "Hi, coz." Renie grinned between the glossy leaves of a fiddle-leafed fig. "Kate and I are being all matey. Sit. You'll lose a pound a minute in this humidity."

Kate Gunn laughed. "Oh, Serena, you're such a tease!" She paused while Judith and Beth sat down on a love seat that matched the other chairs. "I had no idea," she said to Judith, "that your cousin has special powers."

"Ah . . . " Judith was tempted to say, "Neither did I," but suddenly recalled Renie's pretense at reading fireplace ashes a few months earlier in an attempt to elicit information from a murder suspect. "She's a sight, all right. I mean," Judith amended, "she has the sight."

Renie shrugged and made an attempt to look modest. "I couldn't help myself. I felt compelled to study the ashes in the grate at Grimloch and I saw that Kate was in trouble. I had Gibbs bring me over here on his motorcycle. Sure enough, Kate was in peril."

"Oh," Kate Gunn said, "it was incredible! Una, my housekeeper, had gone to the market and I was all alone. I looked outside about an hour ago, expecting Una to be back shortly, and I saw a witch! She was bent over my herb garden, sprinkling something on the coriander and dill. I pounded on the window, but she cackled and rushed off. Serena showed up not five minutes later. Imagine!"

Judith could imagine, though she wondered where her cousin had gotten the witch's costume. "How fortuitous," she murmured.

"A witch?" Beth sounded skeptical. "Did you call the police?"

Mrs. Gunn frowned at her daughter. "Of course not! They never believe me. You know how they've acted in the past when I've had to summon them. They think I'm fanciful or just a nuisance."

Beth smiled wryly. "Well, you have had some odd complaints."

Mrs. Gunn looked indignant. "Nonsense! The midge attacks were frightful last summer. I wanted the police to spray those pesky insects before they clogged up my ears and nose. As for the deer that ate my plants, I had to threaten to poison them before the police would do anything. Not to mention the car that destroyed my nephrolepis fern—and on the feast day of Saint Thérèse of Lisieux, God's Little Flower! Too ironic! That driver should have been arrested for recklessness. If I'd been a heavy sleeper, I'd never have heard the impact and discovered how my poor fern got run over. I'd nurtured it from a small cutting." Her face softened as she looked at Renie. "As for Serena, we've made amends. She said that it was at our awkward meeting in the woolen shop where she sensed my aura and later realized I was in danger."

"Really," Beth said, looking benign. "Speaking of the occult, I don't suppose Master Wass has any insights into Harry's murder."

Mrs. Gunn grew serious. "Not precisely. He did mention a conspiracy, but had no specifics. The planets aren't properly aligned."

"So," Beth said, "you haven't talked to the police at all?"

Mrs. Gunn looked puzzled. "I told you, there was no need to call them. Serena arrived so quickly and quieted my fears."

Judith glimpsed her cousin's smug expression. "She has a calming effect on people." *When she isn't driving them to distraction,* Judith thought to herself, and was aware that she'd begun to perspire.

"I meant," Beth clarified, "have they asked you about Harry?"

"Why should they?" Mrs. Gunn responded, fingering the gold amulet with an odd circular design that she wore on a short chain around her neck. "I hardly knew him."

"Because," Beth explained, "Moira was your daughter-in-law when she was married to Frankie. I thought they might have asked if you knew anything about her second husband."

"I don't," Kate declared, sitting back in the chair and clasping her hands in her lap. "She certainly didn't consult me about remarrying."

"Hey, Kate," Renie said, "are there any more of those scones with your divine blackberry jam?" She licked her lips for emphasis.

"Of course!" Kate exclaimed. "Una can bring more and another pot of tea." She beamed a rather feral smile at Judith. "Your cousin has a wonderful appetite. I like people who enjoy their food." Turning slightly, she spoke into a large rubber plant. "Una—more tea, scones, and jam. Blackberry and Seville orange marmalade."

Una's voice came from somewhere among the plant's large green leaves. "Of course, ma'am. I'll be quick."

Kate's smile was self-satisfied. "I have speakers allowing me to communicate and monitor what goes on in every room. Very helpful."

"Modern technology is amazing," Judith said.

Kate agreed. "I have cameras as well. Much more convenient than the old methods one had to employ. So awkward drilling all those holes in walls when we lived in our previous house."

"Ah . . . " Beth said quickly, "maybe I should help Una with the tea."

"Of course," Kate said with a fond smile. "You're a good daughter. Children are a great comfort as we get older, are they not?"

Renie nodded. "But expensive."

Kate waved a hand. "Why should they not be? How better to spend one's money? Of course Beth married well. So did Frankie, though . . . " She paused and bit her lip. "He was a happy boy, more so than my other sons." She tapped her gold amulet. "His picture is in this locket. It's a talisman symbol, the Shri Yantra for luck, money, and success. The goddess of wealth, Mahalakshmi, resides in it."

"We saw Frankie's grave at the graveyard," Judith said as perspiration began to drip down her forehead and neck. "Your husband's, too. So many people buried there died young."

"Master Wass foretold my husband's death and the cause," Kate said quietly. "I begged Eanruig not to hunt that day, but he ignored me. He often did," she added bitterly. "A bullet went through his eye."

"How awful!" Judith exclaimed, reaching for her purse, which seemed even heavier in the overheated sunroom. She took out a handkerchief and wiped her brow. "Was he shot by a stranger?"

"No, alas," Kate replied. "His close friend, Gabe Montgomery, fired the gun by accident. It drove him mad. He's been institutionalized."

"A double tragedy," Judith murmured, taking another swipe at her forehead. "How many children do you have, Mrs. Gunn?"

"Do call me Kate." She smiled at Renie. "Serena does. I had difficulties conceiving in the early years of our marriage, but eventually I had ten. To my sorrow, Louie died young, even younger than Frankie. My twin daughters Joan and Vicki died at birth. I almost died, too." She looked away as her eyes glistened with tears. "That's why," she said softly, "I'd do anything for the ones who are still with me."

"Goodness," Judith gasped, "you've had your share of troubles."

"The world is a troubling place," Kate murmured. "We merely pass through. Perhaps you noticed my other children buried near Frankie."

"We didn't read all the markers," Judith admitted.

"I'll take flowers this week," Kate said, more to herself than to the cousins. "The past few days have distracted me." She looked up. "Ah—here's Beth. The silver service was made by Cellini. My mother was Italian."

"It's stunning," Judith said, admiring the intricate craftsmanship.

"Ah," Renie said weakly.

Judith realized that her cousin hadn't uttered a peep in the last few minutes. One look at Renie told Judith why: she was sweating profusely and wore a dazed expression. The sunroom was exacting a high price on Renie, but there had to be a reason for her sacrifice.

"Lovely," Judith declared as Beth poured tea and passed around the scones, butter, jam, and marmalade. "We've enjoyed your preserves at Grimloch. You must be very fond of your son-in-law Philip."

"He's an astute businessman," Kate said. "Isn't he, Beth?"

"Brilliant," Beth said, passing the sugar, cream, and lemon. "He's a workaholic. It's very hard to get him to take an occasional break. I warn him to slow down. He's reached a point in his life where he can well afford to enjoy himself. People aren't going to stop drinking whiskey."

Kate smirked. "Of course not. But your Philip needs to seek broader horizons. It's what tells him he's still alive."

"Mummy . . . " Beth gave her mother a warning look.

"Yes, yes," Kate said, holding up a hand. "I'll be quiet."

"You must show our guests some of your orchids before we go," Beth said. "I should be getting back to Grimloch with Mrs. Flynn and Mrs. Jones."

"Of course," Kate agreed, getting up. "Bear in mind, orchids don't all bloom at the same time. There are basically two types . . ."

Holding their teacups, Judith and Renie followed Kate in a daze of heat and humidity. It was difficult to focus on the exotic blooms, despite their beauty. Ten minutes later, Judith felt as if she might pass out. Fortunately, Beth came to the rescue.

"Sorry about the tropical atmosphere," she said after they got in the Daimler. "Mummy's circulation is poor, so she doesn't notice it, and I've spent so much time in Spain that I can tolerate it for a short while."

"Your mother's interesting," Judith said. "She's serious about the astrology thing, I gather."

"Very," Beth replied. "She got into it early on, when she was trying to get pregnant. I'll admit some of the astrologers' predictions have been rather uncanny."

"I noticed," Judith said, "you didn't mention the dustup at Hollywood House."

"What dustup?" Renie asked, still fanning herself with her hand.

"Later," Judith murmured.

"Just as well I didn't say anything about it," Beth said, slowing for the turn to St. Fergna. "Mummy loves conflict. You'd have been in for endless speculation if I'd brought the subject up."

"I see," Judith said, though it occurred to her that Kate's opinions might be interesting. "Beth, could you drop us off in the village? We have to change our money. We'll call Gibbs later to collect us."

"He should have his car back by midafternoon," Beth said. "There's the bank, just up ahead."

"Great," Judith said as Beth pulled into the car park. "Will you be around for dinner this evening?"

"I don't know," Beth replied, "it's up to—" She was interrupted by a cell phone's ring. "That's mine. Go ahead, I should answer."

Renie got out of the backseat, but Judith was still struggling with her heavy purse when she heard Beth let out a gasp.

"That's daft!" she exclaimed. "What could Chuckie possibly know?"

Judith waited.

"I don't believe it," Beth declared. "He wants attention. I'll be there shortly." She rang off and looked at

Judith. "That was Phil. Chuckie's been sulking all day, so Phil finally tried to make up after their row yesterday. But that wasn't why Chuckie was upset. The police haven't interviewed him, and he wants to tell them he knows who killed Harry."

What took so long?" Renie asked as Judith joined her by the bank entrance. "I thought you'd sweated so much you got glued to the seat."

"I would've," Judith replied, "if Beth hadn't turned on the AC. Let's go to the bank and then have lunch. It's been quite a morning. Beth just heard from Philip saying that Chuckie knows who murdered Harry."

Renie stopped on the cobblestones that led into the bank. "Who?"

Judith shrugged. "I don't think Philip knows. Chuckie wants to tell the police. Of course he may be fantasizing."

Renie frowned. "I hope he tells what he knows to the right people."

Judith nodded. "Yes. Otherwise he could put himself in danger."

The cousins went into the bank. Neither knew exactly what to do when it was their turn in the short queue, but the clerk with the shaved head and goatee was patient and helpful. Twenty minutes later, Judith and Renie found a pub off the alley behind the bank. The Rood & Mitre was much quieter and more pleasant than the Yew and Eye.

At almost one o'clock, the pub was busy with customers. The decor was minimal but tasteful, mainly pen-and-ink drawings of local sights, including the castle. The cousins each ordered a glass of ale.

"No Old Engine Oil here," Renie remarked. "I'm going to try the scampi and chips. They come with a salad."

"I'm not very hungry after eating Kate's scone," Judith said. "I'll get a prawn cocktail and a small salad." She put the menu aside. "Tell me what brought you to Kate's house."

"Boredom," Renie replied. "Once I was awake, I realized there wasn't much to do at the castle, and I didn't want to run into Chuckie. Thus I was inspired to tackle Kate Gunn by using my special powers."

"Dressed as a witch?" Judith said with a wry smile.

"Easy," Renie replied. "I borrowed your cape and cackled a lot." She hoisted the shopping bag she'd brought with her. "Your cape's safe, except for some salt sprinklings. I stashed it by her front steps for easy retrieval. I poured the salt on the herb garden while uttering strange incantations that were actually the Notre Dame fight song."

Judith shook her head in disbelief. "And she fell for it."

"Sure," Renie said. "She's credulous enough to believe in astrology. I figured she'd bite like a cat gobbling a canary."

"Some bright people take astrology seriously," Judith pointed out.

"Oh, I know," Renie explained, "but I had a feeling—not from my so-called special powers, but more from my gut—that Kate's superstitious."

"So what did you learn before I arrived? Or were you too busy filling your face with scones and jam?"

"I didn't learn as much as I'd have liked," Renie admitted. "She did talk more about Moira. I got the impression she appreciated Moira's concern and affection for Frankie, but that mother-in-law and daughter-in-law weren't close. When I mentioned we'd met Moira putting roses on Davey Piazza's grave, Mrs. Gunn made a crack about Moira remembering her assistant with more fondness than she had for her first husband."

Judith recalled that there weren't any flowers where Frankie was buried. "He's in the family plot with all those dead children and their father. Maybe Moira lets Kate take care of it."

"Anyway," Renie said, "my theory got shot all to hell."

"What theory?" Judith asked.

"That Kate would do anything for her children—and even an ex-daughter-in-law," Renie explained. "Especially if she wanted to marry Moira off to another one of her eligible sons."

Judith grimaced. "You mean do anything like . . . murder?"

"I think Kate can be devious," Renie said as a lad with shaggy magenta hair arrived to take their lunch order.

"Did you deduce that aspect of her character from the aura you sensed?" Judith inquired with a smirk.

"I deduced it from her spying devices around the house," Renie replied. "Didn't that set off some alarms in your brain?"

"Well . . . yes," Judith replied. "I considered her a control freak."

"It's no wonder her other children don't live at home," Renie noted. "Two are at university, but the older three either live in the Glasgow family home or are on their own. Who'd want Mummy spying on them?"

"True." Judith sipped her dark ale. It was quite bitter, but she'd drink it down. The half hour in the sunroom seemed to have dehydrated her. "Let me tell you what happened at Hollywood House."

"I'm agog," Renie said. "Go for it."

The cousins were halfway through their meal before Judith finally finished. Renie was intrigued. "Wish I hadn't missed all that," she said. "Especially the part where you threw your purse at Seumas Bell."

"That reminds me," Judith said, "I must've overloaded my purse this morning. It feels like it weighs ten pounds."

"Mine does," Renie asserted. "I weighed it at the airport. Of course I still had a pint of Wild Turkey in it then."

"You would. I'm sure it was empty by the time we reached thirty thousand feet." She hauled her purse onto her lap. "When I travel, I tend to toss in things I might need during the—" She stopped as she felt something cold, hard, and unfamiliar. "There's a . . . box or . . . what is this?" She removed a round, footed silver case embossed with gold rose petals and leaves. "Where did this come from?"

Renie stared at the elegant box. "You stole it?"

"Don't be cute," Judith said, trying to open the case. "Honestly, I swear it wasn't in my purse when I left Grimloch this morning."

"Where did you leave your purse unattended?"

Judith was still struggling to unfasten the case. "Let me think . . . At Hollywood House. I left it in Moira's sitting room while I was talking to MacRae. Ah!" The clasp finally gave and the lid snapped open. To Judith's surprise, there were no glittering jewels inside the velvet-lined box. "It looks like a bunch of paper."

Renie put out a hand. "Let's see."

There were at least a half dozen sheets of paper stuffed inside. Judith handed three of them to Renie and kept the rest for herself.

"Emails," Renie said. "Who saves email printouts?"

Judith scanned the first two. "Welcome to the twenty-first century. These are love letters. That is, love emails."

Renie sighed. "There goes romance." She read through the pages Judith had given her. "You're right. No actual dates, headings, or to-and-from names. Very fragmentary," she noted between bites of scampi. "Sign-offs like 'Yours forever' and 'Always together.' Gack."

Judith's eyes widened as she read through the emails she'd kept. "Good Lord! This sounds compromising!" She glanced around the pub to see if anyone was paying attention to the cousins. The other customers seemed involved with their own conversations and meals. Judith lowered her voice anyway. "Listen to this—'Darling— It won't be long now. I'm counting the hours until we're together. Just remember, once my problem is solved, nothing stands in our way. All my love goes with you.' What does that sound like?"

Renie scratched her head. "Well . . . I realize you're putting it in context. It could be Moira, writing to Patrick."

Judith regarded Renie with skepticism. "The only place these emails could've gotten into my purse was at Hollywood House. I've seen Moira's maid. I know you can't always go by looks, but she's not the romantic type. And you've met Fergus. He doesn't cut a dashing figure, either."

"Right." Renie looked glum. "These emails look bad for Moira and—I assume—Patrick. Here's another one. 'I'm making an early night of it and going to bed. Wish you were with me. The sun is setting, but it always shines when we're together.' And how about this? 'Your days are so full and my arms are so empty. I kiss the sprig of heather you gave me, knowing that though it is the last of the season and will wither and fade, our love will not.' Double gack."

Judith shook her head. "It's a wonder we're not gagging on our food. But how did these emails end up in my purse?" She put her napkin on the table. "Let's call Gibbs to have him pick us up. I'm very curious about Chuckie."

Renie polished off the last of her chips. "I can use my cell phone. What are you going to do with those emails?"

"I should turn them over to MacRae along with the silver case. It may be an heirloom," Judith replied, "but I'd like to find out if my purse was a convenient stash or I'm being used." She signaled to their server to bring the bill.

Renie had called Gibbs to tell him where they were. "Shall we meet you on the High Street?" she asked.

Judith waited for Renie to speak again. Their server nodded, and apparently went to fetch the bill.

"Okay," Renie said into the phone. "We know where it is. See you there." She rang off. "He has to collect his car from the mechanic. We'll meet him at Archie Morton's garage. It's only a short walk from here off the beach road."

Five minutes later, the cousins were walking down the High Street. Fluffy clouds flitted across the sun as a fitful breeze blew off of the sea. As they reached the end of the main thoroughfare, Judith glanced to her right at the cottage called The Hermitage.

"I don't see a car parked there," she said. "Patrick must own that red BMW sports model. Maybe he's still comforting Moira."

"I'm not convinced she needs comforting," Renie remarked. "On the other hand, define 'comfort.'"

As usual, traffic was sparse on the beach road. The gawkers who had ringed the cliff in the aftermath of Harry's death had gone to ground. So, apparently, had the media. The only people the cousins saw as they walked toward Morton's Auto Repair were two teenage boys, taking a breather from their bicycles and resting alongside the road.

"Gibbs isn't on the beach," Judith noted as they espied the garage's office entrance. "Maybe he's already here."

The only person in the small, cluttered office was the brawny man who resembled Jocko Morton. "Are you Archie?" Judith inquired politely.

"Aye." He frowned at her from under dark, bushy eyebrows. "What if I am? And ye are . . . ?"

"The Queen of Sheba," Renie snapped, apparently not taking a liking to the man's attitude. "We're here to meet Gibbs from Grimloch." She grinned and looked at Judith. "Hey—I like that. 'Gibbs from Grimloch.' What do you think, coz? Could this be 'Archie of Aberdeen'?"

Embarrassed, Judith stared at her shoes. "Ask him."

"Okay, Arch, ol' bud," Renie said, "where's Gibbs?"

"Gibbs isn't here," Archie replied, still frowning. "King Solomon's not here, either. Why don't you push off?"

"Why," Renie retorted, "don't you f—"

Judith swiftly put a hand over Renie's mouth. "Sorry, Mr. Morton. My cousin's . . . drunk." She winced as Renie bit her. "We'll wait outside."

"Good idea," Archie muttered.

Judith literally dragged Renie outside. "What got into you?" she demanded.

Renie's brown eyes spit fire. "I don't trust that guy. He's not a mechanic. He doesn't have dirt under his fingernails."

"Oh, for—" Judith held her head. "He owns the shop. He probably has mechanics working for him."

"He has pig eyes," Renie said. "Just like his brother Jocko."

"Forget it," Judith said. "You can't antagonize everyone in the village. You're damned lucky Kate Gunn forgave you."

"And vice versa," Renie asserted, looking mulish. "I wouldn't have bothered if I hadn't been bored and wanting to help you sleuth."

"I appreciate it." Judith moved toward the road and gazed out toward Grimloch. "Here comes Gibbs."

Renie was looking in the other direction. Judith followed her gaze. Around the corner from the small office was the repair area. Three men were working on two cars. A black Volvo sedan was up on a hoist; a green SUV had its hood raised. Five other vehicles including a gray vintage Morris saloon were parked behind a chain-link fence. Judith assumed the Morris belonged to Gibbs. A Doberman patrolled the area.

Three minutes later, Gibbs arrived, doffed his cap at the cousins, and went into the office. Five minutes passed. Renie was growing impatient. Judith passed the time by watching the mechanics, who appeared to be as diligent as they were good-natured. Although she couldn't make out the words, she could tell from their manner that they were ribbing each other as they worked.

"What's taking so long?" Renie demanded. "Does Gibbs have to work off the repair bill?"

"Here he comes," Judith said as Gibbs and Archie Morton headed for the chained-off area. "I suggest we stand by the road. I don't want you duking it out with Archie and causing another Ugly American scene."

Almost another five minutes passed before Gibbs got behind the wheel and drove out through a gate Archie had opened for him. The saloon stopped so the cousins could get in. Gibbs merely grunted a greeting. His lined face still showed the ravages of his grandson's death.

As they drove down the dirt track, Judith broke the silence. "Is Archie a good mechanic?" she asked.

Gibbs nodded. "The best. He's kin."

"My," Judith remarked, "there are lots of family links here."

"'Tis a village," Gibbs pointed out. "Little changes in St. Fergna."

"I guess not," Judith said.

"I'll let you off by the lift," Gibbs said. "I keep the car in the shed on the beach. But the shed be gone now, blown up wit' Harry's car."

Judith had forgotten about the wooden shed she'd seen on her first morning at Grimloch. She and Renie had been with Harry at the time. She shuddered in spite of herself. "Oh. Yes. We feel so awful about imposing on you and Mrs. Gibbs at such a time."

"Canna be helped," Gibbs said, slowing down as they neared the foot of the cliff. "Here ye be."

Judith and Renie got out and went straight to the lift. The diving birds roamed the shore just where the low tide was lapping at the sands. More clouds were gathering, but the air smelled fresh and salty.

The lift had already been summoned from above. "Someone must be using it," Judith said, craning her neck to see the cage. "It's coming."

The contraption made its usual rattle-rattle-bang noises as it descended. At ground level, Judith saw Chuckie grinning between the bars. He looked not unlike a chimp at the zoo.

"Hallooo!" Chuckie called. "You going up?"

"Yes," Judith said.

Chuckie shook his head. "Not with me." Still grinning, he poked the button and the lift began to ascend.

"Hey, twerp!" Renie called. "Come back here!"

The lift rose ten feet and stopped. It started again and went up another six feet. Judith could hear Chuckie laughing. At last, the cage came back to ground level.

"Hallooo!" Chuckie cried again. "Do you know the password?"

"It's 'I won't beat Chuckie to a pulp if he lets us in,'" Renie snapped.

"Close enough," Chuckie said, no longer grinning. "Hop in."

"Shouldn't we wait for Gibbs?" Judith said, stepping into the lift.

Chuckie shook his head. "He always tinkers with that old car of his. Fifty years he's had it. Must run on witchcraft." He punched the button to start the lift. "It seems Archie Morton's a warlock."

"I heard," Judith said over the creaking and clattering of cage and cables, "you want to talk to the police."

"Oh, I do." Chuckie smiled slyly. "I know a thing or two."

"You mustn't tell anyone but the detectives," Judith cautioned.

Chuckie didn't respond. His smile faded as he pushed another button. The lift stopped halfway up the cliff.

"Why did you do that?" Renie demanded.

"The view," Chuckie said. "See the waves? Gentle now, but March winds can churn them up to five times as tall as any mere man. Even a man as tall as Harry. See the sands. Tiny grains, each as wee as a flea. But together they ring the rocks and form the shore. Small things can become gigantic. Don't you agree?"

"Sure," Renie said. "I remember my cousin's first husband."

"Coz!" Judith shot Renie a dirty look. "Yes, Chuckie, I understand what you're saying. And the view is impressive. Could we go up now?"

Chuckie didn't seem to hear her. "Birds, dolphins, shellfish, all teeming with life. All those shipwrecks, flotsam and jetsam," he murmured. "Then—boom! Harry is flotsam and jetsam, gone forever."

The wind had suddenly picked up, blowing through the bars of the cage. Judith was getting nervous. "Very sad," she said quietly. "I really would like to go to my room. My purse is heavy."

"So's my shopping bag," Renie said, jiggling the big sack in which she'd put Judith's new cape. "Let's go, before I get really annoyed."

Chuckie scowled. "Don't you want to know who killed Harry?"

"As I mentioned," Judith said, "you mustn't confide in anyone but the police. You could put yourself at risk."

Chuckie hooted. "What do you know about murder?"

Judith didn't feel like telling Chuckie that she knew murder far too well. "If you're sure who killed Harry, you've a moral obligation to tell the police. Why didn't you speak up yesterday when they were at Grimloch?"

Chuckie started to pout. "I wasn't ready. I was hiding."

"Okay," Judith said reasonably. "Let's call them when we get inside the castle. If you could help the police, you'd be a real hero."

Chuckie stared down at his sneakers but said nothing.

The brief silence was broken by a weird yet familiar cry.

Judith looked all around. On a narrow rocky cliff she saw the great northern diver. His white breast puffed out as he uttered that chilling sound from his long, sharp beak.

Chuckie cringed and covered his face with his hands. "I hate that bird! He'll peck out my eyes!"

"Not if we get the hell out of here," Renie said, leaning across Chuckie's bowed back to poke the lift button. "It'd serve you right for stranding us on this damned cliff."

The cage clattered up to the castle level. Gratefully, Judith made a hasty exit with Renie right behind her. Chuckie remained inside, still bent over and covering his face.

"Come on," Judith urged, looking down the cliffside to see the bird fly off toward the beach. "You're safe."

Slowly, Chuckie stood up and dropped his hands to his sides. "If," he mumbled as he walked out of the lift, "I'd had some oranges, I could have thrown them at that awful creature. I like most birds. I watch them with my really special binoculars. But not that one. It's evil."

Judith walked toward the castle entrance just as a light rain began to fall. "Let's ask Mrs. Gibbs to make tea," she called over her shoulder.

"I hate tea," Chuckie said, kicking at some loose rocks along the edge of the walk. "You won't listen to me. I'm going to my special place."

"We'll listen," Judith said, stopping short of the guests' door.

But Chuckie moved away, hands in his pockets, head down.

Judith watched him go past the chapel. "Chuckie's going to the dungeon," she said, sounding worried. "I think that's a really bad idea."

15

When the cousins reached the guest quarters, they went into the Flynns' room where Renie hung the woolen cape in the wardrobe and Judith put the silver jewel case on the bed.

"Now," she said, "I'm calling the cops."

"About those emails?" Renie asked.

"No," she replied, digging out her cell phone. "About Chuckie. He may or may not know who killed Harry, but if he's bragging about it, he could be in danger." A moment later, she was connected to DCI MacRae.

"The wee laddie, eh?" MacRae said thoughtfully. "Is he credible?"

Judith hesitated. "Possibly not," she admitted, "but something occurred to me when we were in the castle lift. My cousin and I went down to the beach after the explosion. When we returned, the lift was up. It shouldn't have been since no one else mentioned using it. I wonder if the killer sought refuge in the castle after Harry's car blew up."

"Ah! We knew we could count on you to notice even the smallest shard of evidence. So this Chuckie lad may have seen that person?"

"He could have," Judith said, "or he might have witnessed something on the beach before the murder and the explosion. Which, do you think, came first?"

"It's difficult to tell," MacRae replied. "The explosion was probably meant to conceal how Harry Gibbs was murdered. However, something must have gone amiss with the killer's plan. The body was virtually unmarked, so we conclude that Harry wasn't in the car when the bomb went off but near a log close to the bank."

"Interesting," Judith remarked, glancing at Renie, who was perusing the emails. "I noticed some people farther up the beach earlier. Maybe someone came along and the killer was afraid of being spotted. Have any witnesses been found?"

"No one's come forward," MacRae said. "Let's see—it's going on three o'clock. Ogilvie and I are just finishing a late lunch in Inverness. If you think Chuckie

Fordyce may have some genuine information, we can come out to the castle before the tide comes in."

"Good," Judith said. "I really think Chuckie should speak with you, whether he actually knows anything or not. If he's bragging about his supposed knowledge, he might be courting disaster."

"Indeed. I'll see you shortly." MacRae hung up.

Renie looked up from the emails. "Well?"

Judith related everything that MacRae had told her. "Isn't it ironic?" she said in conclusion. "Harry was everything a young woman could want in appearance, but totally flawed inside. Chuckie is a physical and emotional wreck in a different way. Which is more tragic?"

"Do I really have to answer a dumb question like that?"

"No." Judith sighed. "Any luck figuring out those emails?"

"Not without names or Internet addresses attached," Renie said. "That's the weird part. Unless," she continued, rubbing her chin, "one of the parties wanted to save these missives but conceal the source. Do modern lovers go all soggy over emails? I find that odd."

"It's the way people communicate," Judith pointed out. "The handwritten or even typed letter is a rarity today."

"True," Renie allowed. "I suppose cave dwellers used to hang on to chunks of rock that their beloveds chiseled romantic notions on, like 'You're the hot sauce to my raw rhinoceros meat.'"

"Maybe." Judith scanned the emails once again. "There's nothing specific. That is, it's all about how much these two want to be together and what they must do to make that happen. It's not exactly a plan to knock off rivals, though I suppose it's implied."

Renie looked inquiringly at Judith. "Do we give these to MacRae?"

Judith grimaced. "Not yet. We don't know how or why they got into my purse. Our priority is Chuckie. The detectives should be here in a few minutes. Let's go down to the courtyard to meet them."

"Okay," Renie said, gathering up the emails and putting them back in the silver case. "By the way, didn't we have husbands when we arrived in Scotland? I seem to recall being with a couple of people who had deeper voices than we do."

Judith frowned. "I suppose they're so caught up in fishing they forgot we were here. Maybe it's just as well. I'm not sure I want Joe to find out we're involved in another murder."

"Wouldn't Hugh MacGowan have been informed by now?"

"Maybe not if he's on vacation. Let's go." Judith went to the door. "I wonder what MacRae and Ogilvie have been doing in Inverness besides eating lunch?"

"Checking out Blackwell's headquarters?" Renie suggested.

"Possibly." Judith moved carefully down the winding staircase. As she reached the bottom, she heard voices. "MacRae here already?" she said over her shoulder to Renie.

But it was Will Fleming, talking to Mrs. Gibbs. "So where is Philip?" he asked. "His car's gone."

"The Master's wife brought it back an hour or so ago," Mrs. Gibbs replied. "He went rushing out not long after."

"You don't know where?" Will inquired in his smooth, soft voice.

"Nae," Mrs. Gibbs insisted with a resolute shake of her head.

Will saw the cousins and smiled faintly. "Good afternoon, ladies. Have you seen Mrs. Fordyce in the past half hour or so?"

"No," Judith replied. "Beth dropped us off a little after twelve."

Mrs. Gibbs started to walk away. "I told ye," she murmured, "Master's lady likes to walk the beach, rain or shine." She kept going.

"Is there a problem?" Judith asked.

Will sighed. "There's very little going on that isn't a problem. The past few days have been chaos."

"How's Marie feeling?" Judith inquired. "Beth told us she was ill."

"Flu," Will replied. "The current strain lasts forty-eight hours."

"Harry's must have been severe," Judith remarked.

"Ah . . . " Will grimaced. "That was different. Moira was worried about the baby catching it. And Harry . . . well, Harry had complications."

Before Judith could inquire about the "complications," Beth came through the door with MacRae and Ogilvie right behind her. "Look who I found . . . Will?" she said in surprise. "What are you doing here?"

"Marie lost her . . . scarf. She thought it might be here somewhere. What's this about?" Will inquired, nodding at the detectives.

"Merely following up," MacRae said blandly.

Beth studied Will briefly. "You look as if you need a drink," she said. "Let's go to the family suite. Phil stashes his special malts there."

MacRae watched the couple go back out through the guest door. "Very deft," he said quietly. "For all her youth, the lovely Mrs. Fordyce is an accomplished executive's wife."

"She seems levelheaded, too," Judith said.

MacRae nodded. "Yes. Beth Fordyce is blessed with a variety of gifts, including common sense. Alas, that's not always the case with beautiful young women. Shall we go into the drawing room?"

Judith hesitated. "You don't think Beth might know where to find Chuckie? She's his stepmother and seems to know how to handle him."

"All in good time," MacRae said with a wave of the hand, indicating that Judith and Renie should precede him down the drafty passageway.

Judith didn't budge. "No," she said, the harshness of her tone surprising her as well as the others. "You have to find him now."

MacRae's thick eyebrows lifted in surprise. "Well!" He turned to Ogilvie. "See if Mrs. Fordyce—or Mrs. Gibbs—knows the wee laddie's whereabouts."

"He was headed for the dungeon when we saw him," Judith said.

"I see." MacRae frowned as Ogilvie nodded and went off on his search. "This Chuckie is an odd one."

"Yes," Judith agreed as they walked along the passageway. "He has both physical and emotional problems."

"Intelligent?" MacRae asked, opening the door for the cousins.

"I think so," Judith replied, "in an offbeat kind of way."

"Cunning is more like it," Renie put in, sitting on one of the settees and kicking off her shoes. "Mrs. Gibbs mentioned that Chuckie will someday take over the distillery from his father. That struck us as unlikely."

MacRae settled into one of the bergère chairs. "Yet Fordyce, I'm told, is a dynast at heart. Keep the business in the family. Still, he's fairly young, and perhaps hopes for children by his present wife."

"Speaking of business," Renie said, wearing what her cousin called her professional boardroom face, "what shape is Blackwell Petroleum in? We heard Jocko Morton went off to Greece to avoid some kind of probe."

"Yes," MacRae replied. "An internal audit, I believe, initiated by Will Fleming, the company's financial officer. Nothing came of it, however, and Morton is back, as you well know." He looked directly at Judith, who had sat down next to Renie. "I understand there was a rumpus at Hollywood House this morning."

"I'm afraid so," Judith said. "Did someone contact the police?"

"An anonymous tip," MacRae said. "By the time a constable arrived, everything was peaceful. The servants insisted it must be a mistake. Your version would be different, I imagine."

Judith nodded, and gave her account of the fight between Patrick Cameron and his two adversaries. "That's another reason I assume all isn't running smoothly at Blackwell. Although," she continued, "last night my cousin and I saw Will, Morton, and Bell go into the cottage called The Hermitage."

MacRae nodded. "That's what you might call Patrick Cameron's bachelor pad before he married Jeannie."

"Not a happy marriage, perhaps?" Judith suggested.

"There are rumors," MacRae conceded. "Gossip is a natural hobby in villages. I grew up in Edinburgh, so I'm not attuned to these small places where everyone knows everyone else's business and may be a first cousin once removed as well."

Judith was puzzled. "Do you mean rumors or connections?"

"Both, actually," MacRae explained. "Blackwell's offices are in Inverness, yet several top executives live in or around St. Fergna."

"Typical of some American companies," Renie pointed out. "When people are transferred to a firm's headquarters, they often play follow-the-leader.

Someone finds a pleasant place to live that's within easy commuting distance of the job, and the next thing you know, all of the newcomers congregate there because the area's a known factor."

"Yes, I suppose that's true," MacRae agreed. "As for the rumors I spoke of, I referred to the ones about the Camerons. Several people have told us that the Camerons are quite happy together."

"He does seem rather intimate with Moira," Judith remarked. "Or maybe I'm reading something into it that's not the case."

"He's ambitious," MacRae said, "but most of the Blackwell executives are. Greedy, too."

"Did you know," Judith inquired, "that Jimmy has gone to Paris?"

MacRae grimaced. "We're not sure he got away. The Inverness police were notified to watch the airport. There are other ways to get to Paris, so the Sûreté has been notified. Taking flight would be very unwise on James Blackwell's part."

Judith leaned forward on the settee. "Is he a serious suspect?"

MacRae's face hardened. "They all are, don't you think?"

Judith couldn't disagree. "I appreciate your candor. So often I've been involved in situations where the local police withhold information."

"Not here, Mrs. Flynn," MacRae said with a warm smile. "We're more than willing to cooperate with someone of your stature."

"I'm flattered," Judith said as guilt pangs stabbed her conscience. *I should hand over those emails,* she thought. But still she hesitated. "Don't you think we should see if Ogilvie has found Chuckie?"

"Yes," MacRae said. "Which way would my sergeant have gone?"

"We only know the courtyard route to the other wing," Renie said, slipping into her shoes.

"That's fine." MacRae rose from the chair and went to the door, opening it for the cousins.

Mrs. Gibbs was in the passageway. "Did ye want tea?" she inquired of the detective.

"No, thank you."

"Have you seen Chuckie?" Judith asked Mrs. Gibbs.

She shook her head. "Not since lunch. If ye'll be wanting Gibbs's car, it won't be ready until late today or tomorrow."

"But," Judith said, "we came with him when he brought it back from the garage."

Mrs. Gibbs shook her head. "Gibbs found something else wrong. Fuss and fret, that's Gibbs. He's gone back to the car shop with Archie Morton. No wonder there's always something awry. That car is auld as the hills."

"We don't need transportation," Judith said. "Although we should have asked Archie Morton if he had a car for hire." She shot Renie an annoyed glance. "A shame we got sidetracked."

As usual, Renie looked unrepentant.

Mrs. Gibbs had been standing stoically, hands at her sides, eyes cast down. Suddenly she lurched forward and grabbed MacRae by the arms. "You will arrest our dear laddie's killer, won't you? Please! Justice must be done!"

"Of course!" MacRae gently disengaged himself from Mrs. Gibbs's grasp. "That's why we're here, to find your grandson's murderer."

Mrs. Gibbs looked stunned. "Do wealth and privilege keep ye from doing your duty? You must arrest Moira at once! Why must we always be the victims of an unjust world?"

Words were futile. Despite MacRae's insistence that there was no solid evidence against Moira Gibbs, Mrs. Gibbs remained adamant. Judith felt sorry for the old lady, who tore at her apron and sobbed. "Not fair!" she wailed, and stumbled down the passageway.

MacRae sadly shook his head. "Poor woman. She's convinced that we'd let Moira go free if we thought she'd murdered Harry. That's not true, of course. But so far we have nothing to go on in that direction. She was at a wedding in Inverness."

In the courtyard, clouds had drifted overhead and a drizzle began to fall. Judith felt as if the towers and battlements loomed above her like reminders of past dangers—and perhaps those to come.

"The dungeon is at the far end," Judith said. "It may be locked."

MacRae looked grim. "Not much use for locks in such a place."

Just as they approached the tower door Judith had seen Chuckie head for previously, Ogilvie came out onto the walkway from the Fordyces' apartments.

"Sir!" he called to his superior. "I can't find him." The young policeman ran down the walk, raincoat flapping behind him. "Mrs. Fordyce hasn't seen him. Mr. Fordyce isn't in."

"You tried the dungeon?" MacRae asked.

"First thing," Ogilvie answered. "Nothing. Just a barrel of dirty water. No point going down there. The dungeon must've been sunk deep into the rock. The room above is for storage with a trapdoor in the floor for the dungeon."

"Chuckie told me he goes there often," Judith said anxiously. "He mentioned a torture chamber, too."

MacRae nodded. "Showing off, perhaps."

Beth Fordyce and Will Fleming came out onto the walk. Will kissed Beth's cheek and moved briskly toward the castle entrance.

"The tide has turned," Beth called, coming to join the others. "Will has to hurry."

MacRae frowned. "Perhaps we should, too, if Gibbs isn't here. We could leave the skiff on the other side, though. Otherwise he might not be able to get back."

"Gibbs has boots," Beth said. "As long as the sea is fairly calm, he can wade to the castle up to his knees." She brushed raindrops from her face. "You still haven't found Chuckie?"

MacRae shook his head. "Perhaps he doesn't want to be found."

"Very likely," Beth said, but she looked worried. "He rarely leaves the castle. He's got to be somewhere. I wish Philip would get back. He might know where Chuckie's hiding."

MacRae looked up, down, and all around the castle precincts surrounding the courtyard. "I should think this place provides all sorts of nooks and crannies for someone who wants to avoid company."

"Indeed," Beth said in a hollow voice.

But Judith feared that Chuckie had already been found—by a killer.

MacRae and Ogilvie left moments later, promising to send more men to make a thorough search of the castle. Beth seemed grateful.

"I always feel like a visitor at Grimloch, not the chatelaine," she confessed, leading the way into the private entrance. A sweep of her hand took in the entry area, which was decorated in a severe modern style with only a couple of abstract paintings and whitewashed walls. "Phil's second wife did this. She stripped it of all the old character. I'd like to change it, but I'm not sure how to go about it."

Renie looked at the space with her artistic eye. "Ghastly. What was she trying to prove?"

"That she was young and hip," Beth replied. "Wait until you see the sitting room," she continued, heading down a narrow corridor with black-and-white photographs of London street scenes on the walls. "Poor Phil. His first wife, Bella, died young from an aneurysm. His second wife, Rosemary, was much older, but very rich, and at the time, Phil was having financial problems. The dot-com crash, 9/11, the whole global downturn hurt business. His second wife died of cancer, only two years after they were married. Phil's always felt guilty about marrying Rosemary for money, which makes him touchy whenever I mention redecorating this part of the castle. I suppose it's his memorial to Rosemary, expressing gratitude for bailing him out of shark's waters."

They'd reached an open archway into what appeared to be the sitting room, all black and white with a couple of red accent pillows to break the monotony. "He's doing well now, I gather," Judith said as all three women sat down on the large U-shaped sofa.

"Yes," Beth replied, "but he got a bad scare when things turned sour. Phil talks about diversifying, maybe merging with Gunn Shipping."

Renie looked surprised. "Is your mother the sole owner?"

"Basically," Beth replied. "My father, like Phil and his father and grandfather before him, believed strongly in keeping their businesses in the family. After my father died, Frankie inherited the position of chief officer, but the will was set up so that Mummy would actually run the business until the eldest son turned thirty. Frankie never lived that long, and all my brothers are under the official age, so Mummy is still in charge. She has quite a good head for business."

Judith recalled overhearing the conversation between Philip and Kate Gunn. "There are no ties to Blackwell Petroleum through either Grimglen or the shipping company, are there?"

"No," Beth replied, "though I've heard Jimmy has been considering some changes. The North Sea is a difficult area for oil exploration and requires investing in very expensive equipment. Production peaked a few years back, but there's been a steady decline since.

All of Blackwell's operations are offshore, and quite far north. Jimmy, I understand, wants to merge with some of the other UK companies. Harry didn't like that idea and thought Blackwell should invest in some of the marginal fields and put money into better exploration and drilling equipment. Jimmy and a couple of the other top executives felt that the initial expense wouldn't be worth the return down the road."

"If," Judith said, "Jocko is the CEO, what exactly is Jimmy's title? He seems to wield quite a bit of power."

Beth smiled faintly. "Officially, he's their legal counsel, though most of the work is delegated to Seumas Bell. But because Moira doesn't always involve herself too deeply in the business, Jimmy acts as her proxy with the right to overrule everybody else, including Jocko. Or did, until Harry barged in and started to interfere."

"Harry was a thorn in many people's sides," Judith remarked.

Beth thought for a moment. "He was young and arrogant. That didn't sit well with the people who'd been with Blackwell a long time. I don't know much about the company. Moira," she added with a wry expression, "rarely discusses it."

Judith had intended to bring up the relationship between Moira and Patrick when what sounded like a pager went off. Beth went to the phone on a side table.

"Yes, Mrs. Gibbs?" she said into the receiver. "Of course. I'll meet them in the courtyard." She hung up and turned back to the cousins. "More police are arriving to search for Chuckie."

Judith and Renie had stood up. "Can we help?" Judith asked.

Beth shook her head. "Thanks, but no. All I can do is suggest some of Chuckie's hiding places. Oh, damn—I wish Phil were here!"

"Men go missing around here," Renie said. "Ours are AWOL, too."

Beth nodded once. "Then they're the lucky ones, aren't they?"

It was three-thirty when the cousins returned to the Flynns' room. "Do you suppose," Renie asked wistfully, "Mrs. Gibbs is serving tea?"

"Good grief," Judith said in disgust, "you can't be hungry again."

"I will be in half an hour," Renie asserted. "I'm thinking ahead."

"Then stop it," Judith said. "Turn off your stomach and turn on your brain. What should I do with those blasted emails?"

Renie shrugged. "Béarnaise sauce might improve their flavor."

Judith shot her cousin a menacing glance. "I'm serious. Should I turn them over to the police?"

Renie brightened. "You think they have better recipes?"

"Knock it off!" Judith went to the bureau where she'd put the silver case. "I'm already frustrated. I'm getting cabin fever. I'd like to tour Speyside and Inverness and the glens and the lochs and do some of things regular tourists do."

"No you wouldn't," Renie said. "You're having a wonderful time trying to solve your latest murder. As a hobby, I suppose it beats stamp collecting and fantasy baseball."

"Shut up." Judith rummaged in the drawer, moving her new sweaters and wondering if the castle had a laundry for guests.

"Just think," Renie said, stretching out on the bed, "you get to go to a real inquest tomorrow. Sound like fun?"

"Coz," Judith said, "didn't I put the silver case in this drawer?"

Renie sat up. "Uh . . . I think so. I wasn't paying much attention."

"It's gone." Judith felt the color drain out of her face as she turned to stare at Renie. "Someone stole it."

Renie jumped off the bed. "That's crazy. Nobody knew you had it."

"Not true. Whoever put the case in my purse knew it."

"But," Renie protested, "that was at Hollywood House."

"So what?" Judith's shock was giving way to anger. "Those emails may be crucial to solving this homicide. Who's been here in the last hour since we got back?"

Renie ticked off the residents and guests. "Mr. and Mrs. Gibbs. Beth and maybe Philip. Will Fleming. Chuckie. The police." Renie shrugged. "We wouldn't necessarily know if someone else showed up."

"True," Judith agreed, sitting on the chest at the foot of the bed. "Now I've got to tell MacRae about the theft—and try to explain why I didn't turn the blasted emails over to him in the first place. Toss me my cell phone. My purse is on the bed. And don't touch anything in this room in case there are fingerprints."

Renie flipped the phone to Judith, who trapped it between her knees. "You think I'm some kind of amateur at this crime stuff?"

Ogilvie answered. Judith phrased her words carefully. "Something has been stolen from my guest room, Sergeant. Could the policemen who are looking for Chuckie check for prints when they get done?"

"Well?" Renie said after Judith rang off.

"He'll get hold of the cops before they leave," Judith said. "We don't have anything worth stealing, which is why I didn't lock the door."

Renie nodded faintly. Judith sat quietly on the chest, watching the pale light cast lengthening shadows across the floor. "It's officially spring," she said at last. "The seasons have changed since we got here."

"A lot has changed," Renie pointed out.

Judith shook her head. "It usually does when we go anywhere. Sometimes I feel like the harbinger of death."

"Don't. You think just because you showed up, somebody took that as a cue to murder Harry Gibbs?" Renie held up a hand to keep Judith from talking. "Don't say it. If you really believed that, you'd think you were the center of the universe. That's not the real you."

Judith didn't argue. "Let's find out how we get from this part of the castle to the other part without crossing the courtyard. We'll take the elevator at the other end of the hall and ask Mrs. Gibbs. I can't figure it out from the castle diagram because they show only the guest section and the rest is marked private or refers to structural features. Even I know a rampart when I see one."

"What if the cops show up in your room?" Renie asked.

"I'll leave a note, along with my cell number. Let's go."

"Tea?" Renie said hopefully.

Writing a brief message for the police, Judith ignored her cousin. "Let's go," she repeated, putting the slip of paper on the dresser mirror.

Looking disappointed, Renie followed in silence. The elevator was a smaller version of the cage on the cliff. It could accommodate two people, or perhaps just one and a service cart. The conveyance made its own strange noises, creaking and squeaking down to the ground floor.

"The kitchen and the pantry are beyond that door," Judith said as they exited the lift. "If you ask nicely, Mrs. Gibbs will give you a biscuit."

"It better be shortbread," Renie grumbled.

Mrs. Gibbs was stirring a big soup pot. "No tea today," she said when the cousins entered the kitchen. "I couldn't bake because the oven broke. Gibbs still isn't back to fix it. Dinner at eight."

"We understand," Judith said. "Excuse us, Mrs. Gibbs. How can we get to the private quarters without crossing the courtyard?"

Mrs. Gibbs brushed a strand of gray hair from her forehead. "Back the way you came, then through the door to the right of the lift."

"Thanks," Judith said. "By the way, have your son and his wife been contacted yet?"

Mrs. Gibbs shook her head. "They'll never find out what's happened to their poor laddie until they get back from the jungle and into civilized parts. That's the way they are. It canna be helped."

"Are their extensive travels work-related?" Judith asked.

Mrs. Gibbs removed the ladle from the soup pot and turned down the heat. "South America, South America—that's all they know. It's a wonder the natives haven't put them in a pot and eaten them."

"How often do they come back here?" Judith inquired.

Mrs. Gibbs shrugged. "Once, sometimes twice a year. What good does it do? Promises, promises— that's all they ever make. A fine way to help us old folk! Banks and such want more than empty words!"

"That's so," Judith said as Gibbs entered the kitchen.

"Car's fixed," he said, and kept going through to the dining room.

Mrs. Gibbs went after him, waving the soup ladle. "Now fix the oven, mon!"

Judith and Renie followed Mrs. Gibbs's directions and found themselves in another narrow passageway where the only light came from a few orange bulbs that had been set in the ancient iron sconces. The three doors along the way had once led to the great hall, but, if Judith remembered correctly, that section was now the Gibbses' lodgings.

At the end of the passageway they found two doors. Judith opened the one on the left. A carpeted hallway with abstract paintings on the walls indicated that this was part of the Fordyce suite. The door to their right was harder to budge. Judith had to put her shoulder against it before it opened with a harsh, scraping sound.

"Where are we?" Renie asked, looking around a large room with two narrow window slits far above the cousins' heads.

Judith scanned the cartons, boxes, barrels, and chests that covered most of the floor and were stacked almost six feet high. The air felt dank and stale. "It must be the storage area." She grimaced at the mounds of various containers, many covered in dust and cobwebs. The room was so crowded that Judith found it oppressive, even overwhelming. "What else could it be?"

"I don't know," Renie replied as thunder rumbled close by. "I can't see anything."

Judith glared at her cousin. "Not funny, coz. Here's the trapdoor," she added, pointing to an area near a pile of wooden crates that were marked with black letters spelling LINENS.

"I'm not kidding," Renie asserted. "I can't see. My chronic corneal dystrophy has come back."

"Good grief!" She was familiar with Renie's problem, involving blurred vision and drooping eyelids. Sure enough, Renie's left eye was half closed. "What brought that on?" she asked in a shocked voice.

"All the gray," Renie replied. "Not to mention the stress from flying, whether I'm drunk or sober. I've got my medication and eye patches with me. I never go anywhere without them. I'll be fine," she said, and walked straight into a large wooden crate marked china. "Ooof! What's this?" she asked, bracing herself on the crate.

"You're in China," Judith replied. "Don't move while I look at this so-called dungeon." She used both hands to tug at the iron grip that was sunk into the trapdoor's well-worn wood. Fortunately, it lifted easily.

Judith stared into the opening. "No cobwebs, no dust, no dirt. It's clean, like it's used often."

"Chuckie?" Renie suggested, feeling her way toward Judith. "He goes into the dungeon to play with his imaginary rack."

"Maybe. I see the rain barrel." She paused. "Why would it be full of water? There shouldn't be any leaks down there."

"Seepage through the walls?"

"Not possible." Judith sniffed. "Can you smell that?"

"Let me move closer," Renie said. "Maybe my sense of smell is better now that I can't see. They say that when you lose . . . Aaack! I just touched something horrible covered with hair!"

"That's my head," Judith snapped. "Don't lean on me!"

"Sorry. Oops!"

"Now what?" Judith demanded, turning to look at Renie, who had stumbled and fallen on top of a carton cluttered with small objects.

"Don't worry about me," Renie snarled. "Now I'm blind *and* feeble." Awkwardly, she righted herself and dusted off her cashmere sweater. "Just carry on with—"

"Open the door."

The cousins both jumped.

"The same voice," Judith whispered.

"Almost the same message," Renie whispered back.

Judith looked around the room but saw no hiding places. All of the storage containers were piled flush against the walls.

"Open the door."

Renie shuddered. "Way too creepy. Let's get out of . . . Aaaaah! I feel something cold and clammy and dead! Help!"

"That would be my hand," Judith said through gritted teeth. "Stop touching me. Where's that voice coming from? It can't be in this hole."

"Who cares? I'm going." Renie tripped over Judith's foot and barely managed to stay upright. "Which way's the door?"

"You can't go without me," Judith retorted. "Shut up and listen." But the voice had gone silent. "It must mean that we should open the trapdoor."

"We already did. It's a ghost," Renie declared. "I don't care if it's giving hot racetrack tips."

"You don't believe in ghosts."

"I changed my mind."

"Bad timing for that." Judith pointed to the trap-door. "Now sniff."

"Medicinal," Renie said after a few seconds.

"Not quite . . . booze!" Judith exclaimed. "It smells like Scotch."

"That figures," Renie said. "Philip owns a distill-ery. Maybe he stores some of his private stash here and it leaked."

"Into the dungeon? That's where it's coming from. Did I see a flashlight on top of one of those boxes by the door?"

"You might have," Renie said. "I can't see any-thing."

Judith went to the carton where she'd noticed the flashlight. She clicked it on and focused its bright beam on the barrel some ten feet beneath the basement floor. "That's odd," she said in a curious voice. "It looks like there's something floating in the water. Or the Scotch. In fact, it looks like a—" Lightning flashed through the narrow windows. Judith sucked in her breath as thunder rattled the casements. "Holy Mother!" she gasped, reeling backwards toward Renie. "It looks like a head!"

16

C huckie?" Renie said under her breath.

"I don't know." Judith was shaking from the shock. "We've got to find the cops." She steadied herself to recover the strength she needed to put one foot in front of the other. Five minutes later they were back in the kitchen, asking Mrs. Gibbs if she knew the whereabouts of the police.

"They went to your rooms," she replied, sorting pippins as she peered at Judith. "Are ye ill? You're verra pale."

"Just . . . tired," Judith fibbed. "Thanks."

The cousins found the constables knocking on the Flynns' door. Glen and Adamson both removed their regulation caps when they saw Judith and Renie. "We're here about the theft," the taller one said.

Judith recalled that he was Adamson. "Never mind that now." She let the constables in as Renie excused herself to fetch her emergency eye medication. "Please," Judith emphasized after she stood near the hearth and tried to sound rational, "don't think I'm fantasizing. But a few minutes ago Mrs. Jones and I went into the storage room and opened the trapdoor to the dungeon." She paused, taking in the constables' stoic faces. "I used a flashlight to look at that barrel in the dungeon because it didn't make sense to have it filled with water."

Adamson's cheeks turned slightly pink; Glen frowned, his eyes avoiding Judith. "A leak," said Glen. "Something spilled from above."

"That is possible," she allowed, "but I saw a head in that barrel. You must look. It's very strange."

"A human head?" Glen said, looking skeptical.

"So it appears," Judith replied. "It could be Chuckie."

The constables exchanged quick, stupefied glances. "We'll check it out," Adamson said. "You'd better stay here."

That was fine with Judith. She had no desire to watch a body being recovered after what must have been a gruesome way to die. "We'll talk about the theft later," she said, seeing the constables to the door.

As soon as they were gone, Judith went across the hall to Renie's room. Her cousin was cussing and struggling with eye patch, gauze, and tape. "I'm out of practice," she complained. "What did the cops do when you told them they had to go bobbing for heads in a barrel?"

"Only one head, I hope," Judith said, sinking into an armchair. "For all I know, they think I'm nuts."

Renie looked in the mirror and realized that the patch was on crooked. "Damn. These things are tricky, but the good news is that the medication is working so that I can see out of my other eye. Sort of."

"Good." Judith shifted restlessly in the chair. "I hate the waiting game. If that's a corpse, Adamson and Glen will bring in their superiors, a medic, and God knows who all. It could be an hour or more before we hear anything." She stood up. "Let's go back to the dungeon."

Renie was aghast. "No! I don't want to see a pickled person! I wouldn't take biology in high school or eat pickled pigs' feet!"

"Then I'll go by myself," Judith said, heading for the door.

"Oooh . . . " Renie tossed the small box containing her eye supplies onto the bureau. "Okay, I'm coming. But I'll gripe the whole time."

"You always do," Judith said resignedly.

By the time the cousins reached the storage room, Adamson had climbed down into the dungeon. Glen, seeing Judith and Renie, held up a hand. "No closer, please. And keep silent." He bent down again to talk to his fellow officer. "Well?"

"A head," Adamson confirmed. "And a body—a dead one at that."

"Chuckie?" Judith said, a hand to her breast.

Adamson didn't answer right away. "A wee laddie," he finally said, his voice lower. "Can you identify this Chuckie?"

Judith blanched. "No. Let his father do that." She leaned against a stack of cartons and prayed. Chuckie had mentioned that sometimes he slept in a barrel. Maybe he'd been joking. But now, Judith thought sadly, a barrel was where he'd gone to sleep for all eternity.

Glen helped Adamson out of the dungeon. Both constables looked embarrassed. "The initial search should've been more thorough," Adamson said, brushing dust and cobwebs from his regulation jacket. "But who'd expect to find a body in a whiskey cask?"

Judith kept from saying that she'd found bodies in stranger places. "It's . . . unusual," she allowed.

"Aye," Glen said somberly. "I'll fetch his father. Mr. Fordyce returned a while ago."

Adamson nodded to his fellow constable. "I'll stand guard and call the guv." He turned sad gray eyes on the cousins. "Do you want to go?"

Renie started to open her mouth but Judith beat her to it. "No. Unless regulations prevent us from staying."

"Nae," Adamson said, dialing his cell phone. "DCI MacRae told us to consider you part of the investigative team."

"He did?" Judith asked, surprised. "That is, I know he—"

She shut up when Adamson spoke into the phone, relaying the message as tersely as possible. Clicking off, he turned to the cousins. "He'll be here as soon as he can get a police launch. The tide's in." He cleared his throat. "Ah . . . what do you think happened here, Mrs. Flynn?"

Judith found the constable's deferential manner unusual. Maybe, she thought, the police in the UK were different from the tight-lipped Americans she knew so well. "I don't think it was an accident. I'm afraid that Chuckie bragged about the knowledge he had—or thought he had—concerning who killed Harry Gibbs. That leads me to conclude that the murderer of Harry and Chuckie is the same person."

"Very logical," Adamson murmured. "Incredible."

"Her middle name," Renie remarked, fiddling with her eye patch.

"Logical?" Adamson said, impressed.

"No," Renie responded. "Incredible."

Judith shot her cousin a dirty look.

"I'm going," Renie said. "That Scotch smell makes me queasy."

"Coz!" Judith began, but after a false start bumping into the doorjamb, Renie was on her way.

"Sensitive," Adamson remarked.

"Not even close," Judith said irritably.

A moment later, Glen returned with Philip Fordyce. The whiskey magnate's usual savoir faire was obviously shaken. He was out of breath and his graying brown hair was unkempt.

"Unbelievable," he said in a hoarse voice. "My God! Not Chuckie!"

Judith discreetly moved as far away from the trap-door as she could. Adamson descended once more, apparently to position the body for Philip's viewing. A wrenching groan was the only sound Philip made when he saw his dead son. For a long moment the bereaved father stood like a statue, staring off into the afternoon's dying light. As Adamson climbed out of the dungeon, Beth Fordyce rushed into the storage room.

"Phil!" she cried. "Phil! Is it true? Gibbs just told me . . . " She threw her arms around her husband. "Oh no! I can't look!"

"Don't," Philip said quietly. He squared his shoulders, and with Beth still clinging to him, he walked away without another word.

Judith waited to make sure the Fordyces were out of hearing range. "Can you tell how Chuckie died? Was there any sign of trauma?"

Adamson shook his head. "Not that I could see. But even with a torch, I couldn't find anything suspicious. And I didn't dare remove the body all the way out of the barrel."

Judith nodded. "I understand." She sniffed at the Scotch-tainted air. "There's another, sweeter odor as well. I've been trying to figure it out." She paused, recalling her nights tending bar at the Meat & Mingle. "Ah!" she exclaimed softly. "I know what it is. It smells like a Rob Roy."

Realizing it might be some time before MacRae and his forensics crew arrived, Judith went in search of Renie. She knew she wouldn't have far to look. Renie was in the kitchen, eating bread and cheese.

"Just a snack to tide me over," Renie said.

"Bring it to my room. Glen's going to check out our . . . mishap," she amended to spare Mrs. Gibbs's feelings. Theft never sat well with an innkeeper. Murder, of course, was worse, as Judith well knew.

"I gathered you didn't tell Mrs. Gibbs about Chuckie," Judith said as they took the elevator to the guest floor.

"I leave that up to the cops," Renie said. "Besides, she might not have given me any food if I'd mentioned it."

Five minutes later, Glen arrived in Judith's room, still looking shaken. "Could Chuckie have had an accident?" he asked optimistically.

Judith shook her head. "Chuckie might have been upset over Harry Gibbs's death. Granted, his emotional state was fragile. He was epileptic and might have had a seizure, but that's a stretch." She pointed to the bureau. "I put the jewel case in the top drawer."

Glen looked inside. "How long did you have it here?" he asked, putting on a pair of latex gloves.

"No more than an hour," Judith answered. "We returned to this room a little after two-thirty and left again close to three-thirty."

"Who," Glen inquired, "knew you had the box?"

"Nobody," Judith replied. "Except for whoever put it in my purse, probably at Hollywood House. Has anyone reported it missing?"

"Nae," the constable said. "Did the case contain jewels?"

"No," Judith didn't elaborate about the emails. "The case looked valuable, though." She turned to Renie, who was sitting cross-legged on the bed, adjusting her eye patch. "Don't you agree, coz?"

Renie nodded. "It did when I could still see. Old, too, and finely wrought. It was polished, as if it had been someone's treasure."

"Mrs. Jones is a graphic designer," Judith explained. "She has an eye for such things."

"Only one, it seems." Glen sounded dubious. "You're certain you don't know how the case got into your purse?"

Judith grimaced. "It sounds stupid, but so much has been happening, not just today, but ever since we arrived at Grimloch, that I didn't check why my purse felt heavy. It's always overloaded when I travel."

Glen nodded absently while working his forensic magic on the bureau. "Given the time frame, who do you know was in the castle between two- and three-thirty?"

Judith thought back. It was going on five o'clock, but it seemed as if hours and hours had passed since she'd discovered that the silver case was missing. "Mr. and Mrs. Gibbs, Mrs. Fordyce, and Chuckie."

"Don't forget Will Fleming," Renie added. "We don't know when Philip Fordyce got back from wherever he'd gone."

"Mmm," Glen murmured. "May I take your fingerprints, ladies?"

"Of course," Judith said. "My husband's are on file with the U.S. authorities because he's a retired police detective."

Glen looked at Renie. "Mrs. Jones?"

She shook her head. "Can't. Don't have finger-prints."

"Beg pardon?" said the constable.

Renie held up her hands. "I have fingers, but no prints. When I was working my way through college I had a civil service job with the city. Everyone had to be fingerprinted, but mine wouldn't take. My grooves were too shallow. Sorry. I'm a freak of nature."

"I'm afraid it's true," Judith said, "in many ways." She ignored Renie's sharp, one-eyed glare. "I'll vouch for her. I've been with her almost the entire time."

Glen gave Judith a sympathetic look. "We'll do our best to recover the case." With a tip of the cap, he departed.

Judith sighed. "I feel just horrible about Chuckie. We should've prevented it, but I don't know how."

"Coz, you know perfectly well that people do what they want to do," Renie reminded Judith. "His murder seems to limit the suspects."

Judith was pacing the room. "Maybe. But we really don't know who was at the castle today. Somebody could've sneaked in. There doesn't appear to be a security system."

Renie allowed that was so. "It's after five. What now?"

Judith considered. "We could find Mr. and Mrs. Gibbs and ask if they know if any other outsiders came to Grimloch."

Renie shrugged. "Okay. But Mrs. Gibbs was going to do some cleaning in the Fordyce quarters before she started dinner."

"Then we'll look for Mr. Gibbs. Go get your coat. He may be outside, though it's almost five and getting dark."

Five minutes later, the cousins met in the passageway and started down the winding staircase. At the bottom they saw Gibbs.

"Message for ye," he said, holding out a slip of paper.

Judith thanked Gibbs and read the brief note before turning to Renie. "We're wanted by the police."

This is odd," Judith said as the cousins hurried across the courtyard. "The message says he'll meet us and take us into the village to talk about the latest information."

"Maybe MacRae sent the message before he found out about Chuckie," Renie pointed out as they got into the lift. "How come you didn't mention that odd voice we keep hearing to the cops?"

"I'd rather they didn't think we're gaga," Judith replied as the lift creaked its way downward.

A jolt that made the cousins cringe signaled that the cage had hit the ground. It was not only growing dark, but the mist had settled in, shrouding the far shore. As the cousins walked out onto the rocky ground, a strange noise startled them both.

"It's that bird," Judith said, peering in every direction. "The great northern diver." She pointed to an outcropping some ten yards above them on the face of the cliff. The bird let out another eerie cry, then flapped its wings and flew off into the mist.

"Creepy," Renie whispered. "The voice of death?"

Judith shivered. "It seems like it. First Harry, then Chuckie. They both hated that bird."

Shaken into silence, the cousins waited for a few minutes before Judith saw a running light and heard the sound of a motor moving toward them. "Here comes MacRae now," she said. "The storm has passed."

"But there's not much visibility," Renie remarked. "Or is that because I'm half blind?"

"Both," Judith replied as the motor went into neutral and the craft floated toward the shore.

"Hop in," said a voice out of the mist.

Judith and Renie helped each other into the runabout. "Thanks, Inspector." Judith settled onto the cushioned sheet. "I can't see you very well in this fog."

There was no immediate reply. Judith waited, hearing the waves slap softly against the boat. The motor purred as they began to move out into the channel. "The inspector couldn't make it," the man finally said. "I'm filling in for him. The name's Patrick Cameron. We've not been formally introduced."

Judith exchanged a quick, wary glance with Renie. "You're not with the police," Judith said.

"Not officially," Patrick said. "Hold on. We're almost ashore."

"Hold it!" Renie cried. "If you're not a cop, I'm not a passenger."

She stood up but Judith grabbed her arm. "Sit. You can't swim."

Reluctantly, Renie complied. "I don't like this," she murmured.

"Give Patrick a chance to explain," Judith whispered.

Renie's expression wasn't just skeptical; she looked on guard, though she said nothing more. The runabout moved smoothly through the shallow water, its running lights dappling the constant waves.

By the time they got to the small dock several yards down from the beach road, the mist had thinned a bit.

Judith finally made out Patrick's form and the familiar leather jacket. "We'll have to walk from here to my
cottage," he said. Patrick tied up the boat, which Judith
noticed was a twenty-footer with an inboard motor and
a fiberglass hull. "Dutch-made," Patrick remarked as
he offered to help Judith onto the narrow dock. "Which
one is Flynn and which one is Jones?"

Judith made the introductions and grabbed
Patrick's outstretched hand. "I saw you at Hollywood
House," he said. "Thanks for the help with those two
thugs."

"Oh." Judith shrugged. "You know Americans—
always rooting for the underdog. They aren't actually
thugs, though, are they?"

"That depends." Patrick grimaced. "The criminal
element sometimes wears an old school tie." He turned
to Renie, who hadn't budged from her seat in the boat.
"Aren't you coming, Mrs. Jones? Or," he added, gesturing at her eye patch, "are you waiting for the Jolly
Roger?"

"Not funny," Renie shot back. "Do I have a choice?
The body count's rising."

Judith winced at Renie's remark. She'd planned to
use subterfuge to find out if Patrick knew about Chuckie's demise. But his rugged features registered curiosity, if not surprise. "Meaning what?" he asked.

"Chuckie Fordyce," Renie said. "He drowned in a vat of whiskey."

Patrick swore, loud and long. "Now why would anyone kill a pitiful laddie like Chuckie? It makes no sense." He made an impatient gesture. "Let's go. We've much to discuss."

Disdaining any offer of assistance, Renie got out of the boat. Patrick motioned with one hand to indicate their misty route. After about twenty yards of careful walking along the beach, Judith saw the base of the cliff, sloping more gently upward than at the end of the High Street. She also made out the bottom rungs of a wooden stairway, and recalled that Patrick had disappeared in that direction after his encounter with Jimmy.

"Mind your step," Patrick urged as he went ahead. "Hold the rail."

Judith followed Patrick; Renie was behind Judith. The stairs looked fairly new, not having yet acquired the worn gray look of ocean-sprayed wood.

"The Hermitage," Patrick said wryly. "My hideaway. Come inside."

Judith was still wary, but even more curious. "Thank you," she said as they entered through the back door. "We noticed this house the other night when we were returning to Grimloch. It looked quite cozy."

Patrick laughed. "Looks are often deceiving." He led the cousins through a cluttered, cramped kitchen and into a common room that appeared to serve as both living and dining room. The big solid table was covered with folders, files, and computer printouts. "It lacks a woman's touch," Patrick remarked. "I bought this cottage years ago, before I married. Sit—if you can find a place." He began sweeping newspapers, magazines, and more folders off of the worn sofa and a couple of side chairs. "It's basically my fishing shack. I love the sea."

"But you work here," Judith noted, sitting in one of the side chairs.

Patrick took off his leather jacket and tossed it on the back of the sofa. "Sometimes. Drink?" He'd gone to a cupboard near the dining room table. "Any kind of Scotch you like?"

"Whatever you've got," Judith said.

"I hate Scotch," Renie replied, making a face.

Patrick looked faintly startled. "Did you tell Phil Fordyce you hated Scotch, so he put out your eye?"

"You ought to see Phil," Renie retorted. "He's in a body cast."

Patrick seemed mildly amused. "Ah. Spunky American females. That's good." He moved some bottles around in the cupboard. "Rye?"

"That's also good," Renie said. "But don't add anything lethal."

"See here," Patrick said, pausing as he started to pour their drinks into glass tumblers. "If I intended to harm you, I'd have done it already and tossed your spunky American bodies into the sea. I'm looking for information, not trouble." He finished filling the glasses. "Tell me exactly what happened to Chuckie."

Judith recounted the discovery in the dungeon while Patrick handed the cousins their drinks and eased his athletic form onto the sofa. "It was ghastly," Judith concluded. "I was afraid something might happen because he was bragging that he knew who killed Harry Gibbs."

Patrick frowned and rubbed at the bridge of his nose, which looked as if it had been broken. He also had a small scar under his left eye. Judith wondered if they were remnants from the night Davey had crashed the Lamborghini. "So Chuckie claimed he knew whodunit. Nonsense, probably. Dangerous nonsense, of course." He shook his head. "Chuckie seldom left Grimloch. I haven't seen him in a year or so." With a glint in his hazel eyes, Patrick leaned forward. "And how did you two get involved in this Harry Gibbs mess?"

"An accident," Judith said innocently. "We're on vacation with our husbands. They've gone fishing with Hugh MacGowan."

"The MacGowan," he murmured. "How strange to have him away at a time like this."

"Strange?" Judith repeated. "This vacation was planned by our husbands. They met MacGowan on a previous fishing trip. My husband's a retired police detective."

"Mine's a nut doc," Renie said. "He could find several patients around here, maybe even a sociopath or two."

"Really." Patrick didn't look at Renie, but kept his attention on Judith. "MacGowan would've made arrangements for time off," he pointed out. "It'd be known when he'd be away."

"I see what you mean," Judith said. "Is MacRae not as capable?"

Patrick shrugged. "Not necessarily. MacGowan knows everybody and everything about this area. He's very good at what he does. MacRae is an outsider, which is a hindrance. That's why I've taken it upon myself to get to the bottom of Harry's murder."

Judith nodded. "In your capacity as security chief at Blackwell?"

"Yes." Patrick took a quick swig of his whiskey. "I started out with the company working on oil platforms in the North Sea. It was dangerous, if exciting, work. In my off hours I figured out ways to improve employee safety. I caught upper management's attention and found myself propelled ever upward. I'm in charge of security, which makes me a sort of corporate policeman."

Judith's first inclination was to say that it wasn't wise for amateurs to get involved. Realizing her own hypocrisy, she nodded. "You think you can help with the official inquiry?"

"I know the players far better than MacRae—or even MacGowan," Patrick said with conviction. He leaned forward, a glint in his eyes and a faint smile on his lips. "So tell me—where's the jewel case?"

Judith was taken aback. "What jewel case?" she asked.

Patrick chuckled. "You know. The one in your purse."

"Stolen," Judith said. "The theft has been reported to the police."

Patrick swore softly. He took another gulp of whiskey and recovered his composure. "Do the police know what was in the case?"

"No," Judith said.

Patrick's shoulders sagged in relief. "Did you read the contents?"

Judith felt the tension build inside as her hold on the cocktail glass tightened. "Yes."

"Love stuff," Renie said.

"Fake," Patrick said.

"Fake?" Judith repeated.

He nodded. "Will told me about them. Contrived to make it sound as if Moira was having an affair, probably with me. It's an obvious attempt to implicate her in Harry's death by providing the motive of a lover." He chuckled and shrugged.

"Do you know who got hold of the original emails in the first place?" Judith inquired.

"Will," Patrick replied. "He didn't know what to do with the bloody fabrications, so he brought them for Beth to read."

Judith nodded. "All I know," she said, "is that I ended up with the case in my purse and then it was swiped from my room. Who'd take it?"

"I don't know," Patrick admitted, getting up and going to the front window. "It's all bosh anyway." He stopped speaking and peered outside. A full minute passed while Judith tried to get comfortable in the too-soft side chair and Renie fidgeted with her unruly hair.

"Are we having company?" Renie asked as Patrick continued to stare through the window.

He didn't answer, but moved to turn off the lamp by Judith's chair. The only light came from the kitchen, casting a pale yellow glow as far as the dining room table.

"MacRae isn't supposed to meet us here, is he?" Judith asked.

Again, Patrick didn't answer. He walked past the cousins without a word, through the dining area and into the kitchen. Two faint clicks indicated the opening and closing of a door. Judith stared at Renie.

"I bet he left." Renie jumped up and raced to the kitchen. A knock sounded at the front door. Judith sat very still. Renie came back into the common room. "Patrick's gone," she said. "Is somebody outside?"

Judith nodded. "Let's sit tight."

The knock sounded more loudly, followed by a masculine voice calling Patrick's name.

"Who?" Renie whispered.

Judith shook her head. "Someone Patrick's avoiding." The pounding made the doorknob rattle. "Maybe we should find out."

"Weaponry," Renie said. "I'll take the fireplace poker, you get a butcher knife."

"Hold off on the armaments." Judith moved to the door as the pounding and shouting continued. "Who is it?" she asked loudly.

The pounding stopped.

There was no chain on the door. Judith couldn't open it enough to see who was there without letting the man inside. She repeated her request for him to identify himself.

"Seumas Bell," he finally said. "Let me in."

Judith opened the door. "Hi," she said cheerfully. "We're just—"

Seumas brushed past her, glanced at Patrick's leather jacket on the sofa, and went straight to the kitchen.

Renie had rejected Judith's advice and was standing on the hearth holding the poker. "He didn't see me. Are his eyes as bad as mine?"

"It sounds like he's gone into another room," Judith said. "I assume he's looking for Patrick."

Renie took a practice swing with the poker. "Shall I whack him when he comes back in here?"

"No." Judith found a table lamp and switched it on. "Seumas doesn't seem interested in us. Maybe we should leave."

But it was too late. Seumas stormed back into view before the cousins could move. Once again, he paid no attention to them, but continued his search, bending down to look under the dining room table. "Well?" he demanded, straightening up. "Where is he?" His gaze fixed on Judith. "I've seen you somewhere. What are you doing here?"

Judith held up her glass. "We're having a drink. Patrick went out for a bit." She wasn't sure why she was protecting their errant host, but having helped defend him in the previous encounter with Seumas Bell and Jocko Morton, Judith decided not to change sides. "Do you have a message for him? We can deliver it when he gets back."

A phone rang, playing familiar notes from Beethoven's Ninth Symphony. Seumas reached inside his hooded jacket. "The Eagle has flown," he said after a moment or two had passed. "The Jackal is trapped." A longer pause followed. "The Leopard? Very well." He clicked the phone off and put it back inside his jacket. "If I were you," he said to the cousins in a low, menacing tone, "I'd get as far away as possible before you get hurt." He looked more closely at Judith. "Yes . . . Hollywood House. Now I remember. Stop meddling! You don't understand the danger!" He turned on his heel and ran out the front door without bothering to close it behind him.

Renie set the poker aside, shut the door, and turned the key in the lock. "Does Seumas think you're Patrick's accomplice from the USA?"

Judith shrugged. "I don't know. He's certainly trying to scare us. I wonder how he thinks we're involved." Her gaze ranged over the folders, files, and printouts that littered the common room. "If we snooped, I have a feeling we wouldn't find any incriminating evidence. Patrick's too sharp to be careless. Blackwell's big dogs were here last night. I doubt that Patrick's coming back soon, so let's go." She unlocked the door and peered outside. "The coast is clear."

The salt air felt invigorating as they stepped along the narrow garden path. Patrick's cottage looked cozy, but Judith sensed its isolation from the rest of the village as it faced the sea. Maybe, she thought, that was where Patrick felt most at home—aboard a ship or on an oil rig or in his little runabout.

The cousins remained cautious as they walked from The Hermitage and onto the High Street. From somewhere, a bell sounded six o'clock.

"Now what?" Renie said as they stood in front of the confectioner's shop that had closed for the day.

"I'm not sure," Judith admitted as her gaze scoured the High Street where the mist was drifting past the lampposts and shop fronts. Two cars went by, driving at a leisurely speed. A white cat crept out from behind a mailbox and disappeared in the scant space between the butcher's and the post office.

"So quiet," Judith remarked. "Who'd think there's a murderer on the loose around here?"

"Who'd think the life expectancy in St. Fergna is about thirty?"

Judith looked up as she heard a crow cawing nearby. The bird sat on top of the High Street clock some twenty yards away. "You mean like Moira's husbands, Frankie and Harry, along with Chuckie and Philip's first wife, Bella?"

"Right. Not to mention," Renie went on, "that Italian guy, Davey, who drove over the cliff. Was that an accident?"

"I've wondered, too," Judith said. "Moira seems to attract men who die before their time. Even Chuckie had a crush on her."

"Bad track record," Renie murmured. "Two husbands, one would-be suitor, and a personal assistant. Patrick should move to Australia."

"He's already married," Judith pointed out, starting to walk up the High Street. "I wish . . . I wish we had more resources. I'm at a loss."

"How about a pub?" Renie suggested. "Drinkers always talk."

"Yes, I'd like to be with seemingly harmless humans," Judith said. "Let's try the nice pub. We've already done Betsy at the Yew and Eye."

The cousins headed for the alley where the Rood & Mitre was located. The white cat zipped out from the shadows and ran ahead of them before disappearing into the mist.

The pub's door was locked. "Odd," Judith said, peering through the small mullioned window. "The lights are on." She knocked twice.

After a long pause, the young man with the shaggy magenta hair who had served Judith and Renie on their previous visit opened the door a crack. "Sorry, we're closed," he whispered. "Private party."

Judith peered inside but the pub was empty. "Please," she begged. "My cousin's going blind. She needs water for her medicine."

The young man's eyes darted around the vacant pub. "Um . . . "

"Oh my God!" Renie wailed, though she kept her voice down as her hands flailed in Judith's direction. "The dark! The gloom! I'm lost!"

The lad stepped back in alarm. "Aye, come in, come in. You're the American ladies from Grimloch." He moved aside and led them to the bar. "I'll pour the water. But then you must go."

"Sit," Renie murmured, collapsing onto a barstool. "Stay. Woof."

With a hand that wasn't quite steady, the lad pushed the water-filled tumbler toward Renie, who was fumbling in her purse. "Weird," he said softly. "She wasn't blind yesterday. No patch."

"It's a condition that comes and goes," Judith explained. "It's brought on by the weather."

Renie slipped something onto her tongue. She picked up the glass and swallowed. "Ahh!"

Judith, leaning on the bar, smiled at the lad. "Now she'll be able to use her good eye on a limited basis. Thanks. What's your name?"

"Ian," he replied, still looking nervous.

"What kind of party? A wedding? A birthday?" Judith asked.

Ian shook his head.

Judith clasped her hands in front of her and gazed up into the beamed ceiling. "Most mysterious. How about a séance?"

Ian's jaw dropped. "How'd you know?"

Judith did her best to hide her surprise, while Renie broke out into a choking fit. "I have my ways," Judith said blithely, whacking Renie on the back several times. "Actually, I'm a medium."

"Actually, she's a large," Renie gasped. "Stop hitting me!"

Ian looked justifiably confused. "You're here for the séance?"

"Only as an observer," Judith said, reluctantly taking fifty pounds from her wallet and placing it in front of Ian. "Where should I be?"

"Uh . . . I'm not sure," Ian replied, timorously accepting the bribe. "I'll check." He disappeared through a hallway at the end of the bar.

Renie had stopped coughing. "You ever try to swallow a breath mint whole?" she demanded of Judith. "That's why I choked. I wasn't going to waste a real pill on your latest nutty masquerade. And how did you make that wild guess about a séance?"

"Hypocrite," Judith chided. "Who played a witch, then claimed to be a seer? As for the séance . . ." She shrugged. "It just popped into my head. I figured it's a gathering of Blackwell's bigwigs. Chuckie's death may have triggered a reaction, which is why Seumas rushed off after he got that call at Patrick's. Maybe they use a séance as a cover. I bet Jocko and Seumas and Will are here. Jimmy Blackwell, too."

"Then Jimmy didn't leave the country," Renie remarked.

"Probably not," Judith said. "The Inverness cops had time to stop him. Remember the animals Seumas mentioned on the phone? The Eagle has flown—Patrick? The Jackal is trapped—Jimmy, stuck in Scotland? I'm not sure who the Leopard is, though."

Ian reappeared from the back of the pub. "They're in the office," he said. "There's a peephole in the storage room next door. I'll show you."

The cousins followed Ian down the hall to the first door on the right. A single bulb dangled from the ceiling. There was just enough room to move single-file between the supplies that lined the walls.

"Here," Ian whispered, pointing to a small space between cartons of crisps, paper napkins, and glassware. "Sort of a bird's-eye view."

"That'll do," Judith said. "They mustn't know I'm observing. It could break the spell."

"Got it. I'll leave now." Ian squeezed past Judith and Renie.

Judith leaned into the peephole area. "Darn. I can't see much."

"Who can?" Renie said with a martyred air.

Judith focused on the back of a man's head. "Seumas, but not Jocko," she murmured. "No Jimmy, either." The third man turned slightly. "Will Fleming."

"Will?" Renie frowned. "Who else?"

Judith wished she had a wider view of the darkened room. "They're at a table . . . four of them . . . Kate and another woman."

"Who's the medium?"

"Nobody's talking. They're just sitting, holding hands."

A moment later a woman's high voice spoke in a slow, drifting sort of tone: "What to do? What was Harry going to do? Answer, Eanruig."

"Earwig?" said Renie, trying to lean closer to the peephole.

Judith shook her head. "Kate's late husband."

"I must know how to act," Kate begged. "Please, Eanruig, speak!"

A long pause followed, broken by Seumas's impatient voice. "This isn't working. May I suggest common sense?"

"No!" Kate snapped. "Eanruig will tell us. He never rushed into business decisions. I insist on more time to reach him!"

"Nonsense!" Seumas snarled.

"Oooh . . . " The woman whose face Judith couldn't see was groaning. *"Buona notte,"* she said in a deep voice. "Who will avenge me?"

Renie stared at Judith. "What? It sounds Italian."

Judith nodded. "It's the woman with her head down."

"No!" Kate cried. "We want no intruder! Eanruig, speak to me!"

A tense silence followed; the unidentified woman rocked back and forth in the chair.

"It's over!" Seumas shouted. "We're done here!"

Will Fleming sighed and leaned forward. "Darling! Wake up!"

The woman who seemed to be acting as the medium jerked in her chair and sat up straight. "What? Where am I?"

"It's Marie Fleming," Judith said, surprised.

"Bedbug City," Renie muttered.

Judith kept her eye on the gathering as the lights were turned up and the quartet rose from the table.

"I told you this wouldn't accomplish anything," Seumas said to Kate. "It's all speculation. Harry had no real knowledge of alternative energy or renewable sources. He was showing off."

Will Fleming turned a stern face to Seumas. "I told you Philip should be here. What can have happened to him?"

"He's lost his only son," Kate retorted. "Where's your pity?"

Judith couldn't see Seumas's expression. He merely shrugged and put on his hooded jacket. Marie spoke to Kate, apologizing for her lack of psychic ability.

Kate nodded. "I'm sorry, too, but you've had flu. It must affect your contact with the spirit world. All those dreadful germs."

They started for the door. "Maybe," Will said, "I should phone Philip to find out why if he—" The door shut behind them.

After their footsteps had gone past the storage room, Judith closed the peephole's flap. "Whose idea was this?"

"The séance? Or the peephole?"

"I figure the answer is the same for both." Judith smiled wryly at Renie. "Kate Gunn. But what's she up to?"

"No good?"

"No doubt."

17

That bunch was in the dark in more ways than one," Renie remarked as they walked into the pub's empty serving area. "If some of them didn't know why Philip Fordyce wasn't there, they haven't heard about Chuckie. Now what?"

Judith saw Ian hang up the open sign. "Let's drink beer."

"And eat. Hey, Ian!" Renie motioned to the young publican. "Who's cooking?"

"Me mum," he said. "She's in the kitchen."

Judith joined Renie and Ian. "How often are these séances held?"

Ian scratched his high forehead. "Once a month? Nae—four, five times a year? I've only worked at the pub since last summer."

"Why have the séances here instead of a private home?"

"This was Mr. Gunn's favorite place," Ian replied, acknowledging a trio of young men who had just entered the Rood & Mitre. "To drink and eat, that is. Mrs. Gunn thinks his spirit is close by." He uttered a short laugh. "People act odd sometimes, don't they?"

"True," Judith agreed. "Did Mrs. Gunn come with her husband?"

Ian cocked his head to one side and grinned impishly. "Never. He came alone." The lad lowered his voice. "Me mum and dad own this pub. They could tell some tales about the local folk. Me dad said Mr. Gunn jumped from the frying pan into the fire when he'd stop for a pint or two." Ian winked. "Coming from the lady friend's, going to the wife."

Judith nodded. "The lady friend who owned the house where Mrs. Gunn lives now."

"Aye. Mr. Gunn built it for Mrs. B.P."

"You mean," Judith corrected politely, "for Porter-Breze, right?"

Ian ran a hand through his shaggy magenta hair. "Aye, but me mum always calls her Mrs. B.P. because Mr. Gunn gave her a big chunk of Blackwell Petroleum." A half dozen other customers had entered the pub. "Pardon, I must serve these regulars."

Judith moved closer to the bar, trying to get a peek at Ian's mother. She could see the service counter at the back, but a canvas flap hid the opening to the kitchen.

"If we ate something," Renie said, sidling up to Judith, "we could offer our compliments to the chef in person."

"True," Judith said. "Ian's mother sounds like a useful source." She gazed around the pub where four older people were sitting down while Archie Morton came through the front door. "Don't look now, but your foe in a potential bar fight has arrived."

"Who?"

"Archie." Judith moved to a barstool and sat down. "Ignore him and order something when Ian finishes with his other customers."

Renie bristled. "Wish I could see out of both eyes. Where is he?"

"Coming to the other end of the bar," Judith replied. "He's sitting next to a guy in a hat."

"What guy? What hat?"

Judith took a quick peek at the man who was a dozen barstools away with a couple of younger men in football jerseys sitting between him and the cousins. "Slouched posture, hat pulled down, raincoat collar pulled up. What some might call suspicious."

"You suspect he's—?"

Ian pushed the food orders under the canvas flap and started pouring drinks only a few feet away from the cousins. "Yo!" Renie called to him. "How about a couple of dark ales and a menu?"

Ian nodded. "Be right back after I set up these pints."

Judith discreetly watched Archie talk to the man in the hat. "I think," she whispered, "the mysterious stranger is Jimmy Blackwell."

"In semidisguise?" Renie nodded. "That figures. It's stupid, but it figures. Jimmy's well known around here. If he doesn't want to be recognized, he should be dressed as a bottle of Scotch."

The pub was filling up not only with drinkers but with supper customers. Judith noticed that no one seemed to be paying attention to Archie and the man she thought was Jimmy Blackwell.

"Typical," Judith remarked sadly. "A terrible murder occurs and causes a big fuss for a short time—then people return to their self-absorption and go on with their lives. It always strikes me as sad."

"They have to make sure that they're still alive," Renie pointed out. "Or else they think death is contagious."

Ian had come back to the bar where he took the cousins' orders for salmon, chips, salad, and two glasses of a reddish-hued beverage.

"What is this?" Renie asked after Ian had given them their drinks.

"Dark Island," Ian replied. "It's a traditional Orkney ale, from the same brewers who make SkullSplitter. Some say it has a magical flavor."

"Mmm," Renie murmured after a sip. "A bit like chocolate malt."

Judith sampled hers. "Nutty, too." She made a slight gesture to her right. "Is that Jimmy Blackwell with Archie Morton?"

Ian shook his head. "I don't think so. Jimmy B never comes here."

"B for Blackwell?" Judith said.

Ian looked embarrassed. "Nae. For 'bastard.' Not his fault, of course, but that's what folks around here call him behind his back."

"We heard," Judith said, "Jimmy hangs out at the Yew and Eye."

Ian shook his head again. "He doesn't hang out at any of the pubs. Not much of a drinker or party type."

"But," Judith pointed out, "he recently got into a fight with Harry Gibbs at the Yew and Eye."

"Oh—aye, so he did," Ian agreed. "But I heard Jimmy B went there not to drink but to . . . well, have it out with Harry."

Judith lowered her voice even more as two older men sat down next to the cousins at the bar. "Over how to run Blackwell Petrol?"

Ian shrugged and started to edge toward the newcomers. "I suppose that, and Harry wanting to run the show." He smiled apologetically before moving on.

"I'm sure that's Jimmy," Judith whispered to Renie. "What's he doing with Archie Morton? And how did Eanruig Gunn get the Blackwell shares for his mistress? The company's family-owned."

"Let me see," Renie muttered, taking a pen out of her purse and sliding a napkin closer. "Phil is currently married to Beth, who is Kate and Earwig's—I'm calling him that because I can't pronounce his name—daughter, whose brother Frankie was married to Moira. So maybe Frankie got some Blackwell shares through his marriage."

"Yes, Eanruig was alive when Moira and Frankie married." Judith tried to peer around the bar customers but the pub was filling up. Her view of Archie and the alleged Jimmy was blocked. "Dang. I can't see."

"Stop," Renie snapped. "You're not making me feel any better."

"They're really busy," Judith said. "Ian's mom might need help."

"Oh God!" Renie held her head.

Undeterred, Judith slipped off the barstool and went to find the kitchen door. It was just to the right off of the bar; she'd passed it when they'd gone to the storage room.

Ian's mother was surprisingly young, an auburn-haired woman of forty with freckles and a plump prettiness. "What's this?" she demanded, flipping hamburger patties on a smoking grill. "A complaint?"

"No," Judith replied, wearing her most ingratiating smile. "I came to help you. Your son says you're overworked."

Ian's mother looked up from the grill. "He did, did he? I don't believe it! Kids these days!" She smacked one of the patties with the spatula. "Go away. The rules forbid customers in the kitchen."

"I'm an innkeeper, a cook, and a bartender," Judith said. "My first husband and I owned a restaurant, and now I have a B&B. I've had decades of experience and I've got dish towels older than you are."

The woman laughed. "That's good, I like it. Make salads. The greens are in that plastic bin." She sighed as she swiftly buttered the buns. "Hard to believe Ian's so thoughtful. Maybe he's growing up."

"Eventually, they do," Judith said, putting on a pair of latex gloves. "I have a son, too."

"What's your name? I'm Grizel. Grizel Callum. Roy—that's me husband—is down with flu. It's going round, I hear."

"I'm Judith Flynn, from the States. My cousin and I are here with our husbands. The men are off fishing."

"Leaving you to work in my kitchen?" Grizel made a face. "Just like men. Where's your cousin? Can she cook?"

"Uh . . . sort of," Judith replied, slicing lettuce. "But at the moment, she has eye troubles. She's half blind."

"Ah." Grizel wiped perspiration from her forehead. "Ian tells me you have the sight."

"The sight?" Judith frowned. "I said I was a medium. I lied."

Grizel looked startled. "You did? Why?"

Judith debated with herself about being candid. Her conscience won. "My husband's a retired policeman. I've gotten involved in some investigations over the years, and discovered I have a certain knack for solving crimes. When Harry Gibbs was killed, I couldn't help myself. I started trying to figure out who had committed such a terrible crime."

"Ah." Grizel's face softened. "You must have a good heart."

Judith shrugged modestly. "Sometimes I think it's an obsession."

"A good one," Grizel remarked, putting the burgers on serviceable beige plates. "Salads, please." She took the mixed greens from Judith and called to her son from under the canvas flap. "Ian! Orders here!"

"You must know the people involved in Harry's death," Judith said, slicing a firm tomato. "Is that Jimmy Blackwell at the end of the bar?"

"Jimmy B? I didn't see him," Grizel replied. "A brassy blonde's sitting on the end stool next to that ornery devil Archie. She's a hairdresser, by the name of Petula."

"But you know Jimmy B?"

Grizel nodded after scanning the new batch of orders Ian had handed to her. "In the way that everybody knows everybody in a village. Not that he and I would stop for a chat. Jimmy B is far too grand for the likes of me. And him born on the wrong side of the blanket! Putting on airs, more so than his sister, whose parents were joined in holy wedlock."

"Moira?"

"Lovely lass to look at," Grizel declared, "though not having the good sense God gave a goose. Unlucky in love. And silly, if ye ask me. It's a good thing we live in a village. So few of us, and not dependent on a big company like Blackwell Petrol." She licked her lips, as if she were savoring the gossip she'd stored inside.

"Up to no good, I figure, like all those greedy oil folk. Might as well live in Saudi Arabia."

"No good?" Judith repeated. "In what way?"

Grizel shrugged. "I've no head for business except running our own. But I hear things. Maybe Harry's doing, maybe Jocko Morton's. As I said, Moira should never have gotten mixed up with Harry."

"I understand she fell in love," Judith remarked.

"She's always falling in love." Grizel made a disgusted gesture. "Oh, Harry could turn a lassie's head, but his own was empty. Come here bragging about how he was the big man at Blackwell Petrol and the rest were past their prime. No wonder Harry and Jimmy B got into it at the Yew and Eye!" She scooped up a handful of sliced potatoes and tossed them into the deep-fry basket with a vengeance. "I wouldn't put it past Jimmy B to have murdered Harry. But then again, the whole Blackwell lot probably wanted to do the same."

"You think Harry was killed by one of his business associates?" Judith asked, chopping scallions and beginning to feel the heat from the grill and the deep fryers.

"It wouldn't surprise me," Grizel replied. "Of course I know it couldn't have been Jimmy B even if he'd be my odds-on pick."

"Jimmy couldn't have done it?" Judith asked in surprise.

Grizel sighed. "Nae. He was here most of that afternoon."

"I thought he didn't drink," Judith said.

"He'll take an occasional pint or a wee dram," Grizel replied, draining grease from a basket of golden-crusted plaice. "On Saturday he came here with his laptop and had a late lunch and a pint and worked for more than three hours. Chatty, too, with some of the regulars, but then I was the only one working that shift and we weren't so busy." She dished up four plates of fish and chips, collected more salads from Judith, and called again to Ian. "A lull," Grizel said, again wiping her forehead. "Ye put in an order, didn't ye?"

"I did," Judith answered, "but I can wait."

"Good thing," Grizel commented, lighting a cigarette. "The woman with the eye patch is eating two orders."

"She's my cousin," Judith said. "That's interesting about Jimmy spending Saturday afternoon here. Has he done that before?"

"Never. Jimmy B told Will Fleming he had to work out some big problem and didn't want to drive into Inverness to the Blackwell headquarters." Grizel flicked ash into the sink. "Jimmy's wife was ailing.

A miscarriage, I heard. Maybe she wanted him out of the house."

"Will Fleming was here all afternoon, too?"

Grizel shook her head. "Only to have a pint. Will works hard, often goes to Inverness Saturday mornings, then stops here before going home." She shrugged. "Nice man. Quiet. Polite."

"I've heard rumors about Moira and Patrick Cameron," Judith said, wishing she hadn't started to perspire in one of her new sweaters.

Grizel laughed. "Oh, Patrick! He does like the lassies! If Moira had married him instead of Harry, there wouldn't be all this nasty talk."

"But Patrick was already married," Judith pointed out.

"Oh no," Grizel insisted. "He was still a bachelor after Frankie Gunn fell off the twig. Patrick and Jeannie were wed only a year ago. Shame on him if he's carrying on with Moira. Jeannie is—what's that?" Grizel put out her cigarette in an ashtray and peeked under the canvas flap. Judith could hear raised voices and a great clatter. "Och!" Grizel exclaimed. "We've got a rumpus!" She raced to the kitchen door.

Dreading the worst, Judith followed. Her fear was well founded. Renie was shoving Archie Morton's face into a salad bowl even as the blonde named Petula attacked her from the rear. A sharp elbow from Renie sent Petula sailing into the lap of an old man who was sitting ramrod straight at one of the tables. He ignored the blonde and took a toothless bite from his fish. Ian dropped a tray of drinks and was attempting to break up the melee. Several young people had taken the opportunity to plug in their iPods and dance on the bar.

"Coz!" Judith shouted. "Knock it off!"

Renie spotted Judith from the corner of her good eye. "The Arch Hog wanted all the salt, let's see how he likes it now!" She leaned her full weight on the man as he struggled to get free. "Hey, Arch! Cry 'uncle'!"

Renie's victim made a muffled noise, though it didn't sound like 'uncle' to Judith. Apparently it was good enough for Renie. She moved off of him and grabbed a napkin to wipe her hands. "Never tangle with a middle-aged woman who's decked a coke addict in the Sacramento bus depot," she shouted, referring to an incident from the past while she and Bill were Reno-bound. "Especially when she's hungry."

Wiping lettuce and dressing off of his face, Archie sputtered as he staggered to his feet. The old man at the table had finally noticed the blonde in his lap. "Get your hand off my tar-tar," he rasped, and gave her a shove. She fell against Archie's legs.

Renie was pointing to what was left of her meal for two, a hodgepodge of scattered chips, salad, and a piece of fish floating in her Dark Island ale. "I'm finished," she called to Ian. "It was yummy."

Ian was busy shooing the dancers off the bar. Grizel was clearing away the spilled drinks from the tray her son had dropped. Archie was working up a head of steam while peeling lettuce leaves from his cheek.

"I'll bring charges!" he roared at Renie.

"Neener-neener," Renie replied, tossing a generous amount of money on the part of the bar that wasn't being used as a dance floor. "You started it, Chunky Monkey."

Judith had gone to help Grizel. "I'm terribly sorry about this," she said. "Mr. Morton must have done something to aggravate my cousin. She's usually very . . . ah . . . refined."

Renie was sashaying out of the pub, head held high, impervious to the mixed cheers and jeers from the other customers. Her exit was marred only by her attempt to open a window she mistook for the front door. Still appalled, Judith apologized again to Grizel and Ian before she followed her errant cousin.

"You!" Archie Morton called. "Which one of you Yank bitches attacked my brother Jocko?"

"Never heard of him," Judith called over her shoulder. Archie's efforts to come after her were frustrated by a bosomy redhead who wanted him to listen to hip-hop on her iPod and exchange a brake job for some other kind of job Judith didn't want to hear.

Out of breath and sore of hip, Judith gratefully got out into the fresh, damp air of the misty night. Renie was nowhere in sight.

"Coz?" she called, wondering if her cousin had decided to hide from Archie in one of the nearby alleys or closes. The white cat crept out from behind a dustbin, haughty with gleaming golden eyes. "You can't scare me," Judith muttered. "I'm Sweetums' human. I've seen it all."

The mist swirled and ebbed through the narrow, winding cobbled side street. The cat was the only living creature Judith could see. There were no customers coming or going from the Rood & Mitre. She could hear a car out on the High Street and a snatch of laughter. Suddenly she was afraid, not just for herself but for Renie.

Feeling a need for the reassuring presence of ordinary people, Judith took a few steps back toward the pub. She felt slightly buoyed by the murmur of human voices, but realized that the sound wasn't coming from the Rood & Mitre some ten yards away, but from outside. Cautiously, she walked past the entrance and turned the corner into a narrow walkway between the pub and the adjacent antiques shop. The voices—or rather the voice of a man—had become quite clear.

"You're lying," he said. "You must stop. Now."

Judith saw the outline of a man whose back was turned to her. She couldn't see the object of his threat, but she recognized the raincoat and slouch hat. It had to be Jimmy Blackwell, she thought with another rush of fear. She was almost certain he was talking to Renie, and his manner definitely didn't sound friendly.

"Coz!" Judith shouted again. "I'm here!"

Renie's head appeared from behind Jimmy's shoulder. "Call the cops!" she yelled. "This guy's assaulting me!"

"I am not assaulting you!" Jimmy retorted angrily. "I'm trying to help you! You're in grave danger!" He glanced quickly at Judith. "So is she. Don't be reckless. It's none of your affair."

Seeing that Renie didn't appear to be in immediate danger, Judith gathered her courage. "Why do you think we know anything?" she asked, moving toward Jimmy and Renie.

Jimmy turned abruptly, looking at Judith from his six-foot-plus frame. He was imposing, with a bearing that was almost regal. "You've been meddling," he said. "Asking questions. Going out of your way to make the acquaintance of any number of people connected to Harry Gibbs. That's not typical behavior of vacationing Americans."

"We're at loose ends," Judith said, shrugging. "What else can we do with no car and our husbands off fishing? We're bored. We Yanks enjoy excitement. That's why we have such a high crime rate."

Jimmy looked more exasperated than angry. "That's ridiculous," he said. "See here," he went on, making an effort to lower his voice and sound reasonable, "I'm not threatening you, but giving a warning for your own good. You have no idea how your meddling can affect the wrong sort of people. I'll be frank—the stakes are very high."

Renie spoke before Judith could say anything. "I'd like to know what these stakes are, since they seem to be worth killing Harry Gibbs."

"No, no," Jimmy responded, looking aggrieved, "I didn't say that. This is no place to talk. We should go somewhere less public."

If no longer frightened, Judith remained wary. "Such as?"

"There's a fine restaurant in a small hotel a short drive from here," Jimmy said. "I have a car parked nearby. Shall we?"

Judith and Renie looked at each other. "Well . . . " Judith began, "I'm not sure. How do we know you don't intend to harm us?"

Jimmy's exasperation returned. "Why would I? For God's sake, I'm already in enough trouble for eluding the police when I tried to leave for Paris. You and one or two others are the only ones who know my whereabouts. I wouldn't be talking to you if I didn't feel you're at risk."

Judith was unconvinced. "A good reason to dump us over a cliff."

Jimmy made a face. "Then why don't one of you drive? Preferably the one who can see. It's a rental, a simple Honda."

"How about this?" Judith suggested. "I drive us down to the beach where we can talk. The tide's going out and there can't be many people strolling along the shore, so we'll have privacy."

"Fair enough," Jimmy agreed. "The Honda's parked near Morton's garage, only a short walk from here."

He led the way, stopping to make sure the street was empty. It wasn't. Archie Morton and the blonde were coming out of the pub, arm in arm. Jimmy held out a hand to keep the cousins back in the shadows. Archie and his conquest went in the other direction.

"This way," Jimmy murmured, heading down to the coast road.

They reached the High Street's dead end where the mist was blowing more heavily in from the sea. Judith's face felt damp by the time they crossed over to the side of the street where the car repair was located. Jimmy pointed out a dumpster not far from Archie's office. "The Honda's behind that," he said quietly.

As they headed in the direction he'd indicated, Judith heard the sound of a car driving on the coast road. She looked behind her to make sure they were out of the way of any oncoming traffic. Due to the poor visibility, the car was creeping along.

They were some ten yards off of the verge when a voice called out: "James Blackwell, stop where you are! This is the police!"

Jimmy swore under his breath and paused for only an instant. Then, before Judith could see who had spoken, Jimmy ran off into the swirling mist.

18

Jimmy Blackwell had disappeared in the vicinity of the dumpster, a few feet away.

Malcolm Ogilvie and his superior, DCI Alpin MacRae, emerged from the gray cloud of fog. "Where'd he go?" Ogilvie asked.

Judith pointed to the dumpster that was almost concealed by mist. "Over there."

"Go to our car!" MacRae shouted as the policemen gave chase.

The cousins hurried to the unmarked vehicle. "Who gave Jimmy up?" Renie asked after they'd gotten in the car.

"Archie?" Judith suggested, trying to settle into the backseat and ease her tired hip. "Maybe somebody else recognized Jimmy's disguise."

Renie had left the door open on her side, but her efforts to see anything were futile. "I thought I heard a car, but I can't tell where the sound's coming from. Say," she said, brightening. "The cops left the keys in the ignition. Why don't we steal this one?"

"Coz!" Judith looked horrified. "That *is* a crime!"

Renie's expression was ingenuous. "Not if you make up a really good fib about why we did it."

"I'd never do such a thing," Judith asserted indignantly. "For heaven's sake, I'm married to a retired policeman! What would Joe say?"

"Why does Joe have to find out?"

"Stop it," Judith snapped. "Besides, even I couldn't come up with a story that would keep us out of big trouble. We could be charged with aiding and abetting a fleeing criminal." She grew silent. "Then again, maybe we should try to find the cops. We could . . . um . . . drive," she added in an uncertain voice. "I mean, *I* could drive."

"Okay." Renie got out of the car and went to the front seat.

Trying to quiet her conscience, Judith also made the switch to the front seat. "I'm serious," she said. "Jimmy had a car. MacRae and Ogilvie are on foot. We'll find them and turn the car over."

Renie stared at the windshield. "Of course we will."

Demonstrating her good intentions, Judith started the car and backed up slowly along the verge until she could see a patchy grass and dirt surface she thought would lead them to the dumpster.

"Where are we?" Renie asked.

"I think we're just a few yards from where Jimmy left the Honda."

There was no car. There were no people, not Jimmy, not the two cops. "Jimmy must have driven off," Judith speculated. "But where did MacRae and Ogilvie go? They don't know St. Fergna like Jimmy does. He'd be able to use all sorts of escape routes."

"It's been less than ten minutes," Renie pointed out. "Maybe the cops are lost in the fog."

"That's possible." Judith glanced at her watch. "It's dark as well as misty. I don't know where to search."

"You might try driving on a road," Renie suggested. "The left-hand side, okay?"

"You're holding out your right arm."

"Huh? Oh!" Renie was chagrined. "I can't see which is which."

Judith turned the car around to head back to the coast road. "No cops," she pointed out as they joined the road almost at the same spot where they'd started. "No backup in sight. I'm nervous. We can get into serious trouble for this stunt."

"You prefer sitting in the mist on a dark night with a murderer loose and we've been warned several times that we're in danger?" Renie shook her head. "It's harder to catch a moving target. Keep driving."

"Okay, we'll keep moving. By the way, I gather Jimmy didn't know about Chuckie or he'd have mentioned it. On the other hand, he was probably in the area when Chuckie was—" She jumped as a female voice came over the car's radio. "This is Control. MacRae, please come in." Judith eased the car to a stop. "MacRae, please come in," the voice repeated as Judith and Renie stared stupidly at each other.

"DCI MacRae," the woman said, slightly louder. "Are you there?"

Renie held up her hand for silence and poked several buttons on the radio. "Yes?" she said in her deepest voice, which even normally was a cross between Tallulah Bankhead and a bullfrog.

"Mrs. Marie Fleming of the Priory on Monk Road has reported her husband, Will Fleming, Blackwell Petroleum's chief financial officer, as missing. Please contact her as soon as possible."

The radio went silent.

"You just impersonated a police officer!" Judith exclaimed in horror. "We're going to prison!"

"I didn't claim to be MacRae," Renie argued. "All I said was 'yes.'"

Fingers clasping and unclasping the steering wheel, Judith shuddered. "I can't believe we're doing this! What's wrong with you? What's wrong with me?" She took a deep breath and sat up straight. "And where's Monk Road?"

Renie clicked open the glove compartment. "Let's see if there's a map. This isn't MacRae and Ogilvie's usual territory. Turn on the overhead light. Ah," she said softly, "here it is. You have two eyes," she added, handing the map to Judith. "You look."

"It's west a couple of miles," Judith said after a brief pause. "It's not on the water. We go through St. Fergna and then hook left twice." She handed the map back to Renie. "We aren't going there, are we?"

Renie shook her head. "Of course not."

The cousins exchanged rueful glances.

"This is so wrong," Judith said as she turned onto the deserted High Street. "But it's possible that somehow MacRae and Ogilvie are at the Priory already. Maybe Marie Fleming came looking for them."

Renie smirked. "As ever, coz, sound logic."

"We have to start looking for them somewhere," Judith retorted. She was almost to the fork in the road and the village green. "What's that?" she said, espying a big banner stretched across the bandstand.

"Bedsheet?" Renie said. "Clothesline?"

Judith slowed to a stop. "It says 'Tomorrow is Judgment Day—Inquest 10 a.m. Women's Institute.'"

"Jocko Morton rallying the troops," Renie remarked. "He's certainly got it in for Moira."

"I suppose," Judith said slowly as she made a left turn by the graveyard, "there's a chance he's right. But I despise his rabble-rousing tactics. Tell me when you see the sign for Monk Road."

"You're kidding, of course," said Renie.

"Oh. Sorry." Judith slowed down. Visibility on the road west was only about twenty feet, and subject to change.

They'd crept along for less than a mile before they saw a cluster of red and yellow lights up ahead. "What's that?" Renie asked. "It looks like a traffic jam, which isn't likely in a village the size of St. Fergna."

"An accident, maybe?" Judith suggested, slowing down to less than ten miles an hour. "They're blocking the road." She frowned, noticing not only cars but bicyclists and pedestrians, some carrying flashlights. At first she thought they were singing, but realized as she rolled down the window that they were chanting in angry voices.

"Can you hear that?" Judith asked.

Renie had also opened her window. "I'm blind, not deaf. Yes—it sounds like 'Jezebel.' Isn't that what the flyer called Moira when Jocko staged his show the other night?"

"Among other things," Judith said grimly. "They must be marching to Hollywood House. We're stuck behind them. If I honk, they might take out their wrath on us—and this police car. I wish it were a real cruiser. We could use the flashing lights and siren to get through."

"We could shoot them," Renie suggested. "Maybe there's a weapon in here someplace."

"You're kidding, I trust," Judith said, creeping along so slowly that the speedometer barely registered. "A cop wouldn't leave a gun in a vacant car. According to the map, Monk Road is about a quarter of a mile from here." She made a disgusted face. "Damn, this is the dumbest idea we've had yet! What were we thinking of?"

"It's all this fog," Renie said. "Our minds have gone. Besides, I kind of enjoy a good riot. We haven't had one at home since the WTO dustup, and I had to watch it on TV. It's not the same."

"Sometimes you're too weird even for me," Judith muttered. "I'll bet MacRae and Ogilvie are somewhere along the way, afoot or—" Loud sounds like gunshots interrupted her. "Now what?"

The parade of putative avengers appeared to wonder the same thing. The chanting stopped abruptly, some drivers honked their horns, and the people on foot ebbed and flowed, with a few ducking for cover. A moment later, two more shots were fired. Several people ran, plunging off the road to seek safety.

"Whoever's firing that gun did us a favor," Judith said, stepping gently on the gas pedal. "The crowd's thinned out a bit so we can move."

"We can also get shot," Renie pointed out. "Oh well."

The marchers had lost momentum, though at least forty people and a couple dozen cars were moving, albeit more slowly, along the road. Judith saw a trio of bicyclists, a skateboarder, and several pedestrians heading back toward the village. The cousins had gone about fifty yards when Judith spotted the signpost for Monk Road.

"Maybe we should see what's going on at Hollywood House first," she said, "especially if MacRae and Ogilvie might be there ahead of us."

"On roller skates?" Renie remarked with a sidelong glance at Judith. "In case you've forgotten, we've hijacked their transportation."

"We borrowed it, remember?" Judith snapped. "Besides, it was your nutty idea."

"At least they've stopped shooting," Renie said. "Hey—listen!"

Judith heard the sound, a faint but angry cry of shrill voices. The car kept moving, following the diehard crowd, which had now reached the gates of Hollywood House where vehicular traffic stopped.

"Damn!" Judith braked, trapped in a virtual blockade of the road. "We can't turn around. We're hemmed in on every side." She stopped, letting the engine idle. "The gates must be locked," she said, "but it sounds as if most of the noise is coming from closer to the house. The protesters or whatever you'd call them are scaling the walls."

"Shall we get out?" Renie asked.

"I guess so," Judith said, turning off the ignition, "if we want to—excuse the expression—see what's happening." The cousins got out of the car. "I hate to leave a police car in the middle of the road, but I don't have any choice." A whirring sound overhead made her look up. "My God!" she gasped. "It's a chopper, and it's practically on top of us!"

"Cops, maybe?" Renie shouted as the helicopter came closer. "With this mist, the visibility must be worse than mine."

Most of the other onlookers were staring up, too. The copter's rotors drowned out the voices of the marchers, who apparently had invaded the grounds of Hollywood House. After a final swoop the chopper gained altitude and flew away.

The throng that had just preceded Judith and Renie was at the iron gates. A few persons were trying to climb up the sturdy bars, either to get a better view or to leap onto the driveway. Judith, being taller than Renie, could see some twenty or thirty people in front of the house. They'd resumed their chanting as soon as the helicopter had departed.

"Guilty, guilty, guilty!" cried the crowd. "Jezebel, Jezebel, Jezebel!"

Renie managed to squeeze between a man and a woman who were shouting themselves hoarse. "Blind person coming through!" she shouted, extending a hand behind her to Judith. "Cripple on my rear!" She lowered her voice a notch and turned to Judith. "Do I detect some good old-fashioned John Knox Presbyterianism running amok?"

"What?" Judith responded. "I can't hear you!" She stumbled and fell against a young man. "Oops! Sorry!"

"That's okay," the young man said, turning around. "Mrs. Flynn!"

"Barry!" Judith exclaimed. She noticed that Alison was next to him and offered a weak smile. "What's happening?"

"Protesters, just like a real city," Barry said, leaning close to Judith so he could make himself heard. "Never seen the like. I dinna ken half these folk. Auld Jocko got the Highlands riled up, didn't he?"

"You mean these aren't all villagers?" Judith asked in surprise.

Barry nodded. "More strangers than locals."

"Do you agree with Jocko about Moira?" Judith inquired.

He shrugged. "Better than watching the telly on a Monday night."

"We heard what sounded like shots," Judith said.

Barry nodded. "It was shots, all right, fired by that butler when some of the mob climbed over the wall. Didn't do much good, though. Think he shot a duck."

The crowd suddenly grew silent, all eyes riveted on the front of Hollywood House. Judith stood on tiptoe to see what had captured their attention. A hazy figure on the second-floor balcony was outlined against the light that came from inside the open door.

"What is it?" Renie asked. "I'm half blind and too short."

Before Judith could answer, a woman's shrill voice split the swirling mist. "Why? Why? Why? I'm your friend, your neighbor! You know me! I'm innocent!"

A chorus of damning denial erupted from the crowd. "Moira," Judith said in Renie's ear.

"It doesn't sound like her," Renie said.

"She's distraught, wringing her hands, pulling at her hair." Compassion welled up inside Judith's breast. "She's . . . unhinged."

Renie shook her head in disgust. "As my father would say, that's ungood. It won't help her with this bunch."

Moira was trying to speak again, but the angry mob wouldn't shut up. A new chant was emerging, though Judith couldn't make it out. It sounded to her like "Caravan," which made no sense. On the balcony, Moira bowed her head and gripped the rail. The cries of the crowd swiftly changed to "Jump, whore, jump!"

"Horrible!" Judith exclaimed. "Where are the police?"

"Looking for their car?" Renie suggested.

"Shut up." More guilt overcame Judith. "What are they yelling besides 'Jump'? 'Caravan'? 'Caveman'?"

"Cameron," Renie said. "Now they're shouting 'Butcher!' They must think Moira and Patrick conspired to kill Harry Gibbs."

"I can't hear you!" Judith cried as the noise grew to a fever pitch and the crowd pressed forward. "Let's go before we get trampled!"

"How?" Renie yelled. "We're stuck! Where are Barry and Alison?"

Judith couldn't see them. She was being pushed closer to the gate, as if the mob intended to crush the iron bars with sheer force. Meanwhile, the driveway was becoming clogged with trespassers who had gone over the walls.

Judith's view of the house had been blocked for the last couple of minutes, but while struggling to keep her balance, she got a glimpse of Moira. The anguished widow looked as if she was weeping, her head in her hands, her hair streaming around her hunched shoulders.

Suddenly the sound of sirens was heard over the crowd's relentless roar. "Cops?" Judith mouthed to Renie, who listened and nodded.

It occurred to Judith that the police might use tear gas or some other unpleasant means to disperse the mob. Somehow, she realized, there had to be a way to escape the crush of irate people. "Can you crawl?" she whispered to Renie, augmenting the question with hand motions.

"Uh . . ." Renie peered down at the ground. "Maybe. But you can't."

"If you move enough people, I can stay upright and follow you."

"Oh . . ." Renie looked aghast. But the sirens were very close. "Okay, here goes," she said, digging into her purse and taking out a pair of small but very pointed nail scissors. "Stay close." She squatted down, got to her knees, and began to crawl toward the road.

As the shouts and jeers became punctured with sharp squeals of pain and hopping feet, Judith was able to squeeze between Renie's victims, who had been caught off guard by the unexpected jabs with the nail scissors. Mouthing apologies and stumbling awkwardly through the throng, Judith had broken into a sweat by the time she got to the road. Fortunately, the crowd was thinning out as two police vans came toward the entrance to Hollywood House.

"I can't get up!" Renie cried, sounding miserable. "About a hundred people stepped on me! I'm a wreck!"

Judith gave her cousin a hand and helped her get to her feet. "You do look pretty ghastly," she said, taking in Renie's disheveled hair, which sported a couple of candy wrappers, a cigarette butt, and an unopened condom. "Let's see if we can move our stolen police car."

The sedan was right where they'd left it, but it wasn't empty. Judith spotted two figures in the front seat.

"Oh my God!" she exclaimed. "Someone else is trying to steal it!"

"No!" Renie gasped. "What's this world coming to?"

Wiping perspiration from her forehead, Judith moved purposefully through the gaggle of onlookers, some of whom had lost their steam as the police vans came to a stop nearby. Reaching the car, she looked inside and saw Alpin MacRae in the passenger seat. Recognizing Judith, he rolled down the window.

"I can explain . . . " Judith began, starting to sweat again.

"Of course," MacRae said with a grim smile. "But not now. Thank God you were able to get here. We had to borrow bicycles from the village after we lost track of James Blackwell and heard about this mob. Would you like to get in?"

"Oh yes!" Judith was confused by MacRae's reaction but needed sanctuary, not explanations. She opened the back door and practically fell into the seat. Renie scrambled in next to her.

"Are you all right?" MacRae asked after swiftly surveying the cousins.

"Yes, yes," Judith replied.

"Speak for yourself," Renie muttered, raking the detritus from her hair. "I've scraped my hands and knees. I'll have bruises all over . . . "

Her words were drowned out by a loudspeaker ordering the crowd to disperse.

"Inverness sent a riot squad," MacRae said. "This is an amazing turn of events, like a rock concert or a football game on a smaller scale."

"I never saw the like," Ogilvie asserted, "except at a Dundee United match against Heart of Midlothian. Hearts is bloody vicious."

MacRae gave his subordinate a faintly patronizing glance. "Aye, lad, but this melee is a wee bit different. I don't like it. I gather Jocko Morton has been stirring up the local folk."

"That's so," Judith said, watching as several riot squad police spilled onto the road and took up positions. A handful of younger people seemed confrontational, but most of the crowd began to break up. "Have you seen the banner on the village green?"

Keeping his eyes on the situation that was beginning to ease, MacRae nodded. "We walk a fine line between free speech and inciting a riot." He turned to Ogilvie. "Stay with the ladies. I'll make sure everything's under control."

As soon as MacRae got out of the car, Judith tapped Ogilvie's shoulder. "Have you been to Grimloch since we found Chuckie?"

"Aye." Ogilvie's expression was somber. "A horrible way to kill someone, poor laddie. Mr. Fordyce is offering a million-pound reward."

"Surely," Judith said, "he has confidence in the police."

"He does," Ogilvie assured her, "but he's that upset over losing his only bairn."

"Do you think that whoever killed Chuckie also killed Harry?" Judith asked as Renie made faces and obscene gestures at the people who were staring at her in the police car.

Ogilvie shrugged. "It doesn't seem like a coincidence."

"No," Judith agreed. She poked Renie. "Stop that! This is an official vehicle!"

"These morons think I'm an official prisoner," Renie declared. "They ought to be cheering me. Why aren't they getting arrested?"

"Only if they resist," Ogilvie said. "They're giving up, it seems."

"Glad you folks don't play much hockey," Renie murmured. "We colonials get kind of fractious at the ice rink."

MacRae, who had been conferring with a member of the riot squad, got back into the car. "We can leave," he informed Ogilvie. "The driveway is clear and constables will be on duty. Mrs. Gibbs's doctor is on his way. She had a fainting spell after her . . . ah . . . balcony appearance."

"No wonder," Judith said. "From what I've heard, Moira's a very emotional young woman. Of course she's been through a great deal. Her health also seems precarious."

"Indeed," MacRae said as Ogilvie drove slowly to avoid stragglers. "Mrs. Gibbs is the Poor Little Rich Girl personified. She—stop!"

A man had flung himself on the car's hood. He was facedown, his hands stretched out as if in supplication.

"Don't move!" MacRae ordered as he and Ogilvie got out of the car.

"Was he pushed?" Judith said to Renie.

"I don't know. I still can't see very well."

Only a couple of people were close by. Judith peered through the backseat window and recognized Barry and Alison. Quickly, she rolled the window down and called to them. "Did you see what happened?"

They both shook their heads. "Too sudden," Barry replied. "Have you been arrested?"

"No." Judith waved weakly and focused on the man who was being helped off of the hood. She still couldn't see his face, but the dark raincoat looked familiar. At last he turned just enough so that Judith could see a bloody gash on his left cheek. When he dug into his pockets to pull out a handkerchief, he turned again.

"It's Will Fleming," Judith said softly. "I guess he's not missing after all."

A sheepish Will Fleming squeezed in next to Judith. "Sorry for the inconvenience," he murmured, dabbing at the wound on his cheek with a white handkerchief. "Did the police rescue you, too?"

MacRae spoke up before either of the cousins could answer. "It was the other way round," he said, twisting in the front seat just enough to look at Will. "Did you get that cut from one of the crowd?"

"I was gashed by a sharp branch while avoiding the mob at Hollywood House," Will said. "I had to crawl through the shrubbery."

"Do you need a doctor?" MacRae asked. "Mrs. Gibbs has called in a Dr. Carmichael for her own problems."

"No," Will replied. "Take me home. Marie must be frantic."

"Of course," MacRae said, then addressed Ogilvie. "Monk Road, the Priory. We reversed for about three kilometers."

Judith was puzzled. "Why is Marie so upset?"

"We'd been to a . . . sort of soiree earlier this evening," Will responded. "After we left, we heard about poor Chuckie Fordyce. I told Marie I'd go to Grimloch to see Philip and Beth. I insisted that Marie take the car and go home. She's just getting over flu. When I didn't come home within an hour, she panicked, thinking perhaps that something had happened to me. We live in dangerous times."

The explanation was smooth. Too smooth, Judith thought. An hour wasn't nearly long enough to make even the most anxious of wives call the cops.

Will also needed explanations. "I don't mean to pry," he said, "but how do you two visitors to Grimloch happen to be riding in a police car?"

MacRae broke in before Judith or Renie could reply. "A coincidence," the DCI said. "They were stranded and needed a lift."

"Oh. Of course," Will said, smiling politely at the cousins.

It occurred to Judith that her fellow passengers were playing a game of evasion, if not outright deception. It was no wonder, she thought, that Renie was looking skeptical.

"I thought perhaps," Will said to MacRae as Ogilvie turned onto Monk Road, "they had to give a statement about finding Chuckie's body."

"They do," MacRae said easily. "This day has been tumultuous. There's been scant time for paperwork."

The driveway to the Flemings' home was marked by two stone pillars and a discreet wooden sign identifying the property as the Priory. As the mist dissipated, Judith saw a large old house that probably had been built for a religious order. The two-story exterior was gray stone, though obvious additions had been made in various styles. The result was an architectural olio, but the overall effect fell short of being ugly.

Will appeared to have been reading Judith's mind. "Rather a hodgepodge," he remarked in a self-effacing manner. "It has its charms, especially the garden. Marie is doing a wonderful job of restoring many original features that had been modernized."

Ogilvie stopped under a porte-cochere on the south side of the house. "Gothic style here," Renie noted. "But nineteenth century, right? Monks didn't drive much before the Reformation."

"A good eye," Will said, unbuckling his seat belt.

"One good eye," Renie responded. "I'm a graphic designer."

"Ah." Will smiled. "Perhaps you can visit during your stay at Grimloch." He nodded to MacRae and Ogilvie. "Many thanks."

Ogilvie kept his foot on the brake as Will entered through an oak door. Judith tried to see if Marie was waiting for her husband, but the figure outlined by the inside light was male. As Will went in and quickly closed the door, Judith recognized Patrick Cameron in his leather jacket.

MacRae turned to look at the cousins. "It's almost nine. We do need that statement. Would you prefer doing that at Grimloch?"

"I prefer a restaurant," Renie said. "I can put my statement on a menu."

MacRae chuckled obligingly. "That could be arranged. It's past our dinner hour, too."

"Speaking of missing husbands," Judith said to Renie, "we haven't heard from ours lately. We should call them from the restaurant."

"For heaven's sake," Renie responded, "they're fishing. You sound like my mother. She always worried herself to a frazzle when Dad didn't get home when she expected him. I learned a lesson long ago that you never worry about fishermen. They can't be bothered with any other activity or consideration as long as the fish are biting."

"Maybe," Judith murmured, "but Joe always keeps in touch."

The same voice Renie had responded to earlier came over the radio: "This is Control. Please come in, DCI MacRae."

MacRae responded immediately. "Yes?"

"Would you stop at Hollywood House?" the female voice said. "Mrs. Gibbs wants to see you."

"Of course." MacRae sighed. "Do you know how many men are on duty to secure the premises?"

"Three now from Elgin, two more coming from Inverness," the woman responded. "Is everything all right with you, sir?"

"Yes, certainly." MacRae sounded mildly surprised.

"Good. You sounded rather odd when I spoke with you earlier." The radio crackled once and went silent.

"That's peculiar," MacRae said to Ogilvie. "I don't recall talking to Annie this evening."

Ogilvie shrugged.

Judith seized the opportunity to tell the truth. "We answered the call," she said, leaning forward. "We didn't know what else to do. She was reporting Will Fleming as missing."

"Ah!" MacRae chuckled. "I'm most grateful. I'll explain to Annie. I didn't know about Fleming until I spoke to the riot force. Inverness also got the call. You can't imagine what a help you've been to us, Mrs. Flynn. You're the best thing that's come out of America since President Roosevelt's lend-lease program during the war."

"Really," Judith protested, "I haven't done much of anything."

"And," Renie said with bite, "apparently I don't exist."

"Now, Mrs. Jones," MacRae soothed as Ogilvie turned onto the coast road, "I didn't intend to ignore your contribution. We know how much support you give your cousin."

"Yeah, right," Renie muttered.

"Sorry about the digression," the DCI apologized, "but we shouldn't be long at Hollywood House. You may stay in the car if you like."

"Oh no," Judith said, ignoring Renie's grumpy expression. "Having a woman . . . I mean, *women* there might make Moira feel better."

As they approached their destination, a handful of people were walking along the road, heading back to St. Fergna. Only one of the two riot squad vans remained, and its personnel seemed to be preparing for departure. A constable stood on guard at the gate. After MacRae identified himself, admittance was granted a few seconds later.

Fergus waited stiffly at the door. "Madam is in her room with Dr. Carmichael," he said, barely giving the newcomers so much as a glance.

The group trudged up the elegant stairway. Elise met them at the top. "Police?" she said, giving Judith and Renie a quizzical look.

"Yes," MacRae responded. "Mrs. Flynn and Mrs. Jones are observing."

Elise's thin face puckered in confusion. "Observing? What sort of observation?"

"Procedural," MacRae answered blithely. "Which way to Mrs. Gibbs?"

Elise indicated the correct door. "The doctor is still with her."

"Maybe," Judith suggested to MacRae, "we should wait while you and Sergeant Ogilvie go ahead."

MacRae considered for a moment, and then nodded. He and his subordinate walked toward Moira's boudoir.

"You know me," Judith said to Elise. "I was here before."

The maid looked at Renie. "Not with Madame Patch-eye. Is she a pirate?"

Renie took umbrage. "Ever see a pirate in a cashmere sweater?"

Elise studied Renie's disheveled appearance. "You are like a tramp. Filthy, unkempt."

Judith moved in front of Renie to prevent another outbreak of violence. "My cousin was trampled by the mob." She paused, narrowing her eyes. "Did you put Mrs. Gibbs's jewel case in my purse?"

Elise looked affronted. "*Mon Dieu!* Why should I do such a thing?"

"If you didn't," Judith said calmly, "who did? Mrs. Gibbs?"

The maid had gone very pale, a hand to one gaunt cheek. "You have the case?" she asked in a hushed voice.

"No," Judith replied. "It's been stolen."

"Oh!" Elise whirled around and covered her face with her hands. "*Non, non, non!* Impossible!" She started to cry.

Judith put a comforting hand on Elise's back. "I've alerted the police. If you made a mistake and put the case in the wrong handbag, I'm sure your intentions were for the best. Mrs. Fordyce and I both carry large black purses."

"I must kill myself!" Elise wailed. "I am the fool most large!"

The door to Moira's room opened and Dr. Carmichael emerged. "What's this?" he asked kindly, his thick gray eyebrows moving up and down as he spoke. "Elise, your mistress needs you. Are you ill?"

Trying to compose herself, the maid shook her head. "I am upset."

"We're all upset this evening," the doctor said. "Becalm yourself and see to Mrs. Gibbs." He patted her once. "Go now."

"We'll see to her," Judith volunteered. "Elise needs a cup of tea."

"Cognac," Elise said. *"Bonne idée."* Rather morosely, she went down the hall in the opposite direction.

Dr. Carmichael's expression was wry. "The French," he sighed. "So emotional."

Judith introduced Renie, who was still looking out of sorts.

"You have an eye problem," the doctor noted.

"Chronic corneal dystrophy," Renie said, softening just a bit.

He nodded. "Then you know how to treat it."

"Yes. I've had plenty of practice."

"Speaking of practice," Dr. Carmichael said with a faint smile, "I should attend to the rest of mine."

"One question," Judith put in. "This may sound strange, but I understand you treated Patrick Cameron the night David Piazza was killed in a car accident. Is it true that Patrick can't remember what happened and how he got hurt?"

Dr. Carmichael frowned. "So he says. And not unusual, really. Trauma to the head. I'd just come home after delivering a baby. I heard the crash as I was getting out of my car. It wasn't the first time a driver had gone over the cliff. It's a treacherous spot. I notified the police and drove to the scene. I could've walked, it was so close, but I was tired." He smiled in a self-deprecating manner.

"Not as young as I used to be. In any event, I could see the car upside down against the rocks. It wasn't easy, but I climbed down to the wreckage." He sighed heavily. "I had my kit and my torch. When I looked inside the mangled car I saw David Piazza. He was dead. While I waited for the police, I wandered around a bit, not far, since the cliffside isn't conducive to a late night stroll. About twenty yards away, I found Patrick, unconscious but alive."

"He couldn't have been in the car, could he?" Judith inquired as the doctor paused for breath.

"I doubt it, unless he jumped out before it crashed," Dr. Carmichael said. "Patrick is very fit, but he doesn't recall anything that happened after he left Hunter's Lodge on foot three or four hours earlier."

Judith recalled that Hunter's Lodge was Patrick's home outside of St. Fergna. "Were Patrick and Davey friends?"

The doctor glanced at his pocket watch. "Not particularly. I'm afraid Davey didn't have many friends at Blackwell. Most of the executives were jealous of his intimacy with Moira."

"Professional intimacy, you mean," Judith said, noticing Renie, who was studying the ancestral portraits that lined the corridor's walls.

Dr. Carmichael smiled wryly. "I assume so."

"Was Patrick hospitalized?" Judith asked.

"Treated and released," the doctor replied. "He refused to stay."

Judith frowned as Renie took a pen out of her purse. "I gather his wounds were consistent with an accident injury."

"Possibly," Dr. Carmichael said, "but I wasn't the attending physician at the hospital." He looked again at his watch. "Forgive me, I must go. I know you're helping the police with their inquiry, but I do have to call on another patient this evening."

"Of course," Judith said. "I'm sorry to take up your time."

"Quite all right," he said, and started to walk briskly away just as Judith realized what Renie was about to do. "Stop!" she shouted.

Dr. Carmichael turned around at the head of the stairs. "Yes?"

"Not you. My cousin. Sorry." Judith marched over to Renie and knocked the pen out of her hand. "How could you? Those pen marks better come off. These portraits must be worth a fortune."

"I doubt it," Renie said, studying the mustache she'd drawn on an eighteenth-century lady with a very long nose and slightly bulging eyes. "Most of them are just one step above paint-by-the-numbers."

"You get worse as you get older," Judith declared angrily, trying to wipe off the mustache with her finger. "You age, but you don't act it."

Renie uttered an impatient sound. "Did it ever occur to you that I get tired of being shoved into the background while you hold center stage? Okay, so I've got some ego, but if we were in an opera, you'd be listed as the star soprano and I'd get a small contralto cast credit as Lumpa-Lumpa, Donna Fabulosa's Drab Companion."

"For heaven's sakes," Judith retorted, "you have your own business, you're a talented artist, you get plenty of credit for—"

"Not to mention," Renie broke in, airing yet more decades-old grievances, "that when we were kids, it always bothered me because on the calendar we got every year from church, your October birthday fell on the feast of Our Lady of the Rosary, not to mention you had both Saint Teresa of Ávila and Saint Thérèse of Lisieux bracketing your big day while I got stuck with St. Willibrord and St. Prosdocimus. Talk about obscure!"

Judith couldn't help but feel a bit sheepish. "How could I do anything about that? Besides, we're grown up now. As for my sleuthing, you usually encourage me. But that still doesn't give you the right to vandalize other people's possessions."

Renie gazed at the portrait, which still showed a faint trace of pen mark. "Frankly, I think it's an improvement."

"I think it's childish of you, and—" Judith stopped. "Saint Thérèse. The French one, the Little Flower of God. Who mentioned her recently?"

Renie frowned. "One of us? When we were talking about that spooky B&B in Normandy?"

Judith shook her head. "No, I don't think so, even though my suitcase had mistakenly been removed from the train at Lisieux, but I got it back before we sailed." She shrugged. "It'll come to me."

Before Renie could respond, Ogilvie came out of Moira's suite. "Come in. We've finished our inquiry about the protesters."

MacRae joined his sergeant in the hall. "Mrs. Gibbs is calmer. Dr. Carmichael's sedative must be taking effect. She was still quite distressed when we arrived. We'll meet you out front." He turned to Ogilvie. "We should speak with the on-duty personnel." With courteous nods to the cousins, the policemen made their way down the hall.

Moira looked very different from the impeccably groomed, graceful, and poised young woman Judith and Renie had encountered in the graveyard. Her red-gold hair lay in tangles on the lace-trimmed pillow;

her fine complexion was ashen and her face drawn; the graceful fingers seemed more like claws as she grasped anxiously at the elegant duvet.

"You must think me an invalid," she said in a toneless voice. "I apologize for greeting you from my bed again. I was up for a while earlier but that mob shredded my nerves. Except for Will, I've made Fergus turn visitors away ever since you were here. Several people have called on me in the past few days, but I simply couldn't deal with them. Curiosity-seekers, if you ask me, though Seumas Bell had the courtesy to offer apologies for the ruckus with Patrick when you were here. I was still upset, so I told Elise to send him away."

"Please," Judith said, sitting in one of the two brocade-covered armchairs that had been pulled close to the bed. "You've suffered so many losses. And the scene this evening was really awful."

Moira nodded once. "I understand you were there."

"We were," Judith said. "We got caught up in the traffic jam."

"You'd come to call on me?" Moira asked.

"No," Renie put in from where she was still standing at the foot of the bed. "We were going to the circus. I've got a gig as a clown."

"We were headed to the Priory to see Marie," Judith said, avoiding her cousin's glare. "We'd heard Will was missing."

"That's absurd," Moira said in a listless voice. "He was here. Marie should've known that. Why didn't she call me? Why didn't she call Will? Marie's usually sensible. It must be the flu."

"Did the ruckus outside disturb your baby?" Judith asked.

"Of course," Moira answered, displaying a trifle more animation. "He cried for half an hour. My governess had to walk him all over the house. Ah. Here she is now."

A plump and plain woman of indeterminate age entered the room. "Master Jamie has finally settled down," she announced, her brown eyes darting between Moira, Judith, and Renie. "Shall I let him sleep through his eleven o'clock feeding?"

Moira gnawed on her thumbnail. "No. Yes! Yes, Euphemia, unless he wakes up and cries for it."

"Shall I bring him to you?" the governess asked.

"No." Tears welled up in Moira's eyes. "I'm exhausted."

"As you wish." Euphemia left as Fergus entered.

Moira cast a weary gaze on the butler. "Yes?"

"Mr. and Mrs. Gibbs have arrived," he said in his stilted voice.

Moira waved a frantic hand. "Please. Send them away. I can't possibly deal with them tonight. Why would they leave the castle?" She put the question to Judith.

"They've probably finished serving dinner," Judith said. "Have you spoken with them since their grandson was killed?"

"No." Moira turned away. "I don't want to. Especially not now."

"Maybe they heard about the riot," Judith pointed out, "and wanted to make sure you and the baby were okay."

"We're not," Moira declared, still staring off into space. "Send them back to the castle, Fergus."

Fergus cleared his throat, a dry sound like crushed autumn leaves. "Your visitors didn't come from the castle, madam. They're the other Mr. and Mrs. Gibbs, your husband's parents from South America."

19

Moira let out an anguished wail. "No! Not Harry's parents! Oh, God help me! Make it all stop!" She threw pillows on the floor, yanked at the duvet, and began clawing at the sheets.

Fergus stood as unbending as a lighthouse. After a long pause, he finally spoke. "Shall I tell them to wait, madam?"

Judith leaned close enough to grab one of Moira's flailing arms. "Please calm down," she urged softly. "You must relax."

Moira tried to pull away but suddenly slumped, her energies spent. "Cruel, cruel, cruel," she mumbled. "Why must I suffer so?"

Renie had moved closer to Fergus. "Let me handle this," she told him. "And one word out of you and we're going to war." She stomped past the rigid butler and left the room.

Judith put her arms around Moira and rocked her like a baby. Fergus turned around in his robot-like manner and slowly walked away.

"Shall I send for Elise?" Judith asked.

Moira gulped and slumped against Judith's arm. "No," she whispered. "Not now. Oh my God!" Moira gasped. "I can't face Mr. and Mrs. Gibbs! They'll blame me for Harry's death!"

"Why?" Judith asked, handing Moira several tissues.

"They've never liked me," Moira said between sniffs as she wiped at her eyes. "Their niece, Liza, lived with them in London while I was away at school in France. Harry's parents treated her like a princess because they'd never had a daughter. When Harry and I started seeing each other, Liza told the most terrible lies about me. They believed her, even though I'd never even met their wretched niece. In fact, I hardly know Harry's parents, but it's obvious they think I'm some kind of silly little slut and was never worthy of their handsome, charming, spoiled boy."

"Spreading vicious rumors is a nasty habit some people have," Judith said as Moira sank back onto the pillow. "I'm surprised that Mr. and Mrs. Gibbs found out about Harry so quickly. They must not have been as hard to reach as I've been told."

Moira scowled and blew her nose. "They can be found if they want to be," she asserted. "I don't believe half their tales from abroad. It sounds too rugged for what I know of them. If they took a trip up the Amazon, they'd hire a limousine."

Renie came back into the boudoir, dusting off her hands. "Your in-laws have left. I told them you were in bed with Fergus."

Moira looked appalled. "That's not very amusing, given their opinion of me."

Renie shrugged. "They don't think highly of Fergus, either."

"We should probably leave you in peace," Judith said to Moira. "You've had very little of that these past few days. Will you be able to attend the inquest tomorrow?"

Moira flung a hand over her eyes and sighed. "I don't know. I'm afraid there'll be another mob. Morton could be behind it. He's always resented me. The police suggested that the demonstration was staged."

Judith wasn't sure how to respond. "Jocko Morton? What would be the point of damaging your reputation? It gives the company a black eye. How can that help him as the CEO?"

"You don't understand," Moira said. "It's not about public image, it's personal. He wants me out. Jocko wants to be in total control."

"But you own the company," Judith pointed out.

Renie leaned against the bedpost. "There must be a buyout in the wind," she said. "Who's making the offer?"

Moira was surprised. "How did you guess?"

"I don't guess," Renie replied. "I work with big businesses. I know the game—or as much of it as I need to in order to not design a pharmaceutical company's logo using a skull and crossbones."

Moira nodded once. "I suspected for some time that something was going on behind my back. Much as it galled me, I asked Harry what he knew about it. He insisted he didn't know anything. Then I humbled myself even further by talking to Jimmy. He can be such a stick, but basically, I trust him. We are kin, after all, and sometimes I feel he acts in my best interests. Jimmy assured me that nothing was happening, and then Morton left for Greece—'on indefinite leave' was the official word. I didn't believe it. I thought he was one step ahead of serious trouble. But now he's back and creating havoc. Or so it appears." She sighed and closed her eyes. "I'm so tired. I wish I could sleep."

"We'll go now," Judith said.

Moira didn't respond.

The cousins left the boudoir. Euphemia was coming down the hall. "Is Madam awake?" she inquired in a husky voice.

"She's trying to sleep," Judith said. "How's the baby?"

"Quiet as a wee mouse," the governess replied. "A good bairn, despite Madam's fussing. Should I fetch Elise to keep watch?"

Judith shrugged. "Is that what Mrs. Gibbs would want?"

Euphemia's strong jaw jutted slightly. "Perhaps. Though what that silly Frenchwoman would do in a crisis is beyond me. Useless, I say. But I'll get her—unless she's had her snout in the cognac too long." The governess turned on her heel and went in the opposite direction.

"Not a happy house," Renie remarked.

"Tell me about Harry's parents," Judith said as they started down the handsome staircase.

"Good-looking couple, mid-fifties, Dad's balding, Mom's got gold highlights in her hair. Well-dressed, well-spoken." Renie smirked. "I wouldn't trust either of them an inch."

"Are they grief-stricken?"

"Hard to figure," Renie answered as they reached the foyer. "I spoke to them for only about ninety seconds."

"What did you really tell them?"

"That Moira had passed out," Renie said. "They didn't act surprised. Peggy—Harry's mother—murmured 'typical,' and Matt—the dad—sort of sneered."

Judith paused at the entrance. "But not crying their eyes out and wringing their hands over Harry's death."

"They're stiff-upper-lip types," Renie responded. "They grieve in private." She leaned against the door. "I'm famished."

"Me, too," Judith said. "Let's see if the police really will take us to dinner. It's going on ten o'clock."

The police, however, no longer had food on their minds. "The tide is almost out," MacRae said after the cousins got into the waiting car. "We'll take you to the castle. Sorry about the restaurant, but with the inquest set for tomorrow, we should speak with Jocko Morton tonight."

"Sure, fine, great," Renie muttered. "Who needs nourishment?"

Making a disapproving face at Renie, Judith leaned forward to speak to MacRae. "Did you meet Harry's parents?"

"No," MacRae replied, surprised. "Where were they?"

"Here," Judith said. "Moira refused to see them so they left."

MacRae considered this turn of events. "Maybe they went to Grimloch. I'd no idea they'd returned from Argentina."

"I thought it was Brazil," Judith said.

MacRae shrugged. "It was somewhere in South America. It all sounded rather vague. We'll check with the newly arrived Gibbses before we leave you at the castle."

The rest of the short trip from Hollywood House to the beach turnoff was made in silence. Renie sulked; Judith pondered. It wasn't until they arrived at the water's edge that anyone spoke again.

"Five, ten minutes," Ogilvie said. "The tide's not quite all the way out." He smiled at the cousins. "Don't want to get your feet wet."

"I'd walk a mile for a camel," Renie murmured. "And then I'd roast it with a side of sage dressing."

"Ha-ha," Ogilvie responded politely.

MacRae was on his cell phone. "Oh yes? Would you tell your son and his wife we wish to speak with them as soon as we arrive? Thank you. We'll be at Grimloch in just a few minutes."

The cousins parted company with the police at the castle. There was no sign of Harry's parents, but Judith assumed they'd agree to meet MacRae and his sergeant. Heading straight for the kitchen with Renie, they found Mrs. Gibbs putting china away in a glass-fronted cupboard.

"You must be glad to see your son and his wife," Judith said. "How long have they been gone?"

The older woman shrugged. "A year, more or less." She made quite a clatter stacking soup bowls. "Venezuela, it was. Lived in something called a *palafito*. Sounds like a sheiling without the sheep. Very lush country, they say. Bugs, I suspect, more than just the wee midges. Spiders, too, and don't tell me different." She banged a couple of kettles together for emphasis.

"They must be terribly upset about their son," Judith said.

Mrs. Gibbs didn't respond. She closed the cupboard with a vengeance and turned her keen eyes on Renie, who was gnawing on a small block of cheese she'd found in the refrigerator.

"Eat what's on hand," Mrs. Gibbs finally said. "I'm for bed."

Judith watched her stalk away. "That woman's made of iron. I can't figure out if that's good or bad."

"Forget it for now," Renie advised. "Lots of sandwich possibilities. Grab something and let's go upstairs. I'm beat."

"Me, too," Judith agreed. "It's been a long day."

"And tomorrow is . . . " Renie looked at her cousin. "Doomsday?"

Judith's expression was ironic. "Let's hope the doom isn't for us."

Mother Nature rose—or fell—to the occasion Tuesday morning with heavy rain and blustery wind. "Looks like home," Renie noted.

"I can barely see the village through the rain," Judith said, gazing out of the Joneses' room while Renie put on her makeup.

"The weather might literally put a damper on a turnout of Moira's detractors," Renie said.

"Like us, the locals must be used to it," Judith pointed out, pausing in front of the dresser mirror to check her hair. "Even Jocko's imported non-villagers shouldn't be daunted."

"I'm daunted by being up, dressed, and fed before ten," Renie complained. "Why can't they hold inquests in the afternoon, say around teatime? Then we could have a Little Something while they droned on."

"A Big Something for you," Judith said with a wry smile. "Ready?"

Renie nodded. The cousins headed downstairs to reach the lift. Wind and rain pelted them as soon as they entered the courtyard. Arrangements had been made to transport Grimloch's residents by police launch at nine-thirty. It would be a short trip, with the outgoing tide.

The lift had just returned to the top of the cliff. Judith saw four people standing below. She recognized Mr. and Mrs. Gibbs, and assumed that the other couple must be their son and daughter-in-law.

Renie nodded as they stepped into the cage. "The funeral's tomorrow."

"There'll be another inquest and funeral for Chuckie," Judith murmured, seeing Philip and Beth Fordyce hurrying toward them.

"Wow, what a vacation!" Renie exclaimed in a low voice while Judith prevented the lift from closing its gate on the Fordyces.

"Thanks," Beth said. "Such a ghastly way to start the day."

Philip said nothing, merely nodding curtly at the cousins and keeping his eyes gazing upward. When they reached the wet, sandy beach, Judith pulled the hood of her cape over her hair and held it in place against the strong wind blowing off of the sea.

Beth also had a hood on her chic mid-calf belted coat. "This will be excruciating," she murmured. "Have you met the traveling Grubbs?"

Judith suppressed a smile. "You don't like them?" she whispered.

"I don't know them," Beth retorted. "But I know how they feel about Moira. I'll introduce you. Try to act pleased."

Judith pulled Renie along. "Be civil," she said under her breath.

Like the rest of the Grimloch contingent, Matt and Peggy Gibbs were wearing black. Matt was tall and angular, with chiseled features and graying light brown hair; Peggy's refined beauty was unmarred by age—or alleged jungle hardships. Her hands had long, manicured nails that didn't indicate recent digging for long-lost artifacts.

"A pity to have your holiday spoiled," Peggy said calmly. "You must be eager to seek the sanctuary of your own home and hearth."

"We can't blame the setting," Judith said, tempted to tell Peggy Gibbs that the hearth at Hillside Manor was one of the few places where a corpse had not yet been found. "We're very sorry about your son."

"A harsh season for sons," Matthew Gibbs muttered, keeping his hands clasped behind his back and glancing at Philip Fordyce. "The Devil's afoot, it seems."

The sound of the police launch was heard before Judith could actually see it. A few moments later the eight passengers were helped aboard by Sergeant Ogilvie and a couple of constables Judith didn't recognize. She wondered if the Grimloch tragedies had strained the local police force's personnel resources.

The trip to the shore took less than three minutes. A van awaited the group, with another constable and a driver holding umbrellas to shield the octet from the driving rain.

"Don't bother," Renie said to the driver who proffered the umbrella. "I come from rain country. It perks me up. I'm almost awake."

Judith and Renie sat together in the van. No one spoke during the short ride up the cliffside and through the High Street. Despite the stormy elements, several residents were going about their business. Judith noticed that the banner over the village green had blown down at one end and drooped like laundry on a broken clothesline.

As the van pulled up in the car park by the Women's Institute, a small group of protesters held up handprinted signs accusing Moira and Patrick of murdering Harry. The dozen or so men and women looked dispirited. They moved their feet constantly, but not in marching tempo. It appeared to Judith that they were trying to keep warm.

"Not a sellout crowd," Renie murmured as they rose from their seat. "Or maybe it is. Some kind of sellout anyway."

"True," Judith agreed, "but where's the media?"

"At the pubs?" Renie retorted.

But as soon as the cousins got out of the van and walked around toward the side entrance of the institute's brick building, they saw a horde of reporters and cameramen standing behind a wooden barricade.

"Fordyce!" several voices called out, followed by a barrage of questions Judith couldn't quite catch. Philip kept moving, eyes averted, staring straight ahead.

Apparently no one recognized the four members of the Gibbs family. Unlike Philip, Judith figured their faces probably weren't known to the out-of-town media.

The meeting room was already packed, but seats had been reserved up front for the Grimloch group. Seated between Renie and Beth, Judith scanned the crowd for other familiar faces: Patrick, sitting with a pretty blonde who was probably his wife, Jeannie; Seumas Bell, looking slightly feral, but alert to every nuance in the room; Jocko Morton, wedging his portly frame onto the folding chair with his narrow, beady eyes fixed on the two vacant places on the dais; his brother Archie, looking pugnacious and untidy in an ill-fitting brown suit; Will and Marie Fleming, handsome and poised, holding hands in the first row.

There was no sign of Moira or Jimmy Blackwell.

"Maybe they're still coming," Renie said. "Obviously the police didn't catch up with Jimmy yet or we'd have heard about it."

Judith nudged Beth. "Is Moira going to attend?"

Beth shrugged. "I didn't talk to her this morning. I doubt she can manage. Frankly, I don't blame her."

A moment later, the crowd's chatter was silenced by the arrival of a white-haired man with a solemn expression and piercing black eyes. With an air of authority, he sat down in the chair that had been placed behind the table. Judith assumed that the other chair was for the individuals who would give their findings.

The inquest started with the police constables who had been first on the homicide scene. Alpin MacRae stood off to one side of the room, arms folded, eyes taking in every detail of the gathering.

There was nothing new in their testimony. Judith's mind drifted, taking in the austere surroundings, including a spinet piano, the flag of Scotland, and the portrait of a grim-looking woman who, judging from the black dress and lace collar, had probably founded the local institute at least a century earlier. Judith also studied the expressions on the villagers' faces. They were a hardy lot, some of them careworn, a few from the younger set who would seem to be more at home attending a rock concert. An honest bunch, she decided, but perhaps a bit judgmental. Their history of strict, old-fashioned Presbyterianism and their life on the edge of the harsh North Sea lent them an aura of rigidity. Or maybe, she thought, it was just her lively imagination.

Dr. Carmichael gave the medical findings. "Death was caused by pressure to the deceased's face with an item that resulted in suffocation." No, Harry Gibbs had not been in the car at the time of the explosion.

A young man in tweeds and an old school tie succinctly described the type of bomb that had blown up Harry's car. "Ammonium nitrate," he stated, and not that difficult to make.

The magistrate declared that Harry Gibbs's death had been caused by the malicious mischief of a person or persons unknown. He immediately adjourned the inquest.

Renie didn't lower her voice. "No doughnuts? No cookies?"

"Shut up," Judith muttered as they began to file out of the meeting room. "I just realized we'll have to give statements at Chuckie's inquest since we found the body."

"Then we can insist on being fed," Renie retorted.

Judith ignored her. The gathering had suddenly stopped halfway to the exit.

"There must be a bottleneck," Marie Fleming said, turning around. "Where are Beth and Phil?"

Judith tried to find them among the dozen or so people at her rear. "Not anywhere I can see. Is there another way out?"

Will Fleming looked over his shoulder. "Yes. Off of the meeting room on the side of the building that faces the green. I suspect the Fordyces want to avoid the media. The reporters must be causing this delay by crowding at the front." He put a hand on Marie's arm. "Let's duck out that other door, darling. I'd rather not get waylaid, either. I'll leave that up to Seumas."

"He doesn't mind talking to the media?" Judith asked as she and Renie followed the Flemings' lead.

"Our Mr. Bell can say less by saying more," Will replied wryly. "He's a very artful dodger, if a rather good lawyer."

There was no chance to question Will further. A few others had the same idea, getting in the way and preventing the cousins from staying close to the Flemings. Outside, the rain had turned into a drizzle and the wind had become only a slight breeze. "Do we have a plan?" Renie inquired after they reached the green.

"Unfortunately, no," Judith replied. "But I really don't want to spend the day at the castle."

"Gosh, no," Renie said in an ironic tone. "It's much more fun standing here getting soaked."

"Okay, okay," Judith said impatiently. "Maybe we should find a way to get to Hollywood House and see how Moira's—" She stopped, spotting a familiar figure entering the churchyard next to the green. "Kate Gunn," Judith said. "I didn't see her at the inquest."

"Why would she be there? Harry had no ties to her," Renie pointed out. "As I recall, we heard Kate and Moira weren't close even when Frankie Gunn was alive."

Again, Judith didn't say anything immediately. Instead she kept walking toward the church.

"Swell," Renie grumbled. "Getting soaked and having a chin-wag in a cemetery. Isn't there a nice gallows around here someplace where we could stand with a noose around our necks and eat lunch?"

"You don't mind the rain," Judith said, leading the way to the lich gate. "Kate's by the Gunn family plot. If she's praying, we'll wait."

"I'm praying for cozy comfort," Renie asserted.

Judith stopped by a guardian angel statue that was patchy with moss and missing a few fingers.

"Kate's lips are moving," she said softly, "but not exactly like a prayer—more like conversation."

"Talking to Earwig?" Renie suggested.

"Eanruig," Judith corrected. "Yes, maybe. Hunh. She's wagging her finger and acting agitated."

"Does she really expect Earwig to answer back?"

"Maybe," Judith allowed, signaling for Renie to hush. Before she could hear any words, Kate turned in their direction. Judith poked Renie. "Pretend to study this tombstone," she whispered.

"It's David Piazza's," Renie murmured. "The roses Moira brought last week look pretty beat up."

"Speak to Kate," Judith urged. "She thinks you've got the sight."

"Half the sight," Renie retorted. "She's better off with Marie playing the part of a medium."

Judith grabbed Renie's arm. "Do it."

With a sigh of resignation, Renie walked over to the Gunn family plot. Judith trailed behind.

"Hi, Kate," Renie said. "The spirits must be on vacation."

Kate gave a start and turned around to scowl at Renie. "You! What happened? Your eye!"

Renie shrugged. "A chronic condition, affecting my vision. In fact, I have no sight at all of the type you mean. I'm a phony. Sorry."

Judith stopped abruptly, unable to believe that Renie would blurt out the truth.

Kate made a menacing gesture. "Fraud! Liar! How dare you? I should've known you were evil when I met you in the woolen shop!"

"That's pushing it," Renie said. "I'm kind of crabby, but not evil. My intentions were good."

Kate looked puzzled. "I don't understand."

"You're a mother, I'm a mother," Renie explained. "Quite a few young men around here, including one of your sons, have died before their time. That's a horrible thing. I felt guilty about getting into it with you at the shop. I wanted to make it up to you after I found out about your background and your inter- ests."

"My interests?" Kate looked even more confused.

"Astrology, for one thing. I . . . well, to pretend I could help you." Renie made a limp gesture. "It was stupid of me."

Kate's gaze moved to Judith, who had come up behind Renie. "That cape! And the hood! She was the witch I saw in my herb garden!"

"No," Renie said, "that was me, wearing my cous- in's cape."

"Americans are very peculiar," Kate muttered. "I find your actions deplorable. You've no idea how vital the spirit world really is. You mock it. You mock me. I can't forgive you."

"Okay." Renie shrugged. "I hope you get a message from Ear—Eanruig. It's difficult to make sound business decisions these days. The real world's all topsy-turvy."

Kate turned her back on Renie. Judith finally spoke up. "I'm sorry, too," she said, "even if you're not in a forgiving mood. We'll leave you in peace now."

The cousins started walking away, but before they got more than a few feet from the Gunn memorial, Kate called out to them. "Wait!"

"Yes?" Judith said, turning back.

"If you don't have the sight," Kate said to Renie, "how did you know I needed business advice?"

Hoping Renie wouldn't reveal spying on the séance at the pub or eavesdropping on Kate and Philip's conversation at Grimloch, Judith held her breath.

"Your husband was a shrewd businessman," Renie said. "If you came here to commune with his spirit, you must be seeking his counsel."

"Ah." Kate's homely features softened. "That's so. You're perceptive, I'll say that for you."

"Good luck," Renie said. "The shipping business is always risky. At least whiskey is one product that rarely has a downswing."

Kate frowned. "Meaning . . . what?"

"Uh . . . " Renie faltered. "Gosh, I don't know. I thought I'd heard that you were involved in some kind of negotiations with Philip Fordyce."

"We've shipped his whiskey for years," Kate said. "That's not new."

"Oh." Renie looked sheepish. "I haven't been here long enough to know all the local commercial connections. I do know that oil and water don't mix, and neither do oil and whiskey."

Kate shot Renie a sharp look. "Why not?"

Renie wore her most ingenuous expression. "I don't know."

"It seems," Kate said stiffly, "that there's a great deal you don't know. Just like the police. It seems they have no idea who killed Harry Gibbs or Chuckie Fordyce. 'Malicious mischief' indeed!"

She stalked past the cousins and headed out of the graveyard.

Renie frowned. "Kate and Philip in a takeover of Blackwell?"

"Sounds crazy," Judith said, leaving the Gunn family plot behind, "but not impossible. It's not the only interesting thing, though."

"Such as?"

"Kate wasn't at the inquest," Judith said. "I know, I looked for her. How did she know the magistrate's conclusion?"

"Aha. Kate has a small hole in the wall of the Women's Institute?"

Judith nodded. "This entire investigation is full of holes. Why do I have a feeling that we could step in one and never get out?"

Renie shuddered. "Not a good thing to say in a cemetery. A really bad thing to say since that's what happened to Chuckie."

Judith nodded again, her expression grim. "That's what scares me. I wish our husbands would come back. I'm worried about them."

The sun was peeking from behind the shifting clouds, but the weather's improvement didn't lift Judith's spirits. "I don't care what you say about fishermen," she declared as they reached the village green, "I'm calling Joe." She dug her cell phone out of her purse and dialed.

After six rings, a message came on, telling her that the person at this number was unavailable. Frowning, Judith stared thoughtfully in the direction of the now deserted Women's Institute. "I'll call the Glengarry Castle Hotel. Where did I put that information?" She did some more digging in her purse. "Ah. Here it is."

"You're nuts," Renie murmured. "They'll be fishing this morning."

"I know," Judith agreed, "but I can leave a message. Hello?" she said as a woman's voice answered on the other end. "I'm calling for Joe Flynn. This is his wife. Is he in?"

"He left yesterday," the woman informed her in a brusque tone.

"Oh." Judith glanced at Renie who had walked over to the drooping banner and was trying to rip it down from the tree where it had been hung. "I assume Mr. Jones and Mr. MacGowan went with him."

"Yes," the woman said.

"Did they tell you where they'd gone?" Judith inquired.

"No."

Judith tried to remember what Joe had told her about their plans. "I thought," she said, "they were going to do some sightseeing in your area. Ben Nevis, Beauly Firth, a castle ruin close by. Didn't they expect to stay at your hotel for at least another night or two?"

"Yes." The woman sounded rather testy. "They were booked through tonight. They didn't bother to check out, so I charged their partial stay to Mr. MacGowan's credit card and added a cancellation fee. It was, if I may say so, quite rude of them."

Alarmed, Judith motioned to Renie, who had succeeded in yanking down the banner and was stuffing it into a dustbin. "Did they take their belongings with them?" Judith asked.

"Not all of it. But they also put at least six fish in our freezer. Shall I send everything on to you?"

"Could you hold for a moment?" Judith said, trying to keep the panic out of her voice and putting a hand over the cell. "Coz!" she whispered urgently to Renie, who was coming toward her. "The husbands are missing!"

20

W hat do you mean, 'missing'?" Renie responded with an anxious expression.

Judith explained what the woman at the hotel had just told her. "Joe and Bill wouldn't walk out of a hotel and leave stuff behind."

"How can they get into trouble when they're with a top-notch policeman?" Renie demanded. "Maybe they intended to come back but the fishing got so hot wherever they were that they decided to stay put."

It was possible, Judith realized. She hesitated before speaking into the phone. "Could you store their belongings for a day or so? It's just not like them."

"If you say so," the woman said, unconvinced. "Twenty-four hours. That's all we can allow to keep their luggage. This is a hotel, not a storage locker." She hung up.

Judith held the phone in her hand. "I don't like this. I told you I had a feeling something was wrong when we didn't hear from them. I'm calling MacRae." After the third ring, he answered. "This is Judith Flynn. Have you heard from DCI MacGowan recently?"

"No," MacRae answered, faintly surprised. "Why do you ask?"

"I don't mean to be an alarmist," Judith said, and explained what she'd been told by the woman at the hotel.

"Rather odd," MacRae agreed. "I hope there hasn't been an accident. Some of the terrain in that part of the country is quite rugged."

The words only increased Judith's concern. "Surely not all of them could have been . . . incapacitated."

"Probably not." MacRae paused. "Don't upset yourself, Mrs. Flynn," he said in a more cheerful voice. "When it comes to fishing, the word 'lure' takes on a strong double meaning."

"Are you friendly with MacGowan?" Judith inquired. "I thought you might know where he was likely to take our husbands."

"I know Hugh," MacRae replied, "but not intimately. I was transferred from Edinburgh to the Moray division only a year ago."

"Oh." Judith's expression was bleak. "Is Ogilvie any better acquainted with him?"

"No," MacRae said ruefully. "Ogilvie was transferred with me."

"Somebody at headquarters must know him," Judith said, growing impatient. "He seems to be quite a legendary figure around here."

"He is that," MacRae said hastily. "Please don't fret. To ease your mind, I'll look into the matter straightaway."

"Thanks," Judith said, and clicked off.

"Zip?" Renie said, still looking anxious. "What can we do?"

"Nothing," Judith said in disgust. She paced up and down on the cobbled street, breaking her thought only to muster a smile at two older women walking past her. "Who thought MacGowan's absence was odd?"

"Patrick Cameron," Renie replied. "He implied that the killer had deliberately chosen a time when MacGowan would be out of the way."

"Patrick may be right." Judith made way for a blind man tapping his white cane as he moved cautiously up the High Street.

"He's worse off than I am," Renie murmured. "But Bill and Joe may be in an even bigger mess. Are the cops sending out searchers?"

"Yes," Judith replied, finally standing still. "I don't know what they do in a case like this, but they're doing something. We're helpless." She scanned the shop signs along the High Street. "MacRae and Ogilvie must be staying somewhere around here, but I don't see an inn."

"There has to be one," Renie said. "Let's go to the source. Alison at the woolen shop seems to know everything."

Judith agreed. Their destination was only three doors down the street, where they found Alison waiting on Harry's mother, Peggy Gibbs.

"Can't you overnight it?" Harry's mother asked in an arch tone. "I must have it for the funeral tomorrow at eleven."

Alison glanced at the cousins but didn't greet them. It was clear to Judith that the girl had her hands full with Peggy Gibbs. "I've never done that with an order from Paris, but I can try."

"Of course you can," Peggy said. "You have my credit card. Tell the express driver to take it to the castle. By nine-thirty, do you hear?" Without so much as a look in the cousins' direction, she walked out of the shop in a decidedly regal manner.

Alison's eyes widened. "Imagine! Buying a two-thousand-quid suit from Paris just to wear for the funeral!"

"I guess she's really rich," Judith said. "Did she seem sad?"

"Sad?" Alison frowned. "Oh—about Harry. Aye, she did, in her way. Angry, too. Maybe more angry than sad."

Judith nodded. "A mother might react that way. By the way," she went on, "is there an inn here in the village?"

"Aye," Alison replied. "The Hearth and Heath, just down the road from the green. The opposite direction of Hollywood House, that is."

"Do you know if DCI MacRae and his sergeant are staying there?"

"They are for a fact," Alison said. "Set up a regular office, I hear. Barry delivered a pizza to them last night."

"How far down the road?" Renie inquired.

"Next to the Women's Institute there's the cobbler shop and the thrift shop," Alison said. "Then the inn. Not far at all. Visit the thrift shop when you've got the time," she suggested. "They've got all sorts of bargains. Barry and I both find things we fancy. He bought that Italian lad's suede jacket for two pounds."

Judith's curiosity was aroused. "David Piazza's clothes were sold at the thrift shop?"

"Aye," Alison replied. "Barry and Davey worked together at Tonio's Pizza Parlor. That was before Davey got his job with Moira Gibbs. Davey had no family nearby, so Moira donated his things to the thrift shop. Part of the proceeds go to the veterans' relief fund."

Judith was surprised. "Davey delivered pizza before he became Moira's personal assistant?"

"No, no," Alison said. "He made the pizzas. In fact, he invented one, being a vegetarian. It's still on the menu—Piazza's Veggie Variation. The Bruce loves it."

"It still seems odd that Moira hired him," Judith noted.

Alison shrugged. "He was hot."

"From the pizza oven, no doubt," Renie murmured. "Or do you mean Davey was handsome?"

"Quite," Alison said. "Not my type, but curly dark hair, huge black eyes, good body. Soulful-looking." She shrugged again. "A pity The Bruce chewed up Davey's suede jacket. Barry was ever so sad."

"No doubt," Judith said, not without sympathy. "Thanks again."

Outside, Judith felt aimless. "What now besides worry?" She looked into the fishmonger's window where a bug-eyed haddock stared back at her. "It's frustrating. There's nothing we can do."

Renie sighed. "I know. Damn!"

"We could have lunch," Judith said.

"I'm not hungry."

Loss of appetite was a measure of Renie's concern. "I don't care much about eating, either," Judith admitted. "I feel adrift."

"Grab an anchor," Renie murmured. "Kate Gunn just came out of the chemist's shop and she's headed this way."

To Judith's surprise, Kate waved. "A moment," she called.

"Yes?" Judith said. "What is it?"

Kate looked all around to see if anyone was listening. Only a half dozen people were on the High Street, and they all seemed to be going about their own business. Still, Kate apparently had qualms.

"We'll go to the Rood & Mitre," she said. "We must talk."

She led the way across the High, back up the incline, and around the corner where the pub was tucked away in the narrow street. Judith realized it was almost noon and was puzzled by Kate's choice of a setting for a private conversation. Lunch hour should be starting at the pub.

Ian was already waiting on a middle-aged couple and two of the booths were occupied. He looked up as Kate entered with the cousins.

"Mrs. Gunn," he said politely, ushering the women inside. "And the American ladies." Ian looked curious. "The common room . . . or . . . ?"

"Or," Kate replied. "This is a meeting."

Ian nodded. "The door's unlocked," he said, heading for the service counter. "If you want food or drink, fetch me."

Kate nodded and wordlessly led the cousins through the corridor they'd traversed earlier when they'd spied upon the séance. "This is the office," she said, opening the door. "It's small and crowded, but ensures privacy. You never know who might be lurking about."

Judith and Renie avoided looking at each other lest they seem guilty for having been numbered among the lurkers. The office arrangement was somewhat different from what Judith had seen through the spy-hole. The table had been moved and apparently was used as a desk. There was an old rail-back chair behind the table. A half dozen folding chairs leaned against the far wall.

"I'm afraid," Kate said as she sat down behind the table, "you'll have to use those metal chairs. The amenities here are sparse."

"No problem," Judith said as Renie hauled out two chairs and set them up. "You look troubled, Kate."

The other woman nodded. "I am. I was very curt with you in the cemetery. Afterwards, I realized you were only trying to help." Kate turned to Renie. "You claim not to have the sight. Yet by my husband's grave you mentioned whiskey and oil and water. It dawned on me after I walked away that you understood my conundrum."

"I was guessing," Renie said.

Kate smiled ironically. "More than a guess." As Renie started to protest, Kate held up a hand. "No. You must be a Scorpio, Serena."

"True," Renie said.

Kate turned to Judith. "You're a Libra, Judith, a social animal, magnetic, charming, and always seeking balance in your life. You're oversensitive, though." She looked again at Renie. "You are competitive, energetic, and hurl yourself into your work, which is often of a creative nature. You do nothing in moderation and you make a fearsome foe. But there is a deeply intuitive side to Scorpios. That's why I had to speak with you." She paused, apparently to let her words sink in.

Judith smiled. "I have to admit your assessment of our personalities is accurate."

"You're perceptive, Kate," Renie said. "But how are we to help?"

"I'll explain," Kate replied. "My children are the most important thing in my life. I've already lost too many of them. Now I may lose my former daughter-in-law." She paused again and licked her dry lips. "I believe that Moira is in mortal danger."

"Why?" Judith blurted.

Kate picked up some paper clips from a small box and began linking them together. "This is very confidential. As I mentioned, Philip Fordyce and my husband had a long-standing agreement to ship Grimglen liquor. That's how Beth met Philip. He's known her since she was born." Kate smiled faintly, as if recalling the moment when her baby daughter was first placed in her arms. "Philip has had some misfortune along the way, not just with his distillery business, but with his family life. He's lost two wives, and his only son was born with severe problems. Now, of course, poor Chuckie is dead. Philip has no heir. If only Beth . . ." Kate dropped one of the paper clips onto the desk and slowly picked it up. "Beth hasn't been able to get pregnant. She's been to fertility clinics all over the world. Philip won't adopt. Like my own husband, he's convinced that bloodlines are all that matter."

"That's ego," Judith remarked. "But how does this affect Moira?"

"Blackwell Petroleum," Kate said, the paper-clip chain now at least two feet long. "Many years ago Moira's father gave shares of the company's stock to his closest friends, including my husband." She grimaced, causing Judith to wonder if Eanruig Gunn had passed on part of his gift to his mistress, Diana Porter-Breze.

"After James Blackwell died, his widow wasn't so generous. The majority shares were left to Moira. If she dies or is convicted of murder, her half brother Jimmy will wrest those shares from her or become her baby's legal guardian. I don't trust him an inch, despite his professed moral rectitude."

"I still don't understand," Judith put in.

"I'm getting to that," Kate said, adding the last paper clip in the box. "As a wedding present, Moira gave Beth some shares of Blackwell. Moira and Beth and Marie were so close, like sisters—and, of course, when Moira married Frankie, she and Beth became sisters-in-law. I won't say that Moira and I had a loving relationship, but I appreciated her care for Frankie, who was never physically strong. Strangely enough," Kate continued, almost as if musing to herself, "when Marie married Will Fleming, Moira didn't attend the wedding, and gave them a rather ugly vase."

"No stock?" Renie asked.

Kate shook her head. "There was a falling-out between Moira and Marie for a time. I don't think Moira cared for Will or trusted him. Recently, they've all made up. But Moira's most significant lack of generosity was her refusal to give Harry any Blackwell shares when she married him. Naturally, he was resentful. The company is in turmoil, possibly because

Jocko Morton had been up to no good. Moira has been indifferent, but she's never had a head for business—which is why Philip and I want to buy the company from her."

"Wow!" Renie exclaimed softly. "That's quite an acquisition."

"Yes," Kate agreed. "But we can manage it financially. My own family is very wealthy—banking, mainly. Now that Harry's dead, the real obstacle is Jimmy Blackwell. I wouldn't put it past him to harm Moira and prevent Philip and me from buying her out. Jimmy is power-mad."

"Do you think he killed Harry?" Judith asked.

Kate held up the paper-clip chain, which she'd fashioned into a loop with a dangling tail. "Perhaps. That's not important to me at the moment. Jimmy must go." She dangled the paper clips from her fingers. They reminded Judith of a rosary.

Or a noose.

Judith still didn't understand why Kate Gunn had unburdened herself so frankly.

"Kate," Judith began, "why are you telling us all this?"

Kate put the paper-clip chain aside. "I have my sources of information. I'm aware of who you really are. That's why I know you have ways to help me solve my problem with Jimmy." Kate's eyes sparkled with apparent excitement. "You're CIA."

"What?" Judith gasped.

"There's no need to pretend," Kate asserted. "My source is above reproach. Let's say that the law is on my side."

Judith was so flabbergasted she couldn't speak.

Renie looked a bit dazed, but recovered quickly. "You're talking about a covert operation," she said to Kate. "We need information about Jimmy's habits, schedule, and so on. We also need lunch. Judith and I will give our orders to Ian. What would you like?"

"Ah . . . " It was Kate's turn to look taken aback. "A sandwich. Fish paste will do."

"Fine." Renie got up and hauled Judith out of the chair. "Let's go. I feel like a burger."

"You act like an idiot!" Judith hissed as soon as the cousins were in the corridor. "Why in the world are you stringing Kate along? And where did she hear that we're a couple of spies?"

"Listen," Renie said, deadly serious. "Kate's got spy-holes all over the place. I'll bet she's got the cops bugged somehow. Maybe she overheard MacRae and Ogilvie talking about your detection skills. Or," she added a bit uncertainly, "they also think you're from the CIA."

"They've never actually mentioned the FATSO web site," Judith said. "It's possible they're confused, too."

"Then make the most of it," Renie said. "Kate probably knows more about what's going on than the cops do. Let's find out."

"Brilliant," Judith said as they went down the hall. "I think."

Renie sought out Ian while Judith poked her head into the kitchen. "Grizel?"

Ian's mother looked up from the grill. "Ah! I hear there's a meeting in the back room. What's Mrs. Gunn up to now?"

"A few tricks," Judith said, offering Grizel a confidential smile. "You know her. Who'd resist an occasional peek in that spy-hole?"

Grizel laughed softly. "Only when I'm not busy."

"Did David Piazza ever come here?"

Grizel flipped rashers of bacon on the grill. "Aye, often. A charmer, he was. Clever, I have to think. Come up in the world, did Davey. He came to this country with nothing, worked at Tonio's, and the next thing we know, he's got an important post with Moira Blackwell. Imagine! And him not knowing the language all that well."

"Sounds like home," Judith murmured, recalling the temporary mailman on the Heraldsgate Hill route who couldn't read English.

Grizel was studying a new order. "Fish paste sandwich and two burgers," she noted. "Mrs. G must want the fish paste—nobody else ever does. Are the burgers yours?"

"Yes," Judith answered. "I can wait and save you a trip."

"Ian will do it," Grizel said.

Judith thanked Grizel and went back to the office. To her surprise, Renie was standing by the open door. "The hen flew the coop."

Judith looked into the cramped office. "Did you see her leave?"

Renie shook her head and pointed to a door marked exit. "It leads to a path that ends at Patrick Cameron's cottage."

Judith was mystified. "Why? I thought Kate wanted our help."

"Somebody called on her cell phone?" Renie suggested.

Judith opened the door. The dirt path ran behind two smaller buildings before abutting Patrick's property. "I wonder if he's there."

"Do we find out?" Renie asked.

"Are you really hungry?"

"No. I'm still too worried about our guys."

Judith went into the office, wrote a brief note to Ian explaining their hasty departure, and left twenty pounds on the desk.

"Since when," Renie inquired as they walked along the narrow path, "did we get stupid? This could be a trap."

"Why? There's no reason for Kate to harm us," Judith replied.

"The trap might be for Kate. Maybe she knows too much."

"Kate can take care of herself," Judith said, opening a gate in the hedge that went around the cottage. "Let's try the back way."

Her knock drew no response. "We'll try the front," Judith said.

The result was also futile, and there was no sign of Patrick's car. "I'm stymied," Judith admitted. "I assume Kate drove to the village, but we've no idea what she drives. Now what?"

Her cell phone rang. Hurriedly, she took it out of her purse.

"MacRae here," he said. "I've good news. MacGowan sent us a text message saying they'd found a hot spot on the Findhorn and changed their plans. They'll be in touch."

"Oh!" Judith exclaimed. "That's a relief! I'll tell my cousin they're safe. Thanks so much." She rang off.

"So we're not widows after all?" Renie said with a big grin.

"No, thank heavens," Judith replied, putting the cell back in her purse. "So where is Kate? And where is Patrick?"

Part of the answer came in the form of Barry, driving his rattletrap car down the High Street. "Hullo!" he called. "Busy time. Lunch hour." Brakes squealing like so many piglets, he managed to stop just short of Patrick's fence. "He's not home."

"How do you know?" Judith inquired, moving cautiously toward the unpredictable vehicle.

"Because he's at Hollywood House, giving a press conference," Barry replied. "I just came from there. Those reporters like pizza."

"What kind of press conference?" Judith asked, one eye on the Bruce, who was nibbling on pepperoni in what was left of the backseat.

"Oh—you know," Barry said vaguely. "The reporters all ask questions at once, and the nob who's behind the mike goes blah-blah and never really answers."

"Patrick must have had a reason for calling the press conference," Judith asserted. "Do you remember anything he said?"

The hamster had polished off the pepperoni and was nibbling on a much-abused suede jacket.

"The Bruce is eating your outerwear," Renie said. "Do you mind?"

Barry turned around to look into the backseat. "Nae, he likes it better than I do. It's too short in the sleeves for me."

"It's getting shorter," Renie noted. "That's the part he's chewing."

Barry shrugged. "It came cheap, being second—" He stopped and snapped his fingers. "Now I remember. Patrick was talking about Davey Piazza. That's who the jacket belonged to before it was sent to the thrift shop. Patrick claimed that Davey's accident wasn't."

"Wasn't an accident?" Judith said.

"Right. Patrick told the reporters that if they wanted to find out who killed Harry they should go after whoever made Davey's car crash." Barry tapped the padded container next to him in the front seat. "Sorry. Got two more pizza deliveries—the post office and the auto repair."

The cousins gave Barry and his car a wide berth. After a couple of false starts, the engine caught and he rattled off toward Archie's garage.

Judith was silent for a few moments. "Davey's death has always struck me as a little too convenient."

"His rise and fall seem odd," Renie agreed. "It's not as if someone immigrating to a new country doesn't have to take a menial job for starters, but they usually spend a long time working their way up. Davey fell into the cream awfully fast."

Judith nodded. "Moira didn't hire him for his ability to toss pizza dough. Her habit of falling in love indicates she was thinking with the wrong part of her anatomy." She paused, shielding her eyes from the midday sun. "This is starting to make sense. I think."

"Ah." Renie smiled. "Your customary logic has kicked in."

Judith shrugged. "I don't understand big business, but I know people. There aren't many motives for cold-blooded murder, but jealousy is a big one." She gazed toward the sea where the sun glinted off of the incoming waves. "There are plenty of reasons for envy with this bunch. You might say," she said wryly, "we've got too much of a bad thing."

For once, Judith was walking so fast Renie had to hurry to catch up with her. "Where are we going?" she demanded as Judith crossed the High Street and headed for the coast road.

"Hollywood House," Judith called over her shoulder. "But we need transport. Maybe Barry's still at Morton's garage."

As soon as the cousins reached the auto shop, they saw Barry's beater parked in front of Archie Morton's office. Judith suggested that they wait outside.

"Why?" Renie said. "Another rumpus with Archie might be fun."

"Not for me," Judith declared. "You're getting ornerier as you grow older. I refuse to spend my twilight years with you in a nursing home. You'd probably get tossed anyway for outrageous brutality."

"I'm learning how your mother drives that wheelchair," Renie said. "She's got some great moves. She should be licensed to kill."

"Don't mention it," Judith said, and winced. "I shouldn't have moved so fast. Now I feel wobbly."

Barry and Archie came out of the office. They seemed to be arguing, but Judith couldn't hear what they were saying. Barry finally shrugged and stalked back to the car. He didn't seem surprised to see the cousins.

"Poor tipper?" Renie inquired.

"No tipper at all," Barry replied, still annoyed. "He says all his expenses at the garage go into the computer and he can't figure in tips. That's bosh. I had two pizzas, one for Archie and one for his main mechanic. Rob's a good lad, always gives me a quid. But Archie wouldn't let me take Rob's pizza to the back shop like I do usually. Just mean, that's Archie Morton."

"We didn't have computers when I worked at the Meat & Mingle years ago," Judith said. "We were lucky to have a cash register. If the help wanted to get paid,

they had to roll the drunks when they fell off of the—"
She stopped. "Never mind. I just had the strangest
thought."

"What?" Renie asked sharply.

Judith shook her head. "It was silly." But she was
suddenly worried, though she tried to hide her concern
from Renie and Barry.

"Last stop," he announced. "Uh . . . Do you want a
lift?"

"Yes," Judith said quickly. "That's why we're here.
After your post office stop, can you take us to Hollywood House?"

Barry considered briefly. "I suppose. No more deliveries just now."

Judith got in the front seat, grateful that the door
had been reattached to the passenger side; Renie again
sat with The Bruce in back. "Sleeve's gone," she said
as the car went forward with a loud *ka-pock-eta-ka-
pock-eta* sound. "He's going for the silk lining and the
inside pocket. Won't he get indigestion?"

"Maybe," Barry warned. "Better move. He may
toss up the suede."

"We'll buy you a replacement jacket," Judith said,
"to thank you."

"Nae." Barry chuckled, heading up the High Street.
"It's been jolly. Most of it, anyway."

"I mean it," Judith insisted. "You're a good guy. Lad, that is."

The post office was two doors down from the confectioner's. Barry double-parked and zipped inside. Renie tapped Judith's shoulder. "What's wrong? I can tell you're upset. You're making rash and expensive promises."

"I'm serious about the jacket," Judith replied, turning to look at Renie. "We owe Barry. But you're right. It's probably a stupid notion, but suddenly I got the feeling that Joe and Bill aren't safe. In fact, I think I know where they are, and I'm certain they're in grave danger. The question is, how do we rescue them?"

21

Renie looked dubious. "Now *you* have the sight?"

"No," Judith said. "But I remembered something after Barry mentioned Archie's computer. When Joe was telling me about Hugh MacGowan, he—" She stopped as Barry raced out of the post office.

"Big news!" he cried, jumping into the car. "Patrick's been arrested!"

"For what?" Judith asked.

"Murder," Barry replied excitedly. "Imagine! Patrick killed Harry!"

"Maybe," Judith said softly. "Where did they arrest him?"

"Hollywood House, after the press conference," Barry replied. "Still want to go there?"

Judith's thought process was hampered by her concern for Joe and Bill. "I don't know . . . Maybe we should go to the Hearth and Heath."

"The inn?" Barry sounded puzzled. "Oh—because that's where the coppers are staying?"

"Yes," Judith said as horns honked behind them. "They'd take him there for questioning instead of to Inverness or Elgin. Do you have a jail in St. Fergna?"

A half dozen vehicles now clogged the High Street. Barry started the car, ignoring the honks and shouts of the impatient drivers. "Nae. No need. The nearest jail is only seven kilometers from here."

The minor traffic jam didn't abate after they reached the village green and made a right turn. It appeared that the media had followed Patrick and his captors from Hollywood House. Their vans and cars and trucks blocked the narrow road as they tried to find parking places.

"Now what?" Barry said, mildly exasperated.

"We can walk," Judith said. "I think."

"Well . . . " Barry snapped his fingers. "I know a shortcut. Hang on." He hit the gas and took a sharp left, driving across the green, beyond the bandstand and onto a rough dirt path that ran behind the Women's Institute. The old car bounced and thumped, causing Judith and Renie to grit their teeth and try to stay upright.

"The Bruce is getting carsick!" Renie shouted. "So am I!"

"Almost there!" Barry took another turn onto a grassy area partially surrounded by shrubbery growing in front of a brick wall. "Back of the inn," he said, coming to a jarring stop just short of a leggy rhododendron. "There's a gate at the end of the wall."

"Not locked, I hope," Judith said.

"Nae," Barry assured her. "We dinna have much crime here."

"Really?" Renie said dryly.

Barry looked rueful. "Well . . . not until lately."

Judith was trying to open the car door. "It's jammed," she said.

"Pull up the string on the handle," he advised.

Judith complied; the door opened. "Are you coming with us?" she asked Barry.

"Nae," he replied. "I should get back to Tonio's."

Renie was already out of the car, holding Barry's tattered jacket. Judith eyed her cousin curiously. "Why did you take that?"

"For comparison shopping," Renie said. "You told Barry you were going to replace it. This is—was—real quality. I assume you don't want to buy a cut-rate item."

"True," Judith responded, keeping an eye on Barry's efforts to back the car away from the grassy area.

"At the moment, all I want to do is talk to MacRae about our husbands."

"Then let's do it," Renie said, marching to the end of the brick wall.

The iron gate was unlocked and led to a narrow brick path between the inn's garden and the main building. Renie stopped at what Judith assumed was the service entrance. She didn't bother to knock, but turned the knob. The door opened easily.

"So far so good," Renie murmured. "The innkeeper must be your kind of person—an open-door policy during the day."

They had entered a small hallway that went into the kitchen. Ordinarily, Judith would have paused to study the layout and compare it with her own at Hillside Manor. But not now, not when her priority was finding Joe and Bill.

The cousins entered the dining room, which was empty though it appeared that the big oval table was being prepared for the afternoon tea. Reaching the parlor, they heard loud voices that sounded as if they were coming from in front of the inn.

"Damn!" Judith exclaimed softly. "Now MacRae's probably having his own press conference."

Before she could look out of the windows, Constable Glen entered through a side door. "Mrs. Flynn, Mrs. Jones!" he said in surprise. "May I help you?"

"Yes," Judith said. "Can you please tell DCI MacRae that we've reason to believe that neither our husbands nor Hugh MacGowan are safe? That text message didn't come from them. It was a hoax, meant to deceive all of us."

Glen frowned. "Pardon? How do you know?"

"Never mind," Judith said, trying to remain patient. "Just tell him. I think I know where they are."

Glen looked disconcerted. "He's with the media. I can't interrupt."

"Then do it as soon as he's done," Judith said, more sharply than she'd intended. "Please. Tell MacRae I think they're at Morton's garage."

Glen looked flummoxed. "The auto repair?"

"Yes." She composed herself and tried to smile. She failed.

"I'll relay the message . . . " He broke off as Seumas Bell came into the parlor.

"Where's Cameron?" Seumas demanded of Glen.

"In our temporary headquarters in the study across the hallway," Glen answered. "You're his legal counsel?"

"No," Seumas snapped. "I refuse to represent him. I'm not a criminal lawyer and I detest murderers. I'll tell him in person." He suddenly seemed to notice the cousins. "What are they doing here?"

Glen's color rose. "They . . . ah . . . "

"I'm going to represent Patrick," Renie declared. "Go ahead, look me up under the American Inns of Court under S. E. Jones. I'm big stuff on the other side of the pond and I've practiced as a barrister over here."

Bell tried to conceal his astonishment but didn't quite manage it. "You're a . . . " He cleared his throat. "Then you're welcome to him." He turned on his heel and left the room.

Glen was staring at Renie. "I didn't realize . . . "

"Never mind. My brother-in-law's the attorney. Bub and I have the same initials. That's because," she went on, "his real name isn't Bub. Still, he's a terrific lawyer, and he did come to England once. For something. I forget."

Glen seemed justifiably confused. "If you'll excuse me, I should—" Shouts and loud noises suddenly erupted, and not, Judith judged, from outside. "What's that?" Alarmed, the constable raced from the parlor.

Judith and Renie followed him to the door from which he'd entered. They saw Patrick Cameron pummeling Seumas Bell before hurling him onto the floor.

"Now, now," PC Glen called. "None of that! Oops!" He lost his balance as Seumas rolled into his legs.

"Keep that swine away from me!" Patrick barked. "He's the one who should be under arrest!" He went back into what was presumably the study and slammed the door.

"We're out of here," Judith said to Renie. "Let's go."

Leaving through the tradesmen's entrance, Judith stopped to catch her breath on the brick path. "Between you and these crazy Scots, I can only take so many brawls in one short span of days. Besides, we can't do anything about Joe and Bill until MacRae gets our message. We'll have to trust him to act fast. I'm sure he will with a fellow cop at risk."

"Let's hope." Renie sighed and clutched at the ruined suede jacket she was still holding. "Damn and double damn. Maybe we should've gone to California after all."

Judith looked askance. "Right. It's so safe. Nothing bad ever happens in California," she said.

"Now what do we do?" Renie asked. "We've no wheels."

Judith studied the inn's well-tended garden and tried to calm herself by imagining how it would look when the bulbs were in bloom and the herbaceous borders had leafed out. At home, she found working with plants, digging in the dirt, and pruning overgrown shrubs was a form of therapy after a difficult day. But just thinking about the process and its results came as no comfort ten thousand miles away from Hillside Manor. "We could sit in the gazebo and pray," she suggested.

"Sounds good to me," Renie said.

They walked the twenty feet to the gazebo with its dark green latticework and sat down after making sure the wooden seats weren't wet from the rain and mist. "I don't hear any noise coming from the front of the inn," Judith said after a couple of minutes of silence. "Maybe the media's gone."

"Good," said Renie. "Then MacRae can find our husbands. What makes you think Morton's got them locked up in the repair shop?"

"Because he wouldn't let Barry deliver the pizza there," Judith replied. "According to Barry, he always takes . . . What was the mechanic's name? Rob?" She saw Renie nod. "Barry always delivers Rob's pizza in person to get his big tip."

"You're scaring me," Renie declared. "Why would Morton be holding our husbands?"

"It has to do with MacGowan," Judith said. "Whoever killed Harry wanted MacGowan out of the way because he's a smart cop who probably knows too much. Somehow MacGowan must've found out about the murder—that is, both murders. Unfortunately, Joe and Bill were with him, and . . . " She shook her head. "I know it all sounds crazy, but I'm sure MacGowan didn't send that text message to MacRae. Joe told me MacGowan detested new technology and refused to use it."

Renie was nervously fidgeting with the jacket. "I don't see how all three of them could've been kidnapped."

"That's what I don't understand," Judith admitted. There was a pause while the cousins fretted in silence.

"Maybe we should go to Morton's garage," Renie said.

"No. Too dangerous," Judith responded. "Let the cops do it."

"Damn," Renie said softly. "The Bruce chewed the label off of this jacket. Now we don't know the maker. The lining's all stained, too, probably from pizza sauce. Let me see if there's a label inside the pockets." She checked the two on the exterior. "No luck." Turning the jacket over, she poked a finger in the half-eaten inside pocket. "No . . . wait, there is something . . ." She pulled out a receipt, which bore The Bruce's teeth marks. "This is from the Dolphin pub on October first. Wasn't that the date of Davey's death on his grave?"

"Yes," Judith said. "I remember because it's Cousin Marty's birthday. Let's see."

Renie handed over the receipt. "Nineteen pounds four shillings and sixpence," Judith murmured.

"Four beverages, one burger, chips, a side of onion rings, and a spinach salad, not to mention a dab of catsup on the—" She stopped. "Let me see that lining."

"Here." Renie gave the jacket to Judith. "It's clouding over. I'll bet it's going to rain again." She looked at her watch. "Good Lord, it's almost three! Where has the day gone?"

"This isn't pizza sauce or catsup." Judith stared at Renie. "I'm no expert, but it looks like dried blood."

"So?" Renie looked puzzled. "Davey must've been wearing this jacket when he crashed his car. Of course there'd be blood on it."

"It's all wrong," Judith said. "Who'd donate a bloodstained jacket to a thrift shop, even for a worthy cause?"

"Moira?"

"I wonder." Judith carefully folded the jacket and tucked the receipt into her purse. "Davey was dead when Dr. Carmichael found him. Patrick was injured, but lying away from the wreck. Let's call Carmichael," Judith said, taking out her cell phone and dialing Alison's number. "It's pesky Mrs. Flynn. Have you got Dr. Carmichael's listing?"

"I know it by heart," Alison replied. "Have to, for emergencies." She rattled off the doctor's surgery number. "Are you ill?"

"No," Judith assured her. "Just an idle query. Thanks so much." She dialed the doctor's number. A pleasant female voice answered. She informed Judith that Dr. Carmichael was seeing a patient and had three more scheduled before the surgery closed at five. "Please," Judith begged, "tell him this is urgent." She gave the woman her cell number.

"But that's not local," the woman said. "Where are you?"

"At the Hearth and Heath," Judith informed her.

"Then come along," the woman said. "We're next door to the east."

Judith rang off and stood up. "We're going to see the doctor."

When the cousins exited the garden through the gate facing the road, they saw what they presumed was the last of the media vehicles pulling away. Only a couple of onlookers lingered by the inn.

"Luckily," Judith said, "we don't look important."

"We're not," Renie asserted as they approached the small whitewashed one-story building that housed the surgery. "How could the cops have missed that jacket if Davey was wearing it?"

"Because," Judith said, ringing the bell, "I don't think Davey was wearing it when the cops got there. That's what we're going to find out."

A slim blonde about forty-odd opened the door. "You're Americans," she said. "I figured it out after I studied your cell phone number. Not traveler's tummy, is it? The water's perfectly safe here."

"No," Judith said as an elderly man shuffled into the waiting room from another direction. "Till next time," he said. "Always a next time." He went out the front door.

"Poor Mr. Murchison," the blonde said. "Old age is painful."

Dr. Carmichael appeared from the same part of the surgery Mr. Murchison had just left. "Susan told me you'd called," he said, nodding at a woman with a toddler who'd just been admitted by the blonde. The doctor nodded at the mother and child. "I assumed it was you ladies. Let's go into my office."

"We won't keep you," Judith assured him as they left the waiting room. "In fact, we can do this right here." She held out the jacket. "Do you recognize this?"

The doctor frowned. "No. It's a bit of a wreck, isn't it?"

Judith quickly explained about the hamster, the thrift shop, and her suspicions about bloodstains. Dr. Carmichael took the jacket from her and examined it more closely.

"Davey Piazza wasn't wearing a jacket when I saw him. Odd, I remember thinking, because it was a chilly night."

"Did you see it anywhere at the scene?" Judith asked.

"Why . . . " The doctor tapped his cheek several times. "No, I don't think so. I discovered Patrick Cameron lying nearby, but I didn't notice a jacket. It was dark and misty, of course." He shook his head. "And now Patrick's been arrested. Such a dreadful past few days."

"Yes," Judith agreed sympathetically. "Are those stains blood?"

The doctor looked again. "Very likely, but I'd have to make a more thorough examination."

Judith nodded. "Thank you. We'll leave you to your patients."

Outside under the encroaching gray clouds, Renie poked Judith's arm. "You have a theory. Let's hear it."

Before Judith could respond, Constables Glen and Adamson came out of the inn, heading for their patrol car parked at the road's edge. Seeing Judith and Renie, they stopped.

"We're off to Morton's," Glen called. "Don't fret, we'll get your husbands back to you safely."

"Thanks! Good luck! Be careful!" Judith's words followed the policemen into their vehicle.

"Shall we wait at the inn?" Renie asked.

Judith thought about it for a moment. "No. I trust the cops. Doing nothing would make me even more nervous than I am right now. Let's take the bus."

"What bus?" Renie asked, mystified.

"That bus," she said, "coming this way." She pointed to her left. "We'll flag it down. We're going to Hollywood."

The driver was the same one who had given the cousins a free ride from Cummings House. Judith insisted on paying him for the previous ride and added a tip. If the man behind the wheel was surprised, he didn't show it, but thanked them in a grumpy manner.

It took five minutes to reach their destination. Judith and Renie had remained silent during the brief journey. As expected, Fergus responded on the intercom. He didn't sound pleased when Judith identified herself, but he opened the iron gates anyway.

"Madam is in her boudoir," he said. "She'll see you now."

"Thanks, ol' buddy," Renie said. "You're a sport."

Fergus looked affronted.

Judith was relieved to see that Moira was alone, lying in bed and looking almost as pitiful as when the cousins had last seen her.

"I'm so sorry to be such a poor hostess," she apologized, "but I'm still very ill. I wouldn't have let you call on me if I didn't think you had news of those silly emails."

Judith couldn't hide her surprise. "Who told you that?"

"Elise," Moira said. Her face fell. "You do know what happened to them, don't you?"

"We know they were stolen from my room at Grimloch along with the case," Judith said. "We haven't heard if they've been recovered."

"Oh!" Moira flung a hand over her eyes. "How could Elise have made such a mistake?"

"Maybe," Judith said, "she told you that to cheer you."

Moira struggled to sit up. "Please, be seated. Oh, I don't understand any of this! It's all a vicious plot! Now Patrick's under arrest, and I know he didn't kill Harry! That bomb was meant for me!"

The cousins sat down in the side chairs by the bed. "You can help us find the killer," Judith said, showing Moira the suede jacket. "You gave this to the thrift shop. It belonged to David Piazza."

Moira frowned. "Goodness, it's ruined. Davey owned a jacket like that, yes. But I didn't give it to the thrift shop."

"I heard," Judith said, "you gave all his clothes away."

Moira shook her head. "I did no such thing." She paused. "Harry may've done it." She paused again. "You see, Davey lived in the carriage house here on the grounds. After his accident, Harry went through his things, making sure there were no important business papers and clearing everything out because I couldn't stand to see the place the way it was when Davey was alive. I couldn't bear to do it myself. Maybe Harry took the clothes to the thrift shop. I really don't know."

Judith nodded. "That makes sense."

"Yes," Moira agreed. "I had a collapse very like this one after Davey died." She moaned softly. "How much more can I endure?"

Judith couldn't help but sympathize with Moira. The young woman had certainly been bombarded with tragedies. Still, her self-absorption caused even Judith's soft heart to harden a bit.

"Life is not easy," Judith declared. "Nobody lives unscathed. You have your son and some devoted friends. You're able to live comfortably—a privileged life, in fact. We make choices, and some of them are wrong. I know—I've made mistakes and paid the price."

"I don't," Renie said. "Only idiots screw up."

Judith was shocked. "Coz! Watch your mouth!"

"Don't start," Renie warned, looking nasty. "You know what happens when we quarrel. I win." She turned to Moira. "Sorry about that. Ever fought with your closest friends?"

Realizing what Renie was up to, Judith waited for Moira's response.

"I have at that," she admitted, falling back against the pillows. "Marie and I had a terrible falling-out a while ago." Moira laughed weakly. "I thought she was marrying the wrong man. Imagine! I'm not one to criticize. I felt Will was too old for her and I didn't trust him. Oh, I had reasons not to at the time." Her expression was rueful. "Will always took Jimmy's side against me in any dispute. Maybe Will lacked faith in my judgment, maybe he thought I relied too much on Davey Piazza, maybe early on he simply felt that I didn't have enough business experience." She shrugged. "But Will's changed in recent months. Now Marie and I are close again and I have complete faith in Will's loyalty."

"That's wonderful," Renie said. She looked at Judith. "Okay, coz, I forgive you. For whatever it was," she added.

Moira's pale face showed some color as she sat up again. "What are you going to do with that jacket?"

"Give it to the police," Judith said.

"No!" Moira's hand shot out to snatch the jacket, but Judith was too quick for her.

"Why not?" Judith inquired mildly.

"I . . . " Moira closed her eyes for a moment. "It seems a silly thing to do." She started to cry softly. "I want the jacket, as a keepsake."

"Sorry," Judith said. "Maybe later. You see," she continued, standing up, "it's not a souvenir. It's evidence."

The cousins had almost reached the door when Moira uttered a plaintive cry. "You don't understand," she wailed as Judith turned to look at her. "Historically," Moira went on, dropping her voice and sounding somber, "we've had three verdicts in Scotland—guilty, not guilty, and not proven. No matter what happens, many people will believe I'm responsible for Harry's death. 'Not proven,' they'll whisper, and for the rest of my life I'll live in purgatory."

She turned her face to the wall and began to sob very softly.

22

I really do feel sorry for Moira," Judith said as they exited Hollywood House. "Living in a village makes gossip even worse."

"I'll bet she moves after all this," Renie remarked, walking along the driveway in a soft drizzle of rain. "Back to France, maybe. These days she could run Blackwell from an ice floe off of Antarctica."

Judith nodded. "Oh well. We found out who the Leopard is—Will Fleming. He changed his spots."

"Power struggle," Renie said. "Harry versus Jimmy. Jimmy versus Jocko Morton. Seumas Bell versus Patrick. Any number of combinations, all struggling for control while Philip and Kate wait in the wings to make their buyout offer."

"Right," Judith agreed, taking out her cell phone. "At least I'm fairly sure who killed Davey Piazza."

Renie stared at her cousin. "You are?"

"I wasn't kidding about this jacket being evidence, though I'm not exactly sure how." She dialed Alison's number again. "It just dawned on me we're stuck here. I got so focused on that jacket . . . Alison? Hi, Mrs. Flynn again. Could Barry pick us up at Hollywood House?"

"He's making a delivery outside of St. Fergna so he won't be back for a while," Alison said. "Can you wait?"

"We don't have much choice," Judith said. "Thanks."

"No luck?" Renie asked as they went through the open gates.

Judith nodded. "Gibbs," she said suddenly. "Maybe he can collect us." She dialed Grimloch's number and got better results. Mrs. Gibbs informed her that Mr. Gibbs would be along in fifteen minutes. The tide was changing; he'd have to take his skiff. Judith called Alison back to tell her not to bother Barry.

"So," Renie said, moving under the shelter of a hawthorn tree, "who killed Davey?"

"Harry," Judith answered simply. "Who else resented Davey that much? His sudden rise was fodder for gossip about an attraction between employer and employee. Jealousy is such a powerful motive. It must have gnawed at Harry. I assume he tampered with

Davey's brakes. Judging from the Dolphin receipt, we know Davey wasn't alone. He paid cash for the meal because Harry never carried money."

"Aha!" Renie exclaimed. "The burger. Davey was a vegetarian, not to mention that even I couldn't eat that much food and drink that many drinks by myself."

"Right," Judith said as a lorry drove past the cousins. "I finally remembered what Kate Gunn told Beth about her fancy fern. Kate mentioned that it was the feast day of Saint Thérèse of Lisieux, which should have dawned on me earlier as the first of October. But all I could think of was Cousin Marty's birthday until you griped to me about the old church calendars and my own birthday. I'll bet that was Harry, driving around in a panic after Davey crashed his car. MacGowan may have checked the garage repair records and discovered that Harry's Rover had been in for a repair—after he wiped out Kate's fern. Harry followed Davey and went down to the site to make sure his rival was dead. He took off Davey's suede jacket, knowing that the telltale receipt was in the pocket. But because Harry wasn't the brightest guy around and flustered to boot, he never removed it."

"Harry also had to deal with Patrick's arrival," Renie pointed out. "That must've scared the hell out of him. I wonder if Patrick saw Harry's Rover before he climbed down the cliff."

"Maybe not," Judith replied. "Patrick was walking from the opposite direction. Anyway, Harry had to act fast, clobber Patrick, and flee the scene. He finally went home, put the jacket with Davey's clothes in the carriage house, and later gave them to the thrift shop without getting rid of the receipt. As I mentioned, Harry wasn't very smart."

"No wonder Moira didn't give him any real power at Blackwell," Renie said. "But he lucked out because Patrick got amnesia."

Judith shook her head. "No." A midsize sedan approached but kept going. "Not Gibbs," she murmured. "I think Moira guessed that Davey's crash was no accident. Harry must have returned that night in some kind of emotional state. She's pregnant, with a husband who's just killed the man he thought was his rival. Think bloodlines. Everybody here does, including Moira's father, who refused to let his illegitimate son inherit the company despite Jimmy's competence. Moira couldn't risk people thinking her baby's father wasn't Harry, so they reconciled, which must have galled her, but was necessary. Somehow pressure was put on MacGowan, who may have had his own ideas about what happened. And Patrick kept quiet for the sake of Moira's reputation. He's always been loyal to her, and arresting Harry wouldn't have been in Moira's long-term interests involving her son."

"But with Harry dead," Renie said, "why would his killer want MacGowan out of the way?"

Judith shrugged. "Maybe Moira didn't exaggerate. It's possible that she was intended to be a victim, too. Harry may have told someone he'd invited her to join him on the beach. Whether or not that's so, his killer didn't want MacGowan around to reopen the matter of Davey's death and link both crimes. Harry was probably gullible. Who fed him tales about Moira and Davey? Somebody was goading Harry to get rid of his wife's alleged lover and go to prison." She paused. "Here's Gibbs."

After getting in the car, Judith thanked Gibbs for coming. "If you don't mind," she added, "could we stop at the Hearth and Heath inn?"

"Aye." Gibbs kept his eyes on the wet road. The rest of the brief trip was made in silence.

Judith and Renie got out, asking Gibbs to wait.

"Do you suppose Bill and Joe are here already?" Renie asked as they entered the inn through the guest entrance.

"Let's hope," Judith responded.

They were in a foyer, replete with framed swatches of tartans of various clans. MacRae was on the phone, standing by an antique table Judith guessed served as the registration desk. Two dried arrangements of heather, thistle, and some plants she didn't recognize stood at each end of a shelf holding maps and tourist guides.

Seeing the cousins, MacRae ended the call after a few brief words. "Sorry," he said. "Your husbands weren't at Morton's garage."

Judith was stunned. "They weren't?"

"No," MacRae said regretfully. "Nor the Mac-Gowan, either."

Judith and Renie exchanged anxious looks. "I was so sure . . . " Judith began, and trailed off, feeling helpless and panicky.

"I must confess," MacRae said, "I had doubts about your idea, but I checked with my superior, who knows MacGowan quite well, and he confirmed that Hugh doesn't use a cell phone."

"They must be somewhere," Judith said in a strained voice. "Are you still searching?"

"Indeed," MacRae replied. "One of ours is missing, too." He grimaced. "The cell number belongs to your husband, Mrs. Flynn."

"I thought so," Judith said. "Bill is like MacGowan— he won't carry a cell phone, either." She glanced at Renie, seeking comfort. But Renie seemed equally shaken, pale and wide-eyed. Trying to dampen her fears, Judith turned back to MacRae. "We have to talk. I've something to show you and a confession to make."

MacRae ushered the cousins into the study, which was lined with bookshelves stocked with popular fiction. There were comfortable chairs and a gas-powered fireplace. Judith figured the room was designed for guests, though the police had made it their own with computers, phones, and file folders. A map of the vicinity hung above the fireplace. Judging from the pushpins and red X's on the beach and at Grimloch Castle, it wasn't there for the convenience of visitors, but to show the crime scenes and other pertinent locations.

"Ogilvie's searching with the constables," MacRae said, sitting at the desk. "What is it you have to tell me?"

Judith and Renie had also sat down. "It's about some emails we found in the jewel case." Briefly, Judith summed up the contents, forcing herself to focus on the matter at hand, rather than fretting about Joe and Bill. "At first I thought the exchanges were between Moira and Patrick. But it occurred to me just now when we came in that those emails aren't as recent as I'd assumed."

Renie stared at Judith. "It did? Why didn't you say so?"

Judith looked faintly sheepish. "It was the dried heather by the desk." She turned back to MacRae. "One of the messages mentioned the last heather of the season. I grow the plant in my garden at home, and heather doesn't bloom past September. There was also something about going to bed early and the sun setting. That sounds more like late summer or early fall than this time of year."

MacRae looked impressed; Renie seemed annoyed. "Do go on," the detective urged.

"That means," Judith explained, "they were written months ago, probably in September, *before* David Piazza died. Those emails were intended to sound as if Davey and Moira were the ones having the affair and possibly plotting to get rid of Harry. Whoever wrote them probably showed the emails to Harry in order to incite him to violence."

"Fascinating." MacRae smiled in approval, cleared his throat, and folded his hands on the desk. "Please don't take this as criticism. I realize you have your own methods when you're on the job."

"I . . . " Judith started to ask if there might be confusion about what the "job" really was, but thought better of it. This wasn't the time to get sidetracked. "The emails were mistakenly put into my purse by Moira's maid, Elise. They were meant for Beth Fordyce, not me. I think Moira wanted Beth to see them and perhaps get rid of them for her. If you ask Will Fleming, I think you'll learn that he found them and brought them to Grimloch. The case they were in ended up at Hollywood House in my purse. I have no idea who later took it out of my room." She paused and put Davey's jacket on the desk. "There's one more important thing," Judith said, and offered her theory about the pub receipt.

"My word!" MacRae exclaimed softly. "You are the goods, Mrs. Flynn! I'll review MacGowan's notes on the accident. Are you returning to Grimloch?"

"Yes," Judith said, getting up. "Gibbs is waiting for us. Unless we can help find Joe and Bill. Doing nothing will drive us crazy."

MacRae thought for a moment. "Really, I don't see how you can help. I've requested extra personnel to expand the search. I'll keep in close touch, of course."

"I understand," Judith said as she and Renie were escorted from the study by MacRae. "I can't believe all three were abducted."

"Very puzzling," MacRae admitted.

MacRae escorted the cousins outside. The Morris saloon was nowhere in sight.

"Where's Gibbs?" Renie asked, looking in every direction.

"Perhaps," MacRae suggested, "he was called away."

"I don't think he has a cell phone," Judith said.

A horn honk caught their attention. "Need a lift?" Barry shouted.

"We do," Renie said. "We've been stranded by Gibbs."

"Come on," Barry said from where he'd stopped in the middle of the road. "Where to?"

"Grimloch," Judith replied, "but if Gibbs went there without us, the skiff's on the other side. We'll be stuck on the beach."

"Let's look," Barry said, making a wide U-turn in the middle of the road and almost running down MacRae, who was still standing in front of the inn. "Whew! Good thing I missed him."

Judith braced herself on the dashboard. "You might be a little more careful," she advised. "The rain is coming down harder and the roads are slick."

"Aye," Barry said blithely. "Sorry I couldn't fetch you earlier. Mrs. Gunn ordered four pizzas, and it takes a bit to go to her place and back. Family doings, maybe," Barry said.

"It's early for dinner," Judith pointed out.

"Mrs. Gunn's different from other folk," Barry said.

"Yes." Judith made no further comment, but she wondered if Kate had called some kind of emergency meeting. Maybe, she thought, the reason was related to Kate's abrupt departure from the Rood & Mitre.

The High Street was almost deserted on this stormy late afternoon. Barry shot through the coast road intersection; the car rumbled down to the beach where the skiff was tied up at the edge of the paved area.

"Guess Gibbs went on a lark," Barry said. "Want me to row?"

"Well . . . you'll have to," Judith said. "We owe you two jackets."

Barry helped the cousins get into the skiff. "What about The Bruce?" Renie asked. "Doesn't he like boats?"

"He gets seasick," Barry said as he plied the oars.

Five minutes later, the cousins were inside the castle. "I wonder where Gibbs went," Judith said as they trudged up the stone stairs to their rooms. "I hope nothing's happened to him."

"Why should he be spared?" Renie snapped. "A lot of us are in danger." She stopped at the top of the stairs. "Your room or mine?"

Judith shrugged. "Yours, I guess. You've got a view of the village."

"If we can see it through the rain," Renie said, leading the way. "It's after four o'clock and I'm still not hungry, but I'm getting crabby as well as worried sick."

Inside the Joneses' room, Renie spotted a piece of paper a few inches from the door. "What's this? A ransom note for our husbands?"

"What does it say?" Judith asked anxiously.

"'Dinner will not be served tonight.' That's it."

"I wonder why," Judith said. "Does this have to do with Gibbs?"

"Maybe it's got more to do with Harry's funeral to-morrow," Renie said. "Both Gibbses must be terribly upset."

"True," Judith agreed, beginning to pace and fight-ing the urge to bite her nails. "I cannot just stay here and have a nervous breakdown!"

"We don't have a choice," Renie pointed out, taking her eye medication kit off of the bureau. "Let's go get a drink."

"I don't feel like drinking." Judith stopped pacing and stared at Renie. "You aren't wearing your patch!"

Renie's smiled wanly. "My eye's much better. I wish my nerves were."

"Me, too." Judith wandered over to the window. "There's a boat heading this way. It looks like the police launch." She turned back to face Renie. "Let's see who it is."

"Bill and Joe?" Renie asked excitedly, heading for the stairs.

"Wouldn't MacRae call us if they'd been found?" Judith asked.

"Maybe the storm screwed up the phones," Renie suggested. "The wind sounds like it's blowing through the chinks in the castle walls."

The cousins waited at the courtyard door. Five minutes passed. Judith and Renie exchanged several worried glances. Judith finally opened the door to peer outside. "Nothing."

Another five minutes passed. Judith looked again. Several people Judith couldn't identify in the gathering gloom were crossing the courtyard, headed for the Fordyce apartments. Except, she noticed, one lone figure was heading their way.

"Gibbs," Judith said, leaving the door open.

Wind and rain blew into the entry area. Gibbs walked slowly, head down, shoulders slumped. He didn't look up when he entered. "Patrick jumped out of the window and escaped," he mumbled, and continued down the passageway.

"Whoa!" Renie said under her breath. "How does he know? Did he help Patrick get away? And why did Gibbs arrive in the police launch?"

Judith leaned against the door she'd just closed. "Patrick probably jumped out of the window at the inn. He's very fit. He could do it easily."

"Did Gibbs help him get away?" Renie asked.

"Maybe," Judith said, "that's why he left us stranded. Come on. Let's ask him."

The cousins headed for the kitchen. When they entered, there was no sign of Gibbs. His wife glanced up from the counter where she'd been peeling carrots. Mrs. Gibbs's red-rimmed eyes indicated that she'd been crying.

"Where's Gibbs?" Judith asked politely.

"I dinna ken," Mrs. Gibbs mumbled, and dropped the peeler onto the floor.

"I'll get it," Renie volunteered.

The older woman's hands were shaking. "Thank ye," she said to Renie. "It's all for naught."

"What is?" Judith asked.

Mrs. Gibbs sniffed twice and wiped at her cheek with the back of her hand. "Everything."

Judith moved closer. "I don't understand."

"My whole life . . . wasted," Mrs. Gibbs declared, avoiding Judith's gaze. "Naught to show for it. A reckless son and a butchered grandson!" Her voice rose. "Work, work, work—and why? This was ours!" She swept a hand in a wide arc. "Then Matthew and his silly schemes lost it for us to that Fordyce! Bought it out from under us for not half its worth! The Master indeed! Och, Philip Fordyce is The Master all right!

Treats us like slaves, he does! And now it's finished."
She looked at the framed MacIver tartan on the wall.
"My clan motto—'I will never forget.' How could I *not*
remember how our lives were ruined?" Mrs. Gibbs
turned on her heel and walked away.

"I'll be damned," Renie said under her breath.

"I've wondered about this whole setup," Judith admitted. "The old folks working their tails off while
Matt and Peggy travel the world."

"Harry's marriage was intended to bail them out?"
Renie suggested.

"Very likely," Judith said. "But there's got to be
more to it."

"Like what?" Renie asked.

"I'm trying to sort through what Mrs. Gibbs meant,"
Judith said, starting out of the kitchen. "Come on. Let's
go to the Fordyce suite."

Renie was right on Judith's heels. "We're party
crashers?"

"Whatever's going on there isn't a celebration,"
Judith asserted as they entered the passageway connecting the castle's living sections. "I'm not sure what
it really is, but I don't want to miss it."

They reached the two doors, one of which led to the
Fordyce suite, the other to the storage room and dungeon. Judith shuddered. "Poor Chuckie." She opened the

other door and walked down the carpeted hallway with the ugly abstract paintings chosen by Philip's second wife. The corridor took a sharp left turn into a wider hall with zebra-striped wallpaper. "Gack," Renie said. "The second Mrs. F had ghastly taste. Why do so many people with money lack the knack for using it wisely?"

"Not our problem," Judith said, taking in several doors along the way. "Where would everybody have gone?"

The answer came when they reached an alcove where Constable Adamson stood at the door. "DCI MacRae was going to fetch you when he got here," the constable said. "They're in the drawing room."

The cousins entered a large, unattractive room decorated in red, black, and white with furniture that looked impossibly uncomfortable. PC Glen stood by a white stone fireplace. Gathered in various states of impatience and anxiety were Philip and Beth, Marie and Will, Jocko and his brother Archie, Peggy and Matt Gibbs, and Seumas Bell.

Beth rose from a red tufted divan and went to greet the cousins. "You don't have to be here. This is going to be ugly."

"It already is," Renie murmured, her eyes roaming around the room. "And I don't just mean some of the people."

"I know, I know," Beth said nervously. "Phil called this meeting."

Jocko Morton lumbered away from a table where drinks had been set up. "It's outrageous!" He shot Philip a nasty look. "You've never invited any of us for a social occasion! Now you have the police haul us here as if we were common criminals! I'll sue!"

"Quiet!" Seumas snapped. "You've made enough mischief already!"

"Haven't you all?" Marie said quietly from the crook of Will's sheltering arm. "I feel as if I'm in a vipers' den."

"Ha!" Jocko cried. "You should know. You married one!"

"Don't speak to my wife that way," Will said calmly, though there was steel in his voice. "Where's that self-righteous villain Jimmy?"

"Slunk off," Seumas said, refreshing his drink. "Slippery bastard."

Archie Morton sneered. "What about Patrick? He killed young Gibbs. Patrick's spent more time in Moira's bed than Harry ever did."

"But not," Seumas put in snidely, "more than Davey."

"That's a lie!" Marie exclaimed. "Moira never slept with Davey!"

"Please!" a grim Matt Gibbs begged. "We've lost a son."

"You'll lose more than that," Jocko threatened, fists clenched. "Your Venezuelan oil gambit is in checkmate now!"

Matt and Peggy exchanged quick glances. "Nonsense," Peggy Gibbs snapped. "You can't undo what's done."

"*You're* done," Seumas asserted with a nasty smirk. "And," he added, looking at Philip, "why are the police here?"

"Venus goo," Judith murmured. "That's what Jocko's note on the napkin meant—Venezuela."

Philip strode to the middle of the room. "I'm your host." His keen eyes moved slowly, taking in each member of the fractious gathering. "I invited the constables because I anticipated tempers would flare."

"What's the point of all this?" Jocko rasped.

"I have also lost a son," Philip said calmly. "Chuckie was as dear to me as any child could be. Perhaps more so, because of his physical and emotional flaws." His eyes fixed on Matt and Peggy. "Your son's flaws weren't obvious. Chuckie might still be alive if Harry hadn't been killed. You're guilty of both of their deaths."

"You're horrible!" Peggy shouted. "We'd never harm Harry! We weren't even in Scotland when he was murdered and we can prove it!"

Philip shrugged. "I didn't say you personally did the deed, but you caused his death. He was your ticket to great wealth and power."

Peggy's brittle façade was cracking. "It's business," she said in an unsteady voice. "Taking risks, seizing opportunities, using—" She stopped and buried her head against Matt's chest.

"You don't cross the line," Philip said sternly. "You don't connive with corrupt foreign officials who have huge oil interests. You don't," he went on, his voice rising, "use your son to sell out his wife's inheritance."

"That's right!" Seumas shouted. "Harry was your frigging puppet! He had to have his strings cut!"

Peggy let out a piercing cry. Matt let go of her and charged at Seumas. Constable Glen moved swiftly between the two men. "That'll do!" he cried. "No violence! Please!"

Matt backed off. Seumas stood still, his expression belligerent. Peggy had collapsed onto an empty chair.

"Where's MacRae?" Renie whispered. "This is really ugly."

"Why don't you bop somebody?" Judith murmured. "It's perfect timing for you to get into another brawl."

Archie Morton swallowed a big gulp of Scotch. "I'm leaving. I've got cars to fix."

"No, sir," Glen said politely. "You're staying. You can't work now anyway. Your repair site is a crime scene."

"*What?*" Archie's face grew red. "Why the bloody hell is that?"

"I think you know," Glen replied.

Archie snarled at the constable and poured himself another shot.

"Bomb," Will said.

Beth stared at him. "What?"

"The one that killed Harry," Will said. "Who else but Archie would know how to make a bomb?" He avoided looking at Archie, who appeared nearly apoplectic. "Isn't that so, Constable?" Will inquired of Glen.

"I couldn't say, sir," Glen answered stoically.

Archie downed three shots in a row before turning to his brother. "It wasn't my idea! It was yours, Jocko! I thought it was a prank!"

"Ridiculous!" Marie exclaimed. "You're all crooks!"

Jocko turned his back on Archie and looked at Will. "You and your wife better keep quiet. You're as guilty as any of us, Fleming."

"We'll see about that," Will said mildly.

Seumas advanced on Will. "You made a deal with the coppers."

"Unlike you," Will said, "I own a conscience. I'd never betray Moira." He patted Marie's hand. "You convinced me where my loyalties lie. You also knew Moira never sent those lovesick emails to Davey."

"Of course she wouldn't," Marie said. "Moira spoke perfect French. When it came to love, she always wrote in longhand and in French. It's much more romantic." She stroked Will's cheek. "Isn't that so, darling?"

"Those emails you gave me when you came to dinner?" Beth asked. "I took them to Moira, but she was ill and irrational, so I decided to wait until she felt better and could deal with the situation. It wasn't until later that day that I realized the case containing the emails was gone from my bag. Knowing what a snoop Elise was, I believed she'd gone through my things, found the case, and put it aside to read the contents at her leisure. When I phoned to ask her about the case, she swore she hadn't kept it."

"That might be true," Glen said. "Apparently the maid removed the case but returned it to the wrong purse." He glanced at Judith. "Then the emails disappeared from Grimloch where they'd been taken inadvertently. Unfortunately, we don't know who wrote them."

"I do," Will said grimly. "Jocko concocted the emails to prove that Moira and Davey were having an affair."

He ignored Jocko's voluble protests and paused to give the other man a venomous stare. "You created those emails before fleeing to Greece. I found them in your safe at headquarters. You forgot that as chief financial officer, I know all the safe combinations. I also turned up some very interesting and imaginative figures intended to bloat the company's bottom line."

"Bloody parasite!" Jocko shouted, and had to be restrained by Glen. "You'd betray your own mother if you thought it'd line your fancy bespoke pockets!"

Renie smirked. "I didn't think Jocko knew words like 'bespoke.' His own clothes look like he bought them at Rummage 'R' Us."

Will's gaze turned to Archie. "The police have found them in your garage. I learned from Moira that you, Seumas," he went on, pointing a finger at the attorney, who had resumed his usual air of smug respectability, "went to Hollywood House to supposedly apologize for the dustup you and Jocko had with Patrick. Elise turned you away—but not before you managed to elicit the information that the maid had erroneously put the jewel case in Mrs. Flynn's purse instead of Beth's."

"*Please,*" Seumas said with disdain. "Leave me out of this farce."

"Are you taking notes?" Renie asked Judith.

"I don't need to," she said. "Beth is Kate's daughter. The apple never falls far from the tree. I bet this whole mess is being taped."

Will was still speaking: "Don't play the innocent with me, Seumas. You relayed that information to Jocko, who had Archie steal the case from Mrs. Flynn when he came to Grimloch about Gibbs's car."

"Of course!" Judith whispered to Renie. "We knew Archie had been at the castle that day."

"Your batting average on this one's pretty high—" Renie stopped, looking startled.

Archie had set upon Will. Jocko broke free from Constable Glen to join his brother in the fracas. Glen blew his whistle, summoning Adamson from outside. Seumas and Matt argued loudly; Philip shielded Beth; Marie smashed a table lamp over Archie's head; Peggy curled up in a ball, sobbing uncontrollably.

"Where are our husbands?" Renie said suddenly. "Joe could shoot these people and Bill could ship the survivors to a mental home."

Judith sighed. "Let's not think about it. I'm getting a headache."

Adamson and Glen had subdued the combatants just before DCI MacRae entered the drawing room, accompanied by Sergeant Ogilvie and two more constables. MacRae turned to Jocko Morton. "I'm placing you under arrest for complicity in the murder of Harry Gibbs," he announced.

Jocko started to bluster but Seumas spoke up: "Don't say a word! I'm your attorney, remember?"

Adamson cuffed Jocko, who glared at Seumas. MacRae faced the other Morton and recited the same charge to Archie. "You," MacRae said to Seumas, "are a person of interest, and will come along, too." He looked at Matt. "The Yard's special unit will deal with you. Don't leave the area."

"What about Patrick?" Seumas demanded. "He's already been charged with homicide and you let him get away."

"Did I?" MacRae smiled slightly. "Careless of me." He herded the group out the door.

A solemn Matt Gibbs went to his wife. "Get up, Peggy." He shook her recumbent figure gently. "It's over." He sighed. "It's all over."

Peggy sat up slowly and let her husband ease her out of the chair. She leaned on him, her eyes half shut. "It wasn't worth it," she mumbled. "The price was too high." Without looking at anyone, she let Matt guide her out of the room.

"My God!" Beth exclaimed. "I'm not sure I understand any of this!"

Philip held his head in his hands. "What is there to understand? A conspiracy of greedy people destroyed the lives of my Chuckie and Harry Gibbs, all for their own gain. The age of the robber baron never ended. It's stronger than ever in big business these days."

"But who actually killed Harry?" Beth asked.

Philip looked at Will; Will looked at Marie; Marie looked at Beth; Judith and Renie looked at all of them.

"I don't know," Philip finally said in a weary voice.

"I think I do." Judith grimaced. "Sorry. I shouldn't intrude."

Everyone, including Renie, turned to stare at her. Feeling a bit foolish and worn out from worrying, Judith sank into the chair Peggy Gibbs had vacated. "First," she began as Renie handed her a half inch of Scotch, "I have to ask you a question, Will."

He looked surprised. "Well . . . of course."

"Why did you really switch sides?"

Will put his arm around Marie. "It was my wife who insisted."

Judith smiled slightly. "That's not the entire reason."

Will laid his head back on the sofa. "No. It was Jimmy. He desperately wanted to take over the company. The man is driven, eaten alive by resentment over his illegitimate birth and deprived of what he feels is his inheritance." Will paused and sat up straight. "Jimmy is astute and competent, with an excellent head for business. Given Moira's indifference to Blackwell,

Harry's meddling, and Jocko urging me to alter the company's books to make him look better as well as richer, I believed it was in everyone's best interests to have Jimmy in charge."

"What made you change your mind?" Judith asked.

"Jocko came back from Greece," Will explained. "Jimmy was furious. I'd told him about Jocko's attempts at deception with company records. Instead of telling the police, he did nothing. I knew something was going on behind my back. It was the South American buyout."

"Which," Philip put in, "would've placed Harry in charge."

Will nodded. "On the day of Harry's murder, I ran into Jimmy at the Rood & Mitre. I thought it odd. He rarely frequented pubs, and when he did, he had a drink and left. Then I heard about Harry. I figured Jimmy was giving himself an alibi."

"But," Beth pointed out, "he *was* in the pub, so he couldn't have committed the actual crime."

"He didn't," Judith said. "But he put everything in motion, including connivance with Jocko and Archie Morton."

"How do you know that?" Marie asked.

Judith shrugged. "All along, I felt jealousy was the motive. It caused Davey's death, the jealous husband angle." She saw the expressions of surprise and incredulity on the two couples' faces. "Jocko goaded Harry into murdering Davey, hoping Harry would get caught and go to prison. But someone—Patrick, I suspect—put pressure on Hugh MacGowan to hold off with the investigation. Or was it you, Will?"

Will sadly shook his head. "Both of us. Moira and the company couldn't afford that kind of scandal, not with Jocko already playing the numbers game. When Jocko left for Greece right after Davey's death, we urged MacGowan to back off until Jocko came back—which we were sure he'd do eventually."

Judith nodded. "Jocko figured the motive for Davey's murder could be used again for Harry's. The work of a jealous lover, this time around it was Patrick. If Jocko could concoct a romance between Moira and Davey, why not do the same with Moira and Patrick? She was very close to both men. But who told Jocko about Matt and Peggy's schemes in Venezuela?"

"Archie?" Will guessed.

Judith shook her head. "He had no entrée into Blackwell except through his brother. It had to be Jimmy. Somehow he found out what the Gibbses were up to, and could only stop them by killing Harry. He wouldn't do the dirty work, so the Morton brothers did it for him. Jimmy and the Mortons were kin. Jimmy's mother was married to Archie and Jocko's cousin. Family—or clan ties, if you will—mean a great deal around here."

Marie nodded. "That's so, even among villains. But who actually smothered Harry?"

Judith grimaced. "Archie Morton is my best guess. His repair shop was close to the beach. No one would question his presence there. I can't see Jocko sullying his hands with murder. But Archie might if his brother and Jimmy promised to pay him well." She shot Renie a wry glance. "My cousin gave me the idea."

"I did?" Renie said in surprise.

Judith nodded. "You mentioned that Archie couldn't be a real mechanic because he didn't have dirt under his fingernails. At the time, I thought that was just you, being perverse and getting into it with Archie. Then I realized you were right. Archie's conscience may have bothered him. Like Pontius Pilate, he literally wanted to wash his hands of the whole tragedy. Not to mention that he'd know about forensic science, being in the car repair business and having to deal with the police about vehicles that had been involved in crimes. He probably spent the next few days after the murder washing and washing his hands and clothes."

"Hunh," Renie said. "Even Lumpa-Lumpa gets an aria."

Philip looked puzzled. "What?"

"Never mind," Judith said. "Jimmy set everything in motion, using the others to get control of Blackwell and going back to Davey's death. The rest of them were his puppets."

"But what about Chuckie?" Beth asked.

Judith sighed. "I wondered if Chuckie had recognized Harry's killer through his binoculars," she said. "I also conjectured that he'd seen the killer here at Grimloch. After the explosion, people rushed to see what had happened. The killer needed time to escape and could have sought refuge in the castle. The elevator had been used after my cousin and I took it. Then Chuckie bragged about his knowledge. At first, I assumed his killer and Harry's was the same person. Then I realized Chuckie's killer knew this castle intimately, which ruled out most of the other suspects. It also dawned on me that someone else could've gone down to the beach and returned before we did." Judith pressed her lips together before addressing Philip. "I believe Gibbs killed your son."

Why?" Philip demanded, rising halfway out of his chair.

"I think you know," Judith said somberly. "Gibbs was torn apart by his grandson's death. A son for a son, an eye for an eye . . . " She paused, looking away. "But more than that, it was your purchase of Grimloch that neither of the Gibbses could forgive—or forget."

Philip looked aghast. "I did them a favor! That was almost thirty years ago. Matthew and Peggy were foolishly throwing the family's money around to finance all their ridiculous schemes. They were both unethical and damned lucky they didn't end up in prison. The price I offered was fair, given all the work that needed to be done to restore and renovate this place. My God, they should've been grateful, not resentful!"

"It didn't work that way," Judith said quietly. "Both of the elder Gibbses had misplaced anger. They definitely resented what you'd done and your presence here. They felt like peasants with you as their feudal lord. It must've seemed so unfair to them when Harry was murdered. To his grandparents, he was perfect, while Chuckie was tragically flawed. The irony wasn't lost on them. Gibbs is old, but strong as an ox." Again she gazed at Philip. "I'm so sorry."

Philip closed his eyes. "God help me, so am I."

Well?" **Renie** said after the cousins went up to the Joneses' room. "Why didn't you tell me your solutions sooner?"

"I wasn't sure until we got to the Fordyce suite and I had time to hear what everybody said," Judith explained a bit sheepishly. "And Gibbs's guilt only came to me after I pondered what Mrs. Gibbs told us in the kitchen."

Renie's expression was sour. "Okay. I think. Thanks for the credit you gave me regarding Archie. Now what?"

"We wait." Judith was staring out of the window, where a heavy rain still fell. "What else can we do?"

Renie was gnawing on her thumb. "Call the American embassy?"

Judith turned around. "If it comes to that—"

"Open the door."

Judith and Renie jumped. The voice was muffled, but there was no mistaking that it was the same one they'd heard on other occasions.

"Holy Mother!" Renie gasped. "I'm going crazy!"

"Open the door."

Judith looked at Renie. "Then we're both crazy. It must be coming from the hall." She walked to the door and slowly opened it.

"My God!" Judith shrieked. "Joe! Bill!" She fell into her husband's arms.

Renie raced to meet Bill. "Where've you been? Are you okay? How—" Suddenly overcome, she let Bill envelop her in a tight hug.

After a few moments, Judith raised her head to see that another man stood behind the husbands. He was tall and stalwart with iron gray hair and deep-set brown eyes.

"MacGowan?" Judith said over Joe's shoulder.

"Aye." The newcomer smiled ruefully. "Sorry to detain Mr. Flynn and Mr. Jones. Of course I was detained as well."

Judith and Renie both moved out of their husbands' embrace. "Come in," Judith said. "Sit down. Oh, I'm so relieved!"

"Who found you?" Renie asked, unable to sit still.

"Nobody," Bill replied. "We weren't lost."

"But—" Judith began.

Joe held up a hand. "Let Hugh tell you."

"Simple enough." Hugh leaned on the mantelpiece and stroked his chin. "Patrick Cameron tracked me down at the Glengarry Hotel. He knew I suspected that Harry Gibbs might have arranged David Piazza's accident. But Patrick felt Jimmy was behind it and was afraid that Jimmy was ultimately responsible for Harry's murder. Patrick knew Jimmy didn't trust Harry, and if arrested, he'd point a finger at the culprit who egged him on to kill Davey. Patrick was at his cottage when the explosion occurred. He started for the beach but saw Jimmy already heading that way and held off for a few minutes. When Patrick went down to see what was happening, he ran into Jimmy, who mentioned how terrible it was that Harry had been killed by a bomb."

"This is simple?" Renie whispered to Judith.

"Hush," Judith snapped. "This guy's good."

"Of course the bomb hadn't killed Harry," Hugh said. "Patrick didn't know that then, but he saw an odd look in Jimmy's eyes that he could only describe as 'triumphant.' Patrick made some crack about Harry's death opening a big door for Jimmy, and they started to argue. Patrick left in a rage, but only figured out Jimmy's role after the autopsy."

"I wish Patrick had told us that earlier," Judith murmured.

Hugh's smile was ironic. "Patrick wanted proof, not just a slip of the tongue. He should have told MacRae sooner rather than waiting until he got himself arrested. But nobody's perfect, and Patrick was determined to solve the crime by himself. The man has quite an ego. He's also brave and conscientious. He figured that Jimmy wanted me out of the way when the murder was committed, and that I might be in danger when I returned, so he sent two of his security people to take us to a safe house. We stayed there until this morning, when I learned Patrick was going to be arrested. A trick, of course, to bring the elusive Jimmy out into the open. I insisted on moving closer to the action. Philip Fordyce arranged another safe house for us nearby."

"Where?" Rene asked.

"Kate Gunn's home," Hugh replied.

"What?" Renie exploded. "You were eating pizza and guzzling God-knows-what while we were driving ourselves nuts with worry?"

"The pizza was second-rate," Bill said. "No sausage. One was vegetarian. What's the point of *that*?"

Hugh moved away from the fireplace. "I must go. Jimmy still hasn't been found. But he will be." He stopped in front of Judith. "And thank you and your agency for the invaluable help." He saluted and left.

"Agency?" Judith repeated. "Not the CIA, surely!"

"Why not?" Joe said. "It's better than being called FATSO."

Judith was stunned. "How could they make such a mistake?"

Joe shrugged. "You know government red tape. I suppose Scotland Yard or British intelligence asked for help in this international oil scam and some bureaucrat lost the memo."

Judith shook her head. "It could happen. But," she said, beaming at Joe, "you're safe. That's the main thing."

"Yes, yes, yes," Renie agreed, still on an adrenaline rush. Suddenly she stood still. "Wait a minute. Where did that voice come from? The one that said 'Open the door'?"

Bill reached into his jacket pocket. "This?" He held out a metal gadget about the size of a matchbook and squeezed the front: "Open the window." He squeezed again: "Open the gate." "It's my latest invention. I brought it along because Hugh knows somebody in the real estate business who's looking for a gimmick to show houses when the agent isn't around. I forgot to take it when we went fishing. I left it on the dresser." Bill frowned at the gadget. "It's got my name on the back, so MacRae gave it back to me. His sergeant found it in the storage room after Chuckie's body was removed. It was on top of some boxes."

"I fell on that box!" Renie exclaimed. "I must have activated it! I'll bet Chuckie loved playing tricks with that, the little—" She stopped and turned somber. "The poor wee laddie."

"My, yes," Judith said, and snapped her fingers as she turned to Renie. "That light in your room that we saw the other evening—I'll bet it was Chuckie, looking for more gadgets."

"He must have been disappointed," Renie said.

"Okay," Joe said, slapping his hands together. "We're not going fishing for a couple of days until MacGowan and MacRae wind up this case. What do you lovely ladies want to do tomorrow?"

Judith and Renie exchanged doleful looks. "Uh . . . " Judith began, "we have to attend a funeral."

"At least there won't be another inquest," Renie put in.

Joe's face fell; Bill scowled at his wife. An uncomfortable silence filled the room.

"Oh," Joe finally said, "let the girls have their fun. We could take a boat out on the sea if it's not too rough."

"The wind's almost stopped," Bill noted as the two men walked toward the window. "I've got the names of a couple of rental places."

"Sounds good," Joe said. "They'll have the gear. We need heavy—"

Renie collapsed on the bed. "I'm starved."

Judith sank into an armchair. "Me, too. And exhausted."

"We need a vacation," Renie declared.

"Maybe we should have gone to California," Judith said.

Renie eyed Judith doubtfully. "You're kidding!"

Judith smiled. "Of course."